Praise for the GARDEN GATES series

"From the opening line . . . debut novelist Hill hooks the reader with this intriguing look at love, faith, grieving, and relationships. . . . Fresh prose, wry humor, an enjoyable protagonist, and strong pacing make Hill a welcome addition to the ranks of inspirational novelists."

—*Publishers Weekly*

"Hill is an author to watch and enjoy."

—Christian Book Previews

"One of the best novels I've read this year."

—*CBA Marketplace*

"Patti Hill is an amazing artist, painting word pictures with her watercolor pen. . . . I have truly enjoyed reading the two novels in this series, and hope for more with bated breath and crossed fingers."

—Romance Junkies

"Like the comforting touch of a good friend, this book captures a widow's journey from pain and grief to growing faith and hopefulness, and does so absorbingly, with gentle humor and realism. Patti Hill is a gifted storyteller who possesses a lovely and engaging way with words. I look forward to future work from this talented new author."

—InFuzeMag.com

"Located in the high desert of Colorado, the setting and gardens are almost like characters themselves. Readers will be able to picture the plants, flowers, and intricate landscapes as if they were there."

—Bookloons.com

"*Like a Watered Garden* is loaded with emotion and imagery. You won't want to miss Patti Hill's debut novel."

—Dancing Word

"This first novel is distinguished by good writing and colorful imagery. . . ."

—*Library Journal*

"Patti Hill has proven she is a master of the written word in this humorous and heart-warming story."

—Focus on Fiction

"If I were searching for a gentle, entertaining, yet intellectually sound way to reveal to the unbelieving world what faith looks like in working clothes, what faith feels like in crises, how faith acts toward others who are hurting, this would be the book I'd reach for. As others have commented, the realism of Mibby's traumas and her intimate, yet not always clicking-on-all-cylinders relationship with the Master Gardener combined with Patti Hill's excellence in creating lyrical prose made me sigh with satisfaction when I finished the last page."

—Cynthia Ruchti,
The Heartbeat of the Home Broadcast

"Those characters . . . are delightfully and truthfully drawn. . . . This is a wonderfully absorbing story . . . an exceptional, fun-to-read novel." (Five Stars)

—Love Romances

"Warm, whimsical, and rich with creative word pictures, Hill uses language the way a master gardener uses plants. I fell in love with Mibby and rooted for her through the struggles and decisions she faced. Mibby won my heart again and again."

—Sharon Hinck, author of
The Secret Life of Becky Miller

IN *E*VERY

*F*LOWER

Also by Patti Hill

Like a Watered Garden

Always Green

In Every Flower

Flower

A Novel

Patti Hill

BETHANY HOUSE PUBLISHERS

Minneapolis, Minnesota

In Every Flower
Copyright © 2006
Patti Hill

Cover design by Koechel Peterson & Associates

Unless otherwise identified, Scripture quotations are from the HOLY BIBLE, NEW
INTERNATIONAL VERSION®. Copyright © 1973, 1978, 1984 by International Bible
Society. Used by permission of Zondervan Publishing House. All rights reserved.

Scripture quotations identified RSV are from the Revised Standard Version of the Bible.
Copyright 1946, 1952, 1971 by the Division of Christian Education of the National
Council of Churches of Christ in the USA. Used by permission.

Published by Bethany House Publishers
11400 Hampshire Avenue South
Bloomington, Minnesota 55438

Bethany House Publishers is a division of
Baker Publishing Group, Grand Rapids, Michigan.

Printed in the United States of America

ISBN-13:   978-0-7642-2939-8
ISBN-10:   0-7642-2939-7

Library of Congress Cataloging-in-Publication Data

Hill, Patti (Patti Ann)
   In every flower / Patti Hill.
      p.   cm. — (Garden gates ; 3)
   ISBN-13: 978-0-7642-2939-8 (pbk.)
   ISBN-10: 0-7642-2939-7 (pbk.)
   1. Remarried people—Fiction. 2. Women gardeners—Colorado—Fiction.
3. Stepfamilies—Fiction. 4. Domestic fiction. I. Title.
   PS3608.I4373I5   2006
   813'.6—dc22
                                                          2006019312

TO MY BELOVED,

DENNIS—

"HIS BANNER OVER ME IS LOVE."

Song of Songs 2:4

Just as a prism of glass miters light and
casts a colored braid, a garden sings sweet incantations
the human heart strains to hear. Hiding in every flower,
in every leaf, in every twig and bough are reflections
of the God who once walked with us in Eden.

—FROM TONIA TRIEBWASSER'S *THE COLOR OF GRACE:*
THOUGHTS FROM A GARDEN IN A DRY LAND

Now faith is being sure of what we hope for
and certain of what we do not see.

HEBREWS 11:1

MARCH
16

Just-for-show clouds remain from yesterday's storm. Forsythias sounding revelry. Apricots and ~~my~~ our Spring Snow crabapple answering the call with breathy pink and white blossoms—nearly 2 weeks ahead of last year. No more freezes, please!

We drove across the Colorado River on a bridge as graceful as a bow. Before us, a carnival sky reflected the flavors of snow cones—grape, cherry, lemon, and my personal favorite, tangerine. Just above the rim of the Uncompahgre Plateau, the setting sun gilded the voluminous remains of a storm.

"We're such a cliché," I said, "driving into a sunset, happily ever after."

Larry drove with one hand on the wheel and the other resting on my knee. A doughy smile tugged at the corners of his mouth. I smiled, too—from the rumble of the floorboard to the top of my head. The wedding had been mostly perfect, and we'd welcomed the late-winter blizzard that extended our honeymoon on Willard Lake by a day. Less than an hour ago, we'd dug through a snowdrift to free Larry's car, and now we passed from winter to spring as we descended six thousand feet from the top of the Grand Mesa to the valley floor. Colorado is crazy that way.

The interstate skirted the barren slopes of the Book Cliffs, a severe escarpment of Mancos shale strewn with boulders the size of houses. Rows upon rows of fruit trees and grapevines filled the south side of the highway, where the river fed the irrigation canals. Their branches were nothing but spindly fingers, except for the apricot trees teased by the balmy weather to unfurl their pink blossoms—such imprudent behavior after only a few warm days. The valley floor lay before us like a calm sea—desert hills scarred by dirt bike trails to the north and farms tilled in a rich red loam to the south. The Book Cliff Mountains and the Uncompahgre Plateau and the Grand Mesa girded the valley like a broad belt. Usually a comforting sight, the cliffs thrummed at an apprehension I'd done my best to ignore in the weeks leading up to the wedding.

The car slowed as we took the first exit for Orchard City and headed south toward home. *Our* home. The inevitable sadness of a carnival rolling out of town nudged me, but I shrugged off the feeling.

When we stopped at the last intersection before turning up Crawford Avenue and home, I squeezed Larry's hand. "You better wipe that silly grin off your face."

His grin widened. "Can't be done. This is what loving you does to me."

I kissed the back of his hand for saying so. "Ready for reentry?"

"Absolutely."

Over my shoulder, the sunset had faded to a nightlight down a long hallway.

Larry's overgrown tabby, Goliath, sat on a kitchen chair grooming herself. Connie, my friend and now my mother-in-law, peeled potatoes with Larry at the sink. Ky would be home soon, and the picture would be complete. The only thing left for me to do was set the table.

I lifted the cat off the chair and opened a drawer to gather the silverware, but tongs and spatulas filled the dividers instead. "Oh my goodness, where's the silverware?" My face warmed at the thought of the crumbs that had accumulated in the silverware dividers. "I didn't mean for you to clean the drawers, Connie."

She quartered a potato into the steaming pot and wiped her hands. "I hope you don't mind. I did a little reorganizing. I'd be happy to put things back. It's just that I nearly wore myself out setting the table every night." She opened the drawer under the coffeepot to reveal the silverware. "Having the silverware near the dining room made setting the table so much easier. And in the upper cabinet, you'll find your coffee mugs and herb teas."

Connie had stayed at the house with my son, Ky, while Larry and I honeymooned on the Grand Mesa. Five days. Maybe she cleaned the attic, too? Better yet, there were Ky's room and the basement.

"I think you'll like how I organized your spice cabinet, too."

The spice cabinet?

"Come see," she said.

Larry dried his hands. "I'll take the luggage up to the room." *Is he scurrying?*

I rolled my shoulders against a growing tension and followed Connie to the cabinet beside the stove. She stopped abruptly and turned to face me. Her eyes glistened with tears, and she smiled like a newly crowned Miss America. She pulled me into a tight hug, a new intimacy for us. "It's so fun to have a daughter," she said. "I couldn't be happier."

"Thank you, Connie. I'm happy, too." *But I liked my kitchen the way it was.*

She released me to check the progress of the roast in the oven. A primal territorial zeal overcame me, and I fought the urge to jump on the island to plant a flag. The kitchen wasn't big enough for another woman. Or was it? I had to admit Connie's changes made sense, and it was wonderful to come home to the aroma of a roast in the oven. So why did I feel compelled to mark my territory? *Get a grip, girl!* I needed water and time to think. I found the glasses in the last cabinet I opened.

Connie had whooped for joy when Larry and I had announced our engagement in February. Surely her manic rearranging flowed from giddiness. The Connie I knew—ever-present, ever-willing, a true friend, and now my mother-in-law—suffered from never-say-no syndrome, not a queen bee complex. Once the sparkle of having a daughter-in-law and grandson faded a bit, she would settle down, and we'd share a laugh when she discovered I'd moved the silverware back to its original place.

When I offered to help Connie with dinner, she said, "You're still on your honeymoon until tomorrow, so sit down and relax." She adjusted the flame under the potatoes and slid a pan of dinner rolls into the oven.

In all the time I'd known Connie, stretching back to our earliest days in Orchard City and Ky's days on the cradle roll at church, she had permed her gray hair into tight ringlets. But like me, she had fallen under the influence of Louise, my best friend, who could talk a bee out of its hum. After an afternoon with Louise at Virginia's Oasis of Beauty just before the wedding, Connie had returned with soft waves of moon-lit copper and a hint of pink gloss on her lips. Picture a daisy's wide-eyed attention to detail—that was Connie, certainly not a meddlesome mother-in-law.

Ky arrived home just as Connie took the roast out of the oven. It still amazed me how he'd grown to fill the doorway. He stood there, disheveled and flush-faced from baseball practice. He looked from Larry to me and said, "Hey, you're home" before he refilled his water bottle.

Connie spoke with the authority of Nurse Ratchet. "Get your hands washed. Dinner's on the table." Something in her voice told me Ky and Connie's days together had not been completely pleasant.

Ky picked up his bag and squeezed past me to the hall. "I'll eat later. I'm not hungry."

Connie leaned toward me, her voice frayed. "I'd make that boy sit down and eat with his family. He hid in his room most of the time you were gone. We only ate together once."

I looked to Larry. He loaded his plate with mashed potatoes, meaning any action was up to me, just as we'd planned. Every stepfamily book we'd read reiterated the same point: the biological parent must be the disciplinarian. All-righty, but parenting an almost-man was difficult enough. I didn't need an audience.

I caught up to Ky as he started up the stairs. "Hey there, how about sitting down with us? It would be nice to hear about your week."

He looked behind me, so I looked too. Connie, wringing her hands, watched us from the hallway. Larry stood behind her. The threat of a storm darkened Ky's eyes, yet he managed to speak with control. "No thanks."

He seldom ate right after practice. He was hot. And, oh boy did he need a shower. But most of all, he needed to decompress from his day. Larry knew that. But still, having dinner together on our first night as a family would be nice. "What's up?" I asked him.

He shrugged and continued up the stairs. "I'm just not hungry."

I believed him, but more than I liked to admit, Connie's approval mattered to me. "Ky?" *Pretty please, come eat dinner with us and pretend like you're interested in telling us about your classes and friends.*

"Stop right there, Ky." It was Larry, sliding past his mother to join me at the base of the stairs. I touched his arm and Larry stopped, but Ky didn't. He continued climbing the stairs, almost with a swagger, throwing down the gauntlet as surely as any rookie knight.

Larry shouted, "Don't walk away when your mother's talking to you!"

The power of Larry's voice startled me. Ky didn't even turn around. "I have stuff to do," he said.

Larry climbed a stair and I caught the crook of his arm, but still his anger flared. "You're not doing anything until you've shown your mother the respect she deserves."

Not only had Larry usurped my command, but by demanding respect from a teenager, he'd given Ky plenty of ammunition for a passive-aggressive counterattack. What was I to do—back up Larry with a fresh offensive or sound a retreat to regroup the troops? Right or wrong, I waved a white flag. "Ky, take a shower and come down when you're hungry."

Connie returned to the kitchen, mumbling, "I don't know about that."

Larry used a stage whisper I could have heard from Kansas. "You can't let him talk to you like that."

Just a handful of hours earlier, I'd watched Larry brush his teeth and declared myself the luckiest woman alive. Had anything changed since then? Only that we'd stepped back into reality. A husband, a son, a mother-in-law, a cat, and a dog. *Where* is *Blink?* I had a family again. That was all good and nothing I couldn't handle. A few more birthdays to remember, personalities to accommodate, the normal stuff of families. *Right?*

Larry slumped to the bottom stair, head in his hands. "I blew it, didn't I? I'm so sorry. You married some kind of Neanderthal."

Who could disdain that kind of humility? Just for him to hear, I said, "Round one to the kid. Tomorrow's another day."

～⌒

I nudged Larry's shoulder to stop his snoring. He mumbled an apology and rolled away from me. His breathing deepened within a heartbeat. I lay atop the new mattress like a magician on a bed of nails. By the time Larry started snoring again, my lower back ached.

I blinked at the ceiling and replayed the day Larry and I had stripped the wallpaper off the master bedroom walls to transform the room from Scott and Mibby's bedchamber to Larry and Mibby's love nest. I'd worked a corner of wallpaper free with a putty knife and pulled slowly like the nice man at the paint store had instructed. A sodden piece, no bigger than a footprint, tore off. "This is nuts," I said.

On the opposite wall, Larry swiped a scoring tool over the wallpaper with broad, confident strokes. "Give the remover time to work," he said and returned to whistling along with the radio.

At first, we'd only planned to remove the wallpaper—Larry had complained it was a little flowery for his taste—and replace it with a manlier yet humble shade of green paint. But once we'd dismantled the bed and removed the furniture from the room, Larry's shoulders had relaxed. He talked about his preference for mission-style furniture and questioned whether the king-sized bed overpowered the space. Larry isn't the sort of man who has style preferences, furniture or otherwise. Not because he lacks an appreciation for beauty—he's downright poetic when it comes to naming his hybrid dahlias. Larry's contentment centers on soft jeans and an uncluttered life, not a magazine-perfect home. In that way, we are perfect for each other.

Talking about mission furniture was Larry's way of saying something without actually saying it. The bedroom's hydrangea wallpaper had wrapped the most intimate of spaces for Scott and me. The king-sized bed and the antique furnishings were remnants of Scott's presence. I should have seen it sooner, no matter that Scott had been gone from this world for more than two years. So I scrubbed the room down to the bones to make it something completely different, not unlike how you wipe out the kitchen cabinets no matter how clean the previous owner left them. We charged the limit on the J. C. Penney credit card and raced to ready the room for new furniture and linens before the wedding.

As I waited for the wallpaper remover to do its job, I wondered how many times the century-old house had been remade to accommodate new residents. Scott and I had removed a wall to join two bedrooms. We'd wanted a modern master suite with an actual closet and a bathroom. I couldn't help thinking that all of our fretting and scraping had made the plain Jane Victorian roll its eyes, knowing someone would eventually come along to replace the wall and dismantle the closet.

The next piece of wallpaper I pried away was the size of Maui—in a pocket atlas—and the paper backing remained adhered to the wall. "There has to be a better way."

Larry wrapped his arms around me, and I leaned into his embrace. "Let's forget all of this," he said. "The Elvis Chapel of Love is only eight hours away—seven if you let me do the driving."

"Does Elvis do wallpaper?"

It had been Larry's eagerness, nay, his exuberance that had persuaded me to move the wedding from the fall up to March eleventh, shoehorning the wedding between my son's basketball season and the beginning of baseball practice. This only perturbed Larry's side of the family, the McManus clan, because the eleventh of March happened to be the fiftieth wedding anniversary of Larry's aunt and uncle. Nevertheless, we booked the church and sent the invitations, but I still hadn't found a pair of sophisticated yet youthful buttercream shoes to wear with my wedding dress. Driving to Las Vegas sounded reasonable.

Standing there with Maui in my hand, I asked, "Are we rushing things?"

That wasn't the first time I'd asked the question. Larry didn't waste words. He tightened his embrace, and I told myself I was crazy to worry. Marrying Larry was the smartest thing I could do. He was earnest and conscientious, possessed an inconspicuous intellect, and was strong in all the ways men liked to be strong, yet tender and vulnerable without being brittle. Loving him had emboldened me to step over the starting line of life. And Larry loved my son—no doubt about that.

Isn't that enough?

Pastor Dale thought so. When we first went to him for premarital counseling, he said our quick decision to marry troubled him. Adult love and marriage is different, he'd said, mostly because the people involved *are* adults—adults who have collected odd bits and pieces of heartache like a decorator crab collects ocean debris on its shell. But Larry and I had talked about everything. Dreams. Money. Values. Wounds. Disappointments. And, of course, Ky. After two sessions with Pastor Dale, he'd taken out his planner and asked, "What date were you thinking about?"

Even with the changes Larry and I had made to the bedroom, all that had been familiar remained: the bar of light projected onto the wall from the streetlight, the hum of the traffic on the business loop, and the incessant yapping of the Bridgewaters' bichon frise. The darkness condensed time and handed a microphone to my self-doubt. I glanced at Larry sleeping beside me. *Do I even know this guy?*

I threw back the covers and headed for the kitchen and, hopefully, a piece of leftover wedding cake from the freezer. When I reached into a drawer for a fork and pulled out a can opener, I flipped on the kitchen light and moved the silverware and glasses and potholders back where they belonged but left the spices in their new order. I wanted to stake my claim, not be spiteful. I sat at the island, eating carrot cake warmed in the microwave. The cream cheese frosting stuck to the roof of my mouth. Before long, the day's should-haves whispered in my ear: You *should have* followed Ky upstairs and talked to him privately. You *should have* waited until the end of the dinner blessing to complain about Goliath licking your bread. You *should have* waited until the end of *Good Eats* to ask Connie if she needed help carrying her luggage out to her car. And you should *not* have groaned when Connie announced that Goliath would be living with you.

Blink, my black Labrador, whined at me from the utility porch. I sat on the floor beside his new bed, a plaid pillow Connie had appliquéd with his name. He hefted himself from the floor to wash my face with his soft tongue.

"I know, I know, everything's different. But trust me, sleeping on the porch isn't that bad. Larry snores. You wouldn't like it. The cat? She's a problem. I'll talk to Larry."

Blink did something he'd never done before. He lay across my lap and sighed. What a conniving dog. "That won't work. You're not getting into bed with me . . . I mean us." But I didn't push him off my lap. I leaned against the broom closet and scratched the silky spot behind his ears.

The computer pinged to announce the arrival of an e-mail. "Sorry, bud, this could be important." *Or it could be the hundredth offer for discount prescription drugs*. When I opened the message, the screen pulsated with smacking lips and swaying wedding bells. I muted the speakers to drown out a mechanical rendition of "Love Is a Many-Splendored Thing." The body of the e-mail read:

welcome home! i wish i was there with you guys :-(i'd make you an omelet with veggies and blueberry salsa . . . remember? ha! :-D just got home from bible study. whoa, did you know that jesus spits out the lukewarm churches . . . he's no wimp . . . Gracie cried for over an hour but nobody said anything . . . Darlia just held her hand. She stopped crying before we shared prayer requests. SHE'S GETTING BETTER!!!!! :o) my only student with promise is truant . . . pray for her . . . name's Lien-hua. She has a boyfriend . . . so young & tough. God wants me here i know it. a new guy in the building asked me out for coffee . . . he likes

iced mochas too . . . match made in heaven? hey, i have an idea
so pray for me too, love andrea
ps-thinking of a septum ring!

Andrea is my stepdaughter—my deceased husband's daughter from
his first marriage. That's a mouthful, but the truth is, God sent Andrea
to me when I needed to learn how to love with an open heart. Scott
never told me about Andrea or her mother, his first wife. Assimilating
that bit of information while grieving my dead husband nearly popped
my cork—until I got to know Andrea. If she was a flower in my garden,
she would be a bleeding heart, delicate with startling details, a jewel
among the ordinary. She lived with Ky and me for two summers but
then moved to San Francisco full-time to teach middle school orches-
tra. I can't think of a more challenging job, and I envy Andrea's buoy-
ancy. For her, every turn in life holds fresh possibilities.

I closed my eyes to pray for Lien-hua. What to pray for a middle
school girl completely confounded me, so I opened my eyes and wrote
a short response to Andrea, making a promise to call her on Sunday:
*All's well here. Yea Gracie! Yea Darlia! God bless Lien-hua! Is this the same
guy you wrote about last week? Nose ring? A garnet stud* and *a ring might
make your nose seem cluttered. Love, Mom.*

I considered telling Andrea about Connie's rearranging the kitchen
cabinets, but I thought better of it. Andrea loved to tease me about
having a gourmet kitchen to make boxed macaroni and cheese. Connie
was just being helpful, as per her usual. Instead, I added a P.S. about
Goliath. *Love the man, love the cat, I guess. Now, go to bed. I love you!* I
hit the send button and hoped she would notice how helpful capitali-
zation and punctuation could be.

The light shone under Ky's door, so I knocked and waited for permission to enter. He deserved at least three seconds of privacy now and
again. He sat bent over the atlas at his desk.

"Ky, it's ten-thirty. Do you have a lot of homework?"

"Mostly humanities stuff."

In his evolution from boy to man, Ky was inching his way past the
midpoint. His limbs, tightly knotted with muscles, grew increasingly

hairy, and he shaved most days, although I couldn't say with certainty that he brushed his teeth for more than five seconds.

"Did everything go okay with Connie while we were gone?"

He turned to me. "She wants me to call her Grandma."

"She does?"

"I told her I'd think about it."

"You're very generous. I appreciate it."

I kissed him good-night—not on the lips or cheek anymore but at the hairline of his forehead, where tiny pimples pricked my lips. I told him to get to bed soon, which I knew was futile but felt obliged to say it. When I lingered a beat too long, Ky said, "What?"

"It's going to take a while to get used to the new—"

"It's no big deal."

"Your happiness matters to us. I'll talk to Connie. And Larry . . . he'll get better. He really cares about you."

"Like I said, it's no big deal." He turned back to his books. "Listen, I have a geography test tomorrow. I have to be able to draw Southeast Asia and label the major cities and geographical features like rivers and stuff. These names are killing me."

As usual, I'd made more of what had happened that night than I should have. "See you in the morning." I waited for his reply, but he was tracing a map from the atlas.

Before I closed the door, Ky said, "Oh yeah, they're hiring delivery guys at Pizza Man. I thought I'd give it a try."

"You have so much going on already. You'll be traveling for baseball soon, and school . . . You hardly sleep as it is."

"My next car insurance bill is due in July. Besides, there's another guy on the team who works there. He says the manager is really good about working around his schedule."

"I don't know . . ."

"Do you have to talk to Larry first?" There was no mistaking the contempt in his voice.

"I'll discuss it with Larry and let you know."

I closed the door softly, more for Larry's sake than Ky's, and returned to my bedroom. A large gray lump snored on my side of the bed. Goliath. When a few nuggets of Friskies didn't entice her off the bed, I sat on my pillow and pushed her to the foot of the bed with my feet. I drew my knees to my chest to lie down. In his sleep, Larry reached out and took my hand.

Love the man. Love the cat? *Not hardly.* Goliath hit the floor, on her feet, I assumed.

I set the alarm for four o'clock, winced, and added fifteen minutes. I wanted to make breakfast for Larry before he left for work at five. Did I need half an hour to make toast and oatmeal? Cold cereal with a sliced banana took three minutes tops. I tapped the minute button on the alarm until the jumbo numbers read 4:45.

MARCH

17

Clouds came around noon. Breezy and cool at 54°. Roses are breaking, but it's too early to prune. Despite my apprehension, hyacinths and Oregon grape and creeping phlox are all blooming.

Dreams are the playgrounds for our daytime emotions. Those feelings of inadequacy that we shoo away by day come back to write absurd plays to be rehearsed at night. That's why adults wish children sweet dreams with wistful sadness. We don't have ambrosial dreams of our own to pass along.

On the first night home from our honeymoon, if I dreamed at all, I would have expected dreams full of rich banquets and vast horizons, perhaps with some flying among the clouds. Instead, I dreamed I was driving an unfamiliar car through a parking lot, probably Wal-Mart at Christmas time. Drivers stalked shoppers with packages in hopes of claiming their parking spaces.

The car had a stick shift like my business truck, the Daisy Mobile, but driving the car was like playing a shell game. Each time the engine revved to a whine and I tried to shift, the function of each pedal had changed. To complicate matters, two extra pedals crowded the floor-board. The car lurched, spurted, and died as I stomped one pedal after another, only to restart on its own and accelerate. Shoppers darted out of my way. An old man in a cardigan sweater shook his fist at me. I abandoned looking for a parking place and groped for the ignition. The car finally came to a stop inside the store, where a man in a blue vest offered the use of a shopping cart.

I awoke to the ringing phone. With one hand I reached for the receiver and with the other I felt Larry's pillow. It was cold.

"Hello?" I said, squinting in the cushiony light of morning.

It was my sister, Margot. "I really thought she would come to your wedding."

Preamble had never been a part of Margot's conversational style. In this case, specificity wasn't necessary. I knew she was talking about our mother, the topic she hated to love. I sat up to concentrate on what she said.

The clock read 6:45, meaning it was only 5:45 in California, where my sister lived. I threw back the covers and headed for the kitchen, hoping to find Larry, knowing he'd been at his job for more than an hour. The shower ran in Ky's bathroom.

"Are you there?" Margot asked, but her words sounded more like a plea.

I stopped at the top of the stairs. "Margot, are you all right?"

"Of course I'm all right. Why wouldn't I be?"

"The tone of your voice. You sound . . ."

"What?"

Every family has its unspoken rules. For Margot and me, the rules were simple: Margot lived to catalog my vulnerabilities and exploit them shamelessly; in turn, I acknowledged her rampart-like strength at every chance, even though I'd known for a long time that Margot's soft underside winced more easily than most. Out of habit, though, I averted my eyes when her protective shell splintered.

I continued toward the kitchen. "You've never called me this early before."

"I expected you to be up, seeing that Larry's a baker."

"He's a bakery delivery driver."

A pink envelope rested against my favorite mug. Larry had written my name in precise block letters and dotted the *i* with a heart.

"Mibby?"

I slit the envelope open with a paring knife. "I meant to be up. I must have forgotten to turn on the alarm."

While Margot explained why she'd called—something about reassuring me that Mother had probably had a good reason for missing the wedding—I read Larry's note. *Good morning, Beautiful! I couldn't bear waking you. You looked like a sleeping angel, so I turned off your alarm. I hope you rested well. I'll be thinking of you every minute of the day. I'll skip lunch to be home before Ky's practice is over so we can have some time alone. I'll be HUNGRY, but only for you. I love you. Larry*

When I sighed, Margot asked, "Are you listening?"

I set the note on the counter and turned my attention to Margot. "I suppose it's possible that Mother didn't receive the invitation, but you know, the invitation wasn't returned, either."

"Did you use the post office box?"

"Margot, having you here made the day special for me."

I'd steeled myself on the morning of the wedding, as I had on so many other occasions, for my mother's absence. Margot's attentiveness had unnerved me more than my mother being AWOL ever could have. Margot arrived the day before the wedding and wrestled control of the buffet from Louise—typical enough for Margot—but she also arrived with a jovial perm, a far cry from her usual somber sleekness. She'd inherited our father's hair, plenteous and pliable. Since the last time I'd seen her, she'd warmed her brown hair with a caramel rinse, a color I would have thought too cordial for Margot, but the change had lit a welcoming flame in her eyes.

Before a gilded mirror in the bride's dressing room of our church, she had zipped me into my dress and adjusted the clasp on Grandma's pearls with an intimacy we'd never before shared as sisters. Our eyes met in the mirror. In the tension of her face, I saw a million words left unspoken. In odd moments during the honeymoon, I'd wondered what Margot would have said if Louise had not tapped on the door to say, "Larry's squirming at the altar like a snake on an anthill. You best get in there, sugar."

I switched the phone to my other ear and asked, "Margot, when we were in the bride's dressing room, was there something you wanted to say?"

"The housekeeper's here."

"At six in the morning?"

"We'll talk later." And the phone went dead, which in a strange way comforted me, because an abrupt hang-up was especially typical of Margot.

Frost coated the straw-colored lawn in the backyard. I shivered and poured a cup of coffee to drink over the floor register in the living room. The warm air rose to billow my gown. I held my mug like a lover. My tummy tingled when I remembered Larry's note.

Goliath swaggered into the room, twitching her tail. I closed my eyes. It was too early in the morning to be snubbed by a cat. Steam from my coffee collected on my face. When I opened my eyes, Goliath lay coiled in a ball, sleeping in my grandmother's damask chair. I don't know what made me angrier—the bloated hairball of a cat taking liberties on a keepsake or that shooing the cocky cat from the chair meant stepping away from the warmth of the register.

I tried pulling Goliath out of the chair. "Scat, you pestiferous cat. Go outside and cough up a hairball."

She dug her claws into the upholstery.

I moved to unhook her claws, and she nipped my hand. "Ow! You sorry excuse for a mammal. Get out of that chair!"

She tucked her nose under her tail and closed her eyes. Such provocation demanded action. I reached for the scruff of her neck, but the cat anticipated my move. She struck the back of my hand, claws extended. Tiny beads of blood rose out of the scratch.

"You beast!" By the time I returned to the living room with a broom, Goliath had disappeared for parts unknown. "Good riddance!"

~⌒

After my shower, I returned to the kitchen in time to see Ky drop Larry's note to the counter. "Good morning," I said, hoping I sounded light and breezy and unconcerned that my sixteen-year-old son had read his mother's love note. Had he gotten to the part about Larry being hungry?

Ky shoved the atlas into his book bag and cinched up the ties without looking at me. "Hey."

Oh yeah, he had read the entire note, all right. An image of walking into the bathroom on my grandmother flashed before me—the startling expanse of white cotton and flesh I'd seen. This was worse. *Pretend nothing happened.* "Are you ready for your test?"

"I think so."

A shaft of sunlight glinted off his blond stubble.

"Did you shave this morning?" I asked.

"No time."

And still he avoided my eyes.

"Listen, Ky . . . the note . . ."

He hefted his book bag to his shoulder and turned toward the door. "I shouldn't have read it."

"You have to understand. Couples—"

"I can't be late." He turned the doorknob. "Mr. Chase docks points for tardies. I'm outta here."

I followed him to his car. "Are we okay?"

He turned to face me, but his eyes fixed on something over my shoulder. "Sure. No problem. I have to go."

He drove down the street, rolled through the stop sign, and squealed into traffic. I leaned against the kitchen door and prayed, "O Lord, get Ky to school in one piece. And . . ." I wasn't sure how to pray. I wanted God to wave His holy scepter and erase Ky's memory of the note's contents. *Fat chance.* There wasn't a rock big enough for me to crawl under, so I prayed, "Lord, forgive me for being so careless. Teach me how to be my husband's lover and Ky's asexual mom at the same time. Amen."

My brain snagged on the image of my son's face as he dropped the note, and in my next heartbeat, my anger flared at Larry. No kid wanted to be reminded that his parents were lovers. I shimmied the anger off

like a dog leaving a lake. Who could fault a man for writing love notes
to his wife?

Not me.

Blink sauntered into the kitchen and studied me with wise, milky
eyes.

"I know, I know. We have to be more careful."

I returned Larry's note to the envelope, carried it upstairs, and
tucked it between my underwear and socks—a no-man's land for teenage boys.

I took my coffee and journal out to the garden. Spring is nature's
grand homecoming, and I wanted to see who had arrived while Larry
and I were on our honeymoon. First, I checked the Japanese maple, a
tree on the frail edge of hardiness for our high-desert winters. Russet
buds filled the delicate tree, so I checked the Japanese stewartia for
signs of life. A bare branch snapped between my fingers. *Bummer.* The
disappointment over the fatality dissipated quickly when I realized the
tree's demise opened up space for a new hardy magnolia I'd read about
in *Sunset* magazine. Gardeners can be heartless that way. I raised my
collar against the chill. Next stop, the roses.

Burgundy leaves as long as an inch filled the rose canes. *Stupid
plants.* A few warm days and they were ready to put on their summer
finery. Spring is a rogue season—one minute pleasantly nurturing, the
next bitingly cruel—especially in western Colorado, where the dry air
can't hold a day's warmth any longer than a secret. Hard freezes sometimes destroyed peach blossoms as late as mid-April. Cautious gardeners, including me, waited until Mother's Day to plant cold-sensitive
plants such as tomatoes and peppers.

The roses weren't the only anxious flowers in the garden. The true
exhibitionists were the daffodils, but they're made for the capricious
nature of spring. They bend with the cold but aren't broken. More
humble, but just as showstopping, the diminutive grape hyacinth
bloomed in the rock garden. Every year, my admiration for Oregon

grape grew. A true performer in every season, clusters of yellow flowers nestled among the holly-like leaves. In a month or two, the plant's blue berries would attract birds to the yard.

The image of Ky's disgust flashed before me. *Argh!* I batted the vision away and returned to the roses. What could happen if I pruned the roses in March? No doubt, the inevitable late frost would come, and I would be caught red-faced and rose-free. *No hurries. No worries.* I slipped my pruners back into their sheath.

Louise called from the garden gate. "Knock, knock. Are the love-birds ready for a visitor? I brought goodies." And to prove her announcement, she walked through the garden, carrying a basket large enough to hold a watermelon. A ripple of joy fluttered my heart when I saw Louise—*and* her basket.

We held each other for a long while, our embrace saying what close friends have such a difficult time putting into words. In the early days of our friendship, back before Ky joined Scott and me, Louise's hugs had overwhelmed me. I'd stiffened without even wanting to. Undaunted, Louise had patted my back and said, "Now, now, sugar," her all-purpose phrase for smoothing over an awkward moment.

Louise had gained back some of the weight she'd lost during her cancer treatments the year before. I liked the softer Louise, especially the way her cheeks made slits of her eyes when she smiled. "Was it wonderful, sugar?" she asked, her eyebrows hopping with innuendo.

"Louise!"

She held my cheeks in her hands. "Gracious, I'm not asking for details. I prayed and prayed for you and Larry to have a simply divine honeymoon. I just want to know if God answered my prayers."

She wasn't fooling me. Louise thrived on details. I put as many as I could into the way I said, "Oh yes, it was wonderful."

"This calls for a feast."

By the time she emptied her basket onto the kitchen table, an array of baked goods and tidy appetizers lay out before me. She pushed a fat slice of white cake encrusted with coconut my way.

Sugary treats made Louise's southern drawl flow like a river of choc-olate around bonbon boulders. "This here is the Coconut Pillow Cake recipe Rhonda Lowell submitted. She says the recipe has been in the family for generations." Louise looked at me over red bifocals rimmed with rhinestones, an ever-present accessory for her editor-in-chief outfit du jour. She pulled a battery-operated fan out of her pocket and pointed it toward her face. She closed her eyes to let the stream of air lift her bangs from her forehead. "Just give me a minute, sugar. The doctor said if I take deep breaths and welcome the hot flashes as a sign of change and new beginnin's, they wouldn't last so long." Her eyes popped open. "I wonder if he would give the same advice with a blow torch pointed at *his* face? Sign of change? New beginnings? That's nothing but hornswaggle, if you ask me. Would you mind opening a window?"

Louise, a breast cancer overcomer, as she liked to call herself, had prayed for a way to redeem the ordeal. She'd tried housing cancer patients in her bed-and-breakfast, the Still Waters Inn, but the memories of her son's lost battle with cancer made that ministry too painful, especially for her husband, Manley. So she'd settled on raising money for the Beauty From Ashes Boutique, a group that provided wigs and prostheses for uninsured breast cancer patients. As editor-in-chief of the *In the Pink* cookbook, she tested recipes full time. For a short while, when the fear of cancer had chased the love of refined flour right out of Louise, she'd stopped baking with anything but whole grains and honey, ending up with concoctions that resembled a glazed brick fresh from the oven. From the weightlessness of the coconut cake before me, I declared Louise free from the tyranny of cancer.

"You go on, now. Give the cake a taste."

I worked the cake over my tongue. "Perfect. All it needs is a touch more coconut."

"That's why I trust your judgment. We're two peas in a pod." Louise slid an evaluation card across the table. "Rate the cake from one to ten, one being 'I wouldn't serve this slop to my dog' and ten being 'I've died and gone to heaven.'"

I gave the cake a seven and cut another bite with my fork.

"Not now, sugar. No dawdlin'. We have lots of tasting to do."

Next up was a plate of mushrooms smothered in a creamy sauce heavy with garlic and some sort of cheese. Romano? Parmesan?

"Karen Wayne, y'all know her, the gal with the hourglass figure and the budget to accentuate every inch the good Lord gave her? You met her at the planning meeting. Her mushrooms are simply to die for." Louise covered her mouth with her hand. "Forget you heard me say that. I don't want to influence your score. She calls her appetizer Mushrooms in Rhapsody Sauce."

Rhapsody made me think of Larry's note again, and my face warmed. "It's a little early in the day for mushrooms, don't you think?"

Louise fanned herself with an evaluation card. "Don't be silly. Mushrooms are a vegetable."

"They're fungus."

"Take a taste before they get cold."

We went on that way until every meatball and sweet treat had been tasted and scored. Louise dumped a rice pudding in the trash. "I don't know what Rosalie Shepherd was thinkin'. Peppermint candies in rice pudding? One must consider texture as well as taste in a well-structured recipe."

Since Larry's doctor had put him on a low-fat diet to lower his cholesterol, I never refused a sugary treat from the "outside." I finished the coconut cake with a second cup of coffee. Louise matched my pace bite for bite. The buttons of her chef's coat pulled at the buttonholes over her bosom.

While she talked, she removed her chef's coat to mop the sweat on her face. "Oh sugar, having Connie next door while you and Larry were away on your li'l ol' honeymoon was simply divine. We had coffee every morning, and she helped me sort through the submitted recipes. She certainly has discernment about the culinary arts." Louise frowned at me. "I know that look. Tell me what's buzzin' under your bonnet."

In the course of our premarital counseling, Larry had voiced concern over the openness of my friendship with Louise. The pastor concurred. "Nothing erodes the intimacy of a marriage like taking issues outside the union." I'd almost snickered when he'd said *union*. Was he talking about marriage or the routing of the South? From the look on Larry's face that day, there wasn't much difference, so I'd promised him to keep the issues of our marriage between us and only us.

Louise, the master interrogator for the South, leaned forward. "Well?"

I turned to butter and melted instantly. Besides, Connie was a mutual friend, not just my mother-in-law. I told Louise the whole story about Connie rearranging my kitchen drawers and cabinets. "I worked for an hour to get things put back where they belonged," I said.

I expected Louise's jaw to drop. Instead, she asked, "Did you ask her why she did it?"

"I didn't have to. She happily told me how poorly I'd organized my kitchen. She claimed that she nearly wore herself out setting the table every night. Can you imagine?"

"Are you about finished, sweet pea?"

"She asked Ky to call her Grandma."

Louise filled the basket with the empty dishes. "You didn't just marry Larry. You married his family. Connie has dreamed of having a daughter-in-law to love for a long time. I'd say you're very lucky to have a mother-in-law who wants to make your life easier."

Louise hadn't grasped the scope of my problem. "Did I marry his cat, too?"

"Does Larry love that cat?"

"Goliath was a gift from his father."

"Then I reckon you married a cat."

I hated to consider what kind of revenge Blink would exact for so blatant an act of disloyalty.

Louise sighed. "I don't know how much more of this flashin' I can take. I soak my nightgown with sweat three times a night, and being in the kitchen all day . . . Let's just say the Lord has some explainin' to do."

"Connie stayed after dinner to watch the Food Channel until nine o'clock, Louise. When are the three of us supposed to learn how to function as a family?"

Louise tapped her temple with one French-tipped finger. "If I remember correctly, you found Larry's love of family one of his most endearing qualities during your courtship. I assumed you included his mother in that assessment." She refreshed my coffee and poured herself a half cup. The steam rose to fog her bifocals. She cleaned them with the hem of her T-shirt and focused the full force of her blue-ribbon eyes on me. "Larry and Connie have a very special relationship, one I believe you hope to have with Ky someday. What would you want Larry to say to her? *Sorry, Ma, now that I have a wife, there's no room for you in my life?* My darlin' girl, in the time it takes to flip a flapjack, Connie will adjust to the new order of things. The two of you will be as thick as grits, and you will be so glad you kept your peace."

I saw the validity of what Louise said. Getting accustomed to new places for the spoons and glasses was one thing. Sending Connie the message that her kindness had been rejected was quite another.

After Louise helped me put the kitchen back the way Connie had arranged it, we warmed our coffee in the microwave and moved to the living room. Louise sat on the sofa. I've never been one for tons of knickknacks, or paddywacks, as Larry called them. Too much dusting for my taste. But photographs cluttered every tabletop, shelf, and bookcase of our home. On top of the bookcase, a teddy bear frame held a picture of newborn Ky. When I looked at that picture, the scent of Baby Magic wafted through my memories, and I felt the warmth of Ky's tiny body against my chest. No crocheted toilet tissue cover could do that for me.

I arranged my photographs the same way I designed my flower borders. Background. Middle ground. Foreground. Tall pictures stood in the back, medium-sized belonged in the middle, and small ones established the foreground. That was how I knew the family photographs on the sofa table behind Louise had been disturbed. Connie must have dusted. I smiled at her kindness.

Louise explained the difficulty of naming the recipes for the *In the Pink* cookbook. "How many fabulous, wonderful, and dreamy recipes can there be, for heaven's sake?"

She chattered on about overused superlatives while I itched to reset the photographs behind her. *What's really bothering you? Are you niggling at details or are you still tweaked by Connie's reorganization of the kitchen?*

Probably a little of both. But still, something wasn't right. Then I realized that the photograph of Scott with Ky reeling in his first fish was missing from the sofa table.

"And there's Rene Johnson and her Fabulous Fudge Fondant," Louise said as I crossed the room to inventory the photographs.

Ky's sports and school photographs remained among other heirloom photographs of my side of the family, including one of my grandmother on her wedding day. I loved that photograph, but what had happened to the fishing picture? Were other photographs missing?

Louise followed me into the dining room. "Too much alliteration, if you ask me. Never mind there isn't one lick of fondant in the fudge. Who would take a cookbook seriously that valued poetry over substance?"

Only a nail marked the spot where the photograph of Scott and Ky with Blink as a puppy had hung. Louise put her hand on my arm. "You're as white as Aunt Pansy's bloomers on washing day."

I led her to the family room. In place of a photograph of Scott, Ky, and me taken among the golden aspens at Haystack Reservoir only weeks before Scott's accident, Larry's high school graduation picture had been slipped into the frame. I slumped onto the sofa.

Louise picked up the frame. "What a precious picture of Larry. He was quite a looker even then. Some men require a little paddin' to soften the sharpness of their youth. I attribute Manley's good looks to buttermilk fried chicken and lots of cream gravy."

Larry and I had talked about all the photographs, and he had insisted the photographs of Scott with Ky and me posed no threat. He only asked that photographs of Scott and me as a couple be removed. Photographs including Larry would be added as we made new memories. Apparently Connie hadn't been notified of the plan.

When I told Louise what Connie had done, she clasped her arms around me. "Now, let's not make more of this than there is. She has surely tiptoed over the line a teensy bit, but she's a lovin' woman of God, sugar. As soon as you talk to her, things will be as right as rain."

I agreed with Louise, but that didn't stop me from lamenting the difference between my imagined new life and the one I'd plopped into.

Talking to Connie was what any mature, reasonable daughter-in-law would do. And yet, an impetuous anger squeezed my heart.

~~~

Later that day, drinking my fourth cup of coffee and munching on a granola bar, I sat down to map out the route for the next day for my landscape maintenance business, stopping now and then to swallow down my anger at Connie. I caught myself staring out the window without seeing, rehearsing my conversation with Connie, revising word choices and reminding myself that *pleasant words are a honeycomb*. I picked up the telephone to call her, but when my heart started pounding in my chest, I realized I wasn't ready to talk to her. Besides, I wanted to talk to Larry first. We'd agreed that I would handle any problems with Ky. I assumed that meant Larry would handle any problems with his mother. Believing Larry would welcome the chance to discuss the missing photographs with his mother settled my thoughts enough to get some work done.

We'd returned from the honeymoon to a message machine full of eager clients ready to see leaves raked, roses pruned, and preemergent herbicides applied. The winter had been mild and wet. Folks were anxious to enjoy their gardens again. Up until the previous fall, I'd been a garden designer, plus a garden maintenance worker to pay the bills, hoping the tedious work of maintaining other people's gardens would become less and less necessary as the garden design part flourished. When Larry and I had taken stock of our financial resources before the wedding, we realized operation of Perennially Yours, my garden design and maintenance business, would have to change. With Scott's life insurance proceeds dipping into the three-digit range, Larry and I decided to minimize the design portion of Perennially Yours, where the income wasn't as dependable as the maintenance side of the business. With a teenager to feed and a lifestyle to maintain until Ky graduated from high school, dependability outranked personal job satisfaction.

I remembered Larry's note and went to the bathroom to brush my teeth before returning to my route planning. I heard a car in the driveway as I folded the map of Orchard City. I looked at the clock. Two o'clock, early for Larry, but he had said he was *hungry*. My heart played patty-cake with my ribs. I stopped to check my image in the powder room. A crease of worry had left its mark between my eyebrows. *Enough of that.* I went to the door to greet him.

Connie stowed the contents of a grocery bag in the refrigerator and pantry while I bit the insides of my cheeks. She said, "Larry called me when he stopped for lunch in Hotchkiss."

"You talked to Larry?"

"He calls me every day."

Really?

"He sounded so harried; I made his favorite for dinner—beef and cheese enchiladas. I had enough tortillas for two pans. We can have one pan for dinner tonight."

We?

"And we can freeze the other pan for later. Would you mind getting the enchiladas from the back seat of the car?"

I stood at the door of Connie's Taurus and exhaled a silent scream. I balanced one pan of enchiladas in each arm. *Connie is a lovin' woman of God.* If I could live with the kitchen redo, I could live through more family dinners with Connie. Surely she'd tire of eating with a moody teenager by the end of the week. Scott's photographs? I prayed Louise was correct about Connie's reasonableness.

Watching Connie work in my kitchen soured my mood, so I insisted on making a salad, even though she had brought a lime Jell-O salad with pineapple and shredded carrot. I didn't realize the force of my chopping until Connie touched my hand and said, "Be careful of your fingers, dear."

Yet another spring storm pressed at the house, making the old timbers creak with complaint. Blink whined from his bed. Out the kitchen window, the trees lashed by the wind danced wildly. Connie hummed an indistinguishable tune, something bouncy and cheerful. It was now or never.

"I noticed you took down all of Scott's photographs," I said.

Connie stopped chopping and laid down her knife. "I'm getting to be such a silly old woman. I meant to talk to you the moment you came home. I figured you'd forgotten about taking the photographs down yourself."

"Larry and I talked about the photographs. We had a plan—"

"He will do or say just about anything for the people he loves."

"The photographs didn't bother him. He told me so."

"That's my Larry."

"The photographs are important to Ky."

"That's why I gave them to the boy. He said he had just the right place for them."

I impressed myself by thanking Connie without moving my lips. After I finished the salad, I went upstairs to pound my pillow before returning to set the table as Connie had requested.

Larry entered the kitchen, breathless and early, but not early enough. He looked from me to his mother. "Are you staying for dinner, Ma?"

"I made enchiladas, your favorite."

When Connie peeked in the oven to check the enchiladas, Larry mouthed, *What's she doing here?*

I could only shrug.

Ky arrived just as we were sitting down to eat and, to my relief, joined us. All through dinner, Larry watched me with questioning eyes. I smiled tightly right back at him, meaning, *We have to talk*. Any woman would have deciphered my meaning immediately and managed to slip away to discuss the problem at hand, but I didn't know if Larry understood. Ky left before Connie served the strawberry shortcake. She raised her eyebrows.

"He's working on a huge project," I said, disappointing myself for thinking Connie deserved any explanation at all.

She chattered on about the most recent winners of the International Barbie Couture Contest and how discouraging it had been to see the same brothers win the evening gown division three consecutive years, the very contest she'd won several years on her own. Although the story of Barbie-fashion intrigue piqued my curiosity, I didn't join the conversation. I was being petty and I knew it, but the woman had jettisoned my first husband's photographs.

After dinner she washed and I dried. When she handed me the roasting pan, she didn't let go right away. "Mibby," she whispered, "I can't thank you enough for welcoming me into your home. My house is so lonely. It helps so much to watch television until I get sleepy. I went home and went right to sleep last night."

I remembered the suffocating stillness of the house after Scott died. "I'm glad you feel comfortable."

With the kitchen clean, Connie poured herself a second cup of coffee. She sat close to the television, watching *Emeril Live* on the Food Network and scribbling notes as the chef chopped onions for an exotic salsa. Upstairs, Ky listened to pounding music and finished his homework. Larry sat by me on the sofa, his arm draped over my shoulders and running his finger up and down my arm. It was past eight o'clock. The audience shouted "Bam!" each time Emeril added another chopped jalapeño to the salsa. My skin felt tight and Emeril hadn't started the dessert yet. I opened *Sunset* magazine to look at a photo spread on small gardens.

In my head, I flipped through five months of dating and engagement memories like pages in a photo album, looking for a time Connie had shown the side of her that fretted about loneliness. I came up blank. But how reliable can the memories of a woman inoculated by love really be? *Not very.*

Larry stretched beside me. Through a yawn, he said, "Man, I'm beat. I'm going up to bed." Then he gestured toward the stairs with his head.

"It has been a long day," I said. "I think I'll turn in early, too."

Connie added to her notes. "Go ahead. I'll turn off the television before I go."

In our bathroom, I whispered to Larry, "We need to talk."

He looked at me as if I were a fresh-out-of-the-oven apple pie. "Okay," he said and kissed me the way I'd anticipated all day. The married kiss. No good-bye. No stifling of longing. No interminable nights of separation.

Downstairs, Connie yelled "Bam!" along with the television audience.

I put my hands to Larry's chest. "We have to talk about your mother."

"When is that cooking show over?"

Hello? "Your mother took all of the photographs of Scott off the wall and gave them to Ky."

"Is that a problem?" His hands moved up and down my back.

Focus! "We agreed to keep the photographs of Scott where they were."

"If Ky would rather have them in his room—"

"He didn't ask for the photographs. It was your mother's idea. She said the photographs make you uncomfortable."

Larry released me to look at his feet.

"You said the photographs didn't bother you."

"They didn't . . ."

"And now?"

"It's hard to explain."

"We agreed for Ky's sake."

"I know." Larry shoved his hands deep into his pockets, and from the way he bit his bottom lip, I knew an inertia as binding as cement had settled in him.

"Would you talk to her?" I asked.

"What would I say?"

Don't make yourself at home in my house! Don't come over for dinner every night! Don't rearrange the kitchen cabinets! Don't sit in front of the TV after we've gone to bed! And don't touch the sacred memories of this house!

"Could you ask her to talk to us before she makes any more changes in the house?" I asked.

"She's awfully lonesome."

"She said you called her from Hotchkiss."

"If I don't check in, she calls the dispatcher to ask if I'm in a hospital somewhere." He kissed my hand and held it against his bearded cheek. "She hasn't always been like this—just since my dad died." I stepped into his arms. Below the scent of yeast and sugar that clung to his shirt, there was a lakeshore baking in the sun, a garden freshly tilled, and something else I couldn't name, something sharp that made me reckless. My knees warmed.

"I stopped to call you in Carbondale," he said, "but a gal with a crying baby was waiting for the phone. The phone in front of Ranch Top Market was out of order, and the phone at the bus station in Montrose had a long line. I put the pedal to the metal to get home to you as fast as possible."

"Maybe we should get you a cell phone."

"I'll stop to call you in every town I go through."

"You'll never get home."

His eyes widened. "Nothing can keep me from you."

Before I could thank him, his mouth was over mine. And like so many conversations do, ours ended miles from its intended destination. There had been a time when I believed love sheltered me from the tyranny of clocks and calendars. That ended with Scott's death. With the taste of Larry's kiss on my lips, I said, "I loved the note you left for me."

MARCH
21

More gray than blue sky. There's a Brandywine tomato planted where the Japanese stewartia failed. Also, the hawthorn has been ~~butchered~~ pruned and so have the roses. Please, Lord, no more frosty nights.

"Put the rake down and come in out of the cold, you silly girl." Margaret clutched the collar of her sweater. "Them twigs will still be here when you come back in two weeks."

Another gust of wind raised goose bumps on my legs.

"I just took some of them molasses cookies you like out of the oven."

Behind her, the clouds swept by at a dizzying pace. "They're still warm?" I asked.

"I knew you was coming."

More friend than client, I'd spent as much time in Margaret's kitchen as in her garden. The red table between us showed its age where the touch of diners had worn past the star design in its laminated top, a testament to her hospitality and prudence.

Margaret sipped her coffee. A gray braid, thinner than I remembered, ringed her bun. I tried to picture a younger Margaret, fresh in the house from hanging clothes to dry. On a March morning much like this, the wind would have tussled her hair around her smooth face, her cheeks pink from preparing her vegetable garden, her back straight, her fingers long and slender. If I had been her neighbor then, would we have met for midmorning coffee and shared recipes from magazines?

"I don't remember seeing a prettier bride than you," she said. "Louise was right about the buttercream dress."

Of course we would have shared everything. Although separated in age by four decades, Margaret and I walked parallel paths. We were both widows and now newly remarried to men we had almost overlooked. We both adored our sons and agonized over them regularly. We both believed God was the most wondrous mystery we'd ever encountered. And we both loved gardens—especially flower gardens. Exchanging iris bulbs had knotted our hearts together the first day we'd met.

At first, Margaret's son, Sonny, had paid me to do the menial tasks of maintaining his mother's flower beds to keep her out of the blazing sun. When she married Walter, Sonny fired me, making me a casualty of a middle-aged man's temper tantrum. I volunteered my services, but the new couple wanted nothing of my charity. Instead, they rented Walter's house to a young couple from their church to augment their income. The young husband mowed both yards, but Margaret wanted me to tend the flower beds and keep the yards tidy. Receiving part of my pay in molasses cookies, soft and chewy like my grandmother had baked, only sweetened the deal.

I dipped a cookie in my coffee to add the flavors of molasses and ginger. "Where's Walter?"

"Where he's always at—the senior center playing cribbage with his cronies." Margaret sighed and smiled on a memory. "You'd think I'd know the man after living next door to him for forty years. I watched Walter leave his house hundreds of times. He practically skipped down the front walk. I'd say to myself, *There goes a man who loves his job.* Come to find out Walter hated working for the power company. All them years, he skedaddled off to play cribbage before the whistle blew. No wonder Agatha threw his boots at him." Margaret laughed and poured me another cup of coffee. "And in case you're wondering, he didn't play one game of cribbage the whole time we was courting, neither."

"Have you asked him to stay home?"

"Sure, I asked and he obliged, as glum as a boy who'd lost his puppy. Whatever Walter gets from playing cards, I figure he needs it more than he needs to be with me every waking hour of the day. Walter ain't like Quentin, not one bit, so we have to do things different. Walter's satisfied going down to the senior center three days a week, and most of those days, I go to the Purl Too shop to sit with the girls and knit. I've completed two afghans, and I'm starting a third, and it's only March. They'll make awfully nice Christmas presents."

Margaret stirred cream into her coffee. "Now if only I knew what to do about Walter yelling in his sleep . . ." She looked at me over the rim of her coffee cup with a question in her eyes.

"Larry flails in his sleep," I said. "He almost knocked me out of bed last night."

"That will get better. Walter gave me a black eye on our honeymoon."

Margaret was prodding me the way a mother does to give a child every opportunity to ask for advice. I downed the last of my coffee. "I better get going. I have a full day."

She emptied the plate of cookies into a plastic bag and followed me to the door. Blink slept where I'd left him, only the clouds had robbed him of his patch of sunshine. His chest rose and fell.

Margaret put her arm around my shoulders and held me close as we walked to the Daisy Mobile. "There's something I've got to tell you, and I can't think of an easy way to say it, so I'm just going to say it. Forget about the way you dreamed being married to Larry would be like. Dreams ain't real, but they're heavy enough to pull you under. You're a smart girl. You know what I'm saying."

~~⌒

Blink stayed in the Daisy Mobile while I walked among the potted trees at Walled Garden Nursery. A few shoppers, bundled against the

chill, wandered through the shrubs and trees. I found what I was looking for between rows of Purple Robe locusts and Autumn Blaze maples:
Timeless Beauty magnolia trees. Fresh from the grower in Oregon, the
trees' waxy leaves shone even under the gray skies, as seductive as any
showroom automobile.

Oh my.

Serious gardeners know their hardiness zone as well as their own
street address. Based on average low temperatures of an area, the hardiness zone determines which plants will thrive in a particular region.
Orchard City is a six. In a gardener's mind, southern magnolias are
grouped with Spanish moss and the syrupy air of a bayou, a solid eight,
not the parched land of creosote bushes that is Orchard City. Knowing
that only made me want a magnolia tree more. True, the Timeless
Beauty was a hybrid with humble parentage, a Virginia cucumber tree,
for goodness' sake. It was a first-cousin magnolia. *Close enough for me.*

I hunted through the foliage for the price tag. Sixty dollars. The
McManus budget disallowed any purchases over twenty dollars without
careful consideration. Still, I allowed myself to picture the tree at its
four-story potential covered with buttermilk blossoms as big as my
head. If I planted the tree as a trial for possible use in my garden
designs, I could justify sixty dollars, couldn't I?

The mortgage was due in a week. *Maybe next year.*

Besides, planting a new tree seemed short-sighted, since Larry and
I planned on moving once Ky graduated from high school. A pang of
regret squeezed my heart when I thought of leaving my house and my
garden but loosened again when I thought of finding a smaller house
for Larry and me to make our own.

Inside the adobe walls of the garden center, my former co-worker,
Kathleen, priced brown bottles of insecticide and herbicide, the weap-
ons of urban gardening. Soon the shelves would be stocked and customers would crowd the sales area pulling wagons full of early vegetables—broccoli and cauliflower—and cold-hardy bloomers—pansies
and snapdragons. Many would ask if the time was right to plant tomatoes, and Kathleen would tell them that planting before Mother's Day
was foolishness. Most bought tomato seedlings anyway. There's nothing

reasonable about longings for a vine-ripened tomato.

After talking with Kathleen about the wedding and thanking her for her gift—his-and-her gardening clogs—I asked if Christopher, the owner, was in his office.

"Trust me, you don't want to talk to him. He just got back from the bank to extend his line of credit. That always makes him cranky, or should I say, *especially* cranky?"

I handed her a jug of Fertilome Rose Food from an opened box. "Is the Walled Garden in trouble?"

She pulled the trigger on the pricing gun and out came a price sticker. Then she looked over her shoulder toward Christopher's office. "He doesn't talk to me. He stomps around, complains that I talk too much to the customers, huffs and puffs over this, that, and the other thing." She lowered her voice. "There have been lots of phone calls from suppliers and delayed shipments of products."

"That doesn't sound good."

"No, it doesn't." She shelved the rose food.

"Think he'll sell the place?"

"He mumbled something about it while he was emptying the cash register a couple days ago. He better wait until Camie graduates in August. I still need spending money for our trip to New Zealand. If I don't get to swim with the dolphins just because Christopher's daddy pulled the plug on his play money . . ."

Christopher cleared his throat from the doorway of his office. Kathleen took the bottle of rose food from my hands and slapped a price sticker on it. "You let me know when you want that delivered, and I'll write up the ticket."

I couldn't be certain what Christopher had heard, so I followed her lead. "Thanks, Kathleen, you always come through for me."

Near the door, a display of summer-blooming bulbs caught my eye. The dead Japanese stewartia occupied a sunny area in my garden, perfect for heat-loving bulbs. I emptied the display of Tropicanna lilies. Their flowers glowed neon orange. Stripes of colors ranging from red to orange to yellow to green fanned from a central burgundy vein—stained-glass windows for the garden. I wished I'd thought of cannas earlier, especially before I planted the doomed stewartia. Planting the annual cannas would hold a place for the magnolia tree until next year.

I checked my watch as I paid for my purchases. Larry had been home for an hour. I pictured him still shiny from the shower. Where his pulse beat below his jaw, he would smell like hot cotton and soap. I looked at my watch again.

"Wake up, Blink. We're going home."

As I left Walled Garden and turned south toward home, my cell phone chimed. It was Larry.

"You sound winded," I said. "What's up?"

"It's a surprise."

My pulse quickened. "Tell me."

"Are you on your way home?"

"Did you talk to your mom?" I asked.

"She's in the kitchen making chicken and dumplings."

"Oh."

The phone was quiet as I waited for the traffic light to turn green. Larry broke the silence. "Asking her to limit her visits doesn't feel right to me, not *honoring* and all. She's my mom."

You can't argue with the Ten Commandments. "That's not what I'm asking. I just want her to talk to us before she makes changes around the house."

"You're right. It's just . . . Can I have a few days?"

I remembered watching a movie about the Plains Indians with Margot. In the winter, when an old squaw could no longer travel with her tribe, she stayed behind, wrapped in a buffalo blanket, and waited stoically for death to take her.

"I like chicken and dumplings," I said.

We talked about our days, how he had eaten lunch with a lonely grocery store owner in Fremont and how I had resisted the temptation to buy a new tree.

"You'll be glad you did," he said. "Hurry home."

True confession. Margaret had read me perfectly. I'd fantasized plenty about my post-wedding life with Larry. Under the torpid stupor of new love, I envisioned Larry and Ky playing catch in the backyard every evening while I showered. Refreshed, I called to Larry from the porch, and he helped me prepare dinner. He did all of the chopping for the salad, my least favorite job in the kitchen, while I stirred the marinara sauce. Without being asked, Ky started his homework at the kitchen table. When he came to a difficult question, he turned to Larry.

Back to reality.

"You're upset, aren't you?" Larry asked, standing over the Brandy-wine tomato he'd planted to replace the Japanese stewartia. Connie stood beside him, wearing my favorite apron, the one emblazoned with *San Diego Is for Beach Bums.*

"I bought canna lily bulbs to plant there," I said, opening the bag to show him the collection of bulbs.

"I thought we should get the tomato in the ground," he countered.

While working at the Walled Garden, I'd faced many an eager beaver, exclusively men, who'd wanted to plant their tomato seedlings during the irascible days of March and April. A tomato plant requires an unequivocal number of long, hot days to bear fruit. Early planting never translates into an early harvest. My words fell on deaf ears. Testosterone-drenched brains insist on making the first opulent bite of a vine-ripened tomato into a race. I guessed Larry couldn't help himself.

"It's okay," I said, knowing I couldn't win. Still, the date of the last average frost was still a month off. Anything could happen. More troubling to me was a tomato vine, heirloom or not, growing alongside my gloriosa daisies and Bonica rose. By the end of the summer, the beauties would be overrun by the tomato vine. Larry must have sensed my apprehension.

"Once the neighbor's ash leafs out, the garden plot will only get a half day of sun," he said. "This was the only sunny place left to plant the tomato." He picked up the shovel. "I'll dig it up, move it anywhere you want."

"You don't have to do that." I scanned the yard for a place to plant the lilies. The perennials filling the flowerbeds—yarrow, Iceland poppies, hollyhocks, and many, many more—were only small mounds of emerging leaves. In six weeks, a cacophony of color would crowd together to compete for attention. No room there. The irises hadn't performed well for a couple of years. "I'll dig up the irises."

"You love irises."

"If it were me," Connie said, "I'd choose a tomato plant over a flower any day of the week. You can't eat flowers."

Broccoli is a flower, I thought, using my na-na voice and hating myself for it.

"There's nothing like an heirloom tomato," she said.

There's nothing like a stuffed nasturtium.

"The heirloom isn't as pretty as the hybrids, but they're sweeter to the taste."

Obviously, you haven't tried Louise's Lavender Tea Cookies.

"I vote for the tomato," she concluded, raising her hand.

Larry and Connie watched me expectantly. I'd planned on adding an heirloom tomato to the garden that spring, *somewhere.* Just not in my flower garden. So why did I feel like a badger guarding its burrow? Then I noticed the awkward shape of the hawthorn tree. Fresh cuts scarred the trunk where two large limbs had been removed.

I asked Larry, "You pruned the hawthorn?"

He stood taller. "And the roses, too."

Sure enough, every rose had been pruned to textbook perfection, a twelve-inch-tall inverted cone. A beautiful job. "I usually wait until the first week of April," I said. "You know, in case there's a cold snap."

"You're angry, aren't you?"

There were too many people present for the tender apologies and promises Larry and I needed to exchange over our garden tug-o'-war. "A little."

"The tomato was an impulse buy," he said, stammering. "There was a sign on a greenhouse in Hotchkiss. I stopped. I thought you'd love an heirloom tomato. The pruning? It was such a nice day . . . and once I started . . ."

Before I could reassure him, Connie spoke pleasantly enough. "I guess Mibby made an impulse buy today with those canna lilies."

Enough!

"You're right, Connie. I blew it. I bought flowers for my garden. What was I thinking?" I grabbed the bag of bulbs from Larry's hand. "No problem. I'll take the bulbs back and get a tomato cage instead."

"I hate to say anything," Connie said. "I know you have your reasons. But I knew it was a mistake for you two to live in this house."

"There are *three* of us living in this house," I blurted, failing to hide my indignation. By then I knew my anger had nothing to do with Larry's good intentions, but poor, befuddled Larry didn't. I headed for the garage and the Daisy Mobile. He followed me. I stopped him with a hand to his chest. "Stay with your mother. I'm going to put the bulbs in the truck. I need to cool down."

Only for my hearing, he whispered, "I'm sorry about the tomato."

"This has nothing to do with a tomato."

"It doesn't?"

"We'll talk later," I said and continued on to the garage. I removed the pruning saw from where it hung on the tool board and hid it in a box of Christmas lights. He wouldn't look there—at least not until December. I paced among the incidental accumulations of my life. I tried to pray. I wanted God the Father to send Connie home and to squelch Larry's enthusiasm to cut things. As soon as the words formed on my mouth, I knew the issues were much bigger than that. "Lord, I love Connie. You know I do. But I can barely breathe around here. I can't relax. She judges everything I do. Well, maybe not everything I do, but she butts into places she doesn't belong. What are you going to do about this?"

I retrieved the pruning saw from its hiding place and hung it among the gardening tools where it belonged, my vote of confidence in Larry's gardening skills, if not his timing.

Over the months of our dating, I'd fought the urge to compare Larry and Scott. They were different men, to be sure. I didn't want to put them on a scale, finding that one outmanned the other. So much for that. When Scott and I had had a misunderstanding, he cajoled me with gifts, flowers, and romantic dinners, baby-sitter included. Scott thought his attempts achieved reconciliation. They really didn't.

Nothing changed. I took pity on him was all. I'd let him suffer for a while, but then I'd pack away the hurt and carry on as usual. Larry was just as helpless, but he coped with dissension differently. When the first shot fired, Larry disappeared into himself, closed the blinds, and turned off the lights. It was my job to ring the doorbell until he answered.

I found him alone in the kitchen. "Where's your mom?"

"She left."

"Can we talk?"

"She was crying." He worked his chin to control his emotions. Anger hiccuped in my chest—at Connie for using tears to manipulate Larry and at him for being so clueless. "I couldn't get her to stay. What she said about buying the lilies, she knows she was wrong."

"I wasn't upset about the lilies."

"But you said—"

Larry and Scott shared one commonality with the rest of the male world. They believed everything women told them.

"At first, I was disappointed about not having a place to plant the bulbs, and when I saw that you'd pruned the tree and the roses . . . It was silly, and I don't feel this way anymore, but I resented your doing my job."

"It was what Mom said about living here, wasn't it?"

"No . . . yes . . . Larry, your mom is always here."

"I know."

"She does things."

"I know. I know."

"We never resolved the photograph issue."

"I'll talk to her." The bluntness of his voice jabbed me in the chest. I rested my hand on his arm. When he spoke again, his voice was soft, matter-of-fact. "My mom and dad had a great marriage."

"What are you saying?"

"There are things we could learn—"

"There's nothing we need to know that we can't learn from having some time together . . . alone."

"She's a good mom. She thinks she's helping. We should give her some time."

"How long?"

"A month?"

A month? Thirty days. Thirty dinners. Countless *Emeril Live* shows. An infinite number of *bams* coming from the TV. "Then what?" I asked.

"I don't know. We'll have to see what happens."

The way I saw it, I had a choice to make. I could be queen of the hill or a loving daughter-in-law—not both. I sighed. "Okay, a month."

The phone rang. It was Ky. He told me he was studying at a team-mate's house. The family had asked him to stay for dinner. I shushed the voice in my head that demanded to talk to the boy's mother. Larry and I needed time to talk.

Finally alone, Larry and I sat down to eat the chicken and dump-lings, only the dumplings now had the consistency of wallpaper paste. Our dinner conversation consisted of polite requests for salt and pepper and to please pass the peas. The air thickened with tension. Every movement caused a ripple.

"Is there more milk?" he asked.

"I'll check."

Larry spent the evening reading a tome on the Peloponnesian War. I watched him for a while, playing over and over in my head what had passed between us. Then I went to the computer in the family room, intending to update my Perennially Yours accounts, a job I equated to stubbing a toe in the dark. Instead, I checked my e-mail. There was a message from Andrea:

hey—good news—lien-hua is back:-) she's disappointed because her boyfriend broke up with her but i'm thinking how cool it is that God loves her enough to get that creep out of her life— wish he'd like stop the rain for one day . . . you really need to be praying for me 1) I need about $500 for a project 2) the band teacher—he's like eighty years old and thinks I'm cute—he keeps leaving apples on my desk—he has ten grandchildren!!!! 3) that guy in my building, the one who loves iced mochas— he's soooooo amazingly good-looking. he's g-a-y! I'm so depressed. HELLO GOD! SEND ONE MAN INELIGIBLE FOR MEDICARE WHO LIKES WOMEN. H-U-R-R-Y! 4) I never get to play my cello other than at school and playing scales with a gazillion kids doesn't count—is my life passing me by or what? I just read this e-mail—it sounds like my life is one bomb after another—not so—I found a coffeehouse that serves decaf chai you have to come see me love you, andrea

Ky's Volkswagen rattled to a stop outside the kitchen door. The part of my heart that stood at high alert whenever my only child flew under the radar stepped down. Only one more client's charges to record.

Out of my sight, Ky came through the kitchen door with enough force to bounce the door off the wall. I cringed when he dropped his duffel bag full of baseball equipment to the floor. I was about to heft myself away from the computer when Larry said, "Why don't you take your stuff upstairs?"

Since the situation provided a low-risk setting for Larry and Ky to work out their relationship, I stayed at the computer, doling out scores for Larry and Ky's performance. I gave Larry an 8.6 for appropriate subject matter and pleasant tone of voice but docked him points for forgetting to ask Ky how well he'd hit at practice. Small details mattered. *5.2 to the ruggedly handsome stepfather.* I cheered him on.

" 'Kay," said Ky. Compliance earned him an 8.1, but sentence structure counted, too. *7.4 for the up-and-coming adult.*

"I'd appreciate if you'd do it now, please."

The *please* earned Larry points for politeness. *Good job, Larry!*

I heard Ky open the refrigerator and rummage through the contents. "In a minute," he said. "I'm hungry."

"I thought you ate at your friend's."

"I did."

"It won't take you a minute to carry the bag upstairs."

It only took him a minute to eat, too. *Faulty reasoning and a definite edge to his voice. A disappointing plunge into parenting. 4.7.*

Ky's response drew a line in the sand. "I said I'd do it in a minute."

I went into the kitchen in time to see Larry step toward Ky, and from the look in his eyes, he was all too willing to cross a line. "I've heard that from you before," he said. "Close the refrigerator and take the bag upstairs."

"Hello," I said in my best tour-guide voice. "Ky, let me warm something up for you while you take your stuff upstairs." *Is everybody happy now?*

He grimaced. "That white globby stuff?"

"It wasn't globby stuff at dinnertime," Larry said. "Your grand-mother—"

Ky slammed the refrigerator door. "Connie is *not* my grandmother. Is that clear?" He picked up his bag and left the kitchen.

Larry's shoulders sagged as if someone had unplugged him.

"It doesn't help to get angry," I said.

"I'm not angry, I'm . . ." He threw up his hands. "I feel powerless; I feel stupid; I feel . . . inept. If I had asked Ky to do something as his coach, he would have done it, no questions asked. I'm beginning to think I shouldn't say anything to him at all. I asked him nicely to take his duffel upstairs, didn't I?"

"You did."

We stood there a long time, not looking at each other or saying anything. "I struggle, too," I finally said. "He's in a hard place right now."

"I thought I'd be so good at this."

"It's harder than it looks." I crossed the room, and Larry opened his arms to me. "You're better than you think you are. Before you know it, Ky will be ready for a new relationship with you. We can't force him, especially about Connie. It's going to take some time."

"One day is as a thousand years."

We laughed and tightened our embrace. Larry's heart thumped against my cheek. The icemaker dropped another batch of ice cubes in the freezer and filled the tray with water. Blink trotted past us and out the doggie door.

"I can't believe we wasted all that time alone stewing over my mother," he said.

"Never again."

APRIL

Low of 29°. Not a cloud in the sky! One lonely anemone blooming. Plant more this fall. Brandywine tomato shows signs of frost damage—limp and wilted. Watch and wait.

I stood in Gordon Webley's backyard remembering an article I'd seen a few months earlier. Just after the beginning of the year, I'd taken the Daisy Mobile in for an oil change. Usually the mundane maintenance chore only gave me enough time to flip through the months-old *National Geographic*s scattered among *Popular Mechanics* and *Sports Illustrated*s in the lube center's waiting area. But apparently all of Orchard City had waited until after the Christmas frenzy to get their cars serviced. It was standing room only. I leaned against the wall, flipping through the pages of a magazine until an article caught my interest: "The Satin Bowerbird's Bachelor Pad."

The male satin bowerbird in the photographs was slicked-back handsome—midnight blue with startling cobalt eyes. He wooed a mate with his mastery of architecture and embellishment. First, he built a U-shaped bower of twigs and moss and grasses on the ground, then he scavenged for blue items such as feathers, berries, shells, and flowers to entice a lady bird inside. The work was constant; he was never satisfied. A tuck of grass here. Another feather there. He even raided adjacent bowers for tantalizing pieces of blue gewgaws, the shinier the better.

The male bowerbird in the photos had done his job well. A female peeked into the bower to watch the male's frenetic mating dance and puff-chested display of machismo. The female appreciated his display, so she flew off to build a nest. Later, she returned to the bower to mate.

Gordon Webley stood cross-armed in the middle of his lawn with the same intensity as a bowerbird. "I know I should be doing something—watering the flower beds, maybe. It's never looked like this before. My wife . . . she cut bouquets, brought them into the house. When she returns to find I've neglected her garden, she'll never forgive me. Do you think a birdbath would dress things up?"

Mr. Webley had no idea his wife's garden told its own story. A debris field of dried flower stems and foliage spoke clearly of neglect since the time of the first killing frost—maybe longer. Last year, the killing frost had come around the middle of October. No one had tended this garden for at least six months. That meant the bulbs hadn't been divided, either.

The Webleys lived on the east end of the valley, where Mount Garfield and Horse Mountain sheltered orchards, mostly peaches, and burgeoning vineyards. Their home, a turn-of-the-century Georgian with a broad, welcoming porch, sat with reliable authority among towering cottonwoods and a weeping willow as alluring as a gypsy. A brick driveway, herringbone-style, bordered the front lawn on one side, and a small herd of cud-chewing llamas watched us from the pasture that bordered the property to the east. A wall, also of brick, separated the property from the country road.

"A birdbath would be nice," I said, "but there's a lot of work to do." I'd seen smaller botanic gardens with full-time maintenance crews. "Last year's foliage needs to be cut back and removed. The roses should be pruned soon. That's a full day right there; maybe another half day, as well." I nudged withered foliage with my toe. There was no mistaking the hefty stalks of dahlias. "Dahlias aren't hardy here. This whole bed will have to be replaced."

"The flowers are dead? That's not good."

"Only the annuals need to be replaced. The perennials will come back." I cleared leaves from the base of a yarrow plant. Feathery sprouts grew in the stubble. "Your wife plants flowers in groupings. The dahlia bed fills this corner. She clustered together Shasta daisies here and a patch of zinnias there, with a row of sunflowers along the fence."

Mr. Webley ran his hands through his hair. Every strand fell back into place. *Good haircut.* "You better replace the . . ."

"Dahlias?"

"Yes, the dahlias."

"Do you know what kinds she likes?" I asked.

"There are more than one kind?"

About a million. "Do you remember colors?"

He widened his stance and studied the horizon. "Are we talking about the tall flowers that bloom along the side?"

"Those are gladiolas," I said gently so he wouldn't think I was being a smarty-pants. I wanted the job because I knew if I didn't get the job, I would drive by anyway to see if the garden had survived Mr. Webley's neglect. Besides, I wanted to tend the garden just as I would want someone to care for my garden if I had to go away.

"My husband is a dahlia expert," I said. "I'll have him put a nice mix together. Your wife won't be disappointed."

Mr. Webley rubbed his chin the way a man does when he's weighing value against the bottom line. "Is the garden too far gone?"

I assured him the garden was redeemable as we walked its full length. I took notes, knowing he would ask for an estimate. Coneflowers and gloriosa daisies needed to be cut back, and about fifty dahlias and gladiolas had to be replanted. Sunflowers to seed. Flowerpots and window boxes to refurbish. My shoulders burned just thinking about a long day of raking the cottonwood leaves out of the beds. By the time we walked completely around the house, I realized rebirthing Mrs. Webley's garden was all about labor.

"Can you start today?" he asked.

I checked my watch. "My next appointment is in fifteen minutes." *Now to test Mr. Webley's commitment to the project.* "To maintain a garden this size requires a weekly appointment for up to three hours, but before I can start a maintenance regimen, I'll need a full day to clear out the leaves and prepare the dahlia and gladiola plots for planting." A wave of self-doubt washed over me. I pictured myself raking and stuffing garbage bags full of garden debris long into the night. "Actually, to be conservative, you should plan on two full days."

"Tomorrow then?" he asked.

"Is there a deadline?"

From the way he sucked in and let the breath out slowly, I knew a deadline had already passed. "I want my wife's garden to be the most beautiful garden in the valley."

"I'll be here before noon."

"Where do they sell birdbaths?"

"Walled Garden Nursery carries birdbaths."

Driving away, I couldn't shake the image of Mr. Webley as an industrious bowerbird. Although the garden had languished from lack of attention, the house and grounds demonstrated meticulous attention to detail. What had compelled Mrs. Webley to fly away from so appealing a bower? An ailing parent? An overseas job? Was she a patient at the Betty Ford Clinic? For all of the unanswered questions and the challenge of breathing life into a neglected garden, I loved my job.

On an impulse, I turned off the highway near the college and drove down Roseanne's street. My good friend had moved to Santa Barbara with her young daughter when a string of involvements with men soured her on the possibility of Prince Charming showing up this far inland. The new owners of her bungalow had already replaced much of the landscape I'd designed for her with spans of stone look-alike concrete. Very sterile. Very symbolic of how I felt losing her friendship. Roseanne had never sent her new address as she'd promised. I parked at the curb and prayed for her. "Prince of Peace, rescue Roseanne from her loneliness as only you can. Amen."

～੭

Louise stood among a jumble of chocolate-coated pots and bowls and spatulas in her kitchen, wearing an apron over her swimsuit, a black-and-white number with a polka-dot skirt. "I declare the mystery of spontaneous combustion solved," she announced. "If hot flashes aren't to blame, I'll eat Aunt Pansy's Easter bonnet, feathers and all." Louise mopped her face with the hem of her apron. "This here is my third attempt at this recipe. First, the balloons were too big, and then the chocolate didn't set up. I've been back and forth to the grocery store so many times I've worn ruts in the asphalt." She dipped a party balloon halfway into melted chocolate. "Martha Stewart has her name all over this recipe. What a mess."

She let the excess chocolate drip back into the saucepan and set the balloon on a parchment-lined cookie sheet. A crumpled pile of chocolate-stained parchment lay on the counter. The balloon slipped onto its side. "Oh, for heaven's sake. Would you believe Susan Paris calls her recipe *Simply* Elegant Chocolate Ice Cream Bowls? Making these bowls is about as simple as wrestling a remote control out of a dead man's hands. I take that back. Making these ding-danged bowls is tougher than wrestling a remote from any man, alive or dead."

I remembered Susan from Louise's chemotherapy treatments. A real estate agent, she brought a briefcase full of work to her chemotherapy sessions. She used her cell phone to call clients, as well as handymen, other agents, and her children, until the rigor of her treatments forced her to trade her briefcase for a quilt and a pillow.

Louise groused about Susan's submissions to the cookbook every few days. A caramel date bar stuck to the roof of her mouth, a banana cream pie required a ladle to be served, a fat-free gingerbread with the consistency of rubber made her jaw ache, and now, chocolate bowls became puddles on her counter. Louise tested every recipe Susan submitted, only to have each fail miserably.

When I'd suggested that she tell Susan not to bother submitting any more recipes, Louise gasped. "Why, sugar, she was one of our fiercest brigadiers. I can't leave her out of the cookbook. Besides, with her connections, we'll sell more *In the Pink* cookbooks than you could shake a stick at."

Another reason to love Louise. She's loyal and a marketing genius.

She swiped the sweat off her face with her forearm, spiking her bangs with chocolate. "Let's try one more bowl, and this time, you hold the balloon while the chocolate sets." She dipped another balloon and placed it on the cookie sheet. I held the balloon upright as the chocolate ran off the balloon to pool on the parchment paper.

"Let me help you clean up this mess," I said.

An hour later, I pulled the plug to drain the sink and Louise handed me a towel to dry my hands. "What time is Ky's game?" she asked. "Do you have time for a cup of tea?"

I hadn't cleaned the bathrooms since the wedding, and a week's worth of Larry's Sweet Suzy uniforms needed washing and ironing. "Do you have any of that orange-flavored tea?"

"Just for you, sugar."

Louise's bout with breast cancer had rearranged her priorities—and her closet. She'd abandoned thematic dressing altogether. Out went the appliquéd ensembles and matching earrings. For a brief time, she wore dusty pastels that flowed around her shrinking frame. Then the idea of the cookbook came to her. She let her hair come back silver and wore red cat-eye glasses. A red pencil sharpened to lethal precision was always tucked behind one ear. At first, she'd worn a chef's coat stiffened with enough starch to repel bullets and a black turtleneck—what she considered appropriate New York food editor garb. But her post-surgery treatments to inhibit estrogen production had wreaked havoc on her internal thermostat. She'd met me at the door wearing shorts in February and her slip in April—always with an apron, of course. I hated to think what she would be wearing by August.

"It's so precious to have this time with you," she said. "Jesus knew I needed the tender care of my sweet friend." She tilted her face toward heaven and closed her eyes. "Thank you." And then her eyes were on me. "How are the two roosters getting along?"

"Larry and Ky?"

"I expect there's been some struttin' and crowin' around your house."

"And door slamming." I sipped the tea. "But really, Ky is rarely ever home, and when he is, he keeps to himself."

"My daddy was no farmer, but he kept a henhouse full of his beloved silver-spangled Hamburgs. They always placed at the Beauregard Parish fair. Daddy called the roosters *dandies* with their black-and-white feathers and red combs. Mammy complained about the hens' eggs. They were itty-bitty things. I could carry two dozen in my apron.

"We had two roosters—Henry Jones and Li'l Ike, an upstart rooster with high ambitions. He wanted to be general and was willing to fight for it. He harassed Henry Jones and his little ladies somethin' awful. Pecked them hard enough to draw blood, he did. How I loved that little ruffian. But Daddy had had enough of him. One summer morning, Daddy announced at the breakfast table that Li'l Ike had to go. And you know, a rooster goes one of two ways: either to another henhouse or to the Sunday table. Daddy left the job of finding that ornery rooster a home to me. I called everybody in Beauregard Parish. Most folks had more roosters than they wanted, and nobody wanted my Li'l Ike due to his reputation. Mammy made up a nice pot of Li'l Ike stew. Of course, no one told me I was eating Li'l Ike until I'd sopped up the last of the sauce with a buttermilk biscuit. I cried all night long, but the girls in the henhouse started laying again, regular as the morning paper."

"Are you suggesting I stew Ky?"

"You know I'm not."

"He was perfectly fine with Larry before the wedding." That was true if you listened to what he'd said, not how he'd said it.

"But you and Larry are married now. Ky isn't quite sure where he stands."

"He's still my son."

"But he's also a man, a li'l ol' pretend kind of man but a man just the same. You can't add a family member without making a few feathers fly. Think about how Andrea shook things up when she came to Orchard City."

Louise had a point there.

"Sugar, a new pecking order will take some time." She sipped her tea, and I could tell she was giving her advice a lot of thought. "In the meantime, make the henhouse the nicest place in the entire world for Ky to be. For a sixteen-year-old boy, that means food and plenty of it. I have just the thing for you."

Louise removed a crowd-sized casserole from the oven. "Here's an eggplant Parmesan casserole I made earlier with a recipe from Cheryl Ooley, an angel of a girl and a wonderful cook." Louise bagged a package of angel hair pasta, a loaf of French bread, and a head of romaine lettuce. "You'll have to tell me how y'all like it. Do I need to send you off with some salad dressing?"

⁓

I walked across the alley and paused before opening the garden gate. The mixed scents of Parmesan cheese and marinara sauce made my stomach growl. Ky's game was early, so we would all be home at a reasonable hour for dinner. I wouldn't need time to cook after the game. That left more time to watch *Emeril Live* with Connie. I preferred the idea of having my legs waxed—with a sunburn.

I leaned against the gate and prayed, "Lord, thank you for a friend like Louise. Help me to appreciate Connie as the gift you intended her to be. May our mealtime tonight honor you because of the love shared around the table. And please, Lord, tame our li'l rooster. Amen."

⁓

A runner crossed home plate. Ky's team, the Eagles, high-fived the runner as he trotted through the gauntlet on his way to the dugout. The Eagles were ahead by eight. *My kind of baseball game.* The opposing pitcher, a lanky kid named Horse, huddled with the catcher and the coach. I hated to see players taken out—even pitchers from the opposing team. That reminded me too much of my own weak performance in girls' basketball. The coach returned to the dugout; the catcher pulled his face mask into place. Horse pitched four consecutive balls.

Ky's high school played baseball at a community stadium built to house a yearly college tournament. That meant bleachers with seatbacks, fresh paint, and a lush playing field. No dust devils stalled the play here. Larry, Connie, and I sat between home and first, but the game competed with the sky for my attention. Snow still glazed the Grand Mesa. The sky was washed with the color of hope, and inconsequential clouds migrated toward the northwest—a spring day made to encourage dreams of grandeur on a clay diamond.

The game drew a light crowd. A few high school students. Cowboys. Businessmen in ball caps who talked on their cell phones. Lots of mothers—some who resisted the urge to call out their sons' names, some who didn't. A woman from the opposing team cheered Horse through every pitch. Only his mother would get away with such devotion. Everyone wore jackets against a biting breeze.

Crack! Horse dove for a grounder and missed the ball by an arm's length. Players advanced to first and second.

"Now batting for the Eagles, shortstop Kyle Garrett!"

I counted on my fingers the number of years Ky had played baseball. If you counted T-ball, I'd sat in the stands through ten seasons. My stomach still fidgeted each time he stepped into the batter's box. The tension teetered between relief and agony. The players leaned on the rail of the dugout so eager for their chance to earn a fleeting moment of glory, yet restrained by the greater probability of a strikeout. I remembered Horse's wild pitches and prayed for Ky's safety. I need not have worried. Horse overcompensated. His pitches flew high and wide. Ky walked.

After the game, Ky crossed the parking lot with three of his teammates, parading the jaunty nonchalance of winners. Another battle won. No big deal. The grass stains on their uniforms were green badges of courage. They had won because they'd held back nothing. Part of me wanted to throw cold water over their swaggers—high school baseball wasn't life. The other part of me wanted to freeze the moment in time, like a baseball card to be admired when the need arose. There would be days of disappointment, even for the Eagles.

Ky looked up to see us standing by his Volkswagen. He rolled his eyes. My pulse quickened.

Larry shook Ky's hand. "Great game, Ky. Your defense was rock solid."

He barely mumbled a thanks. "The guys and me are going out," he said, unlocking the driver's door and sliding behind the wheel. His teammates stood poised at each door.

"Where?" I asked.

Ky reached across the car to unlock the passenger doors. "To eat."

I recognized his passengers. The catcher and the first baseman sat in the back seat; they were upperclassmen, probably seniors, judging from the bulk of their muscles and late-afternoon stubble. The third boy wore street clothes and a cast on his left hand. He'd gone to Ky's elementary school. *Zach?* I remembered going toe to toe with him over proper sandbox etiquette when I was a volunteer in Ky's kindergarten class. I didn't know the other two, except from bleacher talk among baseball moms—and what the moms had said wasn't flattering. Ky rolled his window down.

Our relationship was changing. Ky was the greased pig, and I was the hapless contestant trying to catch him. Food worked. "Louise sent an eggplant Parmesan casserole home with me this afternoon."

"The team goes out after a win." He started his car and revved the engine into a tinny rattle. *Volkswagens.* "It's my turn to drive."

I leaned on his window. The catcher rummaged through the contents of his game bag. The first baseman fidgeted. I didn't know what worried me more—that the boys looked nervous or that they still had plenty of energy.

"We agreed that we'd eat dinner together on school nights," I said.

"*You* agreed."

The boy in the passenger seat bobbed his head in agreement. *Jeremy?*

I spoke out of reflex, like you would grab for a crystal glass nudged off a shelf by your elbow. "Ask your friends to get out of the car, Ky."

Larry whispered my name as a warning, but going out with the boys was all wrong for Ky. Couldn't Larry see that?

The first baseman looked nervously over his shoulder. "Ky, man, we gotta go."

Ky toggled the gearshift. Under his breath, he pleaded, "Mom . . ."

"Your friends can join us for dinner. There's plenty," I said in my best Johnny-on-the-spot voice.

The boy with the cast said, "I'll make sure he doesn't get into any trouble, Mrs. Garrett."

Eddie Haskell?

Larry wrapped his fingers around my arm and tugged gently.

"Ky, why don't you get out of the car and talk to me?" Panic squeezed my voice to a higher octave.

Larry whispered to me, "Let him go. Everything will be all right."

A woman's intuition trumped a man's memory of how he'd behaved in his teenage years. Everything will be all right? The Greeks had convinced the Trojans to accept a certain wooden horse with those exact words.

Since Ky had started playing ball with these brats, I hardly recognized him. The swagger. The way he looked right through me. And the attitude. With a tilt of the head, ever so slight, and a barely perceptible twitch of his upper lip, he said loud and clear, *I'm untouchable, immortal, a higher life form. The rules, well, those are for everybody else—suckers!*

Beside me, Larry asked Ky, "What time will you be home?"

Ky shifted into reverse and backed out of the parking space. He yelled out the window, "Before ten!"

I shook off Larry's grip and turned toward the car. "Let's follow him."

Larry kept up with me. "There was no way to win that battle, Mib." He hooked my arm and pulled me to face him. "You're overreacting. Take a breath."

"Take a breath? What a great idea." I pulled out of Larry's grasp again and walked faster. "Maybe I should sit in the lotus position and reach a deep meditative state while my son goes off with brats who drink like homesick sailors."

"They'll go to Pizza Man with their coach"—Larry spoke like he was trying to explain gravity to a dolt—"have a cheese pizza, and call it a night."

"Are you willing to stake my son's life on that?"

He bent his head closer and whispered, "Mib, Mom is watching us."

Behind Larry, Connie hugged her stadium seat cushion to her chest. I stared after Ky's car, but of course, it was long gone. Around the parking lot, parents and grandparents ducked into their cars. The visiting team, bent by defeat, shuffled onto a school bus for their ride across town. The team manager hefted a bag of bats into the back of a mini-van. All normal stuff. Nothing sinister. I desperately wanted to believe Larry.

"The coach goes with them?" I asked.

"We'll drive by Pizza Man to make sure Ky's there."

"And if he's not?"

"We'll deal with it."

Driving toward Pizza Man, a stew of emotions boiled and popped in my gut. Connie prattled on in the back seat about Larry's Eagle Scout days, insinuating that the Boy Scouts would be the answer to all of Ky's problems. If only Ky believed he had a problem. Maybe Connie could convince him—she did everything else around the house. I awarded myself the daughter-in-law's merit badge of self-restraint for not telling her to shut up. When we drove by Pizza Man and Ky's car was in the parking lot, Larry squeezed my hand. I didn't return the gesture. I looked out the side window, seeing nothing but remembering the ache of Ky's eager leave-taking. I felt like a scorned woman. *How weird is that?*

Ky sat on the floor, leaning against his bed, still wearing his soiled uniform. He'd pulled his ear buds out to listen, which was more than I'd hoped for. Larry had already gone to bed. I leaned against the door-jamb, hoping to convey a casualness that was neither confrontational nor accusatory—just informative, like a weather report. "The whole scene could have been avoided if you'd taken the time to explain your plans."

"I told you the team went out after a win."

He was right. It wasn't what he'd said; it was how he'd said it. "If you want me to trust you, look me in the eye when you're talking to me and answer my questions with respect . . . and don't act so sneaky."

"Sneaky? I told you what I was doing."

"All you told me was that you were going out. I shouldn't have to fish for information."

"I told you we were going to eat."

"Only after I asked."

"Exactly. I answered your question."

"As you were backing away."

"Mom, I need my car."

"You can have the keys on Monday. No sooner."

When I closed the door behind me, something hard hit the door. From the heavy thud and a rustling of paper, I figured Ky had thrown the atlas. I put my hand on the doorknob. Reentering the fray only meant more verbal two-stepping, which meant more stepping on toes and more pain. I put the keys to his car in my robe pocket and mentally added a week to his sentence.

❦

I ran down the stairs to answer the phone. Still ticked at Larry for being male and getting the whole camaraderie-of-sports-guys thing but not the sons-have-to-be-corralled-for-their-own-protection thing, I was happy to delay going to bed.

"So how's married life?" The voice on the other end of the line hinted at a song, one of those rainbow-and-sunshine songs bellowed at the end of a Broadway musical. The last time Margot's voice had held such glee, she had dangled a worm, freshly dug, in front of my face with promises that the worm would taste just like chocolate.

"Good," I said, pacing from room to room.

"Are the two of you getting along?"

I stopped. "Why are you asking?"

The serrated edge returned to Margot's voice. "This is what sisters do."

"Since when?"

The phone line went quiet. I regretted the question immediately. Margot had offered me something delicate, something she'd turned to admire in the light before placing it under glass and dialing my number.

"We're getting along fine," I said, walking through a shaft of light from the streetlight. Goliath slept in Grandma's chair, so I tipped the chair forward, and the cat landed on her feet. She stretched before trotting down the hall and out the doggie door. I brushed the seat off and sat down.

"Not great?" she asked.

I listened to the metronomic ticking of the clock. I loved Larry. He was great. He . . . "We thought we'd talked about everything."

~~~

Larry rose to his elbow and opened the covers for me when I entered the bedroom. "Who called?" he asked.

"My sister." Icicles hung from each word.

"I've been waiting for you," he said, all warm and toasty. He pulled me to his chest. The china plates hanging over the dresser vibrated from the throb of Ky's music.

"Ky's awake," I said, but I meant, *Don't get your hopes up*.

"Does that boy ever sleep?"

"Only when it's time to go to school."

Larry ran his finger up and down my arm, a testing of the waters. I laid my hand over his, the international gesture for, *Not tonight, dear*. He kissed my neck. *Hello?* You can't brush your teeth in an old house without everyone inside knowing about it. "This isn't a good time," I said.

"You feel good," he said and sighed.

We lay there, matching our breathing, listening to heartbeats. Briefly, Larry's arms held my thoughts in the moment like a paperweight, but a nor'easter blew in my head, fluttering my thoughts into wild speculations. My eyes popped open. Talking about what happened at the ballpark couldn't wait until morning.

I knew all of the admonitions about keeping problems out of the bedroom. We could have done just that if Connie hadn't stayed to watch *Good Eats*. Larry had excused himself to go to bed before Alton Brown plated the flank steak roulade. That left me to use a whole roll of masking tape to remove Goliath's hair from Grandma's chair, pronounce judgment on Ky, and talk to Margot, arguably the most pleasant event of the evening. Good ol' Larry had missed out on all of that. But he sure wanted to "snuggle."

Larry's arm grew leaden and his breathing deepened. Within seconds he was snoring. I nudged him. "Larry, we need to talk." I sat up and turned on the lamp.

He shielded his eyes. "Wha . . . ?"

"I didn't appreciate the way you left me hanging tonight."

"Where? Tonight? Hanging?"

"At the *ballpark*."

"Can you be more specific?"

"Parenting isn't good cop, bad cop. We have to back each other up."

He sat up, rubbing his eyes. "Right or wrong?"

"I'm not wrong about those boys."

"Ky came home early."

"Only because he knew I was on to him." I told Larry about the conversation I'd had with Ky and how I'd taken his car keys for being disrespectful.

"Aren't you disrespecting him?"

I threw back the covers and stood at the foot of the bed. "What is that supposed to mean?"

"Come back to bed, Mib. I shouldn't have said anything."

I crossed my arms over my chest. "It's too late to back down now."

Larry stared at the bed. When he spoke, he laid his words down end to end. "What you're interpreting as disrespect in Ky is raw male behavior. We don't extrapolate."

I threw up my hands. "You have to make up your mind, Larry. Either Ky is a brat or a male managing as well as can be expected."

"When did I ever say he was a brat?"

"Maybe not in so many words, but you jumped all over him the day we came home from our honeymoon."

"That was weeks ago."

"And tonight you made me look like a powerless, overwrought fool."

"Honestly, Mib, I thought I was rescuing you."

"From my side of things, it felt like abandonment."

"You're a wonderful mother . . ."

"But?"

"You allowed fear to distort what you saw happening."

"Because I had information you didn't." The wind rattled the window. I slipped between the sheets and pulled the quilt up to my neck. "What are we going to do next time? Shouldn't we err on the side of caution?" I asked.

"The only way we can keep Ky absolutely safe is to lock him in the house. He would be safe, but he wouldn't be the strong man you want him to be. To be strong, he needs experience managing his freedom." Larry took my hand and kissed it. "As much as you're longing for a good relationship with Ky, the Father longs for our companionship even more. He could have built a fence around the forbidden tree, but He gives us all the freedom we need to please Him or to disappoint Him."

"But the Father disciplines the people He loves."

"And we're doing that. All I'm suggesting is that we have to trust him when he's earned it. Putting a stranglehold on him and lumping him together with a bunch of malcontents only pushes him away."

Before Scott's accident, tragedy pounded on other people's doors, not mine. Having the police officer say, *Mrs. Garrett, we have some bad news for you* opened up new possibilities, dark possibilities, possibilities you never wish on anyone. I whispered, "Bad things happen."

Larry drew me into his arms. "I wish it wasn't so."

Free will? Lord, what were you thinking?

APRIL
15

The garden smells like a dime-store powder puff—sweet and flowery, thanks to the Korean Spice viburnum. Intoxicating! The Thunder Cloud plum tree popped open today—black bark and pink blossoms—so Chanel!

Larry sat on the edge of the tub and ran his hands through his hair. "I don't see how this can be a bad idea," he whispered. "Creating a bachelor pad in the basement gives Ky the privacy he wants and we get the privacy we need."

Parenting is not a win-win situation. A mother learns that reality when her fetus first uses her bladder for a punching bag. I tried not to hold Larry's ignorance against him. "Do we have to call the room a bachelor pad?"

"His idea."

Oh brother. "He'll know why we're shooing him to the basement."

"You should see how excited he was when I showed him the plan."

"What would stop him from sneaking out at night?"

"I don't know what to say, Mib. I really thought you'd be happy."

And you keep forgetting . . . "And I thought we were going to talk things over that concerned Ky."

"You were grocery shopping. I was getting the towels out of the

69

dryer. I looked around the basement. It reminded me of the apartment I lived in at college. The idea hit me that we could make an apartment for Ky—not with a kitchen or anything—but with a place for a bed and another area so he could have his friends over. Maybe we could get a pool table. I scratched my ideas down on a piece of paper. Ky asked me what I was drawing. It felt so good to have a pleasant conversation with him. I'm sorry. I guess I didn't think it through."

There I was again, forced to decide in favor of my husband or my son. To endorse Larry's plan was to loosen our influence on Ky. I hated that idea. But to constantly put Larry on the losing side of the equation didn't help our relationship. Maybe Louise was right about the feuding roosters. Maybe someone had to go. If peace could be bought by setting Ky up in the basement, no one would have to end up in gravy with dumplings.

I sat beside Larry on the tub and rested my head on his shoulder. "Thank you for being so patient with me. I worry too much. I know it."

"You don't have to worry alone anymore."

But, of course, I knew I did. At first, I'd seen Larry's objectivity over Ky's behavior as a disappointing measure of Larry's character. He was never going to love my son as much as I did—but how could he? Larry had never cradled Ky slathered with Baby Magic lotion, or seen Ky's face light up at his homecoming each night, or held Ky against his chest through a long night to soothe a raging ear infection—all of the early experiences of parenting that endear children to their parents before they grow coarse body hair and their skin gets oily. The only Ky Larry knew was the one trying to launch himself into the world that had robbed him of a father and created 9/11.

"Let's give the basement a try," I offered. "If it doesn't work—"

"I'll move him back to his room myself."

"We need to be very specific about our expectations for him: who he's to invite over, what they can do, when they go home—stuff like that."

"You bet."

"The computer stays in the family room."

"I agree one hundred percent."

"Living in the basement is a privilege."

"Absolutely."

"One foul-up and he's outta there."

"We should give him three strikes."

"Two."

"Okay, two."

The Daisy Mobile's horn honked. "Who's that?" I asked.

"Ky. He's going with me to the lumberyard."

I'd assumed the basement remodel would start in the near future, not that day. "How are we affording this?"

"I have an extra paycheck in May."

"Oh."

"Are you okay?" Larry asked. "We won't do a thing until you're ready. And when we're done with the basement, we can set up an office for you in Ky's old room."

Ky honked the horn again.

"Sure, go for it," I said.

~~~

Ky moved through the house like a leaf carried along by a mountain stream. The door opened, Ky flowed in, and like a leaf caught by a log, the refrigerator pinned him in place. He stooped to stare inside. "Do we have orange juice?"

"Do you see any orange juice?" I asked.

"Do we have Coke?"

"Do you see—?"

He slammed the refrigerator door. "Never mind. We'll have water."

He filled two glasses of water—one for him and one for Larry—and sat on a stool across from where I stirred a custard simmering on the stove. Sweat soaked his hair, and the chest of his T-shirt was streaked with dirty handprints.

"What's with the foil on the countertops?" he asked.

"Evidently cats don't like the feel or sound of foil when they walk on it."

"We could always teach the kitty to swim in the river."

I stopped stirring. "Ky!"

"Just kidding," he said, raising his hands in surrender. "Whatcha making?"

"I'm testing a recipe for Louise's cookbook." I read from the recipe card. "This is called Citrus Cream Crumble Pie."

"Do I have to eat it?"

"Only if you want to."

"Pass."

I expected the current he rode on to lift Ky off the stool to return to the basement, but he stayed to play with the pastry I'd set aside to make pinwheels. "Larry works like a maniac," he said.

"Is the floor cleared?"

"Almost. He says we can start framing tomorrow."

"That soon?"

"Yeah, and we're gonna install extra outlets and drop the cable into the basement from the living room."

So there it was, the true source of his enthusiasm—the promise of unlimited electricity and cable TV. "Are we ever going to see you again?"

A flash of mischief brightened his eyes. "You'll be able to hear me."

"Just because you're in the basement—"

"I know. I know. God only gave me one set of ears." Ky rolled the pastry scrap into a snake and bit its head off. And like he often did, he finally asked the question he'd wanted to all along. "Do you . . . like . . . ever think you see Dad, but it turns out to be a total stranger?"

I stopped stirring the custard. "Did that happen to you?"

"Yeah." He tilted the stool back. "There's a guy in town with a red jacket. It's like Dad's. You know, the one with the corduroy collar. I've seen this guy a couple times. And . . . I don't know . . . it's like I forget for a few seconds that Dad's . . . you know, gone. The first time I saw him, I watched him cross the street and get into his car. When he turned to open the car door . . . he didn't look anything like Dad. I saw him again this morning at Home Depot. But I forgot all over again about Dad being gone. Freaked me out."

"Are you worried about it?

"Nah, my teacher sent me to talk to a counselor dude right after Dad died. He said he saw his dad in other people all the time."

I didn't know Ky had talked to a counselor.

"So, how about you?" he asked.

Which time? "I saw a man riding a bike—a green one like your dad's. And he wore a Ride the Rockies jersey, too. I think it's the shirt from the first year your dad made the ride. I told myself it wasn't your dad, but I made a U-turn right in the middle of Wingate Avenue to follow him to Ninth Street. I pulled up beside him at a stoplight. I was about to lean over and roll down the—"

"Did you say anything?"

"No. He looked over. I was pretty embarrassed. I turned left and came home." I didn't tell Ky that I'd followed the man on the green bicycle only a few months earlier.

A mound of milky foam rose over the edge of the pan and onto the stovetop. I stirred frantically, but it was too late. The spoon scraped a thick layer of scorched custard off the bottom of the pan. I turned the burner off and looked at Ky, but he was flipping through the channels to check basketball scores. The urgency of the current had already spun him free of me.

"Is Larry waiting for you?" I asked.

"Oh yeah." And he was gone.

The Christmas Ky was six years old, he had barricaded his bedroom door and spent hours creating presents for Scott and me. When I opened my gift on Christmas morning, I found a roll of fabric attached to a loop of elastic with knots of thread. I turned it over in my hands. I had no idea what it was. Ky, exasperated, had stood with hands on hips to say, "It's a bow tie to wear to Christmas parties."

I stood in the kitchen with my ruined custard, wondering over the gift Ky had just given me. He had dropped his mask long enough for me to see that he was still very much involved with the business of grieving his father. We shared a commonness of longing, even though we'd both reentered the flow of life as accidental travelers. What was I supposed to do with the untimely gift? I expelled a breath, but the tightness in my chest remained. I went out to the garden to sit on the ground between a blooming viburnum and a plum tree. Perhaps the humming of the bees and the sweetness of the blooms would organize my thoughts. A mother could dream. At least I wasn't in the kitchen any longer making a pie no one would eat.

～つ

Louise held the screen door open when she saw me walking toward her kitchen door with the Citrus Cream Crumble Pie. "I declare, I've never seen a prettier pie. Come on in, sugar. The teapot just whistled."

"There's something I should tell you about the pie," I said.

She put up her hand. "That wouldn't be fair to Stookie. Let me taste it for myself."

I cut through the layers of cream and custard and crust to lift a magazine-perfect piece of pie out of the pan. I slid the plate toward Louise.

"Aren't you having any?" she asked.

"Too close to dinnertime."

"Bring the teapot to the table, will you, sugar?" With the tea poured and her napkin in place, Louise filled her fork with a generous bite of Stookie's pie. She closed her eyes to reveal shimmery blue eye shadow and eyeliner painted to a sharp point. Her eyes popped open. "This can't be right. How much sugar did you put in this pie?"

I checked the recipe. "Just what it says, two cups."

She took the card from me and slid a red fingernail down the list of ingredients. "Lemon juice?"

"A half cup."

Louise carried the pie to the sink, and with a swift turn of the pie server around the pan, the contents fell into the disposal. "Stookie has avoided givin' me the recipe for this pie for weeks. What she *has* given me is a list of excuses as long as a snake in a hangin' tree." She leaned against the sink. "I've had my suspicions since the first time she brought the pie to pinochle club."

"I'm not the best baker," I said. "I burned the first batch of filling."

"Bless her heart, I do believe Miss Stookie Carmichael buys her pies from a bakery."

Saying "bless her heart" was secret code among southern belles for "I'd like to eat her heart." Louise had told me that herself. "I don't know, Louise. My last culinary triumph required a can opener and shredded cheese. Blink loved it. Maybe I missed an ingredient."

"You don't know Stookie Carmichael. She loves attention, and this pie gets her plenty. There's no telling what you can expect from a woman who is willing to taint a friend's cookbook."

The phone rang and Louise answered. After the usual pleasantries, she handed the phone over to me. It was Connie telling me that dinner was ready.

When I replaced the handset in the base, Louise asked, "Is Connie cooking for you every night?"

"Yes, and bless her heart, she stays to watch the Food Channel until ten." I heaved a sigh and stood to leave.

Louise slid her bifocals down her nose to hold me with her gaze. "Since it's coming on to Easter, I've been reading about the passion of Jesus. These past few mornings, I could barely wait to open my Bible. The sword of the Spirit is a powerful tool in the Master's hands." Louise patted the chair. "You have a minute, don't you?"

She wasn't fooling me. I was about to be splayed by one of her sermons. "I'd hate to keep the family waiting."

"This won't take but a bitty minute."

I sat heavily in the chair.

"This morning, I read about Jesus' crucifixion in the book of John. There was Pilate, such a hollow shell of a man, making his excuses, and the soldiers dividing our Lord's clothes by drawing lots. In the middle of all that posturing and greed, Jesus looked down to see His mama standing there. Just imagine it. Mary came to see her darlin' baby boy nailed to a cross. Why, it hadn't been that long since she felt His milky breath against her cheek or kissed away the sting of a splinter in His finger, all the time knowin' that He was destined for a crushin' great-ness. And there He was, goodness knows, carrying the weight of my sins and yours, hardly recognizable from the many beatings He'd endured, almost emptied of life, and He sees His dear mama weeping below Him. How His heart must have ached to see His suffering reflected in her eyes.

"This is where it gets interesting." Louise took my hands. "Jesus had ten thousand angels at His command. With one word, the armies of heaven would have stormed Calvary to rescue their Prince. Don't you suppose that was the moment of His greatest temptation? One word would have stopped His mama's suffering. I love Him all the more for enduring His pain and hers to save my soul."

I shoved my hands into my armpits. "I think I know where this is going."

"Maybe you do. Maybe you don't."

I watched steam rise from my tea, unable to look Louise in the eye.

"Shall I continue?" she asked.

I nodded.

"I've read that passage a hundred times, and it still amazes me. There He was, our Jesus, hardly able to take a breath for the weight of His broken body. I marvel that He didn't surrender to death, knowing the joy that awaited Him at His Father's side. But He didn't. Instead, when He said to John, 'Here is your mother,' He took care of His mama's need to be looked after and to have someone to love—just what every mama in history has ever needed."

Long fingers of light spotlighted the dust motes' dance in Louise's kitchen. If her sermon was supposed to make me feel better, she'd failed miserably. I was invisible to Ky. If my hair caught on fire, he would open a window to cool down the room.

Louise said, "I think that's what Larry is doing for his dear mama. Taking care of her needs to be loved and to love."

"I know," I said, but of course, I didn't have a clue. I had assumed I was the mama in her story and Ky the dutiful son. I should have known. "I better get going."

～⌒

Connie scribbled notes as Rachael Ray effortlessly chopped, grilled, and tossed a four-course meal featuring beef tenderloins with gorgonzola on her *30 Minute Meals* program. Connie hung on every word. I'd only witnessed such intensity when Blink had cornered a three-legged cat in the backyard.

Be nice! I reminded myself. Connie and I had exchanged apologies and dismissed any suggestion of hard feelings from our encounter over the heirloom tomato. But the more I prayed for patience, the less I possessed. That couldn't be right. I laid the novel I was reading in my lap.

"Mom, there's an e-mail from Andrea," Ky called. "You aren't gonna like it."

Ky carried a mixing bowl full of frosted wheat squares from the kitchen. "We need mo' milk," he said, tipping his head back to talk. Milk dribbled out of his mouth.

"Ky! Be careful! And get those dishes back to the kitchen tonight."

He bounded up the stairs in four strides.

"He really should eat more fruits and vegetables to stay regular," Connie said, looking away from the commercial for Nexium.

I had stopped thinking about my son's bowel habits the moment he went poo-poo in the potty and flushed the toilet himself. I folded down a corner of my book and headed for the kitchen. "I'll take him an apple."

I sat down at the computer and double-clicked on Andrea's username. The mouse was sticky.

i did it!!!! i got the nose ring . . . it H-U-R-T! i can't smile or move my face w/o wincing—must eat soft food for a week . . . totally tofu and yogurt . . . went with tribal style . . . so cool . . . will send pic when it heals. that is so louise to suspect her friend of forging a recipe . . . she loves a mystery! tell her i have some great whole grain recipes . . . i miss you guys too—i'll call on Saturday . . . be nice to the kitty . . . keep praying about the project . . . lots of false turns . . . it's hard not to get discouraged. Sylvie tells me i'm in God's hands . . . he won't drop me will he? love andrea PRAY I DON'T GET A COLD!!!!

I touched a photograph of Andrea I'd taped to the monitor. Her black hair flowed over her shoulder and down her back. The photograph was taken in Louise's parlor at my bridal tea. We ate lemon scones thick with Devonshire cream and Louise's homemade raspberry jam. Bite-sized quiches. Fruit wedges. Gruyère cheese. Buttery crackers. All of my favorites.

Louise had told the story of her and Manley's wedding. "My mama nearly fainted when Manley's family brought pots of homemade ravioli and sausage with peppers to the reception. But for years afterward, my mama visited Mama Giovanelli twice a year to make ravioli with her."

We all laughed. Andrea put one of Louise's tapestry pillows with ropelike fringe on her head. I said her name and she looked over her shoulder at me—smiling, playful. Her strange headdress looked perfectly normal atop her exotic beauty.

I had no idea what a tribal nose ring looked like, but I knew Andrea's face didn't need one to be beautiful. I told her so. I also promised to be as nice to the cat as the cat was to me. She fired back a reply saying, "Remember to turn the other whisker!" It's annoying when your children misquote Scripture to you.

APRIL

30

Life abounds! The Japanese peony is stopping traffic out front. It's r-e-d, red! So glad to see Autumn Joy sedum fleshing out. Phew. Something ate it down to the stems the last two years. Keep an eye on it!

I stood with a jug of milk in each hand, listening to Larry explain how much better the misfit door suited Ky's new basement bedroom, where it could be sanded and painted to cover its dark finish. He promised me a new door at the top of the basement stairs stained to match the others on the main floor.

"Covering the door with paint is the merciful thing to do," he said.

This was exactly why I didn't watch those home renovation shows on TV. They missed the point by talking about crumbling foundations or the excitement of uncovering original wallpaper. The real handiwork of renovation took place in the people whose dreams collided over something as inconsequential as a door.

I remembered the day I'd come home from a baby shower to find Scott standing with his arms crossed in front of a newly stained door. *"The stain is a little dark, don't you think?"* he asked. He had spent most of the weekend scraping through layers of paint and sanding the last remnants of varnish to find the wood of the door. Fourteen more doors needed refinishing in our Victorian, so he had charged ahead. He opened a quart of stain he found in the basement and rubbed it onto the raw door. His recklessness resulted in a door the color of tar rather than the walnut promised on the label and certainly not the honeyed oak I'd dreamed about for months.

"That's the door for the top of the basement stairs, right?" I asked Scott.

"You'll only see it when you come in the kitchen door."

"I like it."

"Really?"

"For the basement door."

"We could go together to get stain for the rest of the doors."

"I'd like that."

Thus, the door had come to represent the delicate dance of forgiveness and grace Scott and I preferred. *Am I willing to hear the music with Larry?*

"I liked the door where it was." I tried but failed to keep the irritation out of my voice.

"It took a long time to remove the door without marring the casing." Larry wiped the sweat off his forehead with his arm. "It's an ugly door, Mib. It belongs in the basement."

"Do whatever you want," I said, turning away from him to put the milk in the refrigerator.

"The door stands out like a sore thumb."

"Leave it in the basement, then."

"Mib?"

I faced him holding a carton of strawberries that smelled wonderful but would probably disappoint me. It was way too early in the season. "It's just a door, for heaven's sake. Put it wherever you want."

"Whatever you say."

When I turned to put away the cornflakes, he was gone. The hollow basement magnified the sound of metal and wood scraping across the floor and plenty of grunting. I stood there frozen in place by the past— unwilling to hurt Larry with the true meaning of the door and too possessive of the past to let it go. He deserved better. I headed for the basement stairs.

The scent of cut lumber and fresh wall-joint compound mingled with mildew and dust in the basement. No longer just a dark place to store our marginalized belongings, three well-lit rooms filled the space—a bedroom, a media room, and a laundry room—Larry's surprise addition. He'd even included a place for a counter to fold clothes. The door of dissension leaned against the new wall of Ky's bedroom.

Larry moved from screw to screw with the drill to remove the door's hinges.

"Larry!"

He dropped the drill to his side. "What now, Mibby?"

"I was wrong about the door. It should stay down here." *Don't ask me to explain.*

"Are you sure?"

"Yes, very."

His eyes held a question I didn't know how to answer.

"I better go put the ice cream away," I said.

"Come back when you're done."

I made Larry a root beer float, my thanks for letting me keep the door's story a secret. He kissed me with lips salty with sweat and sweetened with root beer. We spoke about little things—the garden, the price of asparagus, what color to paint Ky's new bedroom. Safe things that softened the tension between us.

"Shouldn't Ky be helping you?" I asked.

Larry tipped the glass to finish the float and backhanded the froth from his mustache. "He's at work. He won't be home until ten."

"It's a school night."

"He said you knew about it, that you said it was okay for him to work on a Sunday. And to drive his car."

"He never mentioned working tonight to me."

***

I paced from the living room window to the kitchen door, pulling back the shades every once in a while to watch for Ky's car. I called Pizza Man three times. Each time, a girl who I guessed had spent her whole paycheck on a brand new tongue stud mumbled into the phone. I understood Ky's name and *dah-wivery*.

"Have him call me the next time he comes back to the store, please," I said every time I called.

Larry had gone to bed as soon as we'd arrived home from dinner at Connie's. Disappointment roiled in my chest to see how easily he'd stepped from my stewpot of worries to an undisturbed sleep. I stomped up the stairs, intending to wake him to enjoy the "for worse" part of our lives. But more than I wanted his companionship in my misery, I wanted Larry to drive his mountainous delivery route with eight solid hours of sleep, so I returned to the living room.

I sat in my grandmother's chair and ran my fingers over the textured fabric nearly rubbed flat with use. Unbeckoned, a memory of my grandmother catching me smoking a cigarette made me squeeze my eyes shut with shame. Grandma, her face reddened by rage, had wagged her finger at me. "I watched your grandfather drown in our own bed from emphysema."

I'd held the cigarette like a dirty diaper. "Grandma, this isn't my cigarette. I'm holding it for a friend."

She looked up and down the row of corn. "You have an invisible friend now, do you?"

"She went home to take out the trash."

"At ten o'clock?"

I plodded ahead, stammering over every syllable of the lie, compelled by an inner madness that had severed truth and love in my young mind. Grandma took the cigarette from my hand and snuffed it under her foot.

"You holding any more of them cigarettes for your friend?"

"No," I said, but that was a lie, too. The next morning, I threw the last of the cigarettes in the dumpster behind Cox Market. Grandma never said another word about my lone incidence of smoking.

I returned to the front window to continue my vigil. How many times had Ky lied to our faces without flinching? I let my anger at him tumble end over end until the sound of its descent no longer troubled me.

At eleven-thirty, Ky walked through the front door. He'd prepared himself for my questions. "You weren't home," he said. "Larry won't let me do anything unless he talks to you. The manager called. A kid got sick or something. The manager pleaded with me. I knew you'd say yes."

"You could've called my cell phone."

"The manager needed me right away. The orders were backing up. He was desperate."

"Why should I believe you, Ky? You lied to Larry about talking to me *and* about driving your car."

"I have to drive the car to work. I can't deliver pizzas on my bike."

"Then I guess you can't deliver pizzas."

"I have to!"

"If pleasing your boss is more important than obeying house rules, and you can't be trusted to tell the truth, and—"

"I can't believe this! This is great, just great. I try to help somebody out, and you bust me for it."

"Your altruism is truly touching, but helping others doesn't justify lying to Larry or back-talking me."

Ky stood with one hand on the newel post, the other in a tight fist at his side.

"We're trying to build a family here," I said as evenly as I could manage. "We could use your help. *I* could use your help." I stepped toward him, but he turned toward the stairs. "Listen, I know it's different, really different, with Larry here, but he cares about you."

Ky looked up the stairs. "I have homework to do."

"Tonight?"

"Just a few math problems."

"At midnight? You had no business agreeing to work with homework yet to do."

"It's eleven-*forty*."

His attention to detail was no longer amusing. "You're quitting your job tomorrow."

"How am I supposed to buy gas and pay for my insurance?"

"Honey, I'm not even sure you're mature enough to drive a car."

Ky looked off, preparing his rebuttal, no doubt. Fatigue settled in my chest. I suggested we talk in the morning or after school before we both said something we were sure to regret. He ignored my advice. "Without a car, I'll be home a lot more," he said, meeting my gaze. "Larry's not going to like that. I know why he's so anxious to get me into the basement." His lips curled in distaste over the picture he allowed himself to imagine.

Scott had been out of town when Ky asked me the dreaded question around a mouthful of a peanut butter and jelly sandwich. "How does the sperm get from the man to the egg in the woman?" Bread crumbs clung to the peanut butter and jelly at the corners of Ky's mouth. He wore a Teenage Mutant Ninja Turtles T-shirt. He still had baby teeth. I think he was eight, maybe seven. He had no business asking me questions about human reproduction. It had always been my intention to answer his questions with concise clinical terms delivered with a casual off-the-cuff ease. I may or may not have done that. Whatever I said bypassed my short-term memory to be lost forever, but I will never forget Ky's response.

He swiped his mouth clean with the back of his hand and curled his lip in the same way he just had. "That's gross," he'd said as he ran from the table, leaving the rest of his sandwich untouched.

Ky turned and slowly climbed the stairs. I felt like a glob of gum on the bottom of his shoe.

Blink watched me pace around the garden, as uncomfortable with my own company as I'd ever been. I sure didn't want a boy's best friend around. "Go back inside Blink, pleeeease."

Blink sat and cocked his head.

I waved him off. "Go, go!"

His ears lay against his head and he cowered.

I collapsed into a ball and the tears flowed. Blink curled up next to me—his way of saying that he understood. But really, how could he? He'd been neutered years ago. He'd never faced the accusing paw of a puppy over his sexuality. I tried to picture myself looking Ky in the eye when I told him to have a nice day at school the next morning. *Forget that!* I'd leave him a note on his backpack and stay in bed.

I nestled into Blink's back against the cold. He rolled onto his back and offered his belly to be rubbed. When I sighed, he licked at my wet face. I rolled onto my back, too. The night sky, shapeless and solemn, wouldn't let me forget the look on Ky's face. Not only had he acknowledged his mother's sex life, he was aware of my willingness to shuffle him off to a subterranean bedroom at the whim of his stepfather, a surefire premise for an eighteenth-century novel if there ever was one. I longed for the days when I had been invisible to Ky. Too bad I drew attention to myself by remarrying a man with an active libido. But then, is there any other kind?

If only Larry would be more patient. . . . How did he expect us to have time together with his odd working hours and with his mother at the house all the time? He was eager enough to put my son in the basement. He needed to be as willing with his mother.

I found a tissue in my pocket to wipe my nose. Blink followed me into the living room. I stood at the base of the stairs through the twelve chimes of the clock. Rather than join Larry in bed, I slumped into Grandma's chair again.

I blew my nose and sniffed until I found the source of the acrid odor of cat urine on the skirt of the chair.

"Goliath!"

I dragged the chair down the hall to the back door, down the porch steps, and through the garden to where the trash cans stood ready for the morning pickup. When I closed the alley gate, I saw Larry backlit in the doorway, tying his robe closed.

"What's going on, Mib? It sounded like a stampede down here."

"Your cat peed on my grandmother's chair."

He met me at the porch steps and reached for me. I stiffened.

He shoved his hands into his pockets. "You don't have to throw the chair away. We'll get it cleaned."

"Ky *just* came home."

"No wonder you're upset."

"That's not what's bothering me. Well, it is, but it's not why I'm—"

"Upset with me?"

The cold honed the night. It would freeze, and that would be the end of Larry's heirloom tomato. I dabbed at my nose again.

"We can talk inside," he said, extending his hand to me.

I buried my hands in my armpits. "Ky knows why we're moving him to the basement."

"He *wants* to move to the basement."

"Of course he would say that."

"Let's get out of the cold."

"He knows we want him to move to the basement so we can have our privacy."

"He said that?"

"In so many words."

"We're married, Mib."

"You should've seen the look on his face."

Larry expelled a long breath. "What do you want to do?"

I wanted to go back to the morning Scott kissed me good-bye straddling his bike. Instead of harboring a tiff from the night before, I would coax him back into the house. There would be no truck. No intersection. No *"Mrs. Garrett, we have some bad news for you."* That was what I wanted. *Right?*

A red flag waved somewhere in my conscience. This was dangerous thinking, no doubt about it. I made myself remember my first real date with Larry. Just before Christmas Ky had stayed at a friend's house for the night. Larry made reservations at the Riverbend Restaurant, but when we stepped into the night, a gibbous moon befriended us. We held hands inside Larry's jacket pocket. Our breaths were silvery plumes. We walked and walked. And when the cold seeped into our jackets, we drank hot cocoa at an all-night diner. The vinyl booth warmed and softened. I didn't look at my watch once.

Still standing in the doorway, Larry whispered my name, as a question really. His voice worked like a beckoning hand to pull me into the present. "What do you want to do?" he asked again.

I still didn't know.

"Ky's pulling a guilt trip on you," he said, "the oldest trick in the book."

"But aren't we pushing him away?"

"Once the walls in the basement are textured and painted and he moves his stuff down there, he'll be in hog heaven."

"What's the hurry?"

"If slowing down will make you feel better . . ."

"Would you mind?"

"I won't drive another nail until I get the okay from you."

I stepped into his arms. "Thank you."

"Can we go in now?"

"Do you know anything about roosters?"

"Should I?"

"Maybe you should talk to Louise."

MAY
8

Another gray morning, but blooms abound.
The horse chestnut is full of double flower
clusters, trumpet-shaped, and hot pink with
sunshine-yellow throats. Yowza! Something
is eating the Autumn Joy sedum again. Grr!
No sign of grasshoppers or caterpillars.
Do mice eat sedum? Find out!

Kathleen pulled a cart laden with flowers through the plant tables of gem-colored petunias and nasturtiums. I hoped Mr. Webley would approve my selections. A Walled Garden shopper stopped Kathleen to ask for directions to the tomatoes. Normally, I would have helped myself, but Kathleen had insisted on pulling the cart. My stomach gurgled when I remembered the Sweet Suzy Strawberry Cream Balls under the Daisy Mobile's seat. The marshmallow coating would have turned warm and stringy. The shopper thanked Kathleen for her help, and we continued toward the truck.

Mr. Webley had said to make the planters in front of the house special. With all these flowers, they would be that and more. I'd selected two cobalt blue glazed urns as large as whiskey barrels to flank the Webleys' front door. As for the flowers, I'd chosen an eye-popping assortment, just as a bowerbird would do in case the lady bowerbird was to drive by in the next few days. Itty-bitty violas and asters wouldn't do. The Georgian house required equally imposing flowers to maintain a proper scale and balance, so I planned to fill the urns with gallon-sized perennials—Shasta daisies, twinspur, and Summer Sun false sunflowers. The urns would reflect the era of the house, as dramatic as Gibson girls with purple maiden grass and a boa of chartreuse sweet potato vine.

Another twelve pots already lined the driveway. On my last visit to the Webleys', I'd performed a postmortem on the previous year's flowers. And since I'd taken a chance on the entry urns, I selected flowers to match the owner's taste but with my preference for extroverted colors—Valentine-red geraniums, canary marigolds, lacy alyssum for elegance, and my addition, spires of salvia, a purple that leaned toward blue, an embellishment meant to draw in the bowerbird's mate.

Only a few cars filled spaces in the Walled Garden parking lot, fewer than I would have expected on such a beautiful spring day. An older couple bent over a rosebush to read its tag. A young mother and her daughter walked along the rows of container trees. I hoped she considered a linden—such a great shade tree. Next to the Daisy Mobile, a man loaded flats of peppers and tomato plants into his car trunk. When he saw I was watching, he winked and said, "It's going to be a good year for salsa. I can just tell."

I said, "Good luck" and lowered the Daisy Mobile's tailgate.

I loaded the flowers behind the truck's cab to protect them from the wind. "The garden center seems quiet. How's Christopher's mood?"

"Darker than ever. Some guys in suits came to talk to him yesterday." Kathleen hefted the tailgate closed. "Working at Kmart is looking better to me all the time."

We hugged and I promised to pray for her.

"Thanks," she said. "Every morning I pray for Christopher as I'm driving to work, asking the Lord to help me love him and to help him prosper. By ten-thirty, I'm sick with disappointment at my attitude toward him."

"Most people wouldn't even pray."

"Maybe not, but I'm here for a reason, the Lord's reason, and I only want to fulfill His purpose for my life. And then, I'm outta here." She smiled.

Inside the Daisy Mobile's cab, Blink looked out the passenger window completely indifferent to my arrival. I talked to him anyway. "What do you think God's purpose is for me, old feller? Am I fulfilling His plan for me?"

Blink turned toward me. A glob of pink icing perched on his nose. His breath smelled of strawberries. I felt under the truck's seat and pulled out a flattened Starbucks cup and a birthday card I'd bought for my mother but never sent. No sign of the cream balls. I pushed the gearshift into reverse. "That was my breakfast. I don't have a sea of forgetfulness, Blink. You ate the cellophane, too, didn't you? Bad dog—very, very bad dog."

Most of the gardens I maintained were born of practicality over creativity. Grass dominated the canvas; rock provided the middle ground for the requisite junipers and roses; a tree or two planted too close to the house finalized the uptight compositions that looked like something a starving artist might paint. A select number of the gardens, however, I considered works of art—performance art, really. In the span of a day, a brushstroke of tender green deepened in hue, leafy palms opened toward heaven, and dabs of a round brush formed buds to unfold into trumpets with velvety petals. This made the gardener a curator of a divine endowment. That was how I felt in the Webley garden.

A pulse of rain had loosened twigs from the cottonwoods the night before to litter the flowerbeds. The mess kept me from finishing the long list of maintenance tasks I'd prioritized in my planner the previous week, but I managed to plant the large urns on the porch and the row of pots along the driveway. Each time I worked in the garden, tension knotted my muscles—that was how badly I wanted Mrs. Webley to find the garden welcoming. I sat in the Daisy Mobile to write watering instructions for the new flowerpots.

Blink whimpered.

"You were out there for two hours."

He pawed at the door handle.

"You won't get any sympathy from me. Remember, I didn't have my breakfast." I started the truck and shifted into reverse. A car's horn sounded behind me. In my rearview mirror, Mr. Webley waved at me from his black sedan—very shiny and very expensive looking. I waggled the gear into neutral. When I rolled down the window, Blink stepped over my lap to meet Mr. Webley. I put my back to the door and pushed against Blink's chest. "Oh no you don't." Blink cleaned my right ear with his tongue.

Bleh.

Mr. Webley's chest heaved with each breath, and he was flushed from exertion. He loosened his tie. "Stay . . . right there. There's something . . . in the house."

The truck's heater felt good against my legs, but I didn't dare waste gas on anything as frivolous as my comfort, so I turned off the ignition. Mr. Webley trotted up the porch steps to the front door and let himself in. He emerged again less than a minute later with a large glass vase. He hadn't taken notice of the new urns. Even so, I didn't want the man to go into cardiac arrest, so I met him on the lawn.

"I meant to be here sooner," he said, handing over the vase. "The meeting went longer than I expected. The bank is resurfacing the parking lot. I had to park on Elberta." He put his hands on his knees and sucked deep breaths.

"Take your time," I said and felt my pocket for the cell phone and then remembered I'd left it at home on the kitchen counter. *Is it five compressions and two breaths or two compressions and five breaths?*

He blotted his forehead with a hanky. "I'm glad I caught you. I'd like you to take a bouquet of those flowers to . . . a dear friend." He pointed to a bed of iris.

If he intended to impress his wife with the garden, he needed to learn the flowers' names. "The flowers that look like panting poodles are irises," I said.

Mr. Webley considered the irises for a moment and frowned. He unfolded a piece of paper. "I've drawn you a map. Of course, I'll compensate you for your time. It's just that I don't know anything about arranging flowers." He dealt me two twenty-dollar bills from a money clip. "Will this be enough?"

I had three more maintenance clients that day. Still, forty dollars would cover Ky's expenses during his baseball tournament in Denver. I took the money. Once money had been exchanged, Mr. Webley was all business. "She lives off of Peach Orchard Road, just past the fire station, in one of those old Spanish-looking houses."

"I know the neighborhood you mean. I drive right by there."

That's what I said to Mr. Webley with the forty dollars deep in my pocket. When I stood at the door of the red-tiled bungalow, ringing the doorbell for the third time, I regretted my hasty agreement. If his friend didn't answer, I hoped to leave the flowers with a neighbor, but an arborvitae obscured the view of the house across the street. No signs of life there.

One of Orchard City's older neighborhoods, Vista Heights was developed as an artist community. The covenants allowed professional studios on the property and stipulated the red-tiled roofs and adobe walls of Spanish architecture. To the left of Mr. Webley's friend's house, two thick arms of adobe enclosed a side patio and extended to a smaller building with a row of glass-paned doors painted aqua—probably an art studio. One door stood open to the patio. I took a chance and walked along the wall on a path of crushed scoria. A patch of freshly tilled soil filled the space between the path and the wall. I couldn't resist squeezing a handful of the soil in my hand. It was light and moist, yet it poured through my fingers. Whoever had prepared this soil for planting knew what she was doing.

"Hello? Are you looking for me?"

Before I turned to see her tapping her leg with her hand, I'd figured out that Mr. Webley's dear friend was *Mrs.* Webley. She stood with one foot inside the studio and one foot on the patio.

I sputtered like a boiling kettle. "I'm sorry I rang your doorbell so many times. I didn't think you were home . . . but I wanted to make sure. I can't hear my doorbell if the radio is on." Nothing I said softened her gaze.

"What do you want?" she asked.

I remembered the flowers in my hands and extended them over the gate. "These are for you."

She walked to the gate, wiping her hands on a paint-stained rag. That explained her annoyance; painters hate interruptions. And I was probably staring. For weeks I'd imagined Mrs. Webley as an aristocrat, suited in silk and pearls, a carefully managed blonde who never went to the garden without her gloves and hat, not a woman wearing an oversized shirt to protect her faded jeans. Far from the sassy bob I'd given her, Mrs. Webley pulled her salt-and-pepper hair into a pragmatic ponytail. She looked me over with hazel eyes ringed with rust. I wished I'd taken the time to change into clean socks with my Birkenstocks. But then, she wore hot pink Crocs splattered with paint.

"That's my vase, isn't it?" she said, taking the flowers.

"Mr. Webley asked me to bring you a bouquet of iris."

"The truth now—he didn't know they were irises, did he?" As she spoke, I tasted the bitterness of her words.

"I had to remind him."

"You don't have to protect him. I lived with him for thirty-five years. He wouldn't know a rose from a tulip, but that's a bit harsh, even for me." She held the vase at arm's length. "Has my husband hired you to tend the garden?"

"Only since the beginning of last month."

Mrs. Webley stiffened. "Then he didn't have anyone dig the dahlia tubers, did he?"

I shook my head.

"I'm not surprised." She turned her attention to the bouquet and sighed. "I like the way you've jumbled the colors together. Are the peonies blooming yet?"

"No, not yet."

"Not even the Japanese peonies? Well, they always lagged a little." She started to turn but stopped. "Did Gordon have you plant the flowerpots?"

I wasn't so enamored of my additions to her garden under her gaze. "Yes."

"Good," she said and pivoted swiftly toward her studio. I was halfway down the front walk when she called after me, "You'll have to seed the sunflower bed. Make sure you include Moulin Rouge and Ring of Fire."

I recognized the sunflower varieties—one a sultry red, almost black, the other a burgundy red with a ring of yellow around the dark center like a solar eclipse. Perhaps Mrs. Webley's blood still warmed when she thought of Mr. Webley—or at least her garden.

~~~

I nearly tripped over Connie backing out of the powder room on her knees, wiping the floor as she went. "It's my Bible study night," she said, "so I put a roast in the Crockpot. Just add the potatoes an hour before dinner. They're in the fridge, peeled and everything."

"Connie, get up. You don't have to cook for us every night, and you certainly don't have to clean the bathrooms."

"You kids work so hard. I love doing it. Besides, my house gets awfully quiet."

Quiet would be nice.

I followed her into the kitchen, where she poured the water from the bucket into the sink. My face warmed at the sight of the dirty water. "Connie . . . I know you're trying to help, but it embarrasses me when you clean the house."

"Oh, honey, I've known you for a long time. You're a good little housekeeper. There's nothing to be embarrassed about. I just like to help."

"No, really, I don't want you to come over to clean anymore. I can handle it." My voice was lower, a bit harder than I meant it to be.

Connie rested her hands on the rim of the bucket. Our eyes met for a moment before she turned back to the sink to wash her hands. "Are you home for lunch?" she asked. "I could make you something. I picked up some of that Italian roast beef you like from the deli."

I'd worked all morning anticipating the leftover pizza I'd squirreled away in the back of the refrigerator the night before. "I'm home to pick something up."

I took the stairs two at a time toward the bedroom. I stared into the top drawer of my dresser. Panties. Bras. A collection of notes from Larry. Nothing there I wanted to carry out to the truck. *The medicine chest.* I shook two Tylenols into my hand and downed them with a drink from the faucet. I talked to my image in the mirror. "You're being childish. You don't need a reason to come into your own house *or* to leave it." I picked a piece of granola bar out of my teeth before I left the bathroom.

During the summer between my sophomore and junior years in high school, I'd befriended an odd duck of a girl named Janet I'd met at the library—or maybe she'd befriended me. We were more alike than different, only her father owned all of the Taco Bells in San Diego County. When Janet refused to go to camp unless I went along, her father happily paid my way to Camp Wampanoag in Vermont. For eight weeks I was a rich girl sorely lacking the usual refinements. When I blackened the eye of the field hockey coach with my stick, the camp director strongly recommended I try archery. Janet and I cried like two orphans over being separated, but a junior leader walked me solemnly to the archery range anyway. Who knew rich people participated in such dangerous sports? I shot an arrow through the camp director's window. This time, the maintenance man, a burly giant who grunted with the effort of each step, escorted me to the fencing pavilion, saying something about liability issues.

Fencing proved to be the perfect sport for me because the *bouton*, a safety tip on the end of the foil, and the safety garb my opponents had to wear kept everyone safe. Truthfully, it was Valentin LaPierre, our French coach, who made fencing perfection. Butterflies tumbled in my stomach every time he took off his mask and a shaft of black hair fell across his forehead. He refused to speak English. His petulance only deepened my devotion. In an attempt to win his attention, I read the fencing manual until the cabin counselor, a pinch-faced Vassar student with fat thighs and bad skin, confiscated my flashlight. Undeterred, I checked a French phrase book out of the camp library and made Janet rehearse an exchange about the Louvre I'd found in the back of the book. By the end of the week, I was a walking glossary of fencing terms, and I could ask where Mona Lisa went to the bathroom.

Back in the kitchen, when Connie said, "I thought you came home to pick something up," I recognized the *en garde* in her voice.

"I took some Tylenol."

Matching my gaze, she said, "I keep a bottle of pain relievers in my purse."

I parried her *attaque*. "I ran out."

"When I run out of something, I immediately write it on a list I keep on the refrigerator."

Contre-attaque. "I keep a list in my planner."

"If the list is on the refrigerator, anyone can add to it." A *fente*. "You're out of garlic powder. I didn't have any for the roast." And *balestra*.

"I use fresh." A parry and a *riposte*.

"There's none in the crisper drawer."

"You should never refrigerate garlic or onions. Check the bottom shelf in the pantry." *Coup de pointe!*

"I prefer powdered," she said.

Our verbal exchange, as calculated as any fencing *assaut*, left us locked at the guard of our foils. To step back would surrender the point. But what would a *touché* cost me?

"Feel free to leave a note on the refrigerator. I'll go to the grocery store on Friday." I stepped out of the *piste* to stop the match. I told Connie to enjoy her lunch as I closed the door. Something had shifted in my relationship with Connie during our exchange that both satisfied and disappointed me.

I stopped to gather the mail, hoping for a *Smith and Hawken* catalog, the *Bon Appétit* for gardeners, to drool over during lunch. No such luck. I dropped the bundle of mail on the seat beside me and warned Blink not to eat anything but bills.

"It's Taco Bell for us, old friend. Crispy or soft shell?"

I parked under a tree at Pennington Park, broke Blink's taco into bite-sized pieces, and poured water into his bowl. Cooking for a dog was so easy. The first bite of guacamole and sour cream made me moan.

Most of the mail consisted of preapproved credit card offers. A post-

card from Safeway announced a grand reopening and enticed atten-
dance with a ten-percent discount. *Do they still make those individual
tiramisus?* I set the postcard aside. The only catalog came from the
American Dahlia Society. My heart thumped when I recognized my sister's handwriting on a pink envelope. To my knowledge, Margot had
never willingly touched pink since she'd failed to potty train her Penny
Pink doll.

I rewrapped the burrito and wiped my hands on my overalls before
opening the envelope. Inside was a greeting card with a black-and-
white picture of a young girl, probably two or three, in her underwear
and T-shirt, pouting with her fists clenched. Over her, a doctor scowled
and wrote on his clipboard. The caption read, "After six months of
research, scientists postulate that younger sisters are the source of teenage angst and alienation." Inside, Margot had scribbled out the printed
happy birthday sentiment and wrote: "However, after exhaustive
research using sound scientific protocol, the earlier findings have been
revised. Scientists now report that younger sisters give their siblings a
sense of superiority and a place to call home. Love, Margot."

I ran my fingers over the signature. *Love, Margot?*

I stared out the windshield, not daring to own the words. I closed
my eyes, and the first of many hot tears flowed down my cheeks. My
shoulders relaxed from where they had hovered around my ears
since . . . forever.

"Love, Margot."

Blink, never a dog to miss a grooming opportunity, swiped my
cheek with his tongue and panted taco breath in my face. I unwrapped
my burrito for him, knowing I would regret the change in his diet later.

MAY

9

This is May? Low of 35° with rain forecasted for the rest of the week. It's snowing on the Mesa! Woody shrubs and trees—hawthorn, mountain ash, and snowballs—are blooming. I've never appreciated their colors more.

There are good trees and there are fast-growing trees, but there are no good, fast-growing trees. That's a horticultural fact. A globe willow is a fast-growing tree with the same slender leaves as a weeping willow, only the canopy is shaped like it has poked one of its woody fingers in an electrical outlet. Real party trees, globe willows are the first to show their leaves in the spring, but they're less than dependable in tough times. One gust of wind sends a shower of twigs to the ground. Arborists call this self-pruning. I call it job security—and a burning pain between my shoulder blades. Two globe willows grew at the house owned by Walter, Margaret's husband, and now rented by Rex and Jamine. A gust of wind roiled the treetops to pepper the lawn I'd just raked with more twigs.

Stupid trees.

Bad-mouthing a well-meaning tree didn't make me feel any better about the sendoff I'd given Ky that morning. An incident involving a misplaced pair of shoes had turned ugly when he had accused Connie of being a neat freak and nosy and I had countered by suggesting that he was old enough to stop blaming others for his problems. The scene ended with me yelling threats of grounding and annihilation as he dumped the laundry basket full of his neatly folded clothes—thanks to Connie—onto the floor and his shoes landed among his T-shirts and jeans. Not surprisingly, Ky was uninterested in hearing my apologies.

I threw the fourth bagful of debris into the truck bed just as Margaret's front door slammed closed. "I'll get home when I get home," yelled Walter, walking toward his car in the driveway. He backed his Buick into the street without looking over his shoulder. A minivan swerved to miss his car. I turned my back on him and kept raking, embarrassed for him and embarrassed for me. Anger is a fool's sword.

Lord, protect drivers on the road today from Walter's anger.

I quickened my strokes, but cleaning up the willow mess had burned up the twenty minutes I'd gained by not flushing another customer's pond filter, a job I was happy to put off until my next visit.

And protect Ky from mine.

I closed the tailgate of the Daisy Mobile as I mentally mapped out the most efficient route to my next client's home on the north side of town. Before leaving, I scanned what I'd accomplished at Margaret and Walter's two properties. Lawns cleared of debris. Roses on autopilot. Daffodil foliage cut to the ground. I groaned. A forsythia encroached the front steps of Walter's house. Taking the time to trim the shrub would set my schedule back another ten minutes. How pregnant was Jamine? Eight months? She probably couldn't see her feet let alone a misbehaving forsythia. But then again, she might trip over the branches, and then the baby . . . I hefted the loppers out of the truck.

"Let's get the chainsaw," Margaret said, walking up beside me. "We'll cut that there hateful shrub to its roots. Whoever would plant such a dang fool shrub so close to the front door?" Reddened pillows of flesh framed her eyes.

"Margaret, I'm so sorry, but I don't have time to remove the shrub today. I'm a little behind as it is." A rumble of thunder drew my attention to a veil of rain to the southwest. I sure didn't need any more interruptions. I willed the storm to blow to the south.

"I made some molasses cookies," she said, offering the cookies as pleasant as you please, as if I'd just stopped by for coffee. The pleading in her eyes betrayed her calm. A breeze carried the congenial scent of rain, perfect inspiration to partake of coffee and cookies with a friend.

"New clients, the Terrys, are expecting me today," I said, knowing my time with Margaret meant a schedule derailed beyond repair.

"I won't keep you long, I promise."

The remains of a coffee break littered Margaret's kitchen table—two cups, a plate of molasses cookie crumbs, and a crumpled napkin stained with mascara and lipstick. She cleared the table and poured two fresh cups of coffee before sitting across from me. The plate of cookies lay forgotten on the counter.

Margaret massaged her knuckles. "You best enjoy that boy of yours while he's young. Once they're growed, they think they know what's best about everything, like they was the one parenting you." She blinked and her eyes shone with tears. "I thought Walter was going to deck Sonny. And after Sonny left, Walter's anger grew and grew. I finally told him to sit down and be still. I wasn't going to hear no more bad talk about Sonny." Margaret's shoulders trembled. She buried her face in her hands.

"What's going on, Margaret?" I asked, hoping to hear the abridged version so I could at least deadhead the Terrys' Basket of Gold plants.

"You know Sonny was never happy about me marrying Walter. He said I'd forgotten his daddy, asked what the point of me marrying again was anyway, like I didn't have a woman's heart beating in my chest. I told him it was none of his business. Silly me, I thought things was getting better between them two.

"Then Sonny comes over here this morning like he was on some kind of mission. We was just finishing our midmorning snack, a little something sweet. Walter loves them molasses cookies almost as much as you do."

Unfortunately, Margaret was telling the director's version with previously unreleased scenes. The clock chimed eleven.

"I could tell by the way Sonny pounded on the door that something was under his bonnet—and it weren't no bee. He wasn't inside the door but a second when he says he wants to talk to me in private. And like a fool, I told him he could say anything in front of my husband. That just ain't true now, is it? Some things really are best left unsaid."

How very, very true.

"Sonny wouldn't sit down. He crossed his arms, looked down at us all superior like. 'Have it your way, Mother,' he said. Mother? He has never called me Mother in his life. Anyhow, he blurts out like he was ordering a hamburger and fries, 'I want you to go see my lawyer, Steve Gammill. The situation has changed, and you need to bring your will up to date. I won't see what Dad worked so hard for going to Walter on the event of your death.'"

Seeing Margaret's face pucker and her shoulders heave with sobs just about broke my heart, so I cried with her—for how lonely she felt in the contrail of Walter's anger and for how Sonny had belittled her. And I cried for myself, a pitiful excuse for a mother.

Kneeling beside Margaret's chair with my arms wrapped around her shoulders, I remembered the first time I'd experienced the searing pain of separation from Ky. I'd taken him to J. C. Penney to buy sheets for his big-boy bed. He was two. I looked down to show him the sheets covered with dump trucks and bulldozers. He wasn't there. I called his name, but he didn't answer. Instantly, a story from the national news about a baby kidnapping in a department store replayed in my mind. I ran through the store swallowing down panic, looking inside the circles of clothes racks and stooping to check under dressing rooms doors for Ky's red tennies. Through the glass exit doors, a car drove by faster than it should have. I raced to see if Ky's mop of blond hair could be seen in the back seat but changed my mind and headed for the customer service desk to call the police. As I passed a display of luggage, I heard a familiar laugh.

"Ky?" I asked.

More giggling.

I followed the sound to an open-ended cube, where Ky smiled up at me. "Peek-a-boo."

The sickening void from that day had lain inert in my memory all those years. Sitting there with Margaret, I felt the raw edges of the hole tear again. At two, Ky had been delighted with our reunion. Reconnecting with sixteen-year-old Ky would not be so easy, I was sure. But settling for the kind of relationship Margaret and Sonny shared was out of the question. I was even surer of that.

~~~

By the time I crossed Main Street, rain bounced off the pavement. I drove hunched over the steering wheel to avoid looking through a smear of mud and bug goo on the windshield. Blink stood to rest his muzzle on the passenger's window, which was stuck at half-mast. He squinted into the rain, but his nose twitched busily to collect the scents released by the storm. *Doggie heaven.* I leaned toward the driver's door to miss the swing of his tail.

I parked in front of the Terrys' house to wait out the rain. I expected the shower to peter out and die within minutes, as was typical for our valley, but after ten minutes, the rain continued to fall steadily. The clouds roosted over the valley and seemed content to stay a spell. That was enough of an anomaly in the desert southwest to abandon my schedule for an afternoon of sipping tea. I pumped the accelerator and turned the ignition. Blink pulled his head into the cab to shimmy from his nose to his tail, his way of agreeing with my decision. I was too muddleheaded over Ky to work anyway. I headed to what I hoped was an empty house.

I held my breath as I downshifted into second to turn onto Crawford Avenue. Connie and I hadn't talked since our tête-à-tête. I didn't want to beg forgiveness if she hadn't even noticed we'd sparred. And honestly, I didn't want to beg forgiveness at all. I wanted some space. If Connie's car was parked in the driveway, I would continue driving around the block to Louise's. No doubt Louise would be in the kitchen testing recipes. Maybe she had perfected Stookie's pie.

I slowed to check the driveway for Connie's Taurus. Instead, Larry's Datsun was parked by the kitchen door. My watch read 1:40, a full hour before Ky needed a ride home. My heart responded with an explosive thump. I found Larry at the island making a sandwich. He had changed out of his Sweet Suzy uniform and into the slim cut jeans we had bought when cinching his belt gathered his jeans like a gunny-sack. He wore a T-shirt spotted with rain on the shoulders. And my favorite, his hair, a week or so past due for a cut, curled at the nape of his neck from the wetness.

Yum.

"Hey, you're home early." He lifted me off the floor to kiss me deeply before setting me on the counter.

"Is everything all right?" I asked.

"Much better now," he said, tucking a strand of hair behind my ear. "A tire blew this side of Delta, so I cut my run short today." He ran his hands up and down my back. "You feel great."

His words warmed my belly and settled in my deepest parts. "So do you," I murmured.

"I planted the cannas for you," he said.

That explained the scent of humus that clung to his shirt.

"In the rain? I'm impressed."

He pulled me closer, and I looked toward the kitchen door. "Won't your mom be here soon?"

"She's filling in for Sue at the church. She can't leave until the bulletin is done, so she said not to expect her until five or later."

"I don't have to pick Ky up until two-forty." Saying my son's name reminded me of the hurtful words we'd exchanged.

Larry smiled. His dimples deepened. My pulse quickened. We couldn't do anything about Ky until we got him home. "What's on your mind?" I asked Larry, knowing the answer.

He held my gaze with hungry eyes. "You," he said, tightening his embrace.

"What about your sandwich?"

"What sandwich?" He picked me up and carried me down the hall to the stairs.

As we passed the front door, I said, "Wait. Is the back door locked?"

"Yep." He clicked the front door's deadbolt into place and started up the stairs.

"Put me down. You're going to hurt yourself."

He took another step.

"*Larry.*"

He set me down on the stairs. We stood nose to nose. "You were waiting for me, weren't you?" I asked.

"Yep."

"You could have changed that tire yourself, couldn't you?"

"Yep."

Nothing whittled a man's vocabulary quite like desire. Larry closed the discussion with a kiss that turned off the switch in the part of my brain that worried about unlocked doors and unpaid hours. "I'll race you," I said.

We revisited the holiness of the first garden in the intimacy shared by a husband and wife. Created to live in perfect fellowship with the Creator, to live forever without toil or strife, the pleasure of coming together was all we retained from our first parents when they, and so we, their children, were banished from our heritage by the curse. Within the circle of three—husband, wife, Creator—there was no shame in the wanting and the knowing. There was only the pleasure. Marriage is said to reflect the relationship between the Son and His bride, the church. Being with Larry gave me a better idea of what the ecstasy of heaven, of knowing and being known by God, might be like.

Larry sighed, and I turned to him. I inventoried all that was male about him in the light softened by the shade. The day-end stubble below his beard. The pebbled skin of his neck. The vein that traveled along the smooth underside of his arm to disappear into the hard muscle of his bicep. I fingered the coarse hair of his beard and kissed his freckled shoulder.

The phone rang.

"Don't answer it," Larry said, his voice heavy with contentment.

"It could be Ky."

"It's probably my mother."

It rang again.

"Thank you," he said, turning to face me.

"For what?"

"For loving me."

And again the phone rang.

"It's my pleasure," I said, and we laughed.

Another ring.

"Let me see who it is," I said, rolling toward the nightstand to read the caller ID "It's the school." I pulled the sheet up to my neck and pushed the talk button.

"Mrs. Garrett?" asked a throaty female voice.

"This is Ky's mother, Mrs. McManus." I sat up. "Is there a problem?"

"You need to get to the school as soon as possible."

I looked to Larry. His brow furrowed as if to ask, *What's up?*

"Has Ky been injured?" I asked the caller.

"He's not hurt, but he's in a great deal of trouble."

"We'll be right there."

Larry steered the Datsun around carloads of students stopped to talk to their friends and dodged others who ran between cars. A bevy of girls stepped in front of us, too busy making plans for the afternoon to watch for traffic. Larry stomped on the brake pedal. The tires skidded across the pavement. I held my breath until the car stopped just inches from the girls—not one raincoat among them. Short tops and low pants. Bare bellies and shoulders. Larry turned ever so slightly to watch them.

"I would never let a daughter of mine leave the house dressed like that," I said to reel in his imagination.

His head snapped forward, and he shifted into first gear. "Me, neither." He parked in a space vacated by a Honda packed with turning heads and waving arms. Slamming car doors and shouts, both welcoming and profane, sounded around us.

"We should pray," Larry said and bowed his head.

I closed my eyes and a hot tear rolled down my cheek. Larry sat silent for so long, I thought he was waiting for me to pray. *What do I need from you, Lord?* I wanted Ky to be the victim of mistaken identity or a spiteful tattletale, but I knew better. He had left the house that morning with enough angst to launch a war, or at least a small skirmish. And as dumb as it sounded, I felt responsible. Regret tightened my throat.

Finally, Larry broke the silence. "Father God, when we rebelled against you, our perfect Father, you sent your Son to show us your heart and to extend your hand in forgiveness. We choose to do the same for Ky. Holy Spirit, strengthen us to do justly toward Ky, and to extend him mercy, and to walk humbly with you, so he will want to join us. Amen."

Larry squeezed my hand.

"Amen."

~~~

Ky sat alone on the far end of a bench, head in hands, turned toward the distant doors of the hallway. His shoulders bent from the burden he carried. Up to that point, I'd held out the smallest hope that his offense had been menial, maybe being habitually tardy to English Lit 2A, fifth hour, right after lunch. Something in me sagged when I saw him, and I nearly gasped at the thud of it. I fought the instinct to rush to him and hold him to my breast. Larry tightened his grip on my hand and shook his head. For only me to hear, he uttered the four-word solution to everything male, "Give him some room."

"He isn't fainting," I snapped.

Ky looked up to acknowledge our presence with a scowl. We walked in the door marked *Office of the Principal*.

A cheery woman behind a desk asked, "Are you Kyle's parents?" Something hopeful there—the principal and her staff didn't know Ky well enough to call him by his nickname. "Thank you for coming so quickly." She rose from her chair and gestured for us to follow. "Dr. Watt has an important meeting at three-thirty, so we'd better get this show on the road."

Educational attire hadn't changed much since my high school days. The woman wore a capacious jumper with sensible shoes. Timeless.

Dr. Watt looked up from her phone conversation when we entered her office. She waved us to two wingback chairs in front of her desk.

The secretary whispered, "She'll only be a minute. I'll buzz Mr. Rudyard to let him know you're here."

The principal sat behind a large desk, which afforded her instant status and protection. A smart choice. The room reflected the institutional style of the midfifties, when the high school had been built. Steel-cased windows. Steam radiators. Green-flecked floor tiles. A thin layer of femininity had been added by way of mauve paint and a nosegay wallpaper border. Behind Dr. Watt's desk hung a poster of a man running on a rocky slope toward a faraway peak. The caption read, "Anything you can conceive and believe, you can achieve." Just reading the words made me tired. I shifted in the chair, and a broken spring poked my right cheek.

Dr. S. Cynthia Watt, a most unfortunate name for a principal, apologized to the caller for cutting their conversation short with a promise to call the next morning. I recognized her throaty voice as the woman who had called us to the school. The buttons of her cranberry suit strained to hold the fabric together when she reached over the desk to shake our hands. Mascara filled the creases below her eyes. She'd had a long day, too. After a round of introductions and pleasantries, she called Ky from the hall to join us. On his heels, a man strode in, greeted Dr. Watt, and leaned against the radiator. Mr. Rudyard was a man with vigilant eyes and the tautness of a sprinter—a result, no doubt, of being around students with dissecting tools for too many years. He was Ky's biology teacher. His matted toupee, cocked toward his right ear, gave him the aspect of a peevish poet.

Dr. Watt asked Ky, "Do you want to tell your mother and stepfather what happened in biology this afternoon or would you prefer Mr. Rudyard tell the story?"

Ky slouched in his chair, the ankle of one leg propped on the knee of the other. I kicked his chair, but if anything, his slouch deepened. Dr. Watt looked over her bifocals at Ky. He shrugged.

Mr. Rudyard leaned forward from where he sat on the radiator. "As you wish, Mr. Garrett." He spoke directly to Larry. "At the beginning of class, I ask each student a question from the previous night's reading. Mr. Garrett was unable to name the three different types of RNA. Since he was already sitting in the row of F students, I asked him to collect his things and remove himself to the principal's office."

My pulse quickened. "Please explain what you mean by 'the row of F students.'"

Mr. Rudyard pushed his glasses to the bridge of his nose and continued addressing Larry. "Students with Fs in the class sit in the back row."

I waved my hand for his attention. "And the A students?"

"They sit in the front row, of course."

Larry squeezed my hand, and the tips of my fingers tingled. True, I was chasing a red herring. But something had to explain the change in Ky. Maybe Mr. Rudyard's classroom management carried the blame.

"And then B students in the second row and C students in the third?" I asked.

"Yes, with the D students in the fourth row." He spoke with no sense of apology or embarrassment about his management style. I was appalled.

"Let me be sure I've understood you," I said. "The very students who have the toughest time attending to your lectures or understanding the material sit the farthest distance away from you."

He sighed heavily, and for a brief moment, I fantasized about snatching his toupee and using it for a Mexican hat dance. "I have taught high school biology for many years," he said, his sanctimonious voice pinched to a higher octave. "Students respond to the challenge of moving to the front of the classroom through the daily quizzes. The students sit in the places they have earned."

I was about to ask Mr. Rudyard if he'd done his master's thesis on the board game Go to the Head of the Class. Dr. Watt spoke first. "What happened next?"

Mr. Rudyard cleared his throat. "When I told Mr. Garrett to collect his things, he said, 'I'm not going anywhere.' I told him he could go on his own steam or I would call for security to remove him."

Ky looked at the floor.

"I walked to the call button and asked him again, 'Do I have to call security, Mr. Garrett?' He didn't move a muscle. I had given him more than enough chances to do the honorable thing, but because he'd been a good student up until this quarter, I gave him yet another opportunity. He did not utter one word, so I pushed the button. At that point, Mr. Garrett overturned his desk and threw his biology book at me, missing me by only an inch. He stomped out of the room without looking back."

Obviously, Mr. Rudyard had never seen Ky bullet a ball home to tag out a steal. Ky hadn't aimed at his teacher—or he would have hit him.

"Thank you, Mr. Rudyard," Dr. Watt said. "I know you have prep work for tomorrow. You're free to go."

He slid off the radiator.

I stood up to block his exit. "How long has Ky been sitting in the back row?"

"The F row?" He frowned and rubbed his chin. "For well over three weeks."

"And I'm just learning that now?"

"By the time our students are sophomores, they're more than capable of managing the consequences of their actions—or inaction, in his case. He won't have his mommy around forever."

I took a step toward Mr. Rudyard. Larry tried to pull me back into my seat, but my hands were slippery with sweat. "Ky is part of a family, Mr. Rudyard. We're his support system. When he performs with distinction in academics or in sports or in the community, we celebrate his achievements. We are there to help him achieve his goals with our guidance and support. When he fails, for whatever reason, we don't withdraw from him. We draw closer to love him and counsel him. Nobody wants him to succeed more than we do. By failing to call us when the problems started, you've deprived Ky of his support system."

"Mrs. McManus, I have 160 students each day."

"And I only have one son, Mr. Rudyard, so I have the time and the desire you obviously lack to assist Ky through his problems."

Mr. Rudyard looked to Dr. Watt and back to me. "What would you have me do—call every parent when a student has a problem?"

"Yes." Mr. Rudyard had no way of knowing that a call from a caring

Spanish teacher had saved me from educational oblivion in my sophomore year of high school.

"I don't have the time to coddle every delinquent student." He pivoted on his heel and left the office. Larry pulled me into my seat by the
pocket of my denim overalls.

"Mrs. McManus, my teachers really do try within the constraints of
their time and energy to work with parents," Dr. Watt said.

I wanted out of her office. "What happens next?"

She spoke to Ky. "Assault of a teacher is a serious offense, Mr. Garrett."

"Mr. Garrett was my father's name," Ky said without looking up.

"What would you like me to call you?" Dr. Watt asked.

"Ky."

"Ky it is."

I willed him to acknowledge her kindness. She waited, hands
folded, watching him. The clock ticked. The *ca-chug* of the copy
machine beat through the wall. Ky remained as he had been, elbows
on his knees and gazing at the floor. I tapped a leg of his chair with my
foot, hoping he would take interest in what was happening to him.
Instead, he waved me off with a slight flick of his hand. I wanted to tell
Dr. Watt that Ky had learned to say *please* and *thank you* before any of
his preschool classmates and to go ahead and throw the book at him
for humiliating me.

Dr. Watt cocked her head and spoke softly to Ky. "I have no choice
in the disciplinary action in cases like this. The board of education out-
lines clearly which infractions warrant suspension or expulsion. For
aggressive behavior toward a teacher—and you should be very happy
you missed Mr. Rudyard—"

"I wasn't aiming at him," Ky said through tight lips.

"Nevertheless, you are suspended from class for three days, and that
includes all athletic practices and events."

Ky shrugged.

"A suspension gives your coach the right to cut you from the team."

His head snapped up.

"And before you'll be allowed back into Mr. Rudyard's classroom, you'll be expected to apologize to him." Dr. Watt looked to me. "Sometimes problems at home pour over into school. Declining performance and emotional outbursts from an otherwise model student—and Ky has been that—usually mean something has gone wrong at home. It's not my business to pry, but you may want to look for professional help. I'd hate to see Ky back in my office anytime soon."

Knuckles rapped on the back door, but I didn't move out of the chair. I sat there running the scene in the principal's office over and over in my head. As much as I'd wanted Larry to be there, I resented his interference. Mr. Rudyard needed to be put in his place. In my next thought, Ky was nothing but a spoiled brat of my own making. I pulled up memory after memory to support my poor performance as a mother. In the next moment, fear as menacing as any long-fanged monster stalked me with uncomfortable questions. Will Ky graduate from high school? Is he doing drugs? Is he skipping school? Will he slip away never to return? Has my marriage to Larry messed him up for good?

One thing was sure. We needed help.

Another rap on the door, harder this time. I hoisted myself out of the chair. It had to be Louise. No one else knocked on my back door. Louise pressed her face to the screen where the kitchen window had been left open. "Hey y'all, I've rustled up some alluring appetizers for you to try." Her face disappeared, and soon she was standing in my kitchen.

"This isn't a good time."

"It's always a good time for appetizers, sugar," she said, sliding past me to unpack the contents of her basket onto the island.

The meatloaf Connie had made for dinner sat in my stomach like golf balls—the kind they use at practice ranges, all scuffed and raw from being picked up with a range sweeper. "I'm not hungry, Louise."

"Did y'all have a tiff with Larry?"

"Worse than that."

Larry walked into the kitchen. He greeted Louise, but his attention focused on the spread of appetizers. "I thought I heard your voice. These look good." He rubbed his chin. "They're probably not on my diet."

Louise winked at him. "I only use grade A sweet cream butter when I cook. At least you'd die with a smile on your face, sugar."

They shared a laugh.

"These are the finalists in the appetizer category." Louise loaded a china plate she'd brought along with a heaping portion of meatballs, stuffed mushrooms, and wonton-wrapped bundles drizzled with an impossibly red sweet-and-sour sauce.

Larry mumbled a thank-you around a meatball in his cheek and said to me, "I'm going down to the basement to work."

"We *agreed* to wait," I said.

He passed a furtive glance at Louise and looked back to me. "I need something to do."

I said *fine* the way you do when something isn't fine at all but you don't want to look like a shrew in front of your best friend. The nuance of my tone completely bypassed Larry. He smiled, thanked Louise again for the goodies, and turned toward the basement.

Louise called after him, "Be sure to tell me which ones you like best." She looked me up and down. "No tiff, huh? You know I don't like to pry, but I saw a murderess once walkin' into the courthouse with her hands in cuffs behind her back. She had the very same look in her eyes I'm seeing in you this very minute."

Seeing Louise's brow pleated with concern tipped my bucket. "Ky threw . . ." My bottom lip quivered. I swallowed hard and tried again. "He threw a boo—"

"Sweet Jesus, have mercy." Louise stopped divvying up the appetizers and wrapped her arms around me. "Take your time, sugar. Manley's already snorin' like a grizzly bear in front of *This Old House*. He'll never notice I left the house."

Since coming home from Dr. Watt's office, I'd set my emotions on autopilot. We'd collected Ky's assignments from his teachers and gathered his textbooks, and then Larry insisted Ky go to the practice field to explain to Coach Poole why he wouldn't be at practice for the rest of the week. Larry and I stayed in the car while Ky walked like a man heading toward his execution. Ky hadn't said a word since. Connie showed up with dinner. Doors slammed. Forks clanked against stoneware. Then a crushing silence fell on the house, which meant my mind had revved to overdrive.

Louise pulled on my hand. "Come out to the garden with me, sweet pea." She led me down the path to the bench under the honey locust tree. "The air is as sweet as honey. There's nothing as refreshin' as a driving rain. I haven't had a hot flash since lunchtime."

"The bench might be wet," I said.

"I have a hanky."

Louise pulled the hanky out of her sleeve and wiped off the bench while I told her about how Ky had lashed out at his biology teacher, his suspension, and how the silence of my home had only magnified the shame I felt.

"How is this about you?" she asked, sitting down.

"Margot called before dinner. She talked to her therapist—"

"Your sister? Margot? Somethin's happening in that girl's heart. I'm putting my money on the Holy Spirit."

The idea of God's hands warming Margot's heart surprised me so much I nearly let my misery slip away, but I thought better of it. I'd worked hard compiling my list of worries. I wasn't about to drop them without a fight. "Margot thinks marrying Larry has plunged Ky back into the depths of grief."

Louise narrowed her eyes to think on what I'd said. "That makes sense."

"No it doesn't. Larry is good for both of us. Ky is just too caught up in himself to see how much Larry loves him."

Louise tapped her front tooth with a rosy nail. She was dressed in full New York editor style—black, black, and black, except for her rhinestone bifocals. "Boys are the strangest creatures. Right from the womb they're all about the bottom line. For Ky, the bottom line seems to be that you've moved on with your life and he's been left behind, the sole keeper of his father's flame."

"He's so angry."

"He's learning what we all learn—we ain't in heaven yet. Life's rough. People we love go away and don't come back. He's been punched in the gut, and now he's punching back."

"Scott's been dead for two and a half years. Wouldn't you think—"

"Tell me this: aren't there times when you still double over with grief?"

Our eyes met.

"I thought so. Grief doesn't keep time, baby girl. Each milestone we pass—a birthday, a holiday, even making the varsity baseball team in your sophomore year—they're all there to remind Ky his daddy died. Time will make the blows softer, but I'm not sure they ever go away. I can't see a boy's rosy cheeks without aching for my Kevin."

"Was it a mistake to marry Larry?"

"That's a fool's question, and you aren't a fool. You married a good man. Loving him and loving your son are not mutually exclusive."

I shivered against the cool night and closed my eyes to breathe in the sweetness the rain had stirred from the earth, but the knot between my shoulders only tightened. I didn't want to believe Margot's therapist. To do so was to admit I'd abandoned my son to walk through his grief alone. Louise, on the other hand, could be so . . . so . . . so southern.

"Slip Scott into your dinnertime conversations," she said. "He won't disappear just because you fell in love and married."

Didn't I know it? I'd stalked a look-alike cyclist. "I will." *But Larry and Connie aren't gonna like it. . . .*

"That's my girl. Now, let me pray for you." Louise wrapped her arms around me and held me tight. I squeezed right back. Her fleshy cheek touched mine. A faint scent of gardenias clung to her neck. "Mibby is so dear to us, isn't she, Father? You have to be so proud of her desire to serve you as a mama and a wife. You see how she struggles to love as you love and to guide her precious, God-designed boy, Ky, into manhood."

"Louise," I whispered into her ear, "I'm so mad at him."

"No you're not, sugar. You're embarrassed. Ky plumb humiliated you in front of God and everybody. You're not used to that." She rubbed a small circle over my knotted shoulders. "And maybe you're fright-ened. Yes, I think you would be. Your relationship with him is chan-gin'."

I nodded and laid my head on her shoulder.

"That's better. Lean on me." Louise rested her hand on the back of my head. "Holy Spirit, stoke the fires of power and love in Mibby's heart. Make her a mighty warrior for your love to rule in her home. Give her a holy confidence in your ability to heal wounds, old and new. I pray this in Jesus' name because I can't make my prayers pretty enough to move heaven for my friend. Amen."

Ky rolled away from the light when I opened his bedroom door. "Mom?"

"You're in bed already?"

"There isn't much to do." The school had suspended him from attending classes, but Larry and I had cut him off from all electrical entertainment. A few good nights of sleep would only improve his atti-tude, we hoped.

I walked into his room, not knowing if I was welcome or not. The suspense stopped me before I reached Ky's bed. I asked, "How are you doing?" Now, there was a question as useful as spitting in the wind where males were concerned. Ky surprised me. He sat up and ran his hands through his hair. A long strand fell over his face. He needed a haircut. He'd have plenty of time for that over the next few days. I read his gesture as an invitation to sit on his bed. When I neared, he scooted over and lay down. I lay down, too, just as I had done so many times when he was younger and talking to his mother was better than surren-dering to sleep.

"Nothing like this is ever going to happen again," he said. "I'm feel-ing all kinds of stupid."

"Thanks. That's good to hear."

"You know the question Mr. Rudyard asked? I knew the answer . . . but the way he asked the question, like there was no way in the world

I would know it. . . . I don't know, it sounds lame now, but keeping the answer to myself seemed like a victory. But then he got all mad. There are kids in the back row who can't even read, and day after day they get their noses rubbed in it. Rughead is such a jerk."

I bit my cheeks to keep from laughing.

"You're trying not to laugh, aren't you?"

I didn't dare answer him.

"I get it. I know you have to stick with the adults, but you have to admit, the name fits him. I mean, like, we checked old yearbooks, and he's worn the same rug since 1968. Jeremy says he was born with a rug on his head. Rughead keeps a comb on his desk like he actually uses it. What a jerk."

"Ky . . ." I said as a warning.

"I know, but you have to hear this. One day, he was focusing a microscope for some kid and the rug slipped off his head. He didn't even stop talking. He put the thing back on his head, but then he had to walk around like a robot until the bell rang so it wouldn't fall off again."

"Did you laugh?"

"No way, but the toupee looks like one of Goliath's hairballs, doesn't it?"

I bit my cheeks harder. "Yeah, a little." I wanted to make a little speech about how he needed to respect his teacher because doing so would honor God and improve his own attitude toward Mr. Rudyard. But I didn't respect Mr. Rudyard, either, so instead I asked, "Can I pray for you?"

"Sure, I guess."

I put my hand on his arm and waited for the words to come. My laundry list of wants for Ky was long. I wanted the tension and uncertainty between us to dissipate. I wanted to know that he liked me. I wanted the pain he caged in his chest to escape. And a haircut would be good. As I ran a mental finger down the list, I noticed most of the things I wanted for him were really for me, like the Mixmaster I'd bought Scott for his forty-fifth birthday. Most of all, I just wanted Ky to be . . . nice.

Is it even possible for a teenager to be nice?

I remembered my own initiation into rebellion. I'd waited for my mother to pick me up after a Girl Scout meeting long past the other girls' departures. The sun had set below the horizon to take the sheen off the day. Her tardiness bit all the harder because I had begged her to come with me to the meeting. All the other mothers had been there to make matching mother-daughter gingham aprons with rickrack along the hem. I would have surrendered all of my Nancy Drew books—all one hundred of them—to wear something that made my mother and me a matched set.

My mother had long since left the period in which she called herself Jasmine, when she'd been a pesticide-free domestic goddess. As Jasmine, she gardened; she baked; she painted the house the color of sunshine, inside and out; and she planted herbs in a window box. When the afternoon sun heated the rosemary and chives and thyme, the sea breezes filled the house with their dizzying scents. But by my Girl Scout years, she was Diana. She didn't have time for squealing girls in green dresses. She had a world to save.

I sat on the brick planter outside my school until the sky darkened and my stomach ached with emptiness. A policeman stopped at the curb to ask me if I was the Brown girl. All the way home, he lectured me on the importance of letting my mother know where I was at all times. "It's the meanest thing in the world for a child to ignore her mother's feelings," he harped.

Margot greeted me at the door and told the policeman my mother was in the bathroom.

He bent down to issue a final warning. I leaned away from his cigarette breath. "Don't you ever scare your mother like that again, or I'll take you to jail."

His edict pushed me to tears. The officer nodded his approval and left. Margot waited until he pulled away from the curb to sock me hard in the arm with her paralyzer punch. My arm hung limp at my side, throbbing.

"Don't be a baby. He won't put you in jail." She wound up for another punch.

I cowered. "I'm telling Mom."

Margot sauntered to the sofa. "She isn't here. I called the police."

I ran to my mother's bedroom but stopped short when I saw her bed. Only an arched wrinkle where she had sat to put on her shoes interrupted the smoothness of the bedspread. A fly buzzed insistently at the window.

"Get me a limeade," called Margot from the living room.

I opened the top drawer of my mother's bureau, where she kept her dainties and postcards that her eclectic friends had sent her from around the world. Only the postcards and one bottle of red fingernail polish lay on the bottom of the drawer.

"What's taking you so long?" yelled Margot.

I poured the fingernail polish onto the bedspread in the shape of a heart and used my mother's pillow to smear the shape. Behind me, Margot whispered, "Boy, are you gonna get it."

I didn't care. The awe in Margot's voice made the impending punishment all worthwhile.

The memory turned fuzzy, and I dreamed I was walking on an icy sidewalk. My feet slipped out from under me. My flail woke me up.

I blinked a few times in the unfamiliar light. Ky's soft snore reminded me I'd fallen asleep on his bed. I stopped at the door to look back at him. He was still a boy, wasn't he? I reached my hand toward him and prayed, "Protect him. Bless him. Keep him. Make him nice. Amen."

MAY
25

Hot! Snow-melt flood warnings along river.
Russian olive blooms spice up the air.
Despite aphids, Bonica roses are thick.
Sprayed with insecticidal soap. Repeat
in a week or order ladybugs.

I squinted to read the numbers on the nightstand clock. 3:49. I'd slept for two hours straight—the longest stretch of the night. When I'd awakened at 1:20, I'd made a list of all the things I could do that day to make it ordinary. Eat Cheerios. Wear faded pink shirt. Grouse at Blink for tracking mud into the house. Spend too much money for a Caramel Frappuccino at Starbucks. Easy.

It was Scott's birthday.

Larry turned off the alarm before it rang and rolled out of bed without disturbing the covers. I kept my eyes closed, breathing deeply and slowly until the door of the bathroom clicked shut. The toilet flushed and the shower turned on.

Although it was reckless and more than foolish, if not adulterous, I let myself return to the memory of Scott's first birthday of our married life. Scott had come home from the bank that day to find me crying on the bed. "Baby, baby, what's the matter?" he'd asked, pulling back my hair to kiss my cheek.

My sinuses had swollen shut from crying. "I wuined your bird-day pwesent." I was so young—twenty-four—and given to the theatrical.

"It doesn't feel ruined. I'm with the most amazing woman on the planet."

"I burned the cake."

"I had a big lunch."

"I sewed the sleeve of your jacket to the hood." I cried harder.

"You made me a jacket? Wow, that's the nicest thing anyone's ever done for me."

I rolled over to face him. "You're just saying dat."

"You're so beautiful."

"Now you're lying."

Scott dabbed away my tears with a hanky. "Your eyes look like two popovers."

I fought not to laugh. "You hate popovers."

"No, I mean it. I haven't seen eyes this bloodshot since Uncle Ray nearly died of influenza in '62."

I covered my face with my hands, but he pulled them away. "No, I was mistaken," he said. "Your eyes definitely look worse."

I walloped him with my pillow. "You're in so much trouble."

He pinned my hands over my head. "No, my love, you're the one in trouble."

And I was. His hands slipped behind my back; his mouth covered mine. I could hardly breathe, but I didn't care. He unwrapped me with that kiss.

Later, he rummaged the cake from the trash and scraped the burned part into the sink. We lit the tiki torches around the patio. Blooming jasmine sweetened the air. We chased a bite of cake with a spoonful of cream cheese frosting. It wasn't bad. When the chill chased us inside, Scott presented me with a garment bag from Robinson's.

"A gift? For me? That's not right."

"Try it on."

With the addition of landing lights, the shoulder pads of the pink suit would have made excellent air strips. When I walked into the room, Scott said, "You'll be the most beautiful woman at the company party."

I looked at him with every intention of saying *Over my dead body*, but his eyes had turned hungry again and my belly tingled, so I said, "Okay."

The bathroom door clicked open. The scent of Larry's soap reached me on the bed. I watched him through the slits of my eyelids as he eased the door of the closet open to find his work boots and then closed the door just as quietly. There I lay, crushed with longing for a dead husband and playing possum for a new husband tiptoeing in the darkness to let me sleep. Larry opened the bedroom door but turned back to the room. I closed my eyes and made my breathing slow and deep again. The floor creaked under his footsteps as he walked back toward the bed and me.

Please don't.

He kissed my temple. "I love you," he whispered.

The latch of the door clicked into place, and he was gone. His car whined down the driveway. I took a flashlight up to the attic to find the box marked *Baby Stuff*, pulled out a photo album, and headed for the coffeepot.

I sat at the bottom of the attic stairs with only a bare bulb to view the photographs: Scott and me on a Mission Bay cruise. Scott and me during our first Christmas together. Scott and me on our honeymoon, smiling shyly for the camera. A self-portrait, thanks to Scott's long arms, in which I'm holding the wand of a home pregnancy test—we're smiling but a tension pulls at our eyes. A picture of me wearing one of Scott's old T-shirts pulled tight over my pregnant belly as I put the finishing touches on the mural in Ky's nursery. A picture of us hiking with Ky on Scott's back. *Who took this picture?* I studied my image, still full-hipped and bosomy from childbirth, my face relaxed and my hand on Scott's strong thigh. My smile was fourteen-carat gold—absolutely genuine. Not one shadow smudged the clarity of my joy.

I closed the photo album with a smack of plastic. "I can't be doing this."

I promised myself one ring of the doorbell. If no one answered, I would leave immediately. I'd delivered bouquets to Mrs. Webley twice before. The last visit had gone worse than the first. She hadn't liked how I'd arranged the columbines, even though I'd filled out the bouquet with Shasta daisies and coralbells from my garden and used one of my own vases. Pity the woman if she insulted the bouquet today. There was no hope for anyone who found fault in the poof of peonies I carried.

Mrs. Webley's face lost its weariness the moment she saw the bouquet. "I knew the heat would push the peonies to bloom." She opened the patio gate and reached for the peonies. The scent of linseed oil hung on her like a cloak. "The doubles are my favorites. They remind me of the petticoats I wore as a little girl." Mrs. Webley pressed her face into a Duchesse de Nemours and breathed deeply. "Ah, so deliciously fragrant. Are there many buds left on the plants?"

"Enough for two more weeks of bloom, at least."

She turned the vase in her hands, stopping to smell the lone red in the bouquet. "Only one Françoise Ortegat? I'd hoped to paint a whole bouquet."

"They'll be ready next week. The plant is loaded with buds."

She smiled. "There's nothing so passionate as a bouquet of red peonies." She fingered the satin petals of the peonies. "Prim and proper little Mademoiselle Leonie Calot, so extraordinary in her frippery. And Nadia . . . as soft as her name."

She looked up from the bouquet. A rancorous bite honed her voice. "What is Gordon paying you? He can be dreadfully stingy."

Silly woman. She probably thought her exodus from her home had required courage, that her independence heightened her status among humankind. How sad. There had been a time when I would have cheered her on. Not today. Not on a date so congested with memories. Leaving was easy.

"He's paying me well," I said to support the efforts of Mr. Webley's bowerbird ways, "and he pays me extra to deliver the bouquets." In truth, he'd forgotten to leave the cash and a vase for the second time.

Like a hiker tested the strength of an unknown bridge with a few tentative steps, her eyes met mine to test the connection between us. "What's your name?"

"Mibby."

"I'm Elizabeth. You must call me Elizabeth." She settled the vase in the crook of her arm. "Your name, it's unusual."

"My real name is Montbretia—"

"The fiery flower? The name suits you."

I hooked a strand of red hair behind my ear. "Montbretia grows here, but not as well as it did in San Diego, where I grew up."

"I know the flower well," she said. "Montbretia spread like wildfire in my mother's garden. My job was to keep it contained to one corner of the flower bed. I never succeeded, but trying kept me out of her hair for a few hours now and then."

"Then you must be from . . . ?"

"Canada, Victoria, in British Columbia."

Football has the Hall of Fame. Horse racing has Churchill Downs. Flower gardening has Victoria, the home of Butchart Gardens. "My family visited the gardens about five years ago," I said, knowing I didn't have to specify which gardens.

"I worked there summers while I attended university."

"That explains the beauty of your garden."

"But Colorado isn't Victoria."

"All the more reason you should be proud of what you've created."

"And left in ruin?"

"No, the garden looks great. You should go see it."

"I don't think so." A tuck of skin between her eyes deepened and then softened. "Please bring a bouquet each week, and if Gordon forgets to pay you, which he most certainly will, I'll double whatever he's paying you. Everything you've delivered has been scrumptious. You're doing a wonderful job." Elizabeth receded into her studio. The artist in me longed to follow her.

She turned. "Is there a for sale sign in front of the house?"

"No."

"Interesting. I'll see you next week."

I felt silly for hoping before that Elizabeth wouldn't answer the door. Now that I'd seen how she responded to the flowers, my optimism for the couple grew.

Lord, soften the lady bowerbird's heart.

⁓

Ky slumped in a chair behind a one-way mirror, looking with heavy lids from the clock to the door. He crossed his arms and heaved a sigh, probably wondering why it was taking his mother so long to pick him up at the police station. Was Mother Teresa ever tempted to slap an errant boy on the back of the head? Probably not.

Unfortunately for Ky, I'm not Mother Teresa.

The arresting officer, a matter-of-fact woman with her hair pulled tightly away from her face and off her collar, leaned against the window to talk to Larry and me. "He'll receive a summons—"

"Can I talk to him?" I asked with an urgency that surprised me.

"I think it's better for you and me and your husband to chat first—give the boy some time to think."

I looked back to Ky bent over the stainless-steel table. His face now lay hidden in his arms. "It's just that he's never done this sort of thing before."

Officer Frank smiled. "My kid did the same thing. He's a lawyer now." She shuffled through papers on a clipboard. "We mothers want all the credit. When our kids hit the honor roll, we want a rose and recognition. And when they screw up, we volunteer to take the blame." She leaned in. "The truth is, he gets himself on the honor roll, and he gets himself into trouble."

"She's right, Mib," Larry said.

I tried to return her smile, but it felt more like a grimace. All of the reassurance in the world wouldn't convince me I wasn't to blame for Ky's behavior. I had been too lenient in the months after Scott's death. More honestly, I'd been completely unavailable to him. I'd walked around hermetically sealed from life. He'd practically raised himself through the middle school years. Nope, I should have been the one waiting for the world to come crushing down on me, not Ky.

In the interview room, Ky's head lolled to the side, his eyes closed, his mouth agape. Under the fluorescent lights, a pimple with the disposition of Mount Vesuvius glowed red in the middle of his forehead. Thanks to a few beers, he wasn't actually aware that the world was crashing down on him, but he would be soon enough. I moaned.

"We'll have none of that," Officer Frank said, hooking her arm around my shoulders to steer me out of the room. "Let's talk in my office before you take your son home. I bet you could use a cup of coffee."

She fussed with her coffeepot. Pinned above her desk hung a cross-stitched sign, *Cubicle Sweet Cubicle*, along with crayon drawings of smiling stick figures and glittery ponies. The room hummed with activity even in the late hour. Larry leaned his elbow on the partition. When Officer Frank sat down, her bulletproof vest all but swallowed her neck.

"I was telling you that Kyle will receive a summons by mail to appear in court in about a week to ten days. Underage consumption is considered a petty offense. He'll be ticketed and fined."

"How much?" Larry asked.

"A hundred dollars plus court costs, which usually comes out at twenty dollars for these cases. And he'll lose his license for three months."

"He wasn't driving," I said.

"For underage consumption, we try to make an impression on the kids," she said. "The law requires his license to be pulled to reduce recidivism."

"Does it work?" I asked.

She shrugged. "Sometimes."

"Will he have a record?"

"That's the good news. If he pleads guilty and completes the adult diversion program, which in the state of Colorado is twenty-four hours of community service, the case will be dismissed."

"And his record?"

"Completely clean."

Outside the police station, the full moon slid under lacy clouds over the Uncompahgre Plateau, a little too whimsical for my mood. The station's fluorescent bulbs still flickered in my peripheral vision, where a headache pinched my eyeballs. In the car, my seat belt was too tight, so I unfastened it. The radio was too loud, so I clicked it off. I sat with my knees together, hands folded in my lap. I considered rolling down the window to feel the night air, but honestly, I feared the movement would unsettle the calm I worked so hard to maintain.

Larry asked, "Is anybody hungry?"

"No," I said, my face to the window.

"Ky?" Larry asked again, only louder. "Are you hungry?"

"What?" Ky said, as if he were spitting soured milk.

"Nothing."

I glanced over my shoulder at my son. His knees touched the back of Larry's seat as he looked out the side window. Did he see the same things I saw? Ordinary things? Houses dark except for their porch lights? A man and a woman walking hand-in-hand? A lone car at the Taco Bell drive-thru? Was he sorry he had stepped out of the ordinary into the clockless time of chaos?

Before Larry had his seat belt unfastened, Ky had taken the steps toward the kitchen door in one hop and disappeared into the house. At the base of the steps, Larry stopped me with a touch. "We shouldn't blow this out of proportion."

"What do you suggest?"

He shrugged. "I don't know."

I looked toward the house. "I'll talk to him."

"Every kid on the face of the earth does dumb stuff at this age."

"So your take on this is that we need to hunker down until Ky's thirty, when a funeral won't only be tragic for his aged mother but for his wife and babies, too—the old misery-loves-company school of childrearing? That's brilliant."

"You're upset."

I entered the house. The sound of Ky's stereo blared overhead. "That's very observant of you, Larry."

"I said I was sorry."

"You can't be so trusting."

"*I'm* not the enemy—"

"It wasn't me who gave him permission to go out with those creeps he calls friends. I thought we'd agreed they were personae non gratae."

"He said he was going to youth group."

"He hasn't been to youth group in months, and they don't meet on Thursdays. You know that."

"I told you I was sorry. If it will make you happy, I'll never believe another word he says."

"Works for me."

Larry threw the keys on the kitchen counter. "I'm going to bed."

I stood with my belly against the sink as his footsteps creaked through the house and up the stairs. Bile burned the back of my throat. When I heard him walk into the bathroom, I leaned over the kitchen sink and lost what little remained in my stomach. I rinsed my mouth and walked to the bottom of the stairs. Something hit the wall and crashed to the floor in Ky's room. A viscous silence filled the house. It was hard to breathe.

I stood outside Ky's bedroom door, vacillating between charging into the fray or following Larry's advice to hunker down, which sounded better the longer I stood there. I decided I should pray. Isn't that God's job, to be the celestial tie breaker? I modeled my prayer after Psalm 73, the official prayer for whiners. *I am so angry at Ky. He knows better than to lie, to drink, and to get into a car with a bunch of potheads. What was he thinking? That's the problem—he wasn't thinking. And Larry—did he fall off a turnip truck or what?*

I stopped when I heard Ky's muffled sobs.

He turned to the wall when I entered his room. His baseball trophy lay broken at my feet—the one he'd won for MVP the last year Scott had coached the team.

Lord? He answered my prayer by reminding me of how He had spoken to the woman caught in adultery, and how He had opened the door to paradise to the thief, and how He had said yes to the nails for my sins.

I turned off the CD player, slipped off my Birkenstocks, and lay on the narrow bed beside Ky. I held my hand over his shaking shoulder. "Is it okay for me to be here?"

He nodded his head.

"I'm going to put my arm over your shoulder. Do you mind?"

"No."

I scooted closer to hold him. He grabbed my hand and held it tightly. His crying intensified and so did mine. Darkness coiled around us as the moon dipped below the horizon. Ky had crossed some unnamed developmental stage that night, one mothers didn't anticipate or they would surely keep their sons chained to the pipes in the basement. He had discovered how enticing and unforgiving the world could be—the cruelest lesson of all. Finally, his shoulders stilled. I rested my forehead on his shoulder and prayed. *Jesus, Jesus, Jesus . . .*

"I never meant to hurt you, Mom. I didn't think. It was stupid. I didn't know they had marijuana. You have to believe me. This will never happen again."

"I forgive you," I said, the words flowing easily. "But what are you saying about marijuana?"

"Jeremy and Zach had some in the glove compartment. I swear I didn't know a thing about it."

I replayed the vignettes of the adulteress and thief and my own experience with marijuana through my head.

"Mom?"

"Yeah?"

"I've ruined my whole life, haven't I?"

"It only seems that way."

"Coach Poole will cut me from the team. It's in the contract I signed at the beginning of the season. He warns us at practice every week. No drinking. No drugs. No trouble. He probably won't let me play next year, either. The scouts won't see me play. No scouts, no college ball. I'm toast. Oh man, how could I have been so stupid?"

"The sooner you talk to him the better."

"No way."

"He might surprise you."

Ky slipped from under my arm and sat up to look out the window.

"I don't want you to be mad at Larry for letting me go out with the guys. I lied to him, said we were going to youth group."

"Thanks for telling me." I sat up and pushed a pile of papers aside with my foot. "You . . . you were different tonight," I said, sounding like I was commenting about a change in the weather, but a silence settled between us and hardened. I waited. My back ached. Blink whined at the door. The rumble of a motorcycle on the street trebled in my chest.

"I was scared," he whispered, "more scared than I've ever been in my whole life. I was afraid you and Larry would kick me out, or that I was going to jail." He swallowed hard. "Bad dudes go to jail."

I thought about the bad dudes, too, and bile burned the back of my throat again.

"And I was thinking of Dad." The thin line of his voice struggled to stay in control. "I was thinking how disappointed he would be. And Larry, he's pissed, too."

"It's been a long night for all of us."

Ky used the hem of his T-shirt to wipe his face.

"There will be consequences," I said.

"No problem."

"It's your responsibility to pay the fine and the court costs."

"I figured that."

"And you can forget about driving for a long time."

"The police lady said three months."

"The state of Colorado doesn't love you as much as we do, so you can count on a longer sentence from us. Ky, you lied to Larry, you drank beer, and you got into a car with a driver who had been drinking."

"How long?"

"I'll have to talk to Larry."

Ky lay down and turned back toward the wall. "I'm tired."

"We aren't finished yet."

He rolled over to face me. "What?"

How quickly the repentant turn defiant.

"Mom, just say it."

The adulteress, the thief, the tax collector, the leper, the Samaritan woman, and little ol' me, the queen of sinners.

"Getting caught tonight was a gift of love from God's hand," I said.

He heaved a sigh and avoided my eyes.

"You are so dear to God that He let you get caught the first time you forgot how important your life is to Him. You're alive to make better choices about your friends."

"I like my friends."

"Not only did your friends obtain alcohol illegally, they gave it to another minor and then drove around. Not everyone who gets in a car with a drunk driver—"

"Jeremy only had one beer."

"The point is not everyone who gets in a car with a drunk driver gets the opportunity to be caught. They go straight to the morgue."

"You're *not* going to keep me from seeing my friends."

"I'd like to see you reconnect with your friends from church."

"I have plenty of friends."

"You have friends who encourage you to lie and break the law."

"This is so bogus!"

"We'll talk about this tomorrow afternoon when Larry gets home." I hoped to get out of the door before either one of us said anything else we might regret.

"Larry is *not* my father!" Ky screamed.

"No," I yelled back at him, "but he's my husband." I slammed the door.

～⌐◡

Larry exhaled a low moan with each snore. "Larry," I whispered. His breathing quieted but deepened to the moaning again after several beats. "Larry," I said again, louder, "we need to talk."

"You'll have your delivery before noon, I promise," he mumbled in a haze of sleep.

I shook his shoulder as I said his name.

He bolted out of bed toward the bathroom. "What time is it? I must have forgotten to set the alarm."

"It's not morning yet. We need to talk."

He looked at the clock on his nightstand. "It's two o'clock. For heaven's sake, Mib."

"It's important."

"Are you sick?"

"We need to talk."

"Give me a minute." He went into the bathroom and closed the door. Whatever he was doing took longer than usual.

I tapped on the door. "Larry, are you awake in there?"

"I'm awake all right." He sounded weary of life.

"Are you angry?"

"I'm thinking about it."

"You might feel better if you listen to what I have to say." But then again, maybe he wouldn't. That was the question I'd wrestled with in the darkened living room for the last few hours.

The bathroom door opened. Larry stood there in his boxers, heavy with the sour scent of sleep. "I have to get up in a couple hours. Could we talk then?"

"You know that verse about not letting the sun go down on your anger?"

He sat on the end of the bed, shoulders rounded, rubbing his eyes. "We already did that."

"Today . . . no, that's not right, I mean yesterday. *Yesterday* was Scott's birthday. I know it shouldn't matter, but it does. I assumed things would be different when we got married, that all the strings that tied me to Scott had been cut, but that's just not true. I want it to be true. It just isn't, at least not yet."

Larry straightened. "What does that mean—that you're still tied to Scott?"

"I think about him, not like I'm pining for him or anything. Certain days awaken my memories, and I feel guilty and secretive because I don't want to hurt you, but I feel like I can't share those memories with you, either. After you went to bed, I talked to Ky. Then I was too keyed up to sleep, so I went downstairs to think. He's so angry . . . and scared. I never would have believed it, but he is . . . scared, I mean. He says he's afraid of being kicked out of the house or being put in jail, but I don't think he really knows. I think it has to do with his father, even though I haven't figured that part out yet."

"Mib?"

I fell to my knees in front of him. "I'm so sorry for how I treated you today. You didn't deserve it. You've been absolutely wonderful. I'm not trying to excuse myself, but it helped me to understand that this may never be a normal day for me. I will revisit birthday memories Scott and I shared, but today I let my memories drive a wedge between you and me, and for that I'm deeply sorry. It won't happen again."

Larry stood and walked to the window.

"Will you forgive me?" I asked.

"I feel like the fourth wheel on a tricycle. Not quite necessary but interesting to have around."

I stood. "Larry, you're very necessary to me."

He didn't speak for a moment. When he did, his voice was softer than normal. "You're sure about that?"

"Absolutely. I . . . I figure if I was edgy and confused on Scott's birthday, maybe Ky was, too."

"Do you think about Scott a lot?"

"Only on certain days."

"How about May twenty-sixth? Is that a certain day?"

Almost every year, on the day after his birthday, Scott had sheepishly asked for the receipt for whatever I'd bought him for his birthday so he could return it. "Nope, just an ordinary ol' day. But there's August fifteenth."

"What happened on August fifteenth?"

"Scott's and my anniversary."

"Anything else?"

"The day we got engaged, the tenth of January." *And New Year's Day and Valentine's Day and Saint Patrick's Day and the day we went for our marriage license. Easter. Flag Day, because Scott always raced to get our flag out before Mr. Stewart. Andrea's birthday. The day we closed on the house. Ky's birthday. Thanksgiving. Christmas Eve and Day.*

Larry said, "Ma told me there would be days when you'd disappear into yourself to remember your life with Scott. I'd be lying if I said I liked the idea of sharing you, but it would help to know when one of those days comes along."

"Fair enough."

MAY
31

Mystery solved! Caught a pair of sparrows munching on the Autumn Joy sedum early this morning. Trying a pie plate "scarecrow." Take that, you rascally sparrows!

I went out to the garden to take a break from Ky's sour attitude. Of course, there was work to do, so I carried my pruning bucket and tidied up the roses and deadheaded the Prairie Jewel penstemon that had passed its prime. With its bold flowers and silvery foliage, this was my favorite penstemon of all.

A clamorous chorus sounded from the house sparrows that nested in the birdhouse among the salvia and coreopsis. The noise usually signaled the arrival of the mother bird and the parceling out of seeds to gaping beaks. To my surprise, four nestling sparrows, as insubstantial as thistledown, had ventured out to start flight school. They perched on the bench under the honey locust, fluttering their wings to hover briefly before a reckless return to the roost. Within minutes, they'd mastered their flight controls sufficiently to play leapfrog along the back of the bench. Another host of sparrows, further along in their aeronautical studies, joined the young fliers from a neighbor's tree. A daredevil among them flapped wildly to reach a lilac branch an arm's reach from the bench. Every sparrow followed. They perched there, chirping

137

raucously over their achievement, bending the branch until it almost touched the ground.

Had the mother sparrow tired of the insatiable hunger of her brood or the constant bickering over who was served the most seeds? Perhaps the flailing of wings had driven her to the brink, so she'd chirped, "Go!"

I enjoyed the show until I thought of Ky. His attempts at independence were no less brash than the fledglings that had left the nest to follow their rookie commander. Had the fledglings truly proven their flight-worthiness? Had Ky? *Not on your life.*

Blink whined beside me.

"There's nothing I can do. They've chosen their leader."

He complained by chewing on a groan, so I looked at my watch. Lunchtime. "What will it be, Blink? Crunchy or crunchy?"

Before entering the house, I looked back to the sparrow flight school to check their progress. Not one cadet perched on the bench or on neighboring branches. An inky darkness wrapped around my heart.

Lord, keep Ky under the safety of your wing.

Blink nuzzled my hand.

"I heard you the first time," I said, dumping my cuttings onto the compost pile and heading for the back door. Blink led the way, quick-stepping up the walk and through the doggie door.

Since Ky's run-in with the law, Larry and I had consulted with everyone we knew who had children over fourteen. Some suggested homeschooling and others a church-affiliated school, and just as many warned against both of those options. We were told to get tough and to remain a safe place for Ky to land. Everyone counseled us to keep praying. In a fit of desperation, we opened the atlas to find the most remote place in North America where they still spoke English. Moving deep into a fjord of British Columbia appealed to us, but the issue of sustenance nixed that idea, so Larry and I agreed on what we felt Ky deserved: a jail sentence. That meant house arrest, and I was the warden.

At first, Ky had been humbly compliant, asking for chores to do around the house and helping Larry with the basement renovation. That lasted one and a half days. We still expected the same chores to be done, but now he found entertainment value in tormenting his jailers. He discovered bouncing a ball off the wall early in the week. Frequent trips back to school for textbooks or notebooks from his locker soon followed. Taking out the trash, mowing the lawn, and vacuuming were all performed proficiently, yet perfunctorily. The spit wads on his ceiling were a stroke of genius—silent and challenging, but also a swat—or splat—at his mother's artwork. I counted the days left in his sentence. Ten days. Nine nights. *Then what?*

Two days into Ky's sentence, Sweet Suzy reassigned Larry to the north-central route—Craig, Meeker, Rifle, Steamboat Springs—which meant leaving the house earlier in the morning and arriving home after six. Because Connie was happy to come to the house in the late afternoon, I finished my maintenance route after a stint as guard from two-thirty to four.

After lunch, I planned to print invoices for my maintenance clients. Ky was up in his room without a computer or stereo or television—a situation as close to solitary confinement as we could manage. I pictured him hunched over his homework at his desk. Maybe he was thirsty. *Should I take him milk and cookies? Do we have any cookies?* Since Larry had started his diet, the cookie jar had been replaced with a basket of fruit. *I could share a Strawberry Cream Ball from my secret stash, but can Ky be trusted with a secret?* A steady thud reverberated through the house.

"Ky!" I bellowed. "Quit with the ball already!"

"It's Silly Putty!"

"Do your homework!"

"I don't have any!"

Mr. Chase assigned trigonometry every night. "What about trig?"

"I did it in class!"

To believe him or not to believe him, that was the question. "Read a book!"

"There's nothing to read!"

Grr.

I pulled a book off the family room bookshelf on my way up to Ky's room. He lay on his bed, legs up the wall, using a straw to blow spit wads at the ceiling.

One battle at a time, I reminded myself. "Let me see your trig homework."

At the sound of my voice, Ky spun to sit on the edge of the bed, the straw tucked under his thigh.

"I didn't hear you," he said.

"Show me your homework."

"No problem." He pulled a spiral-bound notebook out of his book bag and flipped through the pages. He folded back the cover for me. His name, barely legible, and the date filled one corner of the paper. Behind odd numbers, one through twenty-nine, he'd written equations with squiggles and letters and abbreviations.

"You didn't show your work," I said.

"You only have to show your work if you want extra credit."

"*You* may not want extra credit, but as the mother of a son with an F in trig, I insist that you show your work."

A flicker of panic flashed in his eyes. "I threw my scratch paper away . . . at . . . at school."

"Bummer," I said sincerely. "You aren't eating dinner until you've shown your work so neatly I won't be able to tell if you've handwritten the problems or used the computer."

"I *can't* use the computer, remember?"

This conversation had outlived its usefulness. I should have walked away to leave him to his misery, but I looked up to count the spit wads on the ceiling. I opened my hand. "Hand over the shooter."

"What are you talking about?" he asked, palms opened.

Fully a dozen pulpy globs mottled the ceiling—the very ceiling I'd painted at his request when he still thought of me as human and capable of creative expression. He'd asked for a night sky with a constellation outlining a baseball player in a batting stance. I'd emptied the ibuprofen bottle on that project.

I lowered my voice and metered out my words. "I'm done playing this game."

His eyes widened. "What game?"

"The game where you try to make me sorry for grounding you." I remembered the book in my hand, *Moby Dick*, the fattest tome on the bookshelf. "But I'm not sorry, because now you have time to read one of the greatest American literary works of all time. Melville wrote *Moby Dick* longhand." I threw the book on his bed. "Be prepared to discuss the first chapter at dinner. And get those spit wads off of the ceiling, *now!*" I turned to leave the room, knowing a retort was coming.

"What about my trig homework?" Ky followed me to the top of the stairs. "How am I supposed to get my homework done *and* read a stupid book?"

I was halfway down the stairs when I said without looking back, "You're a smart boy, Kyle Patrick Garrett. You'll figure it out."

Back to printing invoices and stuffing envelopes. With a few clicks of the mouse, I was in the accounts-receivable program and flipping through my logbook to gather hours and supplies used at each address. I wondered if the same part of my brain that juggled numbers also stored overflow resentment, because as I entered the time I had spent weeding Gloria Langston's sidewalk border, I blamed Larry for letting Ky go out carousing with his friends. That kind of thinking wasn't helpful.

I filled my lungs with a deep breath and held it, just as the therapist on *Oprah* had suggested. I checked my watch. My guard duty stint expired when Connie arrived at four to relieve me. Another hour and I would be out of the house to finish my maintenance jobs for the day, including the small yard belonging to Harlan Chandler, my neatnik client. Since I'd told Mr. Chandler that the hairlike interiors of rosehips caused diarrhea in dogs, he called me every time the new berries ripened. As his dog's bathroom functions improved, so did Mr. Chandler's tips. Daydreaming about spending today's tip on a Caramel Frappuccino kept me from my invoicing. *Get back to work!* It took less than an hour to print, stuff, and stamp the invoices—a new personal best.

Goliath mewed behind me. A juvenile house sparrow, one from the flight school, no doubt, lay at Goliath's feet with its head cocked unnaturally to the side, perfectly still, lifeless.

"You stupid, stupid, evil cat!" Goliath snatched the rejected gift and darted through the doggie door. "Don't eat it! Don't eat it!" I pleaded from the porch. Goliath stood in the middle of the patch of lawn we called the poop deck, watching me with the sparrow hanging from her mouth, poised to flee if I moved toward her.

"I hate you! I hate you, you—!"

Ky's footsteps drumrolled down the stairs as Goliath trotted into the shrubs. "Mom? What happened?" he asked.

For a heartbeat, the boy standing before me was the boy with sweet milk breath sleeping in my arms. The boy who had tickled my chin with a dandelion. The boy who had cheered me with songs when I'd miscarried his little sister. Taller. Muscled. Hairy. But still a sparrow of a boy.

"Come with me. We have some pruning to do."

"That shrub nearly killed Buttons. I never should have listened to you. And the gas . . . I can't take him in the car unless I drive with all the windows down."

Harlan Chandler stood on the top step of his porch, neck veins pulsing, his bald head reddening, his arms crossed over his chest. I'd worked for Mr. Chandler long enough to know his posture meant the whole world had soured in the week since my last visit. A bandage over his brow and a black bruise on his forearm probably didn't help matters. Reminding him that I was the one who had discovered the link between Buttons' bowel problems and the rosehips was useless. This wasn't the first time he'd forgotten something we'd already discussed. Mild kowtowing to appease his sense of injustice was all Mr. Chandler needed. It was Buttons I worried about. The dog eyed my pant leg and his lips quivered over a snarl.

"I'm sorry, Mr. Chandler," I said. "But now that we know what's causing Buttons' intestinal problems, I'm happy to keep the rosehips pruned for you. If you take Buttons inside with you, I'll be done in a jiffy."

"I won't be needing your services much longer."

Again?

"My daughter's convinced I'm a hazard to myself and to just about everybody else in the county. She's signed me up to move into one of those assisted-living places."

Mr. Chandler has a daughter?

"That signal was not red," he said. "I don't care what the accident report said. I'm not blind. That nincompoop was going too fast to stop, I tell you. The punk has a hole as big as a quarter in his ear—on purpose! Dressed all in black like some kind of—what do they call them?" He tapped his temple. When the word he wanted didn't come, he blinked a few times and opened his mouth again, only to shake his head. "That boy looked like an idiot, I can tell you that. I suppose the keepers at the home will want to drive me around in a bus with a bunch of drooling old folks. Those places smell bad."

"Several folks from my church live in assisted-living situations," I said. "They have their own apartments with a kitchen. You can fix your own meals or eat in the dining room with your neighbors. You just might like it."

"That's what they said about Lyndon Baines Johnson, so I voted for him. He's doing a terrible job. Any man who picks his dog up by the ears can't be trusted. You didn't vote for him, did you?"

President Johnson was elected in 1964. I was born in 1965. "Absolutely not, Mr. Chandler."

"Good." He hiked up the waist of his pants. "A Realtor's coming to see the house."

"I'll miss coming to see you." And strangely, I knew I would. He'd been my client since before Scott's accident. "Mr. Chandler, I'll make the yard look real nice for the Realtor. Would you mind taking Buttons into the house? He doesn't like me very much."

"He probably thinks you voted for Johnson." Mr. Chandler gulped for air. I felt for my cell phone in my pocket to call 9-1-1, but his laugh settled into his belly. His eyes closed. His head went back. We laughed until our eyes watered. He wiped his eyes with his hanky. I used my sleeve. When I looked up, he looked lost, as if he had walked into the wrong class on the first day of school.

"Is there anything else I can do for you while I'm here?" I asked.

"You can plant those roses like I asked and leave me in peace."

"I'll do that." Poor Mr. Chandler. He wasn't agitated about rosehips. He was afraid. *Walk with him through all of his fears both real and imagined, Lord.*

As I filled a bucket with rosehips, it dawned on me that Ky would be the one to look after me when my driving became a hazard and my memory flickered in and out like a shorted bulb. I hoped my synapses kept firing until the sting of his grounding was long passed—at least a few weeks. I'd read or heard somewhere—and how quickly I'd forgotten—that chocolate improved memory . . . or was it mood? No matter. I stopped at the Starbucks in Barnes and Noble for a Mocha Frappuccino while I read the *CliffsNotes* on chapter one of *Moby Dick*.

Chuck Moreland looked at his watch. "Looks like our time is about up. Is there anything you want to add, Ky?"

"I'm never coming here again."

Chuck, the only marriage and family counselor who had openings in his schedule before October, threw back his head and laughed. "If I had a nickel for every time I've heard a kiddo say that, I'd be a rich man. Mom? Dad? How about you? Is there anything you'd like to add?"

The rust and gold upholstery of Chuck Moreland's office furniture had faded long ago. Furnished with castoffs, circa 1972, the room had mummified under a gray layer of dust. Butcher-block coffee table. A swag lamp. Beanbag chairs stacked in the corner. A snail that plowed a trail through the algae on the aquarium glass behind the desk.

Chuck fingered a hooked-rug pillow as he spoke. "You haven't said much, Dad."

Ky released a moan, but Larry remained silent. In fact, he hadn't said a word in the forty-five minutes we'd sat in the counselor's office. Chuck held his pen poised over his clipboard. If at all possible, Ky shrank deeper into the sofa cushions.

"We need some strategies for becoming a blended family," I said. "Any ideas?"

"I don't believe in blended families, just like I don't believe in Santa Claus." Chuck slapped Ky's knee. "Sorry, bud. I hope that wasn't a shocker for you," he said and he laughed again. When he regained his composure, he continued, "A fruit salad is a better model for what happens when people with children remarry. The oranges are still oranges. The bananas are still bananas. The strawberries are still strawberries. The different textures and flavors make eating the salad more interesting, just like individuals with their various strengths and weaknesses, likes and dislikes, make a family more interesting, only you don't eat your family. I don't advocate cannibalism." He guffawed loudly. "I never get tired of that one."

Ky groaned. Larry stared at the floor with his elbows on his knees. At two dollars a minute, we couldn't afford to waste our time. "There's a lot of anger in our house," I said. "We're not sure how to deal with it."

"*Au contraire,* I think we've gotten a great start here," Chuck said. "I suggest we schedule another session. Same time next week?"

Larry finally spoke up. "How many sessions, exactly, do you think we'll need?"

"It's difficult to say. Making a new family isn't like baking a cake, but I can assure you that most families get excellent results in a year."

~~~

From the back seat of Larry's Datsun, Ky said, "That guy's a moron."

"Ky!"

Larry looked at me. "He has a point."

"So this guy didn't work for us. We can try someone else. Maybe someone at church?"

Larry frowned at the road ahead of him. "I think we're smart enough to figure out what it means to be a family."

"There are other families out there that've already met the same challenges," I said. "It seems foolish not to take advantage of their experience."

"I'm not throwing money away like that again."

"Think of it as an investment."

At a stoplight, Larry let me know he wanted the subject closed with a slight turn of his head and an arch of his brow.

"There's a group at church," I said.

"Mib . . ."

"It's for blended families."

The light turned green. Larry shoved the gearshift into first and gave the Datsun more gas than it needed. The wheels squealed.

"Cool," Ky said.

Larry looked straight ahead. He mumbled, "Let's talk about this at home," which meant not in front of Ky, as if my son didn't know we were having problems. Since we hadn't achieved much at the counselor's, I figured we should use our time in the car.

"Okay, I know what you won't do to help us become a family. What are you willing to do?"

Larry's knuckles turned white on the steering wheel. I turned toward the passenger window. We drove under amber streetlights past homes where families had already eaten dinner and were settling in front of the television. All I saw was the dead sparrow in Goliath's mouth. "Your cat ate one of the fledgling sparrows today. I want you to think about taking Goliath back to your mother's."

"Fine."

We drove the rest of the way home in silence.

~

Connie's car engine turned over. I waved and went about shutting down the house for the night. A typical end of the day at the McManus house, only this night I could taste my disappointment with Larry, who had been in bed for an hour. Rather than join him, I checked my e-mails. I'd received one—a poem promising good luck if I annoyed five of my friends by sending it on. *Delete.* The computer pinged to announce that the Desert Horticulture Society newsletter had dropped into my mailbox. I read every word about the tamarisk invasion of White Sands National Park. Andrea deserved a response to her last e-mail, but instead, I played solitaire until my eyes burned and I couldn't stop yawning. I tiptoed into the bedroom and slid under the covers with my back to Larry. I could tell from his breathing that he was awake. I was still too angry over his nonparticipation at the counseling session to say good-night without sounding peeved, so I lay in the dark as stiff as a plank.

"Mib?"

"I'm *really* tired."

JUNE

6

Wonderfully cool! Lydia broom is a
sunshine-yellow beach ball. Note:
Gloriosa daisies overwhelming
Moonbeam coreopsis. Thin in September.

My cell phone rang as I scouted Main Street for a parking space. I was ten minutes late already. By the time I wrestled my cell out of my pocket, the screen message said I'd missed a call from Andrea. I pushed the redial button and scrounged for quarters in the glove compartment to feed the parking meter.

I'd left Andrea a message on her voice mail several days earlier, hoping to pinpoint her arrival date for her summer visit. My motives were mostly selfish. I needed another jailer to keep an eye on Ky during his summer vacation. The other part of me longed for her clemency. I didn't bother hiding my disappointment when Andrea laid out her summer plans.

"You're not coming?" I sat on the curb and leaned against the parking meter.

"I can't," she said. "I've agreed to teach summer school, and . . . well . . . there's the project I'm working on."

The *project* again. I'd never seen Andrea flinch from anything—not

149

hunting down her long-lost father or facing his combative widow—but I'd lectured her about the guys she'd dated several times. Maybe she was involved in another male fix-it project like the dimwit who had heard God tell him not to work.

"Does your project have a name?" I asked.

"My lips are sealed."

Whatever this project was, I had not been invited to participate, and it was killing me. My imagination invented and discarded threatening scenarios. That was the old Mibby, I reminded myself. The new Mibby, the one who squared off daily with a teenaged detainee, charged ahead with a new strategy. More delicious tidbits have been shared around a prayer circle than in the sealed rooms of CIA headquarters. "How can I pray for you?" I asked.

"My Bible study is praying for me around the clock, and a friend put me on the prayer chain at her church. I'm covered."

"You know, don't you, that you're being—"*tight-lipped? secretive? evasive?*—"ambiguous."

"I don't mean to be. The time isn't right yet. But I'll tell you everything, I promise."

"You're not sick or anything, are you? You wouldn't keep anything like that from me, would you? I could be there tomorrow."

"You'll be the first one I call if any of my appendages blacken with gangrene, but it isn't anything like that, so stop worrying."

"I pray for you every day."

"I know you do."

A beat of silence finished the conversation about the project, so I dropped the only quarter I'd found into the meter and headed for Rosie's. When Andrea spoke again, her voice was buoyant. "I'm looking forward to summer school. The students come from all over the Bay Area to keep their music skills sharp during the summer. It's a dream job—twenty-seven students who really want to learn. It's quite an honor to be offered the position. We'll perform at the mayor's birthday party in August."

"I'm so proud of you. I wish we could be there."

"Come! You and Larry can sleep on my bed, and Ky can sleep on the futon."

As wonderful as a trip to San Francisco sounded—Ghirardelli chocolate, sourdough bread, and honest-to-goodness dim sum—I knew a vacation wouldn't happen this year. Money was tight, and Larry had used up his vacation days on our honeymoon. And the real reason? I couldn't think of a more torturous way to spend twenty hours than driving across Nevada with Ky.

"We can't this year," I said.

"I have a week between summer school and the start of school in the fall. Maybe I can come then."

"I hope so."

"There's another call," she said, breathless. "I better take it. Give my love to Larry and tell Ky I miss playing Brain Drain with him on the computer, so he better be cool so he can get his computer back. And tell Louise to send more cookies. I love you."

⁓

I brushed dirt off my overalls before walking into Rosie's, a new restaurant reflecting Orchard City's shift from small town to a metro area as surely as any population census. Starched linens. Richly colored walls. Impossibly small halogen lights hanging from threadlike wires over each table. Serve staff—not waitresses—in black pants, white shirts, and neckties. Daily specials with goat cheese and reduction sauces. They also made the best French fries in town.

Louise sat in the reception area, waiting to be seated. She wore her sunglasses inside the restaurant, even though the lights were kept fashionably dim. Add a jewel-toned silk scarf on her head and a plum blossom brocade blouse, frog buttons and all, and you had a movie star on the lam from the paparazzi *or* Mata Hari. As long as we didn't end up on the evening news, I didn't mind. I was used to standing out in a crowd with Louise.

"Sugar, you're filthy." She put her hanky to her mouth.

"You're not giving me a spit bath," I said, backing away. I'd spent

151

the morning planting twelve flats of pansies in Gloria Langston's back-yard in the wind. "I'll wash up in the ladies' room."

"Good." She handed me a boutique bag. "There's a clean top and socks to match in the bag."

I peeked inside the bag—yep, a peach and green T-shirt with socks to match. She probably found them at a Garanimals store for adults. At least she hadn't brought me a sarong.

"And sugar, I took the liberty to include deodorant and a sample of Espionage perfume." Louise lowered her sunglasses and winked. "Now, isn't that just perfect?"

Mata Hari, definitely.

A malnourished hostess in a sleeve of a dress approached us and looked me up and down. "Miss Giovanelli, party of two?"

Louise turned my shoulders toward the ladies' room and pushed. "I'll order you an iced tea. Hurry now, we don't want to miss her."

I found Louise watching the front door from behind her menu. "Something tells me we're not here for the food," I said.

"Quick, change places with me. I don't want Stookie to suspect anything."

The waitress brought the iced teas. Louise pulled her sunglasses down. "We're going to need a teensy-weensy minute more to decide on lunch. Do you mind?"

"Of course, take your time," she said in a deferential tone.

"I slipped the hostess a ten," Louise whispered. "This table is perfect to watch Stookie Carmichael buy one of Rosie's Lemon Crème Crumble Pies, what Stookie calls a Citrus Cream Crumble Pie."

"How do you know she'll be here today?" I asked.

"I do declare." Indignation made Louise's Louisiana accent as thick as gumbo on rice. "The pies have been out of the oven—" Louise looked at her watch—"for forty minutes. Perfect to be whisked home to the refrigerator and no one need be the wiser—especially not the pinochle group meetin' tonight."

I'd been dreaming of Rosie's grilled portabella sandwich and a mountain of golden steak fries since eight o'clock that morning. "We *are* going to eat, aren't we?"

"Why in heaven wouldn't we? Just don't order anything that would block your view of the door."

All right, a half order of steak fries.

Louise swirled her iced tea with the straw. "My daddy taught me to give folks the benefit of a doubt. I was so sure I'd misread the recipe. That's when I asked you to bake the pie. I knew you'd follow the instructions to a T. You could have stripped paint with the fillin', it was so sour."

"Maybe Stookie copied the recipe incorrectly," I said.

"Oh, sweet pea, I wasn't born in a cabbage patch. I called her before I took my rollin' pin out. Stookie swears she sent me the original recipe from her grandmother's recipe box."

I remembered the recipe card had been yellowed and stained with grease.

"I was completely bamboozled until she let it slip at our last pinochle game that she was the prop manager of her senior class musical." Louise pushed her iced tea aside and leaned over the table. "And you know as well as I do that theatrical types know everything there is to know about falsifyin' documents. I'll kiss a long-toothed catfish if that recipe card isn't a forgery. Li'l Miss Stookie most certainly won't get away with sabotaging the integrity of my cookbook."

Clearly, Louise watched too much *Law and Order*. "So, we're here to . . . ?"

"Catch her in the act, dumplin'."

"Have you considered asking her about the recipe?"

"And hurt her feelings? I would never . . . no, we're going to sit here until Stookie opens her purse to pay for the pie. That's when we'll yoo-hoo and wave." Louise demonstrated and nearby diners looked over. "I hope y'all are enjoying your lunch," she said to them. It took Louise another ten minutes to explain the roundabout southern method to save face. If she noticed me squirming, she didn't let on. After all, I bought lemon cream pies for Larry from IHOP.

"Stookie will know," Louise continued, "even though we don't tell her we know that she doesn't bake her own pies, but since we don't actually say anything about the false representation of the pie, she'll have enough doubt swimmin' around in her head to wonder if we really do know, so she'll withdraw her pie recipe for consideration. I don't see why you're having such a hard time understanding this."

The fries and the sandwich came. Nothing disturbed digestion quite like Louise's application of southern mystique, so I said, "It must have been low blood sugar. I understand now, Louise."

She reached across the table to dip one of my fries in a puddle of catsup. "Did I ever tell y'all the story about my brother's huntin' dog, Raineau?"

I'd heard countless stories about her dimwitted brother and his good-for-nothing hunting dog, but Louise would eat fewer fries if she kept talking. "I don't think you have."

"Y'all keep your eye on the door while I'm talking."

I assured her I would.

"As long as Junior had Raineau on a leash, he was the picture of submission. He followed every command my brother uttered—actually seemed to read his mind. But you and I both know you can't keep a huntin' dog on a leash. God created them to retrieve vanquished prey so a gentleman doesn't muddy his boots."

Louise swirled another French fry through the catsup. She wagged the potato wedge for emphasis. "Once that dog was off his leash, he was his own master. Junior begged and pleaded with that dog to come, but Raineau pranced, head high in the sky, with a li'l ol' duck in his mouth just out of reach of Junior. I always knew when Junior had been hunting. He came back to the house red-faced and swearin' like a sailor. That usually earned him the hard end of the broom from Mammy.

"One day—I remember it was just before prom because I was helpin' Mammy sew tiny pearls all over the bodice of my dress—my daddy came out on the veranda just in time to see Raineau trotting away with a fat wood duck in his mouth and Junior stomping on his hat. We stilled our needles to watch Junior get a lickin'. Instead, my daddy said to Junior, 'Son, the surest way to get a dog to come to you is to make his coming worth the while. You have to make him glad he came, boy.'

"Daddy cupped his hands to his mouth and gave a call just like a wild turkey, and Josephine—have I told you about Josephine? She was

Daddy's state champion huntin' dog. Her whelps went for a pretty price, I can tell you. Where was I? Oh yes, Josephine came running like her tail was on fire. She stopped at Daddy's feet and sat stone-still waiting for his next word. Daddy cooed and praised that dog like she had just recited the Louisiana generals in alphabetical order. And then he tore off a piece of dried beef no bigger than a pea and gave it to Josephine. '*That's* how you train a dog to come to you, son.' Daddy said to my brother.

"Junior never did train Raineau to come when he called, but Junior wasn't the welcoming kind, if you know what I mean. But I listened that day, and Daddy's wisdom has never failed me. If you want a dog— or even a boy—to come when you call, the arms of hospitality must always be open with abundant praise and a table overflowing with good food."

Her story had been a sermon all along. I should have listened more carefully. We sat there for another hour, waiting for Stookie to show up to buy a pie. Between us, we drank enough tea to float a paddleboat. I told Louise I had to finish my maintenance route. She pouted a little but said she understood. "I'm going to sit here a little while longer. Now, when you get to the door, sugar, turn to look at me. I want to be sure Stookie won't recognize me. I dressed as inconspicuously as I could."

I turned to look just as she'd asked. With her colorful scarf and red silk jacket, she had the low profile of Dolly Parton.

～

The most difficult part of building a trap for Goliath was finding a box big enough. Once I'd dumped a file box of tax returns, it was only a matter of propping the box with a lilac branch and attaching the fishing line.

Here, kitty, kitty.

Since the incident with the sparrow, Goliath spent most of her daytime hours prowling the neighborhood or hiding among the tangle of flowers that grew in my garden, venturing out of hiding only after

Larry's Datsun came to a stop in the driveway. I wanted the matter of Goliath's exile settled before Larry arrived home that day, so I emptied a can of all-white tuna into Goliath's bowl and slipped it under the box. The fishing line unwound from the spool as I backed toward the Lydia broom for cover. I waited on my hands and knees, never taking my eyes off the cardboard trap.

And waited.

And waited.

Cedar bark dug into my knees. An ache in my lower back stoked into a fire from my hips to my thighs. My feet tingled. I doubted Navy SEALs withstood this much pain to complete a mission. No matter. Goliath had committed an unpardonable sin.

After Ky and I had shared an after-school snack and reviewed his homework planner, I'd gone out to the garden for the pure joy of working among my own flowers while Ky started his homework. I could've spent the time dusting, or ironing Larry's uniforms, but the Elfin Pink penstemon needed deadheading. One garden task led to another. I nipped a few miniature rose blooms starting to brown and weeded another wave of the invasive Liriope spicata I'd planted the previous year. I couldn't remember the common name, and it was just as well. I held nothing but murderous thoughts for the intruder. Then I noticed that the montbretia hadn't sprouted yet.

I pushed aside the mulch, looking for the tardy sprouts. The soil was beady, like it had been tilled. The moment I disturbed the soil with my hand, the scent of cat urine belched from the earth. Of all the places Goliath could have staked her claim, she had chosen the square foot of the garden most crowded with meaning. The montbretia bulbs had been a gift from Scott, ordered from a seed catalog the day before his accident.

Goliath had to go.

I caught the twitch of gray tail out of the corner of my eye and sank lower behind the broom plant. I tightened the slack of the trip line. On my belly, I inched past the maiden grass to improve my view. Goliath approached, stretching her neck to test the scent of tuna. My heart beat wildly in my chest.

Focus.

Goliath stooped to sniff the tuna but remained beyond the cover of the box. She settled onto her haunches.

Here, kitty, kitty.

She stood to stretch like a furry wave.

It's all white meat.

She groomed the fur of her ruff.

I hope you get a hairball.

She licked her paws and washed the backs of her ears.

Stupid cat!

The burn in my lower back twisted into a fiery knot.

Goliath, pleeease eat the tuna.

The cat finished her grooming session and strode toward the tuna, full of confidence and doomed by her false sense of immortality. Nine lives, indeed. She eased herself under the box. Head. Shoulders. Haunches. Her tail lay on the ground outside the footprint of the box, swaying nonchalantly as she picked at the tuna.

Tuna is yum, yum, yummy.

She lay in front of her dish and wrapped her tail over her paws. I pulled the line. Goliath disappeared. She nearly toppled the box, so I sat on it, satisfied to hear her plaintive meows. Blink trotted over to drop a ball at my feet.

"You're very welcome, my friend."

Ky called from his window. "Way to go, Mom!"

~⌐

"I don't understand," Connie said, puppy-faced. "Goliath has always been the best cat, not one bit of trouble. But if this is what you want, I'm happy to take her home with me." Goliath rubbed her head under Connie's neck. Larry scratched Goliath behind her ears.

I smiled woodenly as I stood on the curb, thinking I looked like the mother of all cat haters. I liked cats—most cats. Cats that stayed out of flowerbeds, didn't pee on the furniture, and kept to the floor.

Connie kissed Larry and touched her cheek to mine. "Good night, you two. Sleep well."

Goliath sat in the front passenger seat of Connie's Taurus. It was probably my imagination, but the cat looked smug, as if somehow she'd gotten just what she wanted.

Larry said, "I hope you're happy" and opened the screen door with enough force to hit the house. In the pure light of retrospect, begging Larry's forgiveness and calling Connie to do the same would have been the right thing to do. I didn't do that. I followed Larry into the house. "Goliath is a *cat*. She hates it here. How many ruined flower beds and pieces of furniture will it take for you to see that?"

He emptied the coffeemaker of wet grounds. "You didn't have to trap her."

"We never even discussed Goliath living here. You just assumed—"

He filled the reservoir with water. "We never discussed Blink living here, either."

"He belongs here. This has been his home since he was a puppy."

"And if he hadn't adapted well to *my* being here?"

"Dogs are trainable. They're social. They're a part of the pack."

"All I'm saying is you could have handled this with a little thought as to how trapping the cat would make Mom feel."

It all went back to Connie. I was the one covered with cat scratches. "The way I was raised, animals didn't rule the house." This was not the time to tell Larry my only childhood pet had been a goldfish I won at my school's harvest carnival. Since it had died by the next morning, the issue of a fish-held monarchy hadn't been a question in my childhood home.

Larry pressed the auto button on the coffeemaker and a red light shone. "The way you were raised wasn't normal, Mib. Normal mothers don't change their identities with every shift of the wind and walk away from their families. My mom is trying to connect with you. *That's* normal. Maybe you should cut her some slack, that's all I'm asking. I'm going to bed."

I followed him down the hall, flailing my arms. "By all means, Larry, go to bed. That's your solution to everything. Everything will be hunky-dory in the morning."

He held my gaze, his hands deep in his pockets. "Good night."

Outside, I sat on the porch swing and gathered my legs under my sweatshirt. No moon shone, and the chill made my nose run. I'd already absolved myself for trapping Goliath. The cat had been destructive, after all. But the look on Connie's face and the sight of Larry walking away from me . . . Tomorrow, I decided, I'd offer to take the cat back with humble apologies. Maybe.

JUNE

18

Day 3 of record high temperatures. Here we go again. Don't forget to add polymer crystals to containers next year! Heirloom tomato loves the heat, growing well. Cannas have aphids.

"I'm not wearing the hat," Ky said, holding a frayed straw hat at his side.

Connie watched us from her kitchen window.

"Connie is bestowing an honor on you," I said. "The hat belonged to Larry's father."

"That's just great."

A mother secure in her role as family safety coordinator would have issued dire warnings about high-altitude sun exposure and the threat of skin cancer. But tiny blisters peppered my shoulders from my own recklessness. "Wear the hat until you're around the corner of the shed. Then you can put your cap back on."

"I'll look like a dweeb."

"Yes, but you'll only look like a dweeb for ten yards, maybe twelve. I think you're up to the challenge, don't you?"

"I wanna go home."

"Everybody knows that. You'd better get going. Larry probably wonders where you are."

Ky walked down the path, bent from the weight of wearing the hat and my expectations. He dropped the straw hat on the edge of the lawn and snugged his ball cap into place. My chest tightened around an ache. I raised my eyes to the far-off cliffs. As promised in the Psalter, no help was forthcoming from hills *or* sandstone cliffs. Burnished smooth by years of wind and sand, the ridges and monoliths only reminded me of how long it took for sandstone to be sculptured. I hated to think what kind of pressure it would take to reshape Ky's heart and how long I would wait to see the results.

My help comes from the Lord.

I sat on a plastic chair under a cottonwood tree with the hat on my lap. The shade, deep and sheltering, relieved the sting of my shoulders, but soon after sitting, my legs were slick with sweat against the seat. "Lord, I'm not looking for grandeur, only a boy who finds his family worthy of modest respect. And that look of nausea on his face . . ." I closed my eyes against a sting of tears, wondering if my happiness mattered to God at all.

I remembered the autumn Margot had made the drill team at her junior high. While she sliced the air with knifelike precision, I checked the mailbox daily for the J. C. Penney Wish Book. The book arrived in mid-September. I ripped the brown paper cover off in the privacy of the bathroom. Starting from the back of the catalog because I had no interest in velour robes or artificial fireplaces, I circled the toys I wanted for Christmas and marked them with my initials, M.I.B. I considered the exercise a favor to my father, who usually spent the precious pre-Christmas shopping weeks fighting fires in the blistering Santa Ana winds. God wasn't Santa Claus, but He was my Father. Of course He would want to know what would make His daughter happy.

"I want a happy son. I want him to pick up his feet when he walks. I want him to respond to kindness. I want him to say *please* and *thank you* when other people are around. I want him to smile from that place where boys marvel at collared lizards and crawdads. I want him to lay his burdens down at your feet." I turned to see Connie still watching from the window. I brushed off the straw hat and walked toward the house. "And I want the forging of this family to proceed in a painless and timely manner. Amen."

Another Sunday, another dinner on the dahlia farm with Grandma Connie, as she had started calling herself. She performed all the grandmotherly functions with great heart. She baked cookies, watched Rockies games to commiserate with Ky, and suggested a haircut as if she were offering a stock tip. She bought him small gifts—a magnetized Rockies schedule for the refrigerator and a Christian CD performed by a group she'd heard on K-LOVE. Best of all, she fried chicken and coaxed a gallon of gravy out of the drippings. I'd hoped Ky's mumbled thank-yous had heartened Connie. When she told me she was thinking about getting a puppy from the shelter, I knew she'd decided to look elsewhere for adoration.

Connie and I set the table while Larry and Ky spent time in the dahlia garden, bonding in the heat. The dahlia plants had reached a foot tall. From the kitchen I heard someone, probably Larry, pounding the T stakes into the ground. He hoped to set the guy wires to support his growing plants.

I jumped when the screen door slammed against the house. Larry threw his cap onto the kitchen counter without looking at Connie or me. He washed his hands with his back to us, working up an impressive lather. Either he'd dipped his hands in sulfuric acid or his plan to teach Ky about growing dahlias had proved disappointing. My money was on Ky exasperating Larry, partly because Ky had begged me to release him from coming with us to the McManus farm and partly because a niggling pessimism had hummed about me like a swarm of gnats since Ky's school had let out for the summer. It had been the longest week of my life.

I sidled up to Larry at the sink. "What's up?"

He turned off the water. "He doesn't know a thing about working."

"Not many kids do at his age."

"I was working alongside my father from the time I could walk."

"Ky hasn't had the advantage of his father to teach him."

Larry finally looked at me. Flushed from the heat or anger, his jaw barely moved when he spoke. "I wasn't saying—"

"It's time to eat," Connie said. "Call the boy in."

"Ky won't be joining us," Larry said, drying his hands.

"What now?" I asked.

"The rule on this farm has always been, If you don't work, you don't eat. He didn't work." Larry sat at the table and loaded his plate with chicken and potatoes and gravy. "This looks good, Mom."

Connie joined Larry, served herself from the platter of meat, and passed a napkin-lined basket to him. "I used Grandma Kerr's recipe for the biscuits."

I looked out the door toward the dahlia plots. No Ky in sight. Maybe missing a member at the dinner table had been usual enough for the McManus clan, but the Garretts didn't vote their family off the island—or the dinner table. "Excuse me, Larry, but I have a son sitting out in the hot sun. Could I get some details?"

Larry tore open a biscuit and slathered it with butter. "There's not much to tell, if you don't count Ky's whining and complaining."

Larry and Connie bowed their heads to offer thanks for their dinner. Before they said amen, I was out the door. I found Ky sitting in the shade of the toolshed.

"I wanna go home," he said, his face buried in his arms, looking much younger than his sixteen years.

I slid down the wall to join him and rested my hand on his arm. "Tell me what happened."

He shrugged my hand off. "I *said* I wanna go home."

"Not until I know what happened out here."

"There's nothing to tell," he spewed.

"Ky, Larry's trying to build a relationship with you. What would it hurt to be pleasant for an hour or two? You might find—"

"I told you already, I didn't do anything. Maybe you should tell *Larry* to be pleasant."

Ky was good—plant a seed of doubt, divert attention. I batted his goad away. "As I was saying, you might find that Larry has something to teach you."

"Like what? To be a farmer? To deliver Twinkies?"

I tried empathy. "You know, son, this isn't the life I planned on, either. I expected to grow gray and wrinkly with your father. I dreamed about you coming to visit with your own family so you could grind up our food when our teeth fell out. I figured your father would always be around. I'm sorry our story changed, but it did, and we're darn lucky to have people like Larry and Connie who love us both."

Ky stared off. I couldn't read him anymore. When he finally turned to me, I saw a red welt in the shape of a handprint on his cheek.

"Come on," I said, "we're going home."

~~~

I sat in Scott's chair in the dark, waiting for Larry to come home. Ky had sulked up to his room an hour earlier and cranked up his stereo. I wasn't about to make the volume an issue. Besides, the carping beat of the music fed my anger. How dare Larry hit my son and sit down to eat a meal without telling me!

Unbidden, another day billowed the folds of my memories, the day Andrea had picked up Ky from school and taken him for ice cream. At the time, I'd only known her as the Earring Girl, and there she was chummying up to my son. I slapped her hard across the face for saying that Scott was her father. The mark of Larry's hand had already vanished from Ky's cheek. And really, it didn't take much imagination to see Scott doing the very same thing in light of Ky's insolence.

But that was Scott. This was Larry. I tried to pray. I asked God to give me wisdom and courage, but I was too busy flagellating myself for believing Larry's gentle-giant act. The thrumming music pressed me to ask scary questions. *Should I ask Larry to leave? Maybe I should take Ky to a shelter before Larry gets home. Am I being melodramatic?*

Definitely. Maybe not. I doubt it. Maybe I'm being reckless.

The sound of Connie's car idling in the driveway stopped the questions. A car door slammed, and a moment later, the kitchen door clicked open. Larry walked through the dark house softly calling my name. The floor creaked under his weight in the kitchen, the family room, and down the hall. I pulled myself into a tight ball to sit unseen in the darkness. He stood with his hand on the newel post and one foot on the bottom stair, listening.

"You have some explaining to do," I said.

He sat on the edge of the sofa, the seat farthest from me, shoulders rounded. "I'm not proud of what happened," he said, his voice low and rough.

"You shouldn't be."

"He needled me, Mib."

"So you hit him?"

"At first he complained about having to work in the heat. That didn't bother me. I'd expected it. Then he questioned the masculinity of a man having a flower garden. I knew he was goading me. I gave him a history lesson about Cato, a military leader in Rome who catalogued cultivars." He wiped his hands on his pants and laced his fingers together. "By then I was pretty ticked, but I held it together. Then he made lewd comments about us. If he had been any other man—"

"But he isn't any other man. He's my son."

"He's getting out of hand, Mib."

"He's lost his father, and now his mother has married a—"

"Stop right there unless you're going to call me a frustrated man because that's all I am. I don't deserve a label for what happened today."

"You don't deserve a medal, either."

"No, I don't. I blew it; I admit that. But rather than talk about it now, I think we should—"

"We're talking about it now."

Larry looked toward the stairs. "Maybe we should go someplace else to talk."

"I'll put on my shoes."

We drove west over the river and turned south until the road bent toward the Uncompahgre Plateau. Larry downshifted to third for the steeper grade. The road wound through hills dotted with homes, discernable only by porch lights and the glow of lit rooms. The grade steepened. A crescent moon paused askew in the sky. Signs warned of 15 MPH turns with scant guardrails. Larry wasn't taking the danger seriously enough.

"Maybe you shouldn't take these turns—"

"I've driven this road a million times in the dark. I dated a girl in high school who lived up here."

I watched Larry as he drove, lit by the dashboard lights. He looked the same—soft, kind, strong, and a little shell-shocked. Was he a brute hiding a short fuse? How was I supposed to know that? I chided myself for agreeing to marry so quickly. Surely his rougher side would have come out over time. I worried about not being able to see his true nature, and I worried about his ability to hide his capricious side.

Will the real Larry please stand up?

A river of lights in the valley caught my eye and disappeared behind a wall of sandstone when I turned to look. The scattering of houses thinned, and still we climbed into stands of juniper and pinion.

"Where are we going?" I asked.

"It's not much farther."

We turned off the paved road and past a sign that designated the expanse of gravel as a staging area, whatever that meant. The gravel ended where a rutted road of red dirt picked up. My head hit the window when Larry steered around a washed-out section of the road. "Ouch!"

"Are you all right? I'll drive slower."

"Are we almost there?"

"You won't be sorry. I promise."

A section of washboard nearly loosened my fillings. I was about to insist we stop when the valley appeared below us, an amber wash of lights from one end to the other. Larry stopped the car and opened his door. I followed him to a broad, flat boulder and took his hand for a hoist up. Crickets chirruped in the brush. Below us, the shapes of buildings were undefined behind the sparkling lights, but the mountains stood black against the star-riddled night. *Amazing.*

"Did you bring your girlfriend up here?" I asked.

"Sometimes."

A breeze like a breath melded the scent of juniper resin with the pinion and sage in the cooler air of the plateau. Larry shifted his weight. His shoes scraped pebbles against stone. "I need to know before we say anything. Do you think you can forgive me?"

"I don't know. I haven't tried." *If your brother asks for forgiveness . . .* "I'm still angry—and scared."

"Of me? Oh, Mib, please don't say that." He threw his head back. "Oh my God, how did this happen?"

"Ky says you treat him differently when I'm not around."

Larry wiped his face with his sleeve. "He's probably right. I'm more direct with him, authoritarian, like my dad. But I've never hit him before, I swear, and although I was tempted, I never belittled him . . . ever."

"Are you willing to say that in front of him?"

Larry nodded and wiped his face again. "Do you want me to move out for a while? I'll talk to Pastor Dale. I'll read a hundred books on stepparenting. I'll even go back to the counselor if you want."

"Not the counselor. I love you too much for that."

He offered his hand as if he expected me to bite it. I took it and brought the back of his hand to my lips to kiss. Touching him refreshed my memory of who I'd married. We stood there for a long time, our foreheads touching.

"Ky's a smart kid," I said. "He knows how to push the right buttons to get us working against each other. We can't let him do that. Something has to change."

"Mom had a suggestion."

I stiffened. "Yes?"

"They have camps for kids like Ky—angry kids who need the strength of something bigger than his anger to push against. If I dipped into my retirement IRA, we could swing it."

"I'm not sending him away to be fixed like some watch with a bad spring. Absolutely not. And you can tell your mother—"

"I'll tell her we're sticking together."

"Thank you."

When we embraced it felt like we were clinging to one another at the edge of a deep precipice. Larry prayed, "Father, in front of Mib, I want to ask you again to forgive me for striking Ky in anger. I ask you to redeem my bad judgment to accomplish your good will for Ky. Lord, I don't have a clue of what I'm doing. I want to get along with him. I just don't know how to make that happen. Teach me how to love him the way you love him."

"Thank you for bringing Larry into our lives. Amen."

"What do you think about giving his license back?" Larry asked. "Maybe cutting him off from his friends was a bad idea."

"I think giving his license back now would look like his temper tantrum worked, but we need a plan. Trust me, nothing but trouble can come from him lying around the house all day and going out with his friends at night."

I'd never questioned Scott's ability to love Ky through the tough times. I assumed he would. After all, Scott had diapered him as a baby after some of Ky's most explosive bowel movements. That's devotion. Could I expect the same from Larry? I was glad I didn't have to answer for every misjudgment I made as a parent.

And I'd never dared to wonder how the death of his father might score Ky's heart and what would eventually stick to that raw place—a greater understanding of the fleetingness of our lives and the hope that comes from living toward eternity—or something else? Bitterness? Cynicism? A spine-shattering loneliness?

Sitting in the front seat of the Datsun with Larry, the heater warming us, remembering the hope of eternity strengthened me. Now I needed the faith to believe God could do the same thing for Ky.

JUNE
23

Humdinger of a thunderstorm today—
brief but intense, another 1/4 inch to push us
past average precipitation for June. Yahoo!
Carine gladiolus—creamy white with
splashes of raspberry-pink—be
still my beating heart.

"I won't have you getting struck by lightning," Margaret said.

"A car is the safest place to be in a storm," I replied. My heart pounded in my chest just seeing the Family Dentistry Center sign over the door of Sonny's office.

"I'm not so sure about that." Margaret whispered, "Truth be told, I could use some moral support." A rumble of thunder sounded in the distance. "We best get going," she said, using her shoulder to push against the Daisy Mobile's passenger door. She climbed the steps to the dental office, a weary box of brick and cedar. The no-fuss landscape of junipers and more junipers filled a railroad-tie retaining wall, a landscape fixture as timeless as leisure suits and just as worthy of being forgotten. Margaret turned at the top of the stairs to wait for me, a hand on her hip. In the other hand, she carried her purse like a shield.

Since a dentist's drill had zinged one of my nerves when I was a child, I sang "Marching to Zion"-type songs the week prior to my once-a-year cleaning appointment. Margaret had caught me unprepared by asking me to take her on an errand when I'd arrived to do her garden maintenance. I hummed "Some Trust in Chariots."

Margaret tapped her foot. "What are you waiting for?"

My dentist gives me a nice little pill to take an hour before I visit her office. With its soothing effect, my breakfast stays in my stomach and the tray with the pokey tools seems much less menacing. A true gift from God. I looked at the tin of Altoids on the truck's seat, a powerful mint to be sure, but not at all what I needed.

I yelled out the window. "Margaret, this is between you and Sonny. He won't be happy with an audience."

"I ain't asking for no audience, just your company."

She deserved that and more. As I climbed the stairs and held the glass door for Margaret, I strategized. If I sat with my back to the receptionist and imagined myself at the gynecologist's office—a preferable experience to the dentist any day—and repeated the Lord's Prayer, I would be able to keep my seven-layer burrito where it lay in my stomach. Just in case, I felt my pocket for the doggie waste bag I carried for Blink's untimely movements.

Some trust in chariots . . .

Pale-blue wallpaper and artwork that surely fell off a starving artist's truck covered the walls of Sonny's waiting room. One cliché after another—a barn, a covered bridge, lots of pine trees in the snow— homey images, all meant to reassure patients their dentist wasn't squandering his fees on frivolous decor. I happened to know Sonny spent his decorating budget on a Mercedes sedan.

The receptionist, a pretty girl wearing a lace-trimmed top that resembled my grandmother's best slip, smiled tentatively and ran a French-tipped fingernail down the computer screen. "Is Dr. Simpleman expecting you?"

"Dr. Simpleman is my son."

"Ohmigosh, no one told me you were coming. Like, today's my first day. I don't even, like, know how to put calls on hold." The more flustered the girl became, the brighter her cheeks flushed. "I'm, like, so sorry."

Margaret reached over the counter to pat the girl's hand. "There's nothing to be sorry about. I'll show myself in."

The girl stood. "He, like, has a patient."

Margaret grabbed my hand and walked past the reception counter. "I won't be long." Margaret pulled me close enough to whisper. "Pretty girl. Not too confident. Chances are she'll be my daughter-in-law before long. Do you think I should warn her?"

Somewhere very close by, a drill whined. . . . *and some in horses . . .*

Margaret tightened her grip. "You've come this far."

My stomach swayed. . . . *but I will trust in the name of the Lord my God . . .*

We passed a small room where a hygienist worked over a patient. With protective glasses and a mask, only her eyes asked a question about our presence over the noise of her tool. Margaret waved at her and continued down the hall. When Margaret opened the door of a supply closet, I asked, "You *have* been here before, haven't you?"

"My dentist don't charge as much as Sonny."

Sonny's assistant saw us first. She looked to Sonny, but he was hunched over his patient, intent on drilling and drilling and drilling.

I leaned against the doorframe. *Sing it again. Some trust in chariots . . .*

The assistant moved around the chair to push a square button on the wall. It lit, and down the hall a buzzer sounded. "As you can see, Dr. Simpleman is busy. The receptionist will show you to the waiting room."

Margaret squared her shoulders. "I'm here to see Sonny."

The drilling stopped. "Mother?"

Margaret spoke to the assistant. "He'll only be a minute."

"Mother—"

"We can talk in the hall."

I half expected Margaret to grab Sonny by the ear, but she didn't need to. Sonny told his patient he'd be right back and shot a questioning glance at me. I shrugged. The assistant excused herself. "Thank goodness you came. I haven't had a break since lunch."

The room tilted to the left and back again. I steadied myself against the counter. In the exam chair, a man in a mechanic's uniform—Ron, from the name patch sewn to his shirt—lay with a metal brace holding his mouth open. A square of latex stretched over the frame to expose one tooth. A rubber dam. I slid down the cabinet and put my head between my knees.

The man in the chair asked a question I recognized only by its cadence.

"I'll be better when I get out of here," I assured him. . . . *and some in horses . . .*

In the hall, Margaret spoke to Sonny. Her voice was a cotton quilt. "Sonny, darling, you're the only son I have. No one—not Walter, not anyone—can fill the place in my heart that belongs to you. Not even the memory of your father, and you know how dear your father was to me, don't you, Sonny? There's nothing you can do to earn my love or lose it. I don't love anyone like I love you. Now, honey, you're a grown man, so you will understand when I tell you that I also love Walter—not with the love a mother has for a son, but with the love a woman has for a man."

I looked up. The man in the chair had heard Margaret's speech, too. We sat there for a long time, waiting and listening, but not one word came from the hallway until Margaret said, "Now, Sonny boy, I didn't mean to make you cry."

❧

Parked at the curb of Rocket Park, I nibbled on the remains of my lunch. Raindrops accumulated on the trees above the Daisy Mobile and plopped on the cab. With the chaotic rhythm of the oversized drops as background, I replayed Margaret's speech to Sonny. Nothing she'd said had required working knowledge of thermal dynamics or even a doctorate of dental science. Surely, Sonny already had known everything Margaret told him. He *was* her only son. He couldn't lose his mother's love. But there was knowing, and then there was *knowing*—the kind of surety that comes when the truth we hope for is finally put into words. It happened to me when Larry first said he loved me. If a simple declaration of the obvious had softened Sonny's heart, would the same work for Ky?

Lord?

I cranked the ignition key and pumped the accelerator to start the truck. It was too late to cook Ky a gourmet meal myself. I headed for Louise's kitchen, praying she had created a masterpiece even a teenage boy would appreciate. She intended to include corn dogs in her cookbook, didn't she? Ky would be home at about six. We'd loosened his grounding so he could help out at a youth group fund-raiser. He was that desperate to get out of the house. That gave me a little over an hour to be ready.

Louise winced when I asked her about food for Ky. "I have a Wheat Berry and Watercress Quiche in the oven. Will that do?"

I scanned the kitchen. "Anything else?"

"I made a simply divine lemony dill egg salad from a recipe submitted by Janet Sheehan."

I groaned as I dropped onto a chair, but Louise didn't notice.

She continued, "The combination of the lemon and the dill creates a multilayered palette of flavors. I served the salad on rye toast for lunch. On the side, a spinach salad with goat cheese tossed with an orange balsamic vinaigrette balanced the flavors perfectly. Manley loved it. I think there's enough left for one sandwich, maybe two if you spread it thin and use lots of lettuce."

"Louise, we're talking about a boy who eats peanut butter out of the jar."

"You're absolutely right, sweet pea. What was I thinkin'?" She shuffled through a pile of recipe cards. "Here's something promising, a taco frittata recipe from Susan Paris."

"Isn't she the one—"

"According to the recipe, it only takes ten minutes."

"Maybe I should take Ky out to dinner. He likes the Happy Dragon."

"There is nothing more powerful in a mama's arsenal than a home-cooked meal. This is no time to be turning your bloomers into a flag of surrender." She waved the recipe card at me. "Ky loves tacos. I've seen him eat half a dozen when he wasn't even hungry."

I knew him better than she did. He would never mistake a taco frittata for six crunchy tacos from Taco Bell. "Don't you have a steak marinating in the fridge?"

"I start testing beef entrées next week."

"How soon can you have the frittata ready?"

Louise pushed me toward the door. "You go home; set the table with that embroidered tablecloth I gave you for a wedding gift."

I stopped. "The one that requires ironing?"

"You'll have time. Be extravagant. Don't hold back. Use those candlesticks you keep in the hutch, and for heaven's sake, lay out your best china. Remember, you want Ky to feel like a prince returning home after a long journey." Louise buttoned her chef's coat to her throat and assembled her cooking tools—bowl, cutting board, measuring cups, a cleaver the size of Florida. "If Larry doesn't have plans for dinner, you can send him over here. Manley would appreciate the company."

"Larry offered to go to his mother's."

"What a honey bear he is." Louise swiped her cleaver across the cutlery steel with impressive speed. "You better skedaddle. I have cookin' to do. The frittata will be out of the oven by 5:45. That way you can take a shower and put on a dress."

Shower? Yes. Dress? No. I kissed her cheek and turned to leave.

"Wait a minute, sugar." She disappeared into the dining room and makeshift office. "Those rating cards are here somewhere. Who knows? This taco frittata may be Susan's masterpiece. It would be a shame not to be prepared." Louise slid a card into the bib pocket of my overalls. "Do you want to take a couple place settings of my mama's china?"

"I have my grandmother's Havilland."

With the tablecloth in place and the table set, I dimmed the light over the dining room table and lit the candles. I'd picked a bouquet of coreopsis, blue veronica, Shasta daisies, and cupid's dart, a flower even Ky could appreciate with its electric blue petals and nearly black centers. It was a spirited bouquet, especially since I'd passed on my favorite filler, a rosy twinspur, a bit too delicate for Ky's taste. I sorted the biggest corn chips out of three opened bags and arranged them in a napkin-lined basket. With the salsa poured into a silver gravy boat, it was time to claim the frittata from Louise.

I returned to the garden just in time to see Ky pedaling his bike down the driveway and out of sight. I ran after him, jostling the frittata and a carton of sour cream, calling his name. Just as I cleared the side of the house to see which way he'd gone, my shoe caught on a crack in the pavement. The frittata and I hit the pavement at the exact same time, jolting the lid off the frying pan onto the pavement, where it shattered.

I sat there, a hollow barrel of a woman, condemning myself for letting Louise list the adjustments she'd made to the recipe and for taking the time to try on one of her dresses. More than that, I was embarrassed for believing a meal and a few rehearsed words could erase all the recent trouble with Ky. It was clear he had walked into the house, seen the table set for an intimate dinner for two, and assumed he was the odd man out. I threw the frying pan against the fence.

The longer you believe something to be true, the more it becomes the truth no matter how much evidence proves otherwise, especially if you want to believe that the familiar world of home and family are against you. That's teenage angst. I pulled a chair to a front window and prayed Ky would return quickly. When he didn't, I gathered the phone book and the telephone and the graham crackers. I called Ky's friends to ask if they'd seen him. They hadn't.

When Larry came home, he looked over the list of people I'd called and added a few more. While I made the calls, he blew out the candles on the table and returned the china and goblets to the hutch without one clink. As I talked to the third baseman's dad, Larry kissed my forehead and set a grilled cheese sandwich on the table next to me.

"He's usually home by now," I explained to the father.

"Take my advice," the father said. "The tighter you hold on to Ky, the harder he'll squirm to break free. My wife and I, we learned the hard way. Our boy—"

"Thank you. Thank you so much for the advice. I better free up the line in case Ky tries to call. He usually calls. That's why I'm worried. Good night."

At nine-thirty, Larry knelt before me. "Would you mind if I went to bed? I'm beat."

I looked at him, blinking. "Go ahead. I'm okay." And in saying so, I released him from the difficult parts of parenting. "I won't be up much longer."

"He's at a friend's house, Mib, watching videos or playing computer games. He's lost track of time."

"Yeah, you're probably right."

Larry kissed my hands and studied my face. I smiled weakly. I wanted him to go to bed so I could call the hospitals without his calling me a hysterical mother, although, honestly, Larry had never said such a thing.

"Do you want to pray?" he asked.

All I wanted was a chance to reconnect with Ky. I wasn't sure who was to blame for the missed opportunity, but I wasn't all that happy that God hadn't slowed the rotation of the earth a nanosecond or two to accommodate my plans.

"You do it," I said, lowering my head.

"Father, we don't know where Ky is right now, but you do. Protect him from harm and from doing anything that would cause him shame in the years to come."

"Are you trying to make me feel better?" I asked, raising my head to meet Larry's gaze.

"Is there anything Ky could do tonight to lose your love?" he asked.

"Keep praying."

"Lord, help us to welcome him when he returns home just as you welcome us. Amen." He kissed my temple. "Don't stay up too late."

Twelve-forty. Seven hours. A couple videos. A competitive game of some truer-than-life video game. He should have been home. I pulled back the curtain again. No Ky. I sat on the stairs, looked up the numbers for the hospital emergency rooms, and asked Blink if he thought I was being hysterical. I dialed anyway.

"Let me check," said the proficient voice on the other end of the line. There was a tapping of computer keys and she said, "No one by that name has been admitted tonight, and no John Does to fit your son's description."

I thanked her and called the sheriff and the police department.

One-fifteen. I slid a pan of brownies into the oven, an impetuous act meant to be a homecoming gift for Ky—or a source of comfort for me. I played a game of solitaire on the computer. Lost. Cleaned up the spam on my e-mail account. As I tapped the delete key, I almost deleted an e-mail from Andrea sent several days earlier.

don't be too hard on ky . . . there is so much pressure to be cool . . . whatever that means . . . we prayed for him last night at small group . . . darlia told us the story of abraham and isaac. do you know the story? just be glad God never asked you to sacrifice ky on a mountain somewhere.

Thank you, Lord, for never asking me to do that. I couldn't, you know. I just couldn't.

creepy story but cool how God provided the sacrificial lamb in Isaac's place . . . what will God ask me to do? my students sound better every day . . . i'm a teacher!!!!!;-) Are you sure you can't come to a concert before school starts? i'd like you to meet somebody!!!!!!
i love you guys
andrea
p.s. gracie has been working at the bookstore for one whole week THAT'S A MIRACLE!!!!

I scooped a corner of brownie out of the pan while it was still warm and chased it down with a chug of milk. I sufficiently washed the sticky remnants of chocolate from my teeth, but enough milk remained in the glass for another crispy brownie corner. I misjudged the amount of milk I'd need to wash down the second serving. I poured milk to the rim of the glass to cleanse my palate, only to be left with more than enough milk to justify a third corner. I sure liked the crunchy edges and the warm, soft middle. That was how I ate my way around the pan of hot brownies. I cut what remained into two large brownies for Ky.

Two-ten. I sat on the porch swing wrapped in a blanket. The night, spotlighted by a waning moon, seemed too benevolent to hijack my son, but it had. The screen door opened. Larry stepped half into the moonlight, wearing only his highly reflective white boxers.

"Why don't you come to bed?" he said.

Whether it was the regret that follows the binge eating of chocolate or the tenderness in Larry's invitation, a knot tightened in my throat.

"Mib? Honey?"

"I'm scared."

He left the cover of the shadows. I opened the blanket to him.

"I know you are."

I wet his shoulder with my tears until fatigue dragged me into a shallow dream about walking up the stairs with Larry and crawling under the cool sheets. His chest hairs tickled me awake to find that we still sat on the porch swing. I looked up and down the street.

"He probably crashed at one of his friends' houses," he said. "We'll work this out in the morning." When I didn't move, he added, "You'll hear him when he comes in."

Even though fatigue had long since replaced the panic that had tightened my throat, I followed Larry upstairs feeling like a deserter. What kind of mother went to bed when her son wasn't home past midnight?

Three-fifteen. I left the bed and dressed in the clothes I'd dropped on the bathroom floor, only to stare into the night. I cataloged all of the random acts of futility I could accomplish by driving through the dark neighborhoods of Orchard City. I put my pajamas back on and went to my desk in the family room to write Ky a note that included all of the things I'd wanted to say to him over dinner. I went back upstairs. Moonlight cast a silver veil over the inelegant refuse of Ky's room. I couldn't find his pillow, so I pushed a pile of clothes from his bed and set the note and the brownies in the middle of the bed.

With more hopelessness than faith, I surrendered the outcome of the night to God's care and returned to bed. Larry's sticky snores wakened me to hear heavy steps on the stairs. The clock read 3:40. I stood outside Ky's bedroom door but could not rally the courage to open it.

As much as I wanted him to be home safe and sound, I wasn't sure I wanted to know what shape he was in. Drunk or sober, he was safely home. There would be time enough in the morning to talk to him, find out where he'd been, prescribe yet another round of lost privileges.

And yet . . .

I cracked the bedroom door open. "Ky?" I whispered into the darkness.

"Huh?"

"Nothing. I just wanted to know if it was you."

"Who else would it be?"

I switched on the light. He cowered behind his arm from the brightness. The note and brownies I'd left for him lay scattered among his clothes on the floor.

"What the—" he started until he squinted to see me holding the plate of brownies in front of his face. Standing that close to him, I knew he'd been drinking.

I shoved the note into my robe pocket. "I didn't want you to step on the brownies." I saw myself as Ky saw me. Unraveled. Feeble. Wounded. *Mission accomplished.*

I gathered myself like crumbs swept off the table into a hand. "See you at six," I said and closed the door.

JUNE 29

Hot Lips sage is putting on quite a show.
Now that the highs are in the 90s, the flowers
are pure white. Will the blooms revert to red
and white when it cools down? What a hoot!
Please be winter hardy.

I paced the kitchen until the microwave's digital clock read seven and then I dialed Margot's number. She greeted me with her usual warmth.

"Why are you calling me so early?" she asked.

Fortified by sparring with Ky over the past few days, I refused to recoil. "You're the one who wanted to be sisterly. Well, this is what sisters do, Margot. They lose their minds and then they call their sisters to talk about it."

"Tell me."

"Really?"

Margot allowed a long pulse of silence to hang between us. "Yes, I really want to know."

I told her how Ky had bolted from the house and not returned until the wee hours of the morning smelling of beer and how Larry had taken a sick day the next morning to "discuss" Ky's behavior.

"Did Ky listen?"

He had scowled and grunted and swore at us. Larry and I retorted

183

with down-the-nose lecturing, huffing, and name-calling. I cycled through fear, anger, and rage, but they all felt the same from the inside. In a fit of frustration, Larry and I had emptied Ky's room of everything but his mattress, a blanket, and a pillow and loaded his stuff into the Daisy Mobile.

"I'm not sure we did the right thing," I told Margot.

It had taken three trips to the McManus farm to store all the stuff in the dahlia shed. For the last load, Larry pounded the hinge pins from Ky's bedroom door and carried it to the truck.

We pushed the mattress into the corner of his room. Although Larry and I disagreed on the fine point of a pillow being a need or a luxury, Larry prevailed and the pillow stayed. We bought a windup alarm clock that ticked loudly and woke up the neighbors at six o'clock sharp. The cellblocks of Alcatraz had been better appointed.

Over the next few days Ky's anger had only escalated. He cursed at us, blamed us for everything but global warming and athlete's foot. An odd confusion pocked my thinking. I drove past clients' houses, stashed a full gallon of milk in the pantry, and ran out of gas on the interstate. I recognized the symptoms, all right. I was grieving again, only this time the "corpse" enjoyed my misery.

"This is exactly why I didn't have kids," Margot said.

"Short of chaining him to the register, I'm stumped."

"Have you considered sending him away?"

"Do you have room?"

Margot gasped. "I'm never here. Besides, there are camps for messed-up kids. I saw a TV show. They make them ride horses and rappel down cliffs."

Messed up? "Out of the question. I'm not sending Ky away."

"Then consider this: the human brain cannot fully assess risk until it's twenty-five years old. You have nine more years of harnessing his bent on self-destruction. What's your plan?"

Good question.

I enjoyed the solitude of my job, especially when I had a lot on my mind. Most of my regular maintenance customers worked during the day, so I came and went as it suited me. I knew the yards well enough to schedule for optimal working conditions, which meant generous shade for a redhead like me. If I wanted noise, I listened to a CD. If I didn't, I listened to birds sing; I played catch with lonely dogs; I breathed the fresh air. Best of all, I lay in the grass in the deep shade of Mr. Webley's cottonwood tree. The leaves fluttered when a breeze ran its finger along a branch. Otherwise they hung motionless in the afternoon heat. Beyond the tree's canopy, the sky was a bowl inverted over the valley with only a few fragile contrails to relieve the stark blueness. If the Colorado sky had a personality, as I'd heard so many people say, this day it was a cheerless choleric bent on sucking the joy out of Elizabeth Webley's garden. Or maybe out of me.

By 7:21 in the morning, Ky had successfully derailed my sincerest efforts to be my best self—a new record. Larry and I didn't trust him alone in the house, so each day meant arranging supervision while we worked. At first, I stayed home with Ky until noon, when Connie showed up to relieve me. That worked until I found Connie crying and Ky drawing on his walls with a permanent marker. Time for a new plan. I arranged for him to spend the afternoon with one of his old youth-group buddies and his family, the McDowells, at the lake, boating and fishing. What kid wouldn't love that? I pictured Ky laughing as the dad pulled him the length of the lake on an inner tube, and I prayed faith cooties would rub onto Ky from the son, Douglas.

I bolted to a sitting position when a male cleared his throat over me. Gordon Webley looked like he'd been standing there for some time. Sweat deepened the blue of his shirt under his arms and his face glowed red. His car wasn't in the driveway. Had I prayed out loud?

"I walked home," he said. "The car is in the shop. I didn't want to miss you again."

"I can explain." I slipped on my Birkenstocks and made to stand.

"Don't get up," he said. "I can't remember the last time I lay in the shade like that. You looked so peaceful; I didn't want to wake you."

"I was taking a break."

"Mind if I join you?"

Mr. Webley lay a few feet away, looking up into the branches of the tree. "Look at that sky. Have you ever seen anything so blue? I haven't done this since . . ." His sentence hung like the languid leaves above us. Once I stopped expecting him to say more, my muscles softened and I closed my eyes to enjoy the play of light and shadow on my eyelids.

Mr. Webley spoke again, and my eyes popped open. "Elizabeth stayed home with the kids. I traveled almost every week, had paperwork to finish on the weekends, so she kept them busy. I missed out on the good stuff. I envied her for that."

The grass made my back itch, so I sat up. "I feel great. I think I'll get back to work now."

He sat up, too. "It's awfully hot to be working."

"I'm used to it."

"I suppose you are, being outside like you are all the time." He tore stems of grass and shifted them through his fingers. "Are you still taking bouquets to Elizabeth?"

"Is that all right?"

"Is she pleased? I mean, does she understand that the flowers are from me?"

Careful. "Oh yes, she enjoys the flowers."

Mr. Webley sighed. "Thank you. I was afraid you'd stopped, seeing how I forgot to leave the vases. There's a lot going on at the office. A merger's coming." With a start, I think he realized who he was talking to. He stood up to brush off his clothes. "Add the cost of delivery to my monthly statement, will you? And if you've had to purchase a vase—"

"That hasn't been necessary." Elizabeth had an empty vase waiting for me when I delivered her flowers each week.

He wiped his forehead on his sleeve. A car drove by, and he turned to watch it, welcoming the distraction, I supposed, from trying to make conversation with the gardener.

"You should probably get yourself a tall drink of water," I said to relieve him of his duty.

"I appreciate what you've done. I probably should have sold the place. Nothing has changed . . . or will. I should be grateful for the years she gave me and leave her alone." His shoulders rounded from the weight of his words. He looked off toward the rotund Mount Garfield. Hands on hips, he surveyed the flower garden. "Well . . . uh, you're doing a great job."

"Thanks."

"I sit on the porch almost every night to watch how the setting sun changes the colors of the flowers. It's amazing. I don't know why I never noticed it before." Mr. Webley looked at his watch. "I'll leave you to your work. A meeting, you know." He looked down at his shirt. "I better change."

He was nearly to the front steps when I stood up. "You can count on me to deliver the flowers for you."

He turned. "Good, and leave a bouquet for me . . . for the table, I mean."

Not once in all of the weeks I'd been maintaining the Webleys' garden had I been invited inside. That didn't stop me from imagining what lay beyond the few glimpses I'd caught of warm cherry wood floors and the startling white molding of the entry. The garden was an ocean of green with islands of color and texture. Bloom times overlapped as effortlessly as the coming and going of the tide. If the inside of her house reflected the garden, each room in Elizabeth Webley's home evoked a tiptoe respect to the calm and wonder of balance.

Visiting Elizabeth's studio shattered the peace of my imaginings. Canvases leaned against one another like books at a yard sale. Metal shelves were stuffed with toolboxes labeled for oils and pastels, art books and magazines, and crocks full of pencils and brushes. Paintings in various stages of completion leaned against easels. One painting—a canvas about four feet square—took center stage. On it she had painted one daisy to fill the canvas, slightly askew with a few petals missing, as if out of frame a young girl had paused in the middle of "He loves me, he loves me not."

Elizabeth loaded her brush from a line of paints squeezed onto a glass palette. "I want the paint to wiggle and squish, to be free," she said, working her brush with a loose hand. "Speed is my friend." She reloaded her wide brush and held it out to me. "You try."

"I don't know—"

"You can't ruin it. Honest."

"Where?" I asked, taking the brush.

"Inside the dark outline I scrubbed onto the background. Leave a stained-glass edge. See the sketch?" She pointed to a sketch no bigger than a matchbox taped to the easel. "Start with the petal at three o'clock. Remember, the point is fast and loose."

I gaped at the canvas.

Elizabeth put her hand over mine. "Let me do the work. Feel the shape of the stroke." She guided my hand to crosshatch, dab, and swirl the paint across the canvas. "This technique kills the perfectionist in you. Very therapeutic. Now you try."

I reloaded the brush and looked to Elizabeth.

"Perfect. Go for it."

In the time it takes to sneeze, I emptied the brush of paint with strokes I mimicked from Elizabeth. The petals absorbed the colors of a sunset, but to the eye, the daisy radiated white—so simple, so friendly. Paint gliding onto the canvas released a bubble of joy along my spine.

"Keep going until you fill the space."

A dull headache started over my eyes.

"You're doing great. Wipe that frown off your face."

"It's the linseed, I think."

"Oh! You should have said something." She took the brush from me and dropped it into a glass of milky liquid. "Let's get out of here."

Elizabeth brought a pitcher of lemonade to the patio. "Today's your lucky day. My daughter sent a box of lemons from Florida. I made lemonade."

"You have a daughter?"

"And a son. Todd is in a managerial internship at Microsoft in Seattle—very much like his father, the poor dear, especially since he inherited a bit of my artistic soul. He's a little conflicted, but he'll figure life out. Lily is at the University of Florida—an art major and psychology minor. She wants to work in the area of therapeutic art."

"Do you get to see them very often?"

Elizabeth tilted her head and narrowed her eyes. "Has anyone told you how transparent you are?"

"Only my sister. She punched me frequently for thinking hateful things about her, and she was right."

"Well, you are transparent. You're worried about my children. Has Gordon said something to you about them?"

"I didn't even know you had children, remember?"

"About me, then?"

"Only that he regretted letting the garden go."

Elizabeth sipped at her lemonade. "Does he say *anything* about us?"

"I rarely see him. Today, he walked home to make sure I had a vase to bring you a bouquet."

"He walked home? In this heat?"

"His car is in the shop."

"Oh my, Gordon walked home," she whispered and leaned her chin against her hand.

Whatever I'd said to confound Elizabeth kept her thoughts encased behind her hazel eyes. She grew quiet and thoughtful. I sipped at the lemonade and slipped out of my Birkenstocks. Shaded by a burr oak, her patio lulled me into a *mañana* state of mind—tomorrow, tomorrow. Groupings of pots, painted the laughing colors of a fiesta, filled every corner of the patio. She'd chosen ornamental kales and grasses, miniature roses, canna lilies with purple stems, verbena, and fragrant heliotropes. She designed flowering pots the same way she painted: fast and loose, uninhibited yet balanced.

We didn't speak of Gordon or her children again. We talked about gardening as an extension of our art, and she asked me to look at an ailing wood sorrel in her kitchen window. I told her to move the plant to a room lit like a forest floor on the Olympic Peninsula.

When Elizabeth walked me to the Daisy Mobile, she said, "I'll drive by the house to see the gardens before you come again. The gloriosa daisies and the hyssop and the Chinese plumbago should all be blooming. Could you bring me an armful of each?"

The homeowner's lips were drawn in place with red lipstick, and her black hair fell unceremoniously past her shoulders. She gestured for me to follow her. Her footfalls were soundless on the wooden treads of the stairs. I followed her but stopped to step out of my Birkenstocks and look where I'd walked to see if I'd left dirt on her maple floors.

She spoke over her shoulder, and I hurried to catch up. "He does wonderful work. If you're thinking about having him remodel for you, don't let his appearance put you off."

I laughed. "Droop extended the back of our house and remodeled the kitchen."

She pointed down the hall. "You'll find him in the guest bathroom. Third door on the right."

The door was closed, so I tapped lightly. On the other side of the door, Droop set the lock. "This is not a good time, Mrs. McCourt."

"Droop, it's me, Mibby."

"I don't care if it's the Queen of Sheba. You ain't coming in."

Maybe he wasn't wallpapering as Mrs. McCourt had suggested. I whispered where the door met the casing, "I can wait until you're . . . *finished.*"

"It ain't nothing like that," he shouted back. "I'm working above the door. If this ain't the ugliest wallpaper I've ever seen."

The woman startled me with a tap on my shoulder. "I heard shouting. Is there a problem?"

"No, he's working above the door. He can't open it just yet."

"I see."

I smiled, tight-lipped, hoping she'd see that while I needed to shout to be heard, my conversation with Droop was private.

"Did you say something?" he asked. "You're going to have to speak louder if you expect me to hear a word you say."

I looked back to the woman and shrugged.

She smiled to reveal translucent white teeth smeared with her lipstick. "It's awfully warm today. Would you like something cold to drink?"

"No, thank you. I'll be on my way as soon as I talk to Droop."

"I see," she said, but she didn't see at all because she stood erect, her ear cocked toward the door.

"Maybe I am thirsty," I said. "I'd love a glass of water."

"I'll be right back." And she was gone.

I knelt on the floor to whisper under the door. "Droop?"

"Hang on to your britches. I have a tricky cut here." The scritch of a razor cutting along a straightedge was followed by mild cursing. The door opened. Droop stood before me in his painting togs and cap, wiping his hands on a paint-stained rag. "It's good to see you, honest it is, but I've never had a harder time getting wallpaper to stick to a wall. If I don't finish this here job today, I can kiss my profit good-bye. You have five minutes."

I bypassed the rhetorical arguments I'd developed driving from Elizabeth's studio to Droop's worksite and went directly to the summation. "Can Ky work with you? I'm desperate. You wouldn't even have to pay him. Nothing seems to get through to him. Larry is working long hours and so am I. I'm terrified that Ky will do something stupid. Everyone seems to think he needs to go away. I don't know. It's awfully expensive. And how do you choose—?"

Droop held up his hand, palm toward me. "T.M.I., young lady. Stop right there. I'd be happy to help you out." He looked over his shoulder at the bathroom. "But it's pretty tight in here."

"How about your next project?"

"Before you came, I was set to finish this job in time to do some fishing up at Vega this afternoon. I suppose it's no great loss since the water's so murky, but I sure was looking forward to Honey's picnic supper."

"Ky needs something constructive to do this summer."

"So you're looking for a baby-sitter, are you?"

"He's sixteen."

Droop let out a long whistle. "The sheriff knew me by name the summer I turned sixteen."

"Ky's gotten himself in trouble with the law, too."

Droop removed his cap to rub the dome of his head. "Is he running with a bad crowd?"

"Mostly older kids. A few have graduated. He's sneaking out to party with them."

"Is he drinking?"

"Yes, and maybe doing pot."

"I'm set to renovate a bunch of rental cabins up on the Mesa. I figured the job would take me the rest of the summer, with some minor finishing work next spring. With Ky's help, I could finish before the aspens turn. The work will be hard. Up and down ladders. Demolition. Framing. Concrete work."

"The harder the better, I say."

"Okay then, he's hired." Droop looked toward the ceiling. "Let's see now, it will take us about an hour to get there, and you know I like to be home to Honey by four. That means I'll have to pick Ky up at . . ."

"Six?"

"Yep. That gives me an hour for lunch to contemplate the world's problems with a fishing pole in my hands and to catch my dinner. Honey greets me real nice if I come home with fresh trout, if you know what I mean."

"Thanks, Droop."

"Before you go calling me Sir Galahad, you better know the rules of employment with Droop the Handyman Quality Services. First of all, I expect Ky on the curb at six A.M. with his hair combed, his face shaved, and his shirttail tucked in. It's up to him to get himself up and ready to go, and that means packing his own lunch. You ain't doin' it for him, you hear?"

I nodded, thinking I'd better stock up on peanut butter and saltines.

"Now, if he don't get up on his own, rousting the young rooster out of bed is my job. And just so you know, I won't be singing him no rise-and-shine song, neither. If you dislike watching your son being pulled out of bed, you best go eat muffins with Louise." Droop hiked up his pants, but his buckle still hid under his belly. "I won't cotton to no interference from you. Are you okay with that?"

"I think so."

"And what about the Sweet Suzy man? Should I expect any inter-ference from him?"

"Larry? He's out of the house long before six."

"The job starts next Monday. No, make that Wednesday. I promised Honey a visit to her mother . . ." Droop rolled his shoulders, and I heard a pop. ". . . for the long weekend, being it's the Fourth and all." In the meantime, take Ky to the co-op store for a pair of steel-toed work boots and a pair of leather working gloves—the thicker the better. I don't want him crying over a splinter every two minutes."

"Thanks so much—"

"I got wallpaper to hang." The door slammed closed. I turned to see the homeowner standing in the hallway as straight as a pillar with a tray of iced tea and cookies. The cookies lay on the plate like paper cutouts—no nuts, no chocolate, no coconut.

"I didn't mean for you to trouble yourself." I drank the glass of iced tea straight down. "Thanks for your kindness. I have to go." I eased past her to descend the stairs.

Droop opened the door to yell after me, "And get the boy a fishing license!"

~~~

I carried a large tub of fabric swatches and trims out to Connie's car. The sun beat down on our heads and radiated up from the side-walk. As we walked, she told me about Pastor Dale's daughter marrying in the fall. Whenever someone in our church married, Connie made a Barbie doll look-alike dress to present to the bride as a keepsake, Barbie doll included. Connie had spent the afternoon sewing teeny-tiny beads on a Barbie-sized cathedral train to match the daughter's dress. Accord-ing to Connie, the bride had chosen a gown three sizes too small in hopes of being motivated to lose twenty pounds. "I've known more than one bride who shortened the train to expand the waist," she said, opening the car trunk for the box. "I hate to see girls put so much emphasis on their waistlines."

Louise had refused to let me wear Birkenstocks for my wedding, so I'd snipped the waist of my control-top panty hose to make wearing pumps easier to bear. Sometimes a woman has to create her own relief.

Connie slammed the trunk. "Love is a heart issue, plain and simple."

Plain and simple? Love?

The heat off the asphalt burned my eyes. This was no time to contradict my mother-in-law, especially since she played an important role in making my love for Larry both elaborate and complicated. In a rare moment of common sense, or eagerness to return to the air-conditioned house, I held my tongue.

Connie leaned against her car. "It was a good thing I was here when the McDowells brought Ky home early. I was just about to leave. I only dropped by to get dinner started in the Crockpot."

I stepped onto the grassy boulevard strip and deeper into the shade. I'd already heard the story twice. "I really appreciate your help, Connie."

"I'd never seen Wade McDowell so flustered. Nothing he did seemed to please Ky. And I'm sorry I can't be here tomorrow. I've made plans to take Jane out to lunch for her birthday." Connie blotted the sweat off her forehead and lip with the sleeve of her T-shirt. "But you know, Jane's an understanding girl. If you can't find anyone, all you have to do is say the word."

"Don't change your plans. It's only one day. I'm sure we can work something out." *Maybe Visigoths will gallop through Orchard City and need a stableboy.*

Connie turned to unlock her car door. I caught myself before I released a sigh. She left the keys hanging in the lock and turned back to me. "You better give Droop my phone number, just in case he runs into a problem with Ky."

Droop wasn't the kind of man to be bamboozled by an upstart rebel like Ky. "Droop has my cell phone number," I said.

"Even so, I'm available if you need me."

"Thank you."

And still she hesitated.

"Connie?"

"I'm nothing but a dreamy old woman when I'm tired."

I'd never once considered how the tension of our house weighed on Connie. "I'm so sorry. Would you like me to drive you home?"

"It's just that I wanted to say . . . That is . . . I *know* you appreciate how hard Larry is trying to be a good father to Ky. It isn't easy to father another man's son."

If anyone else had said this to me, I would've found an insult aimed at my lack of appreciation for Larry and a jab at Scott's ability to father. This was Connie, I reminded myself. "Larry's doing a great job."

"I'm praying for the two of you."

I hugged her and whispered thank-you in her ear.

She smiled and said, "You're a sweet thing." I waved at her until she turned the corner. I'd never dreamed loving a mother-in-law could be so much work.

Ky sat on his mattress, leaning against the wall. *Moby Dick* lay spread-eagle beside him. He wore a look of detachment common to teenagers when their parents behaved unpredictably. And Larry was doing just that by setting up a cot in front of Ky's bedroom door.

Larry snapped the cot's legs into place. "I got the idea from the reading in Nehemiah today."

Sure enough, had I remained on the reading-through-the-Bible-in-a-year regimen Larry and I had started at the beginning of January, I, too, would have waded through the rebirth of Jerusalem that morning. My good intentions had been bushwhacked just a week into the exercise by the story of God commanding Abraham to sacrifice Isaac on Mount Moriah. The Genesis passage made my soul itch. A little too close to home for my comfort.

Larry unfurled a sheet with a snap. "It's a great passage. Nehemiah led the people to rebuild Jerusalem. Nothing but rubble lay where the walls once stood. Their enemies enjoyed mocking the efforts of the Israelites, but they changed their tune when the gaps in the walls started closing. A plan was hatched to stir up trouble among the Israelites to stop their progress." Larry looked from Ky to me. "Sound familiar?"

"I can't believe this," Ky said.

Larry shimmied a pillow into a pillowcase. "The laborers were exhausted. A battle meant certain defeat for the Israelites."

"Now, *exhaustion* sounds familiar," I said.

"This is the good part: Nehemiah posted guards at the lowest points of the wall and grouped the people by families. The guards carried swords and spears and bows because they took the threat seriously."

"If you're expecting a siege tonight," Ky said from his dark room, "I can put your minds at rest."

Larry ignored him. "Listen to this advice about the plotting enemies." He read from his Bible. "'Don't be afraid of them. Remember the Lord, who is great and awesome, and fight for your brothers, your *sons* and your daughters, your wives and your homes.'"

"You're going to sleep out here all night?" I asked.

Ky shoved *Moby Dick* to the floor. "Larry won't let me turn on the light. How am I supposed to read?"

"There's another cot in the basement," I said to Larry. "You don't have to sleep out here alone."

"This is my job."

He was right about that.

"Can I at least have a flashlight so I can read?" asked Ky.

"Should we?" I asked Larry.

"We wouldn't want to exasperate him."

I kept a flashlight in my nightstand. I threw it to Ky. "Don't leave it on when you go to sleep."

Larry stretched and his feet poked out from under the sheet. I knelt beside him. "I'm sure going to be lonely tonight."

"That's enough of that," called Ky. "You don't want me to get sick, do you?"

I kissed Larry good-night and patted my leg to beckon Blink. "Come on, boy. You can sleep with me tonight."

Blink stared at me with his milky eyes.

"Just like old times. Come on, boy."

Blink lifted his head to yawn.

"Don't make me beg."

He rolled onto his side and stretched.

"Pleeease."

"It sounds like you're begging," Ky said.

Larry reached down to pat Blink. "You better go with her or we're not going to get any sleep tonight."

Blink hefted himself off the floor, pausing to stretch and yawn again before he sauntered into the bedroom and jumped onto the bed. By the time I'd brushed my teeth, he was on my pillow snoring.

"It's a good thing you're not a cat."

I lay in the dark, listening to Blink's snores and missing the comfort of Larry's hairy calf where I tucked my foot to fall asleep. I scooted my leg against Blink's back. Not the same thing at all. I clicked on the light. Blink looked over his shoulder at me.

"I'm going to read for a while," I said. "Is that okay with you?"

Blink jumped off the bed and put his nose to the bedroom door. Before he could bark and wake up Larry, I opened the door to let him out. He crawled under Larry's cot and moaned. Larry's bare feet still hung over the edge of the cot. I nearly touched them to wake him up to join me, but a yellow circle of light lit up my hand.

"Hi, Mom."

"Shh, I was just letting Blink out," I whispered and returned to bed.

My choices of reading material were the Bible or a referendum pamphlet on water issues in Colorado. My Bible fell open to where I'd left the bookmark listing the read-through-the-Bible assignments for each day. Genesis 22, the story of Abraham and his son, Isaac.

In the margin, I'd written that Isaac had been twenty-five when this story occurred. I now rejected that little tidbit of information. When I read the story, Isaac's skin was smooth, except for a scrape on his knee. He was eight, maybe nine years old with a tumble of black curls and two wise onyx eyes that gladdened Abraham's heart when they caught the light of Sarah's cooking fire. Did Abraham stop while collecting firewood for the altar to watch Isaac play games with the other boys? Did he leave his bed with Sarah to study Isaac's face by moonlight before they left for Moriah? Did the knife tremble in his hand?

I slammed the Bible shut and let it slide off my lap onto the floor. A wave of emotion crested. Not wanting to waken Larry, I closed the door of the bathroom and slid into the bathtub. The cold porcelain intensified my ache. I whispered into the darkness, "Don't ask me to do this."

Surrender.

"I can't. He's sixteen, for goodness' sake. I can't. I *won't.*"

Surrender.

I slid lower into the tub. "Please, please, please don't ask this of me." When I closed my eyes, the freshly honed edge of Abraham's knife stood at the ready to slash Ky's throat. My eyes popped open.

Surrender.

I sat up. With my head in my hands, I played out the future my sputtering faith envisioned for Ky—drunkenness, failure at school, clashes with the law and his family. I threw in a string of disastrous live-in girlfriends and a couple of grandchildren living in far-flung cities to darken the play as any Irish playwright would.

Surrender.

I crawled back into bed and closed my eyes tight, willing sleep to come. Instead, I cross-examined God. *How in the world am I supposed to surrender a sixteen-year-old boy to you in these days? Give him the keys and say adios? Sit back twittering my fingers and wondering what he will do next to destroy himself? He'd be dead in a week.* A shudder ran through me. Finally, I struck a workable compromise. *I'll surrender Ky to your care when you promise me nothing bad will happen to him.*

JUNE

30

*Early monsoon season? Yet another afternoon
storm darkens the valley. No complaints here.
Hyperion daylily opened today—a study
in contrast—a delicate scent from
a screaming-yellow flower.*

I stepped out of the shower to hear the doorbell ringing. I wrapped a towel around my hair and slipped into my robe. From the top of the staircase, the dome of a bald-headed man was visible through the transom. The clock chimed six a moment before Ky's alarm rang.

I opened the door. "You're early."

"Now, ain't that typical," he said with smiling eyes. "You complain when I'm late and you complain when I'm early. There's no winning with some people." Droop obviously enjoyed catching me off-guard. He scooted me aside with a wave of his hand. "I'm here for my worker."

"He's not expecting you until next week. We haven't bought the boots yet."

"That don't matter. He'll be wearing waders for the next few days." Halfway up the stairs he stopped and turned back to me. "It might be best if you went on out to your pretty garden until the boy and me get on our way. Or better yet, mosey on over to Louise's."

"I don't know . . ."

"You best decide right now if you want Ky to work like a man or not because that's what I'm here to teach him."

What choice did I have? "Okay."

Droop stomped up the stairs and thought of something else. "You wouldn't happen to have any of them Sweet Suzy strawberry thingies, would you?"

Since Larry had started his diet, I'd kept a box of Strawberry Cream Balls in the freezer—under the lima beans—for emergencies like this. "Yep."

"Now, that's a good piece of news, little lady. And how about some of that good coffee you make?" He walked down the hall to Ky's room and pounded three times on the wall. "What are you doing in bed when there's work to be done?" he yelled.

With a great deal of stumbling and mumbling, Ky prepared himself for a day of work while I made a fresh pot of coffee and headed for the freezer in the basement. I pushed aside the economy-sized bag of lima beans and retrieved two packages of cream balls for the guys and one for me. After all, I was the one who thought of asking Droop for help.

I don't know how he did it, but by the time I'd filled a Thermos with coffee and threw cheese and crackers and apples into a bag with the cream balls, Ky was dressed and sitting in Droop's truck.

"Don't worry none about the boy. I'll take good care of him."

I watched them drive down the street and turn out of sight. In the patina of a new day, golden fingers of clouds reached for the west. I prayed and fretted until the sun topped the Mesa like a cherry on a sundae.

"Come on, Blink! Daylight's burning!"

~⌒

Living in a region that receives only eight and a half inches of rain a year, it seemed strange to be rained out of an afternoon of work two days in a row. At home, I followed the sound of pounding up to the master bathroom. Blink's claws tapped down the hall to his bed. Poor fella, he'd nearly run himself ragged chasing thunder around the Pooles' yard.

Larry was too engrossed in his work to notice me clenching my chest at the bathroom door. He knelt in the shower with his utility belt low on his hips, tapping a chisel with a rubber mallet. The tile fell away from the shower wall into his hand. He added the tile to an impressive stack on the bathroom floor.

Scott had put in the master bath's shower tile after we'd poured buckets of water over our heads in lieu of a shower for almost a year. The tiling job intimidated him that much. With a *Sunset* magazine how-to book in one hand and Ky bouncing in his doorway jumper, Scott had installed the tile while I'd attended a women's retreat—my first time away from my husband and toddler.

Larry had complained about the crooked tile many times, saying in less than a day he could have the tiles down and reinstalled as good as new, which meant straight. I'd managed to redirect his energy to other projects until now. After all, you didn't hear people talking about painting over the Mona Lisa because *her* smile was crooked. Larry scraped at the grout and positioned the chisel where the tile met the wall.

Panic rippled in my chest. "Stop!"

He looked over his shoulder, smiling until he saw my face. "Hey," he said with the caution of a swimmer testing a mountain lake, "you're home."

"What are you doing?"

"I had some time. These tiles have been driving me crazy for months."

The tiles had driven me crazy at first, too. I'd almost insisted Scott hire a professional to remove them and replace them in nice straight rows. That was before I saw the square of Scott's shoulders and the approving nod of his head. To him, the tile looked professional already. Once the shower door with opaque glass was installed, I reasoned, who would know? After a few years, I'd hardly noticed the wavy line of tiles. They backdropped my life, as typical as a sweater hung over a kitchen chair.

I asked Larry, "Did you ever stop to think that I liked the tiles the way they were?"

His hands, chisel in one, hammer in the other, fell to his sides. "You *like* crooked tiles?"

"They're . . . they're homey. Straight tiles are so institutional."

He hung his head, probably thinking his wife had lost her ability to reason. But he was smarter than that. He looked up, girded for conflict. "Did Scott tile this shower? Is this yet another square of sacred ground you haven't told me about?"

"This has nothing to do with him."

"Right," he said, pushing past me into the bedroom, where he threw his tools in the toolbox. He stood before the window, arms crossed over his chest, his stance wide, poised for action.

"We should talk before you start ripping things off the wall," I said.

He settled his hands on his hips. "We talked plenty before we agreed to live in this house, and you told me you were fine with it, fine with me, fine with this being our home, Mib—yours and mine."

"I was . . . I *am* fine with living here. This is your home, *our* home. We need to talk things over is all I'm saying."

"I feel like a visitor here, Mib. I never know when I'm going to touch something or do something to upset you."

"What are you talking about?" I knew exactly what he was talking about. More problematic was telling Larry that the emotional ties I held to Scott still surfaced when I least expected them, wanted or not.

"This is more than a house to you. It's a holy shrine, and Scott is on a pedestal in every room."

"That's not true. We made the changes you wanted."

"Then let's talk about the tile, shall we?" Larry looked at the floor for a long time before he met my gaze. "Mib, honey, have you noticed that the tiles in the shower are crooked?"

I barely squeezed a yes between my lips.

"I've done a fair share of tiling in my time—never had any complaints. May I pretty please fix it?"

"Do whatever you want," I said and left the room.

He followed me down the hall.

"While you're at it," I said, "take down every photograph so you and your mother won't feel uncomfortable."

I patted the newel-post at the top of the staircase. "Scott loved this staircase. Let's rip out the balusters and handrail while you have your tools out. And the front door—it took him a month to remove the layers of paint off that door. Tomorrow's trash day. I say we take the hinge pins out this minute."

Larry leaned against the wall with his chin touching his chest. I wanted him to open both barrels at me. I deserved it, didn't I? *Come on, Larry, give it your best shot.*

"Yoohoo, is anybody home?" Connie called from downstairs.

~~~

I hadn't hidden in Scott's closet for a pity party in a long time. The timing seemed right to me. On the floor of the closet where Scott's sport shoes used to lay in a jumble, the totality of Larry's shoe inventory stood in ordered pairs. Winter work boots, a pair of cross-trainers with a broken shoestring, and then a blank space where he parked his summer work boots every night. A pair of Birkenstocks I'd given him for his birthday but he'd never worn, a pair of brown dress shoes and a pair of black dress shoes, more suitable for a bass fishing convention than a night of dancing, and a pair of navy slippers covered with cat hair. No way was I going to lie on cat hair to feel sorry for myself, but neither was I going downstairs to have Connie look at me sideways and then at her son, only to shrug and peel the potatoes like a good little soldier. I slammed the closet doors shut.

I sat on the toilet seat and stared at the shower. Besides a touch of mildew in one corner and several rows of missing tile, the shower looked the same as the day Scott had first tiled the walls. The shower-head still dripped, and the shower spray still blistered backsides when someone flushed a toilet in the house. Idiosyncrasies.

The first tile came off with one solid whack of the mallet. The second tile resisted until I switched to a heavier mallet from Larry's toolbox. Of the first ten tiles I removed, half of them broke. At that rate, only Blink would be able to use the shower, but I didn't stop.

"Are you sure you want to do that?" asked Larry, leaning against the vanity.

"More than anything."

"I see you've broken a few. Would you like some help?"

"It's cathartic."

"It's expensive."

"Cheaper than therapy." He couldn't argue with that. For the generosity of his understanding, I asked the question I'd avoided since we clashed over the kitchen door. "Can you live in this house until Ky graduates?"

"It's hard sometimes."

I'd watched Larry move through the house, looking unsettled, like someone would ask him why he was there. "I know," I said.

"I can't see how staying here has helped Ky."

"Staying here was the one thing everyone agreed on. Even the counselor we saw emphasized the importance of place in Ky's life right now."

"I wouldn't cite Dr. Laughing Hyena if you're trying to make a convincing argument."

Larry could always make me smile.

"This is an expensive house to maintain. Moving to a smaller house would reduce our expenses," he said as if offering me a dessert tray. "The mortgage alone is a killer. Natural gas is expected to double this year."

"You want to move before winter?"

"That would be preferable to moving *during* winter."

"It's a lot of work to sell a house, and who knows if it would sell or not."

"It's a nice house in a desirable neighborhood," he countered. "We won't have any trouble selling a house like this."

I slid down the shower wall to sit among the clutter of grout and broken tile. "I don't know, Larry."

"I could never give you a house like this."

"So this is a male ego thing?"

He swallowed hard before he answered. "I want to provide for you."

"You're doing that."

"In another man's house."

"It's our house. See? I'm fixing the tile."

Larry took the mallet from me and helped me stand. "You're breaking the tile."

"Can we take some time to think about this?"

"I *have* been thinking about it."

"It's just that we agreed—"

"It's time to reevaluate a lot of things."

A lot of things?

"Maybe we can go away for a weekend, take time to pray through some decisions." He kissed my forehead. "I'll be okay. *We'll* be okay. This is fresh ground we're plowing. We'll get it worked through."

I walked to the door.

"Are you hungry?" he asked. "Ma's making a sandwich for me. I'm sure she'd make one for you."

"No thanks. I think I'll go weed the garden."

~~~

Weed *schmeed*. I walked to Louise's back door.

"What a nice surprise. Come on in, sugar. I just took Virginia Prodromide's whatchacallit"—she read from the recipe card—"span . . . ah . . . ko . . . pee . . . tah, spana*ko*pita, out of the oven. Try to say that fast five times."

Louise's face glistened with sweat. She fanned herself with a magazine. "Are you hot? I'm dying. Y'all wouldn't mind if I took my blouse off, would you?" She unbuttoned the top button and wiped her hands on her pants. "Oh, for goodness' sakes. Follow me." She opened the freezer compartment of her refrigerator and unbuttoned her blouse to the cool air.

She spoke over her shoulder. "I have a new theory about global warming, and I'm dead serious about this, so don't you go pooh-poohing it. You know, don't you, that there are 40 million baby boomer women in America, all being taken off their estrogen at the same time? Every room I walk into shoots up thirty degrees. Now think of 40 million women hot flashin'. I know I'm right. Get yourself somethin' to drink, sugar, while I cool down a bit."

"Not everyone's convinced global warming can be blamed on anything but a natural cycle," I said as she buttoned up her blouse and set a plate of stuffed triangle pastries in front of me.

"On the instructions for this recipe I'm going to strongly suggest these appetizers be made with a partner. I destroyed two boxes of phyllo dough before Manley arrived home to help me. You would've thought I'd asked him to waltz down Main Street in a strapless gown, but only until the first batch came out of the oven."

The spanakopita melted in my mouth, and why wouldn't it? Butter separated the layers of phyllo dough, and warm feta and spinach oozed out of the center. "You better add cardiac paddles to the ingredient list while you're at it."

"But sugar, that's why they're so good." She bit into a triangle and dabbed a greasy smudge off her chin. "Is Larry over at his mama's working in his dahlia garden?"

"He's home repairing the tile in our bathroom."

"The tile Scott slapped up like a drunken sailor?"

I reached for another spanakopita. Louise slapped my hand. "You best get back there and give your husband a hand."

"The shower is too small for both of us."

She narrowed her eyes. "Is it now?"

"When you're swinging a mallet, it is."

Louise tipped her chin—her coy debutante pose. "Tell me this, sweet pea. Why did you marry Larry?"

I wasn't up for a game of twenty questions. "Because I loved him?"

"You love me, and you didn't marry me. You love Ky, Margaret, Andrea, and that dog of yours. But you only married Larry. Why?"

"He met a need in me no one else could meet." Never mind that he was reneging on agreements we'd made in the stupor of infatuation.

"You were a lonely little bug. It killed me that our friendship, no matter how much I loved you, could never meet that need in you. From that very first day when Larry saved you from suffocation, I knew he was the one. I nearly swooned with relief in front of the house."

I reached for a spanakopita. Louise slapped my hand again—harder.

"Ouch!"

As she talked, she tore off a piece of aluminum foil to cover the plate of appetizers. "When Adam finished naming all of the animals and saw that there wasn't a companion suitable for him, God took a li'l ol' rib out of his chest to make a woman because it wasn't good for man to be alone. It still isn't good for a man to be alone. You best get yourself home and do what God created you to be—a companion—even if that means sitting on the toilet seat and talking about a whole lot of nothing."

Ky would be home soon, and Connie was still there. I opened my mouth to protest. Louise turned me by the shoulders and slapped my bottom. "Git on home now, ya hear?" She pushed me out the door and slammed it closed behind me.

~

Ky opened the kitchen door with enough force to hit the wall with a bang. Connie dropped a freshly speared shish kebab on the floor. Ky didn't flinch. He headed for the sanctuary of his basement bedroom. I caught a whiff of his wake. I yelled after him, "Put your clothes in the washer! And use the long cycle."

"You might want to add a little bleach to the wash water," Droop said from the door, just as mud-caked as Ky.

"How did he do?" I asked.

"Once we came to an understanding, he worked real good. His attitude didn't sweeten none, but that's not your problem, and it certainly ain't mine. Work ain't always a bowl of cherries, and he sure learnt that today." He turned to go.

"Wait a minute. What did you guys do?" I asked. "You smell . . . awful."

"I best be getting home to Honey. She gets ornery if I'm late. Tell Ky I'll meet him at the curb at six A.M. or else. And he knows what *or else* means." He flashed a self-satisfied grin. "Ask your young man about fishing for finless browns. He caught a bundle of 'em." Droop ambled down the driveway toward his truck.

Larry and Connie laughed behind me.

"What?" I asked, annoyed to be on the outside of the joke. "I thought he went up there to work, and he's been fishing all day?"

"He's been fishing all right, but not for fish," Connie said. "Sounds like Droop had Ky mucking out septic systems."

Ky emerged from the basement with a towel around his waist. His hair stood glommed together in crusty spikes. Mud? Whatever it was, it caked his arms and neck. He mumbled as he walked through the kitchen, "Don't expect me for dinner. I'm never eating again."

I went down to the basement and added a few glugs of bleach and another cup of detergent to his laundry.

Humidity and mosquitoes—my scourge!
Dinner plate hibiscuses undaunted. Great
colors—burgundy, a cha-cha pink, and a yellow
showoff with a chocolate center.

Some people talk to a priest or a bartender or a counselor when their troubles mount up. In a pinch, a gardener will do. The Webleys' daughter, Lily, pulled the petals off a Shasta daisy one by one as she talked. "I keep thinking I'm going to get used to them being apart. I was totally clueless about Mom wanting to leave. I went away to school thinking time would stand still while I traveled off to Florida, and then Mom came to parents' weekend alone. 'I have something to tell you,' she said like she was going to travel or open a gallery, not move out of the house. I'm questioning everything. If my mom and dad can't love each other—these two amazingly smart and warm people—what chance do I have of finding a love to last a lifetime? The worst, though, is how totally betrayed I feel, like they left me. Crazy, huh?"

"It's not as crazy as you think." During the night a woolly layer of clouds had settled over the valley to press the heat and humidity to the valley floor. I twisted my hair onto the top of my head and pulled on my straw hat.

"Really?" Lily broke off a Shasta daisy to slide behind her ear. "I'm the one who's supposed to be in a weird place. But it's my parents who are completely out of context—Mom in her little hacienda, Dad here alone. All that I've ever believed has turned to gray. Everything has a question mark behind it."

"Have you told your parents this?"

"I could never . . . It would kill them."

Is that what Ky thought, that the truth of his feelings would crush me? "The greatest honor you can show your parents is to trust them with your heart."

Lily passed her hand through a stand of cosmos as tall as her shoulders. "What would it matter?"

I stood up to stretch my back. Lily had inherited her mother's hazel eyes but the broad analytical forehead of her father. "Maybe they can shed some light on the gray areas."

She closed her eyes to a breeze as intriguing as a whisper. More than likely, she was trying to picture herself being frank with her parents.

I batted away a mosquito humming by my ear. "You should go back inside," I said. "The mosquitoes are getting worse."

The first week Droop had come to roust Ky out of bed and take him up the mountain to work, I'd managed to be out of the house by the time he arrived all but one morning. I stood on the back porch, letting my coffee get cold and cringing at the force of Droop's tirades to wake Ky. The profane give-and-take between the two made me doubt the wisdom of asking for Droop's help. I wavered between stepping into the barrage on Ky's behalf and then Droop's. I left messages on Droop's cell phone, telling him I would understand if he wanted to back out of having my son work for him. He never returned my calls.

By the second week, Ky was washing his own clothes and putting them in the dryer. By the third week, he was packing a lunch the night before. On Tuesday of the fourth week, he stampeded down the stairs at 5:58 to be on the curb before Droop turned the corner. He'd forgotten his lunch but never complained about going hungry that day.

At the dinner table, we heard stories about Ky's work on the mountain, how he had installed more windows than Droop one day and about the property owner's preference for his tiling work over Droop's. Ky sat taller and ate voraciously everything set before him, including trout he had caught during his lunch break. So when he asked me if he could go to his friend's house for a night of movies and video games, I sat him down for a heart-to-heart.

"I want you to have fun times to remember from your high school days. But more than that, I want you to learn how to weigh the value of your life against some of the choices you're bound to come across," I said.

"I'm done with drinking, if that's what you're worried about."

"This will go a lot faster if you just listen for a while." Ky looked up at me, and I continued on. "I've seen a change in you. You're stronger physically. You handle yourself with confidence. More importantly, you're . . ."

He looked up again, waiting. Would it matter to him that he had remembered to say please and thank-you for the last few days? "You're demonstrating remarkable responsibility," I said.

"Does that mean I get my license back?"

"That's in the state's hands."

"Oh man," he complained.

"But you're not grounded anymore. You can see your friends in public or in supervised situations."

"Which are?"

"You can go to sporting events, your friends' houses if their parents are home, or organized events, like a youth group outing or—"

"Can I hang out at the mall?"

Larry and I had hashed over the hang-out-at-the-mall issue for more than an hour before I talked to Ky. To me, hanging out at the mall meant trawling for babes. No mall. No babes. Larry, however, had a history at the local mall. His first independent outings had been hanging out with his friends in the food court. He assured me that Ky strutting his stuff at the mall was a safe place to see and be seen.

"As long as you stay inside. When you leave the mall, you have to call us about your plans. *And* we want you home by ten-thirty on Friday and Saturday nights; nine the other nights."

He looked at the floor for a long time. "Okay."

"If you want to go to a friend's house, you're going to have to plan ahead. I want to talk to one of the parents before you leave the house, so don't call me from the mall and say you want to go to Jeremy's or Ryan's or—"

"I get the point."

"Bud, I wish you could see this from my point of view. It's scary to turn you out into such a crazy world. You're going to fall down—"

"I already did."

"And you got back up. That's what matters. I'm proud of the job you're doing with Droop. He says you're doing great work."

"Are we about done here?"

"I'm going to pray for you." He bowed his head when I touched his knee. "Heavenly Father, thank you for Ky. What a great young man. Bless him with many friends who respect him and think he's cool."

"Mom?"

"Yes?"

"Get to the point."

Fine. "Lord, give Ky lots of friends who think *I'm* cool and who would never do anything to make me mad. In Jesus' name—"

Before I finished the prayer, he had swung his leg over the back of his chair and headed for the phone.

"Amen."

Five minutes later, Ky handed me the phone. "It's Jeremy's dad. He wants to talk to you."

"Hey there, Mrs. Garrett. This is Rick, Jeremy's dad." He cleared his throat. "The boys want to get together for some movies at the house tonight. I don't think I've ever had a parent call to check up on me. I didn't know I had such a wild reputation."

Oh brother. "We appreciate your giving Ky and the boys a safe place to get together."

"Well, thank you. It's nice to know I'm not the only parent who's keeping an eye on the little whippersnappers."

Whippersnappers?

"I'll be here all night," he said. "I lead the most boring life on earth."

I cursed my overprotective tendencies and thanked the man.

"Jeremy wants to set things up with Ky," Rick said. "It's been real nice talking to you, Miffy."

~~∽

A pride of Ky's friends stood in the entryway, avoiding eye contact and shifting their weight from one foot to the other while Ky changed clothes upstairs.

"What are you guys doing tonight?" Larry asked.

The guys exchanged glances. "Hanging out," said Jeremy. "Play video games. Watch some movies. You know."

"What movies?"

Another exchange of looks. "Dunno."

"Where will you be tonight?" I asked to corroborate what Jeremy's dad had told me.

Much darting of eyes. "We'll be at my house, I think," Jeremy said.

Larry crossed his arms over his chest and widened his stance. "Why don't you guys talk amongst yourselves, decide where you're going before you leave the house? We like knowing that kind of stuff."

Jeremy stepped forward. "We're definitely going to my house."

"Your folks are home?" I asked.

"My mom won't let me go anywhere unless the parents are home, so it's less hassle to go to my house."

I gave him a piece of paper and a pen. "Write down your phone number and address."

"I'm at my dad's this weekend. He won't be home until eight, so we're going to the mall to hang out until he gets home."

"But I talked to your dad."

Every boy's head turned to Jeremy. He didn't miss a beat. "One of Dad's workers called from the hospital, said his wife was going in for emergency surgery. She was in an accident or something. The guy sounded pretty upset, so Dad went down there to sit with him until his family could get here from Montrose."

I looked to Larry to see if Jeremy's story registered red flags for him. Larry said, "Sounds good to me."

Apparently not.

Ky pounded down the stairs. "Let's go." He all but pushed the boys out the front door. My mind, my heart, and my mouth froze. Everything Jeremy had said sounded plausible and responsible. Why was my heart racing in my chest?

Larry closed the door behind them.

"Are you sure we should let him go?" I asked.

"He's already gone. What are you worried about?"

"I've never seen a more conniving group of boys. That Jeremy is up to no good. Did you see the way he avoided eye contact with me?" I peeked through the curtains. "Look at them. They're high-fiving one another. I'm telling you now, that father will not be home tonight."

"You read too much into things. The kid answered your questions. His dad sounds like a good guy."

I'd married a clueless man.

"Would it help if we prayed?" he asked.

What will help is to sink Ky into ten years of cryogenic sleep. On his twenty-fifth birthday, when his brain and auto insurance rates regain a sense of reasonableness, we'll wake him up for a party. "I think we should."

Larry covered my hands with his. Connie entered the living room, wiping her hands on a dish towel. "Are you praying for Ky? Let me in on this."

It had been a challenging week for Larry. Another driver quit at work and that route had been divided among the remaining drivers. That meant even longer days on the road. Plus he'd spent three evenings in the dahlia garden de-budding and weeding. His weariness weighted his prayer.

"Lord, we entrust Ky into your hands. Watch over him. Thank you for keeping your promise to complete all of the good work you've started in him. Amen." He kissed my forehead. "I'm going to get cleaned up. I may or may not come back down. If not, I'll see you in the morning."

Connie said, "I'm beat, too. I can't wait to get my nightie on."

I washed my face and put on my jammies to settle in front of the television. No cooking shows for me. I flipped through the networks, finding mostly crime shows too vivid for my tastes. The cable networks were littered with explosions and motorcycle fabricators. *Yawn.* On HGTV, a couple quibbled over sink styles for their spalike bathroom. Too frivolous. I pointed the remote at the television. Sports, sports, and more sports.

"Forget that." I pushed the power button.

I pulled the curtain back to look up and down the street. I considered calling Louise, but it was half past nine. I didn't want to wake Manley, another male in the brotherhood of early risers. Blink hefted himself from his place by the front door and walked down the hall toward his bed. The worst kind of loneliness is when your dog won't stand watch with you. I needed to distract myself.

Ice cream!

Surrendering my child into God's hands wasn't any easier while picking chunks of almond toffee out of ice cream, but the task gave me plenty of time to rethink the story of Abraham and Isaac. The father had bound his son's hands before he laid him on the altar. He surrendered Isaac, all right, but not without restraining him first. Just how was a mother supposed to apply that bit of wisdom?

I knelt beside Larry's head in the dark. "Honey?" I ran my hand up and down his forearm. "Larry? Are you awake?"

"Wha—"

"Abraham tied Isaac's hands. Yes, you surrender your children to God, but you don't let them knowingly go out and do something stupid, like remove themselves from God's care."

"I need a glass of water."

I followed him to the bathroom. "Surrender isn't enough. We still have to be smart. Abraham bound Isaac's hands so he couldn't jump off the altar. And did you ever notice that Abraham didn't know which mountain he was going to when he headed off with Isaac? God told

215

him what he needed to know as he went along, including, 'Hold it right there, Buster!'"

Larry sat on the end of the bed. "This would have made a great topic for the morning, Mib."

"I don't feel good about Ky being out with those boys."

Larry fell back on the bed. "You talked to the kid's father."

"There was something not quite right about that guy. A bit too earnest, if you ask me."

"He said he'd never had a parent call before."

"He called the kids *whippersnappers*."

Larry sat up. "Get me a shirt."

⁓

Jeremy's dad lived among the gentlemen farms that dotted the north end of the valley. In the green dashboard light, I tried to read Larry's expression. Either he was humoring the little lady or Connie's enchiladas had given him heartburn again.

"I'm probably crazy," I said.

He worked his jaw as if he were trying to swallow something bitter. "You let your imagination get the better of you sometimes."

"It's not like I'm seeing giant rabbits. I heard a man on the phone trying to sound parental. By the time you have a sixteen-year-old son, sounding parental shouldn't be that hard. Besides, I've heard of parents who actually provide alcohol for their kids and their friends. And then there are those boys who came to the door—especially Jeremy. The more I think of him, the way he acted . . . He wasn't telling the truth."

"What are you going to do when we get there?"

"Maybe we should stop by the market for some potato chips. We could say we wanted to provide the snacks."

Larry set his jaw, meaning he couldn't think of one nice thing to say about that. I let go of my hair and let the night air whip it about my face. I saw something. "Stop!"

"What?"

"Stop the car!"

"What did you see?"

"Back up, back up. Ky was sitting on a guardrail back there."

~~~

Back at home, the three of us sat around the kitchen table. Blink ambled out and sat beside Ky. I filled my largest mixing bowl with warm, soapy water for Ky's feet.

"I can take a shower," he protested.

"This will feel good." I lowered his feet into the water. "What happened?"

"First of all, you didn't talk to Jeremy's dad. You talked to his older brother, Jared. He's in college."

"Did you know that when you left the house?" Larry asked.

Ky expelled a long breath. "Yeah."

"So why were you walking home?"

"Jared handed me a beer. There was a keg and tons of kids—some college kids, too, but mostly kids from school—the popular kids. Kids I've known since middle school. I couldn't believe I was there. A kid dreams about stuff like that."

"Go on."

"Anyway, there was a girl there. She's in my trig class."

"Do you like her?"

He rolled his eyes. "Me and about a million other guys."

"She's real pretty, then?"

"Oh yeah."

"And?"

"I thought she was coming over to talk to me, but she just wanted another beer. I could tell she was smashed already, so I asked her if I could get her a Coke or something. She laughed, and then she threw up on my shoes."

"Where *are* your shoes?"

"I tossed them into the drainage ditch in front of Jeremy's house."

Eighty-five-dollar shoes into a ditch? "We could have washed them."

"Mib," warned Larry.

"I didn't want to see them again."

"So you left the party because this girl threw up on your shoes?"

"Yeah, it was pretty humiliating."

"I can only imagine."

"You can do pretty much whatever you want to me," Ky said. "I totally blew it. If she hadn't thrown up on my shoes, I would have stayed there and broken my probation. I'm not going to make any more promises to you 'cuz you won't believe me anyway. And that's completely what I deserve."

I wondered if I'd ever be able to trust him again. "I don't know what to say to you. I hardly recognize you as my son. I don't understand anything you do anymore. One minute you're—"

Larry kicked me under the table.

"What?"

"What a bummer," Larry said to Ky with heartfelt emotion. "You're looking after that girl when obviously no one there cared about her one bit, and she throws up on your shoes."

"The worst part was the way she looked at me when I offered her a Coke."

"Was it like she'd swallowed a bug?"

"Like she'd stepped in dog—"

Larry's hand flew up to stop Ky. "That's brutal, man, way brutal."

"She didn't even know my name, and I let her copy off my trig homework practically every day."

"You let her—?"

This time Larry's hand stopped me like a conversational traffic cop. "That chick's heart is ice," he said to Ky.

"She didn't even say she was sorry."

"It was cool, though, what you did."

"I guess."

"You better say good-night to your mother."

Ky kissed me good-night, right on the lips for the first time since I could remember. When I heard his door click shut, I said, "Just because a girl threw up on his shoes doesn't excuse his behavior."

"He knows that. He said so."

"So he's grounded?"

"Yep, and he knows we understand how he feels." Larry slipped down in the chair, his long legs spread out before him. "There was a girl in my earth science class, my lab partner. She had this long blond hair that caught the sunlight coming through the window. I'd noticed her around school, but I didn't have a prayer of knowing her, let alone dating her. She surprised me by being the nicest girl I'd ever met. She shared cookies from her lunch, told me funny stories about her kid brother. She had a way of moving . . ."

"And the point to your story?"

"I slipped her the homework assignment before homeroom. She'd have it copied by the time earth science rolled around. I really thought she liked me." Larry rubbed his eyes with the heels of his hands. "I asked her to the homecoming dance. She didn't even think about it. She laughed in my face. She said, 'You're kidding, right? For a minute there, I thought you were serious.' That was October. We had seven more months of class together. I kept up the whole homework thing so she wouldn't know how much she'd hurt me. I hated my junior year."

"Do you remember her name?"

"I remember she'd gained about eighty pounds by our tenth reunion."

"She could've lost it all by now."

"She'll never be as beautiful as you."

The phone rang. Ky was upstairs, Larry beside me, and I heard Blink snoring from his bed. All present and accounted for. I answered the phone.

"Mom?" came a voice pinched with emotion.

"Andrea, what's wrong?"

"Nothing, I just wanted to hear your voice. Did I wake you up?"

I told her about Ky's misadventure.

"Poor kid, and the worst part is he'll never forget her name."

"Maybe she'll get fat."

"That's real generous of you."

"Fat people can be happy." Mournful cello music played on Andrea's end of the phone line. "Andrea?"

"I shouldn't have called. I'm sorry. There's nothing you can do. This is something I have to figure out for myself."

"Would it help to talk about it?"

"I've already done too much of that already. I've made up my mind. It's time for action."

"You're not enlisting in the French Foreign Legion, are you? Because I can tell you that those hats with the flaps look good on camera, but in the Middle East, most goat herders wouldn't be caught dead in one."

"I'll keep that in mind, crazy lady."

"I love you. I'm here to listen. I'm not one bit sleepy." That was a lie.

"I love you, too. It's no big deal. I'll call tomorrow."

AUG
21

Wonders of wonders—high of 88°. New favorite sunflower: Apricot Twist! Ruffled orange-yellow petals. 2nd place goes to Ring of Fire, a burgundy red with a touch of yellow—looks like a solar eclipse. 3rd is Moulin Rouge—deep red with black folds.

Around four o'clock every summer morning, give or take an hour, sleepers in the desert southwest awake to cover themselves with the cotton blanket kept at the foot of their beds and fall back asleep to the crickets' serenade. I covered my chilled arms without opening my eyes in case the clock displayed a time disappointingly close to the time set on the alarm. In matters of sausage-making and the accuracy of pre-dawn time, ignorance truly is bliss.

I opened one eye at the sound of a car traveling down Crawford Avenue. The beam from the car's headlights slid over the ceiling and stopped briefly right before the driver hit the house with a newspaper. Then the room was dark again. My foot swiped the cool sheets on Larry's side of the bed, and a sinkhole swallowed my heart. I opened the other eye.

A quarter to five. *Maybe he's still here.*

I left my robe on the chair. The old floorboards ticked off my every step. Yellow light spilled out of the kitchen into the hallway. I found

Larry, pen in hand, waiting for me at the kitchen table.

"I was writing you a note," he said, surrounded by wads of crumpled notepaper and one sheet, still flat, poised for use before him.

I opened the cabinet over the coffeemaker. "G rated?"

"Nothing like that."

For Larry to miss a chance to volley innuendos made me turn my back on the coffeepot. He wore his hangdog look, the one that meant he'd been mining his thoughts for the right words to say and hadn't found what he was looking for. I guessed his note had to do with his feeling neglected. In the weeks since Ky's trouble at Jeremy's house, Ky had been grounded—*again*. To Larry's credit, he'd been the one to suggest we use the time to rebuild our relationship with Ky, which meant keeping him too busy to get in trouble and making him so desperate for company he would be inclined to have a conversation with his parents. During the week, we had Ky's favorite meals waiting for him when he got home from his workday with Droop. Grilled hamburgers. Tater tots. Pizzas with pools of yellow grease in the pepperoni saucers. Lots of ice cream—the chunkier the better. Nachos. Larry grilled himself salmon and ate fat-free sorbet for dessert. After dinner, we watched movies of Ky's choosing. *Napoleon Dynamite* completely baffled me, and I worried about my sanity when I started laughing at *Army of Darkness*.

On the weekends, we camped along the Crystal River and hiked to the marble quarry or drove up to Silver Jack Reservoir, where the aspen trees purred us to sleep at night. At first, our efforts proved as pleasant as slow dancing with a saguaro cactus. Ky moped and slumped and groaned, but the number and severity of our clashes dwindled. Larry and Ky regularly maligned the Rockies but watched their games religiously. I began to believe we were over the worst of Ky's bad-boy season.

For Larry to be writing a note about his feelings meant whatever was going on inside his head had reached the boiling point or he would have avoided the issue altogether, the modus operandi of three billion men around the world. I demonstrated true love and sacrifice by leaving the coffeepot behind and pulling a chair close to him. He turned the note facedown.

"What's up?" I asked.

"It's nice to see you." He leaned over to kiss me. His lips, warmed by coffee, covered mine. "Good morning."

"Something's on your mind?"

"Nothing earth-shattering. I was just hoping we could go away this weekend, just the two of us."

"We talked about taking Ky golfing in Rifle."

"I wanted to surprise you. I sold a bundle of dahlias to a florist for a wedding in Aspen. Maybe we could use the money to stay at a nice place in Glenwood Springs or that B and B we heard about in Cedaredge."

"What about Ky?"

"My mom said she'd stay with him."

That hadn't worked so well in the past. "Being alone with you for two days sounds heavenly, but—"

Larry pulled me to him, chair and all, and kissed me hungrily. He definitely didn't have his Monday morning safety meeting on his mind. Before surrendering to the vortex of passion, I liked my ducks in a row, my privacy secured, and all interruptions forestalled. Larry, and all males for that matter, didn't seem to have those same concerns.

"Don't you have a safety meeting this morning?" I asked when he finally took a breath.

"Not until five."

"It's five till."

Larry looked at the microwave clock. "Isn't that thing fast?"

"You reset it, remember?"

"Oh man." He tightened his embrace. "Safety is the last thing on my mind right now."

"Sorry, tiger, you better set your parking brake."

At the door, we kissed again, a long drink of a kiss meant to assuage our thirst for the long day ahead.

"I'll call Mom to set things up." He released me and walked down the garden path toward the garage. He turned abruptly and walked back to me. His arm went around my waist and he pulled me into another kiss. "I'd rather have my heart ripped out than leave you right now."

"That won't look good on your safety record."

"I could call in sick."

"Only five days until Glenwood Springs."

Bolstered, he ran to the garage. A slam of a car door. The rev of an engine. The whine of backing out of the garage. And he was gone.

~~

I followed the throb of a bass guitar to the bathroom. Ky flexed his bicep and eyed himself approvingly in the mirror—until our eyes met. "What are you doing home?" he asked.

"I dropped a melted cream ball in my lap."

"I thought you and Larry made a pact not to eat those things anymore."

Never mind. "And I thought you worked until four."

He turned from the mirror—a real sacrifice, duly noted. "There was a mix-up with the shingles and the floor sealer wasn't dry, so we came home early. You should come up and see the cabins. They're looking pretty good."

"Working in the mountains agrees with you."

He glanced at the mirror again, tightening his abs as he turned to admire his profile. "Yeah."

"You have a ponytail." It was a small ponytail but a first for Ky.

"My hair kept falling in my eyes. Droop suggested it. It's cooler, too."

"A haircut would help. My treat."

"Maybe before school starts."

Ky took the stairs three at a time. I followed, hoping I had another pair of clean overalls to wear. He waited for me at the top of the stairs. "Andrea called. She wants you to call back."

"Did you talk to her?"

"Nah, she left a message."

In the family room, the answering machine whirred and clicked.

"Hey, it's me, Andrea. Call me when you get home. I could use some—"

Beep!

"What? What do you need?" I asked the machine.

Ky shouted, "She can't hear you. You have to pick up the little black thing."

Choose your battles.

I looked at my watch. If I weeded the Keeneys' flower garden next and waited to fertilize Mr. Chandler's shrubs until my next visit, I could call Andrea and finish work by dinner. I punched in her phone number.

"Is there any way you can come out to see me?" she asked.

"Are you okay?"

"Sure, but something's come up."

"Is it something bad?"

"I'd rather not say."

"You're scaring me. Are you sick?"

"No, nothing like that."

"You have to tell me something."

"You know that project I've been working on? I finally found what I was looking for."

I'd never liked guessing games, mostly because I'd always suspected Margot changed the answer when I got too close in Twenty Questions. "And what would that be?"

"My mother."

Scott and Andrea's grandmother Victoria had collaborated to hide Andrea from her mother as a baby. Andrea's mother was that unreliable. I hadn't even known Scott was married previously until Andrea found Ky and me just months after Scott died. I still didn't know if Scott had ever divorced Tina before marrying me.

"Hello? Are you there?" Andrea asked.

"I'm here." Secretly, I'd wished Tina was living in a nice patio home in Siberia—not the western hemisphere. "Are you sure you want to open yourself to her?"

"People change. I'm not a baby anymore."

"Have you talked to her?"

"I have her address and phone number. The guy who tracked her down took pictures. She lives just north of here in Colonia. I can't believe we've been so close all these years."

"She may not want to see you."

"Neither did you."

That's true. I'd thought of Andrea as a stalker before I knew her. I'd slapped her when she claimed to be Scott's daughter.

Andrea continued, "It's all I can think about. I can't sleep. I can't eat. I can't stand knowing where she is, and I can't stand wondering if she cares. There's only one way to find out, but I need some backup. Would you go with me?"

"When do you want to do this?"

"The sooner the better."

⁓

"Take a look at this!" Louise held a pie over her kitchen sink and poured a swirl of pink and white down the drain. "This is another one of Susan's recipes, bless her heart. I'm completely bewildered. I've never known a woman who worked so hard at being so bad in the kitchen."

Strawberry stems filled a colander; a sugar scoop lay on the bottom of an empty canister. Rivulets of sweat streamed down Louise's face. "I'm puttin' a DNR on this Strawberry Cream Pie recipe—do not resuscitate. It's OOTR and ITT."

"Which means?"

"Out of the runnin' and into the trash."

I helped Louise clean her kitchen. No one should experience such a complete cooking disaster and then have to clean the mess alone. The activity worked in my favor. I didn't forget why I'd come to her kitchen, but talking about the advantages of cornstarch over flour as a thickening agent and the difficulty of determining the proper ratio of strawberry puree to sugar grounded me.

"Oh, for pity's sake, can we talk about something else?" Louise finally said. "I'd offer you a glass of strawberry smoothie, but honestly, I'd rather sit on an anthill than look at another strawberry. Iced tea?"

We took our drinks into the parlor. On the fireplace wall, a strip of rose wallpaper hung like a lolling tongue. Louise fanned herself with a magazine. "Sugar, when it comes your time to go through the change, take a piece of advice from me. Stay out of the kitchen."

"Are you redecorating?"

"I don't know what I'm doing. One minute the room is cluttered and tired looking. The next minute I'm a sentimental fool, sobbing over the wallpaper. Have you ever heard such drivel in your life? The wallpaper stays where it is. I have plenty to do with the cookbook. The printer wants the manuscript by October first or he can't promise to have it ready for Christmas. I'm beginning to wonder if I haven't bitten off more than I can chew—pun intended." She dropped the magazine to her lap. "Please, tell me something about your household, as long as it doesn't include a stove or an oven."

"I heard from Andrea this afternoon." I told Louise all about Andrea finding Tina and wanting me to go along to meet her.

"When are you going?"

"It's not that simple. There's the cost. I'd have to fly, because neither of our vehicles would survive the trip. Although I suppose I could rent a car. But then there's rearranging my maintenance schedule. I'm behind as it is. Folks have been patient, but I can't expect that to last. Maybe this winter."

"Sugar baby, all I'm hearing is fear—fear that your truck will break down and fear that your clients won't understand. And I suspect, even though you haven't said as much, you aren't thrilled about meeting Miss Tina, either. The Father didn't give you a spirit of timidity, but a spirit of power and love and self-discipline."

"I'm talking reality and responsibility, Louise."

"You're right about that, baby girl; fear is definitely a real thing. If I was you, I'd walk to San Francisco to be God's hand on our sweet Andrea. It's like a reverse birth. First, Tina dreamed and fretted over the life growing in her and along came Andrea. And now it's Andrea bubbling with anticipation over meeting her mama. The questions she must be turning over in her head. What color of hair does my mama have? Are her eyes like mine? What kind of woman is she? Is she a musician?"

The questions didn't matter to me. I wanted to love Larry, see Ky live long enough to have children who would exact the appropriate revenge upon him, and more than anything, I wanted to see Ky fall head over heels in love with God. I didn't want to go to California. I tried to explain my feelings to Louise.

"I hear what you're saying," she said. "But I've never heard Andrea complain for lack of friends. She asked you to go with her for a reason."

I hoped Andrea trusted me to understand the disorientation of losing and finding a mother. I opened my mouth to say so, but Louise interrupted me.

"Look at the time! I have an editorial review meeting in twenty minutes, and I'm sweatin' like a piano mover. Sugar, I'm sorry. Can we walk and talk?" I followed her up the stairs. "Andrea is as vulnerable as a newborn kitten. Her heart is reachin' out for someone who can answer to the name *Mother*. You've done a wonderful job, and so did Victoria. But now she's crossing a swollen creek on a log that's sure to bend under her weight."

Louise opened her dresser to rummage through a drawer of harem-colored satin panties. She selected a pair of fuchsia lace, and out of the next drawer retrieved the bra to match. "On this side of the creek, Andrea is safe with you. She wants to hold your hand until she can reach out for Tina's hand to feel the welcome or denial there, all the while knowing you're there to return to. But you knew that, didn't you, sugar?"

Louise clenched her dainties over her heart at the bathroom door. "I—"

"I'll be praying for you the whole time I'm in the shower, sugar." She closed the door.

"Okay," I said to the door.

The door opened again and Louise popped her head out. "I'm so glad you're still here. Can a woman die from estrogen deprivation? My brain is saying yes. Anyhoo, the cookbook committee is expecting a classy lemon cream pie. Stookie has left me in desperate straits. And the owner of Rosie's Restaurant wouldn't give me her recipe, either. Would you mind terribly submitting your lemon cream pie? I know it nearly melted Larry's heart."

"But I'm not a cancer survivor."

"No, but you're a cancer survivor's best friend. Will you?"

AUG
25

Phew, down to 94°. Hot Lips sage is two-toned again, red and white. Inchworms are eating the buddleia leaves. Applied permethrin. Don't mess with me!

We sat with the windows and doors open to the beckoning day, the sky still a soft gray, the air still cool and gentle. An ambitious robin chirped from its nest in the neighbor's ponderosa pine. Soon it would wake the thirty or so house sparrows roosting in the hawthorn, bringing an end to the halcyon hours of the morning. Larry sat across from me at the kitchen table, his Sweet Suzy shirt not yet buttoned, his neck still raw from shaving. He dug another bite from the center of the Sunshine Pie I'd baked from my grandmother's recipe. "This is the best lemon cream pie I've ever eaten," he said. "You did something different."

"This is my grandmother's recipe. She taught me how to make it when I was about ten. I'd nearly forgotten about it until Louise asked me for a recipe."

He lowered his fork. "I'm sorry I didn't get a chance to meet your grandmother to thank her from the bottom of my heart for sharing her pie recipe with you."

"She would have loved you."

"Not as much as I love you."

"But I love you more," I said.

Larry savored a huge bite of lemon cream. When he spoke again, his voice lost its playfulness. "You came to bed late last night."

"Andrea called again after you went to bed. Tina's behaving just as I feared. One moment, she sets a place and time to meet with Andrea. Before the time comes, she cancels, only to call ten minutes later to reschedule. Rather than toss and turn, I baked the pie."

"To heck with Tina."

"That's easy to say, but this is Andrea's mother. It cuts like a knife to feel unworthy of a mother's love. She begged me this time. She really wants me to be there when she meets Tina."

Larry reloaded his fork. "That's probably a good idea. If the meeting goes badly, she'll need you there." Cream stuck to the bristles of his mustache. I dabbed his whiskers with a napkin. He held my hand to his lips. I felt his warm breath. "Ten more hours."

"And we'll be zooming toward Glenwood Springs."

Before we could leave, five maintenance clients expected me. There were bills to pay, several loads of laundry to do, and a meeting with a prospective client. Most important, I planned to shop for a new swimsuit to wear in the hot springs pool. The first one-woman tent I tried on would be the winner. And I needed to pack. We'd be lucky to leave by midnight, but I didn't say so.

Larry waggled his eyebrows, and my face warmed. "I didn't expect you to eat the whole pie," I said. "Your doctor will send me hate mail."

"Not if you bake him a Sunshine Pie."

I raised a fork. "Give me a taste before you eat it all."

"Sorry, this is my pie. You said so."

I shook my fork at him. "What's mine is yours, and what's yours is mine. That's marriage. You have to share." I reached for a bite of crust and custard. Larry mantled over the pie.

"You should take a look at your schedule to plan a trip to see Andrea," he said.

"I don't see how I can get away until Ky's back in school." When it came to whipped cream, it took more than a verbal distraction to dissuade me. "Isn't it time for you to go to work?"

"I'm taking the pie with me."

I hated to beg. "Come on, just one bite."

"Nope."

With the speed of a desperate woman, I scooped a bite of custard and cream onto my fork. The custard nearly stripped the enamel off my teeth. My face puckered and the room got all watery. "How can you eat this?"

"What do you mean? This is the best pie I've ever eaten."

What have I done to deserve Lawrence Edward McManus? My face puckered again, but this time I was crying.

He stood over me. "Don't cry, Mib. Please don't cry," He raised my face to meet his, and he swiped my tears away with his thumbs before he kissed my eyelids. "Ten more hours," he whispered.

I mentally crossed everything off my list except my clients and one load of laundry—my underwear, what else? The bills could wait.

"There's something I have to tell you." I couldn't bear to look at him. "All those lemon cream pies I told you I baked. I bought them at IHOP."

"I know."

"You knew?"

"I didn't marry you for your pies."

~~~

Ky stood over me as I emptied the dryer of my underwear. "I want to stay here on my own," he said. "I won't let you down."

"We'll be gone two nights. You could slip and fall in the shower and no one would be here to call the ambulance."

Larry was zipping his suitcase closed when Ky and I entered the bedroom.

"Mom, please. I'm not a little kid. I don't need a baby-sitter."

I closed the lid on my suitcase to cover the black lace and chiffon that lay on top.

"This has nothing to do with me falling in the shower," he said. "You don't trust me. You're never going to let me live down my mistakes."

"He's right, Mib. We have to trust him sometime. Why not now?"

Why not *now*? Because I knew how hard it would be to relax while wondering what Ky was doing; because I already resented Larry's pushing me toward a decision I didn't want to make; and because I remembered a weekend I was left alone in the house at Ky's age. Who knew the upholstery on the kitchen chair would melt like that?

"I'm not saying yes, but if you stayed here alone, things would have to be different. Absolutely no friends over," I said.

He nodded. "I can deal with that."

"I don't want you going out after dark, either."

"I thought about going to a movie with Douglas." Douglas was a kid from youth group who had disappeared from Ky's map of friends. "Early show. Straight home afterward. I'll call," he promised.

I looked from Larry to Ky. You would have thought I held the power of life and death in my hands. For a boy longing for independence, I supposed I did. My last stand was an appeal to his stomach. Perhaps the threat of starvation would repress his enthusiasm. "Okay, but there isn't much to eat in the house."

"I'm a working man. I have money. I'll go to the store."

I opened my mouth to remind him of his revoked license.

"I'll change the tire on my bike. Honestly, Mom, I promise, you won't come home to a cadaver."

"Poor choice of words, Ky." Leaving him on his own for forty-eight hours would give him plenty of time and opportunity to spread his wings to fly—or to crash and burn. "You can expect random phone calls and courtesy checks by Louise and Connie."

"So it's okay? I can stay on my own?"

How much confidence or lack of confidence should I express? I leveled with him. "This is hard for me. I've lived long enough to be pessimistic about the world. This can be a dangerous place for the unwary. You must remember to turn on the porch lights, lock all of the doors day and night, and if you bake anything—"

"I won't bake anything."

"Thank you."

Larry called Connie to explain our change in plans while I finished packing my suitcase. The doorbell rang. I figured the pizza we'd ordered for Ky had arrived. Larry called up from the front door. "Mib! It's for you. You better come down here."

From the tone of his voice, I expected to see the angel of death at the front door. Instead, Margot fanned herself with a folded map. "How do you live in this heat?"

In the kitchen, I poured Margot an iced tea.

"Do you have any lemon?" she asked.

"I used them all. Sorry."

"I'll take a glass of water, then."

Margot wore a tailored linen suit, jacket and pants, with heels and hose. No wonder she was hot. "So what are you doing here?" I asked.

"I didn't have plans for the weekend, so I hopped on a plane. That's okay with you, isn't it?" She shoveled three heaping teaspoons of sugar into her water and stirred. "Actually, my therapist suggested I come."

"Oh."

Larry came into the kitchen and poured himself some iced tea. He laid down his words like a stone path. "What are you girls planning?"

"Margot's here for the weekend," I said.

"The *whole* weekend?" He downed the glass of tea. "That's . . . that's real nice." If Margot noticed Larry's sarcasm, she didn't show it. "Maybe the two of you should drive out to see Andrea," he suggested. "She'd love for you to come."

"What are you talking about?" I asked him. "We have plans. Besides, Margot hates to travel by car."

"I don't throw up anymore. I went to a hypnotist," Margot said. "Actually, I'd enjoy seeing the great American desert. I spend too much time indoors. I love San Francisco."

Who are you and what have you done with Margot?

I told Margot about the romantic getaway Larry and I had planned. And then she wanted to know about Andrea.

"Now that you're married, you can go away for a romantic weekend anytime, right? I think you should be there for Andrea."

What would I come home to if I canceled our romantic weekend for a trip to San Francisco with Margot? And how much faith could I put in a hypnotist to cure Margot of car sickness? I'd never forget the strawberry cake and ice cream she'd lost on our way home from a birthday party.

Larry came back into the kitchen. He filled his arms with popcorn-making supplies and laid it all on the counter next to the stovetop. He dribbled a thin line of oil into the pan. "With two drivers, you can drive straight out. You'd get to San Francisco in time for dinner tomorrow. That gives you all day Sunday to arrange a meeting or . . . whatever."

Did he *really* want me to go?

Did *I* really want me to go?

I'd worked double-time at my clients' homes and rescheduled my meeting with the prospective clients to get home early. I'd loaded the washer with my underwear, showered, and driven to the mall. I'd tried on approximately three hundred bathing suits to find just one that kept most of my cellulite a well-kept secret and provided invisible support without making me look like a trussed turkey. I'd believed the bathing suit I'd purchased was a travel gift from God.

"We'll be like Thelma and Louise," Margot said.

"Tell me you didn't bring a gun."

"I'm neurotic, not psychotic. But I insist we take the rental car."

"You're already packed," Larry said. "You and Margot will get to spend time together."

I heard the disappointment in his voice, so why was he encouraging me to leave?

A car trip to San Francisco was not a weekend trip. By the time I'd called my Monday and Tuesday clients to change schedules and then talked to Andrea and the hotel in Glenwood Springs, Larry and Ky were engrossed in a Rockies game. Seeing them on the sofa, eating popcorn out of a bowl between them, made me want to join them.

Larry lowered the volume with the remote. "Are you leaving?"

"I have a few things to add to my suitcase," I said and motioned with my head to invite him to follow. He filled his mouth with popcorn.

"Maybe you could help me," I said.

"Now?"

I looked at the television. From the scoreboard, I knew the Rockies were in trouble. At the bottom of the eighth inning, they were down by one with the tying run on third and one out—not a good time to have a meaningful conversation with a baseball fan. *Nevertheless* . . .

"We have to get going, Larry." I leaned hard on his name.

"Sure . . . sure, I'm coming." He stood up but didn't take a step in my direction.

"Larry!"

Ky groaned. "I can't believe he struck out. Typical."

"It's not over until the fat lady sings." Larry tossed Ky the remote. "Was there something you needed?" he asked me.

As I exchanged lingerie for jammies in my suitcase, Larry sat on the bed and peppered me with questions. "So how long do you think you'll be gone?"

"Don't forget, this was your idea."

"I didn't think you'd take me up on it."

"You're kidding. If you want me to stay, I will. I'm sure our room in Glenwood Springs is still available, and I'll tell Margot to go home."

"Andrea's expecting you. I want you to go."

His words said go, but his voice said, *Choose me! Choose me!* There was something in the begging that I resented.

I closed my suitcase. "I better get going."

~⌒

Margot drove and I gripped the door handle of the Mustang on our trek west on I–70 along the great arch of the Grand Valley toward the Utah state line. We passed farms to the north and skirted the Colorado River to the south until the river bent away from the highway to wind through the walls of Ruby Canyon. We climbed a swell that swayed through tumbles of red sandstone and juniper. When we passed the sign thanking us for visiting colorful Colorado and another sign welcoming us to Utah, the Beehive State, the landscape turned callous, with only saltbush and rabbit brush growing along the road and a range of barren mountains raking the skyline in the far distance. The highway lay before us, a rod honed to a fine point at the horizon.

"We should take Highway 50. It's more direct," insisted Margot, glancing at the open map book on my lap.

"It's a two-lane road with hundreds of miles of nothing—and I mean nothing."

"Fifteen and 80 take us too far north."

"But 15 and 80 are interstates . . . with gas stations . . . and bathrooms."

"Have you ever taken 50?" she asked.

"I've heard about it." The speedometer quivered at eighty-five. "You won't be able to drive as fast on a two-lane road."

"Let's look at the map—"

I slapped the map book closed. "You look at the road and I'll look at the map."

"We're taking Highway 50," she said, and short of wrestling the steering wheel from her, there was nothing I could do about it. "I'll stop for gas in . . . What was it? Green River? We should be fine."

We drove in silence, mostly because I was inventorying our survival gear. We'd stopped by the grocery store on the way out of Orchard City. We'd bought a six-pack of Diet Pepsi, a large bag of corn nuts—in case Margot's stomach started churning—four apples, and a bag of grapes. I had also sneaked a strawberry cream cake out of the basement freezer. But there was no snakebite kit. No broad-brimmed hats. No sunscreen. No jugs of water. We were toast.

"I never realized how isolated Orchard City is from the rest of the world," Margot said as we passed a sign warning us to watch for eagles on the highway. "There's nothing out here. It's a little creepy." The speedometer rose to ninety. At least death would be instantaneous.

"If you think this is creepy, wait until you see Highway 50. They call it the loneliest highway in America."

Margot turned on the radio and hit the scan button. It found only one radio station, and that station was playing country music. "No NPR? No wonder no one lives out here."

AUG 26

Creosote bush and rabbit brush. Blech!

"Wake up! This can't be right." Margot yelled and threw the map book into the back seat, where I slept. "We took the wrong road. There's nothing here. Check the map." She pushed frantically at the dashboard buttons. "I can't find the stupid lights!"

"We're okay, Margot," I said, sitting up. My eyes felt like cotton balls and a buzz sounded in my ears from drinking three Pepsis. "I feel great. Pull over. I'll drive so you can rest."

"Are you kidding? Who knows what's out there? I haven't seen another car for two hours. The last town we went through had an all-night truck stop. That was an hour ago. I wasn't about to stop there."

I climbed between the bucket seats to join her in the front of the car.

"We need gas—the sooner the better." Tears streamed down her face. She wiped her palms down her thighs. I weighed the danger of an anxiety attack at seventy miles per hour against a teeny-tiny white lie.

"I know exactly where we are," I said, hoping she was too busy inventing the unimaginable to remember I'd never been on Highway 50.

"You do? Really? How much farther to civilization?"

"Not far at all. . . . Maybe ten, maybe fifteen miles."

"That far?"

I feigned studying the map. "No, wait, five miles. Margot, pull over. You don't even have to get out. Crawl over the seat. I've created a nest of pillows and blankets. It's very comfy in the back seat."

"You know I can't sleep in the car."

"Don't you have sleeping pills?"

"I've been trying to quit."

"I always take one when I travel."

Margot slammed on the brakes, and I slid to the floor. She parked in the middle of the highway. Not one pair of headlights shone out of the blackness in either direction. She climbed into the back seat. When I turned on the car, the gas gauge rose lazily to indicate a quarter tank. I looked at the map again. I heard the pop of a medicine bottle and pills being shaken out.

"How many pills do you take?" I asked.

"Two . . . or three, sometimes four."

"Take two. Promise me you'll only take two."

"I already took three."

Gray tufts of creosote bush and broken glass lined either side of the two-lane highway. The half moon had long since set. The only color in the night was the yellow dash down the middle of the road. For fear the monotony of the line would lull me asleep, I kept my eyes sweeping from rearview mirror to side mirror to the reaches of the headlights.

"Margot," I whispered, "are you awake?" My voice grew louder. "Margot, are you sleeping yet?"

I slowed to fifty miles per hour to save gas and clicked the radio on and then right off again. If ever there was a time to pray, this was it. *Lord, you know how much gas we have and how far we have to go to get more. You know every obstacle, every escaped convict, and every nail on this long stretch of highway, and every belt and cap and doohickey in the engine*

of this car that might snap, pop, or blow. . . . Get us to the next town, Lord,
and let there be a gas station. Amen.

The dashboard clock shone three-thirty, but of course, that was
Mountain time. Three more hours to sunup. I turned the radio back
on, but the twangy song it played only served as a background to my
fretting—not so much about the road but how I'd left Larry. He would
be up, wondering where we were. I fished my cell phone out of my
purse. No service.

"Just as well," I said to the crushing blackness. Larry's behavior had
been childlike, not to mention rude. He'd barely greeted Margot. He'd
told me to go but didn't really mean it. What was I supposed to do?
Tina had been like the bogeyman to me, threatening but never encountered. Andrea said she was pretty. I remembered the one picture I'd
seen of her, enormously pregnant with Andrea on the Fourth of July.
She sat next to Scott, holding a sparkler. Now that time had separated
me from the shock of Tina's existence, I agreed that she was beautiful
in an academic sort of way. And here I was, on my way to meet her.
The dashboard pinged and a small gas pump lit up under the gas
gauge. The needle pointed steadily at the midpoint between a quarter
tank and the huge *E*.

A sign announced the junction of Highway 361 in five miles. *Lord,*
I've always thought of highway junctions as splendid places to put gas sta-
tions. A hand-painted sign, cracked and peeling, promised full services
at the Hardy Gas and Convenience Stop two miles ahead. The gas
gauge needle pointed insolently at the *E*.

I can walk two miles, but you know, Lord, I'd rather not.

The Hardy Gas and Convenience Stop blazed with lights. I parked
by the pumps. A sign read, "NO CC AT PUMPS! COME IN FOR FREE
CUP OF COFFY AND PURSNAL SERVUS." Inside, a woman with a
coal-black braid draped over her shoulder looked up from watching
Happy Days.

"Do you have a bathroom?" I asked.

The cashier lowered the volume on the television. She handed me
a key and directed me back through the doors and around the corner
of the building. "Do you need a fill-up? Unleaded or regular?"

"Unleaded."

"I'll wake Tiny."

"I can pump my own gas in just a minute. It's no trouble."

"Tiny doesn't like no one touching his pumps," she said, waddling toward the back of the shop. "We'll both be better off if I wake him up." She waved over her shoulder and disappeared past a bucket and mop. I followed her instructions to the bathroom.

The store was empty when I returned, but I heard the woman cajoling Tiny to wake up. The wait gave me a chance to look for a sugary snack. I squeezed a Sweet Suzy Coconut Dream Cake. Hard as a rock. The image of the little blond girl on the cellophane made me remember the way Larry carried the scents of dust, sweat, and sugar home from his delivery route. I sighed and poured myself a cup of coffee as dense as ink. Three hazelnut creamers and a French vanilla didn't help. The coffee remained the color of dirt, so I added a raspberry creamer to make things interesting, and hopefully, lighter. No such luck.

The woman with the braid and full-moon face returned. "Tiny's moving like a snail this morning. He'll be out in a minute. That coffee's burned. I'll make new."

I waited for Tiny to make an appearance with more than a little dread. Before long, the scent of coffee awakened my appetite. I gathered one item from each food group. When I spotted trail mix with raisins and M&M's, I returned the cheese crackers and raspberry-filled chocolate balls and picked up a teriyaki beef jerky. What would Margot like? I selected a bottle of Evian water. Out the front window, a man, stoop-shouldered with tufts of white hair rising inharmoniously from his head shuffled toward the Mustang. Tiny? I laid my purchases on the counter.

"He'll wash your windows, too," the woman said.

Tiny wore overalls and had bare arms as pale as rising baguettes and a look of perplexity as he fumbled with the gas cap. "Maybe I should go out and help him," I said.

"I wouldn't do that," she said quickly, and then she shrugged. "He likes to work alone."

Thirty minutes later, Tiny finished filling the gas tank and cleaning bugs from all of the windows and the side mirrors. By then, the gossamer light of dawn lay soft and hopeful on the desert. I paid the woman and squeezed past Tiny toward the car, learning exactly why he liked to work alone. I revved the engine and watched the needle climb to F. I pressed the accelerator to the floor. When I hit eighty, I set the cruise control and sipped at my coffee. My goal was to reach civilization by the time Margot woke. According to the braided woman, Fallon was only fifty miles farther, and Reno another sixty. *Two hours?* Behind us, the sun rose to turn the tufts of rabbit brush golden. Alkaline salts powdered the ground like snow. I listened to an all-news radio station and ate half of the trail mix. When I passed a sign saying three miles to Fallon, I decided to wake up my sister.

"Hey, Margot, we're coming into Fallon. Do you want something to eat? How about a bathroom break? Margot?"

Not one sound came from the back seat. I turned down the radio and looked over my shoulder. An empty pillow lay where her head should have been.

~~~

Margot sat on a pile of newspapers and leaned against a magazine rack, sleeping and snoring with a pitiful moan on each exhale. The corner of her mouth glistened in the low beam of morning. Drool.

"She was pretty upset when she came out of the bathroom and you were gone," whispered the cashier. "I told her you would notice sooner or later. She tried calling your cell phone, but cell phones are pretty useless out here. Tiny comes out and I think to myself, 'Uh-oh, there's gonna be trouble now.' He whispers to her, 'Sit down, little sparrow. It's not time to be alarmed. It's time to rest.' She looked just like my cousin Esther when she found out she was pregnant with her ninth child, but she sat down. And pretty soon, I hear her snoring."

An empty Twinkie wrapper lay at Margot's feet. "What do I owe you?" I asked.

The braided woman waved away the question. "I should pay you. We haven't had this much excitement since a truckload of turnips turned over on the highway. We got plenty tired of turnips, I can tell you."

Margot woke with a start. "Mibby? Mibby! You came back! You came back!" She was about to embrace me when she stopped, blinked, and wound up a paralyzer. She nailed my arm where the muscle barely covered the bone. My arm hung at my side. "You left me, you brat! You drove off without me. You didn't even ask if I wanted anything."

"You were sleeping! I didn't want to wake you!" I said, bent over. I chanced a look at her.

Her face softened. "You came back."

I stood up. "Of course I came back. You're my sister."

Margot embraced me and kissed my cheek. "I knew you'd come back."

The woman behind the counter said, "Tiny ain't using his bed in the back. Maybe you should rest before going on."

Margot and I spoke in unison, "No, thank you."

"Don't miss the shoe tree," called the woman as we reached the door. "Drive down the highway a piece. It's the only tree; you can't miss it. Some folks say there's five hundred pairs of shoes on that tree. It's really something."

Margot got behind the wheel. I said a silent prayer and commanded myself not to look at the speedometer. After several miles and some drifting over the center dividing line, I asked, "How's work?"

"The same."

"Are you dating anyone?"

"No."

"I'm really sorry I left you behind."

"You are?"

"Of course I am."

"It's just that . . . you know, I'm sorry I hit you."

Margot sped toward what had to be the shoe tree, since it was the only tree in a sea of ashen earth. Two cars were parked in the shade of the cottonwood, and a cyclist posed for a picture in front of the tree with his bike. The braided woman hadn't exaggerated. Hundreds of pairs of shoes, mostly tennies, hung over the tree's branches by their laces. Almost as many shoes littered the base of the tree.

"Maybe we should stop," I said. "Take a picture."

Margot glanced sideways at me and the car accelerated.

The shimmer of heat rising from the road made my eyes ache to close, but I feared Margot would fall asleep at the wheel. I drank the last of the coffee and swallowed a mouthful of grounds. Then I picked the M&M's out of the trail mix. If I fell asleep at my post, at least I would die fully chocolatinated and happy.

We finally hit I–80 and then stopped in Sparks to eat, ordering root beer floats to go. Billows of smoke from forest fires rose against the colorless sky above the mountains to the south. The highway between Reno and Truckee, California, was congested with travelers heading west toward the cooler temperatures of the High Sierras and the coastal regions of northern California. When we passed a sign welcoming us to California, we cheered.

Margot took a long draw on her root beer float. "Do you remember going to the Beach Hut for root beer floats with Dad?"

I remembered Dad carrying me on his shoulders and Margot complaining the whole way. "Sure, and watching the sunsets on the breakwater."

"Do you know why we did that?"

"We always celebrated when Dad returned from a fire."

"That's what he told us, but I know the real reason," Margot said.

In big and small ways we remained the children we had been. Margot had always loved dumping bad news into my lap to see my reaction. But I wasn't ten years old anymore. "The past is both lighter and darker than we remember it," I said. "It's best to leave it alone."

"Dad wasn't going to fires. They sacked him for drinking on duty."

"That's ridiculous."

"Is it? I heard him talking to his girlfriend."

"His girlfriend? Are you nuts?"

I instantly regretted both of the questions. The first one because in the asking, I'd given Margot a club to pound memories of my father. The second because the answer might be yes, and Margot was driving fast.

"Dad brought Denise to the house lots of times when Mother was off to her meetings," she said, passing a black Mercedes on the steep grade. "I caught them making out in the kitchen one night. Dad had his hand—"

"You're making this up!"

"And why would I do that?"

"You're right. You wouldn't."

"I told Mother what I saw, the two of them clutching and practically chewing each other's faces off." Margot darted between a Humvee and a sports car to pass a minivan towing a trailer. My heart pounded. Margot pressed the accelerator. "That's why I didn't go places with Daddy unless I had to. His drinking and infidelity are what drove Mother away."

"Why haven't you told me this before?"

"Because I would have told you to hurt you."

We sped along between the granite cut of the mountain and a plunge to the Truckee River below. I couldn't see how running into the mountain or falling off of it could hurt any more than what Margot had told me, so I asked her, "So why are you telling me now?"

"You're not a child anymore, but you still like your heroes spic and span. Dad wasn't a monster, but he wasn't a saint, either. Perhaps Tina isn't the wicked witch of the west or the tooth fairy. Maybe she's just a woman carrying baggage no one can see. Maybe she had a good reason to leave Andrea in the care of her grandmother, and especially for not coming back to claim her."

Since when was Margot an expert on motherhood? "Just how many good reasons can you think of for leaving a child?" I asked her.

"Part of my job at the hospital is doing spot checks on the wards to make sure the nurses follow protocol. I do random reviews of charts and interview patients. A few years ago, I met a girl named Danica. Her mother got tired of her asking when dinner would be ready, so she threw hot bacon grease in her daughter's face. The only good news in the story is that Danica won't be able to see how disfigured she is because the grease blinded her. I wish *that* mother had left her child."

"You underestimate me, Margot. I have nothing but pity for Tina. She lost out on raising Andrea. I figure Tina has some kind of mental issue going on. Maybe she's bipolar."

"But are you willing to credit Tina for giving Andrea a safer home, or are you too afraid Andrea will love her more?" Margot glanced over to gauge the effect of her question. I recognized the look in her eye. Like so many times before, Margot had stalked me, waiting for the moment when my heart was about to deflate from exhaustion. "Also, you should know," she said, "Dad didn't die in a wildfire. That was Grandma's story. He was moving to Redlands with his girlfriend and Roger, her little brat son. Dad lost control of the car. He hit another car head-on. The people in the other car died, too. They think he'd been drinking."

"Stop the car!" I screamed. "Stop the car!"

"Calm down. I'll get off at the next exit."

Her calm voice scraped my bones like a knife. I turned toward the passenger window. I couldn't bear for her to see my tears. She slowed to exit the interstate. The rumble of the road stoked my anger. I opened the door before the car came to a stop. Margot grabbed my arm and held it until we parked in the shade of a ponderosa pine.

"Let go!" I shook her hand free and grabbed my purse in case she exacted revenge and drove off without me. Shame on me, I wished she would. I walked into the trees a stone's throw from the interstate on a cushiony bed of pine needles. It was hot—hotter than I imagined the mountains could be. My steps released the sharp scent of pine resin. A steady flow of tires on concrete droned on the interstate. Not exactly the most private place to grieve the dethroning of my first prince, my father.

"I'll wait for you here!" Margot called after me.

Fabulous.

I leaned against the rough trunk of a pine and slid to the ground. For all of Margot's faults, she never lied. She didn't have to. She wielded the truth as treacherously as any sword.

There are two periods of my life scored by a precise cut: before Dad died and after. The memories that ran on either side of the line remained crystal clear in my mind, like the night Dad had come into our bedroom to say good-bye. The squeak of the door hinges woke me before he leaned over the bed to whisper. His breath showered my face with the familiar scents of beer and cigarettes. "I'm going to be gone for a long time, pumpkin." He spoke slowly and deliberately.

When he'd left for fires before, his words had tugged at him impatiently, so I asked, "Where are you going?"

"Redlands."

"Where's that?"

"Near San Bernardino."

"That's kind of far, Dad."

"It is, but I'll call you when I get there so you'll know how to get in touch with me. You can call me about anything, pumpkin. Just because I'm far away doesn't mean I'm not your dad."

"I know that," I said with the self-assurance of a fifteen-year-old.

"You're a smart, sweet girl. Don't ever change." He stroked my bangs away from my forehead, which I hated. "You can come and see me anytime you want. Just say the word and I'll buy you and your sister a bus ticket, or I'll come back here. We can work that out."

A knot of panic tightened my throat. "How long are you going to be gone?"

"I don't know."

"Be careful."

"I will, baby. I will." He kissed my forehead and turned toward the door.

"Aren't you going to say good-bye to Margot?"

"I'll call her when we stop."

And he was gone.

Dad had awoken me to say good-bye, not her. That was something I could wad into a tight ball and throw in her face. *Ha!* Like two strong hands on my shoulders, a verse I'd memorized with Ky during his Awana days turned me away from revenge. *Even if my father and mother abandon me, the Lord will hold me close.*

My anger at Margot collapsed into a heap. A jumble of shame and gratitude and marrow-sucking fatigue compressed me into a two-dimensional cutout of myself.

Margot napped in the reclined car seat. Her mouth hung open, and I didn't even wish for a fly to land on her tongue. Instead, I prayed for my sister. "Lord, holder of the fatherless and motherless, embrace Margot. Swipe her hair away from her face and kiss her forehead to awaken her sleeping faith. In Jesus' name, amen."

"Margot, honey, wake up," I said, rubbing her shoulder through the driver's window. "I have something to tell you."

She opened one eye. "Do you have a gun?"

"No, but hear this. I won't be your clay pigeon anymore. Do you know what I mean by that?"

She nodded.

"I promise to hold your heart like a sleeping child to my chest."

Margot pulled up on the door handle with such force I feared she would tackle me and sock my arm again. Instead, she clung to me like a drowning woman. A miracle happened in the tears of our regrets. In that moment, Margot and I became sisters, the kind you read about in *Reader's Digest* and *Parade*. The kind of sisters who give kidneys to one another. They drop everything just because one of them needs to talk. They climb Mount Everest or trek through rainforest or sail around the world, just the two of them. More than likely, but no less wondrous, they are completely safe in each other's company. No more paralyzing punches for me. No more suspicion for her.

Back on I–80, a river of cars traveling above the speed limit pulled us along in their current. The steeper the downgrade, the faster we hurled toward the Sacramento Valley. "I saw a billboard for an In-N-Out Burger in Auburn," Margot said.

We drove several blocks beyond the restaurant to find a parking space. Margot parked the car in the shade of a eucalyptus tree. My muscles resisted attempts to stretch. There would be time for stretching later, after a cup of hot coffee. I flung my purse over my shoulder and headed for the restaurant with java on my mind, and yes, a boatload of French fries.

Margot took my hand. "Let's walk for a while. My muscles are like knots."

"I've never been this tired in my whole life."

"Sure you have. Remember the year you graduated from high school? We drove to Oregon to visit Mother. We didn't have enough money for a motel, so we drove through the night."

I remembered, all right. "You threw up six times."

"Thanks for reminding me."

We lengthened our strides as our muscles warmed.

"We sang 'Found a Peanut' from Grants Pass to Eugene," I said.

"Just thinking about that song makes my stomach queasy." Margot and I exchanged a glance. We'd never mention the song again.

In the restaurant, Margot showed me how to drink down a chocolate shake and add a cup of coffee. "Voilà, a mocha!"

I sipped on my drink as the interstate expanded to eight lanes. We traveled with ten million of our closest friends—and I mean *close* friends. Margot drove with one hand on the wheel, accelerating and braking, dodging into faster lanes, swearing at drivers who beat her move, all the while tapping the beat of a song on the radio against the steering wheel. I crushed the sides of the cup.

"Have you called Larry since we left?" she asked.

"Maybe I should." The answering machine picked up the call. I was relieved and disappointed at the same time. "Hey, you guys, you aren't having fun without me, are you? I don't mean to rub it in, but I just finished a cheeseburger, an order of fries, and a chocolate shake from In-N-Out Burger. Eat your hearts out. Anyway, we're creeping up on Vacaville and doing fine. I'll call when we get to the motel."

AUG 27

Every plant that requires deep shade in Colorado thrives in the sun and fog of San Francisco—fuchsias, rhododendrons, azaleas, ferns—the list goes on and on. I'm so jealous!

It took me ten minutes to maneuver the rental car between two colossal SUVs in front of Andrea's apartment. Margot had stayed at the motel, saying she needed to make some phone calls. Andrea and I walked to Delphia's Cajun Restaurant for a late breakfast. We sat in the morning sun with a well-dressed couple, college students with dreadlocks and opinionated sweatshirts, and a tourist toting a Ghirardelli Square shopping bag. San Francisco.

Inside the restaurant, the waitress welcomed Andrea by name and poured coffee. Andrea ordered a plate of beignets. The waitstaff, harried yet blasé, turned sideways to carry plates heaped with food between the tightly packed tables. A ceramic bowl of rhubarb and strawberry jam and a bottle of homemade ketchup marked *Hot* sat on each table. The waitress set the plate of beignets between us.

"Stop staring at my nose ring," Andrea said.

"It's bigger than I expected."

"I like it." Andrea tore apart her beignet. Her hair hung straight, past her shoulders. She looked younger to me. Not one trace of the red stripes Louise had dyed into her hair remained, but the nose ring was as big as a door knocker. What was she thinking?

"You look beautiful," I said. The beignets were pillows of pastry heavily dusted with powdered sugar. Andrea's nose ring was soon sugared, as well.

"I talked to Tina yesterday," she said. "We're supposed to go to her house between two and three. That way her husband won't be home. He's not too excited about me. He thinks I want money. He's the reason Tina called off our meetings, so her reluctance had nothing to do with me. That's a relief."

The menu listed eggs Benedict with trout and red beans and sausage, so I ordered rice pudding porridge with currants and raspberry sauce. Something safe. Andrea ordered a vegetarian omelet with a buttermilk biscuit.

"What do you want from meeting your mother?" I asked and sipped the hot coffee with chicory. *Not bad.*

"*Not* her money, that's for sure."

"I know, but you need to be aware of your expectations. Do you want a traditional relationship with her? Do you want friendship or just a few questions answered? When you came to me, you were concerned about health-related issues concerning your father."

Andrea smiled. "I was playing on your motherly instincts."

"Your plan worked."

The waitress set our breakfasts before us. A spiral of raspberry puree topped my rice porridge. I sprinkled currants over the top and flooded the bowl with cream. "I don't want you to get hurt."

"I'm counting on being hurt. I'm not doing this to feel good."

"Then why *are* you seeing her?"

"I have to. She's my mother, whatever that means. I want to look into her eyes, see if I got my flat chest from her, smell her skin to see if her scent awakens a part of me that's been asleep." Andrea filled her fork with egg and avocado. "I want to know if she's crazy. I don't know, maybe I inherited something from her."

"You didn't. You're perfectly fine. You have a beautiful mind."

"Sometimes I . . ."

I reached across the table to still her hand. "You aren't crazy."

She lowered her eyes and shook her head. "I've felt crazy since I started looking for her. I wanted to find her. I didn't want to find her. I dreamed about her. Sometimes in my dreams she welcomed me with open arms and smelled of lavender water. Another time, she chased me with a hoe."

"That would've been me."

Her eyes smiled. "Yeah, that's what I thought when I woke up, too."

"Nothing you've said worries me."

"I've driven by her house fifty times."

"You're curious and tenacious, that's all."

"I stole a letter I wrote out of her mailbox."

"That's a felony, not craziness."

Andrea pushed a piece of potato around her plate. "I don't know."

"I wouldn't mention any of this to Tina, but no, you're not one bit crazier than I am."

Finally, she laughed.

~~~

We drove north on Highway 101 through a wide trough of a valley between rolling hills chenilled by oak and bay laurel trees and the golden grass of summer. This was the California that still teased me into believing the state held a place for me. Margot had begged off joining us. I wanted to include her, but she insisted she wanted to do some shopping in the city.

"Turn left at the bottom of the off-ramp," Andrea directed.

Since discovering Tina's link to my life, I'd pictured her living in a small bungalow in the college district of some espresso-driven town, probably Berkeley. Tie-dyed curtains covered the windows. A Volkswagen van was parked over the remnants of a lawn. Once we'd passed the quaint downtown area of Colonia and wound our way into the hills, I seriously doubted my assumptions.

"This is it. Pull over here," Andrea said.

We parked in front of a house with the biggest roof I'd ever seen. A broad stone path led to a massive front door. "Are you sure?"

"Two-six-one-four Avenida de los Robles. This is it." She held her hand over her heart. "Do you think we should pray or something?"

Stuck in the twilight between my expectations and reality, I said, "Sure."

"You go."

"Well . . . uh . . . Lord, prepare a place for Andrea in Tina's heart and stand guard over Andrea, as you promised you would." *And me, too.* "Amen." When I opened my eyes, the rearview mirror flashed with red and blue lights. The officer tapped on my window.

"Hello, officer, is there a problem?"

He scanned the contents of the car. "The resident of this home has logged a complaint about you."

I hoped he didn't notice the extra sugar and creamer packets I'd pilfered from Taco Bell.

Andrea leaned across the console to talk to the officer. "We were invited by the woman who lives here. We haven't been here more than two minutes." She opened the passenger door and got out.

"Ma'am, I'm going to have to insist that you get back inside the car."

Andrea turned and walked toward the front door. The officer hurried after her. "I'll straighten this out," she said. "I'm visiting my mother. She'll tell you."

I left the car, too, but when the front door opened, I stopped at the sidewalk. A man, Andrea's height, redheaded and balding, spoke from the porch. "I don't know who this young woman is, Officer. She hasn't been invited to this house. I want her gone." He spoke with the disdain of a man returning his overcooked steak back to the kitchen.

"Is this the Tidwell residence?" Andrea asked the man.

When the man didn't answer, the officer prompted him.

"Yes, this is the Tidwell residence," he said, speaking to the officer.

Andrea stepped toward the man. "Does Tina Tidwell live here?"

"No one named Tina lives here."

"Maybe you know her by another name," Andrea said. "Could you tell your wife that her daughter is here to see her?"

"I live alone."

"That's not possible. I have pictures of my mother in front of this house."

The officer tipped his hat at the man and ushered Andrea by the arm toward the car. "It's best that you leave."

She yanked her arm from the policeman's grasp. She faced the man on the porch. "You're lying! Is my mother all right? What have you done to her?"

The front door slammed shut. When it did, Andrea collapsed into a ball to weep. The officer looked up and down the street as if he were expecting backup. I said to him, "I'll take care of her." Andrea's shoulders heaved under my embrace.

The officer removed his cap and wiped his brow with his sleeve. "Maybe you wrote the wrong house number down. Avenida de los Robles goes on for three to four miles, at least." He looked to be the same age as Andrea, and I could tell that he'd been captured by her exotic beauty, even with the door knocker in the middle of her face. "I could check on my computer for other Tidwells in Colonia, if you like."

I urged Andrea to stand. "That's kind of you," I told the officer, "but that won't be necessary."

Andrea and I traveled in silence down the winding road back to the highway and south over the Golden Gate Bridge and into the tangle of the city. "He found out somehow," Andrea said with a voice thick from crying.

"Tina probably said something."

"She wouldn't. Maybe he came home and saw that she was expecting someone. You don't think he's some kind of control freak, do you? Maybe he threatened her if she didn't tell him who was coming."

"That's possible," I said, not believing the scenario was possible at all.

"Maybe she'll call when he goes back to work. Not today, but tomorrow when he wouldn't expect her to call. Do you think he has a private investigator watching her?"

"That would make him paranoid."

"I saw a movie—"

"Andrea?"

"Yeah, I know."

"You were very brave."

"My knees were shaking the whole time."

"But you didn't stop. You kept going. That's brave."

"Do you think she'll call?"

"I hope so."

"I'm sorry. You came all this way for nothing."

AUG
28

*Humidity—love it and hate it. The flowers seem
bigger, their color more vibrant. A non-
horticultural observation, however—my hair
frizzes and I sweat more, so I'm bigger and
more vibrant, too. Not a good thing.*

I tucked my bare legs inside the sweatshirt and pulled up the hood. The twenty or so ducks on the pond watched as I opened the bread bag. One of the ducks quacked and then another joined in, yet they watched warily from mid-pond, paddling to the left and right to observe me with both of their beady eyes. Canopies of oak trees, some varieties I couldn't identify, some as familiar and comforting as old friends, spread their long arms to shelter the park, a grassy place meant to set the mood for people coming home to Colonia after a long day in the city. My plan was to sit on the grass feeding ducks, hoping to see a balding redheaded guy drive by on his way to work. Hopefully, that would mean the coast was clear for an early-morning visit to Tina. I planned on using the phone number I'd taken from Andrea's purse to call Tina. It was a long shot.

I tore a slice of bread into small pieces and scattered them on the water. Much quacking and frantic paddling and the bread was gone. The ducks stormed the beach. I threw quartered and then halved pieces of bread on the shoreline. The ducks pressed forward and poked at my legs with their beaks.

"Hey now, let's not get out of hand."

A latecomer, a mallard with a jaunty gait, waddled through the hoard. I dropped a piece of bread at his feet. He must have preferred whole wheat. He caught a piece of my shin in his beak instead.

"Ouch! Stop that, you nasty duck."

I jumped onto the picnic bench. A warm stream of blood ran down my leg to show I'd battled a bunch of ducks and lost. I emptied the remaining bread onto the ground and ran. Just as I reached the sidewalk, a two-seater sports car, Italian-looking with its wire-spoked wheels and sleek body, drove by. At the wheel sat Mr. Tidwell.

I punched Tina's phone number into the cell phone and pulled into traffic. The phone rang five times before she answered. "Hello?"

I had stared at the motel's ceiling to rehearse my first words to Tina over and over. At the sound of her voice, all the poetic words of gentle persuasion vanished from my mind. "This is Mibby Garrett, Scott's widow. I'm in Colonia. I can be at your house in five minutes." Static filled the silence. I waved another car through the four-way stop and waited.

"The girl told me about you," she finally said. "The garage will be open. Park in there. I'll be in the garden." She hung up.

Tina turned at the sound of the garden gate opening. Backlit by the morning light, she looked angelic. No horns or tail. She wore a celadon green tunic covered with white cranes flying helter-skelter—very Asian, especially with the slim line of her capri pants. Most surprising of all— Tina was a blonde.

"The girl isn't with you?" she asked.

"Your daughter? No, she doesn't know I'm here."

She wrung her hands. "I don't know how to apologize for what happened yesterday. My husband wasn't supposed to be in town. He took an earlier flight. He's very protective." She motioned toward a patio table and chairs. A pitcher of tea and three glasses of ice sat on a serving tray. "Please, won't you sit down?"

I would have preferred a cup of coffee to replace the one I'd left on the picnic table. "That would be nice." While Tina poured the tea, I took in her garden. Beyond the stone patio, a narrow swath of grass ran the length of a waist-high stone wall, the first of three walls to terrace the hill behind the house. Roses, azaleas, and a saucy bougainvillea all seemed to bow toward the patio, waiting for the drama to begin. The garden was colorful but not terribly imaginative. Only a haphazard selection of surefire performers filled the space. At the top of the hill, a line of mixed conifers screened any evidence of a neighbor. A giant deodar cedar stood among them with tiered skirts of boughs. How I envied the gentle coastal climate that nurtured the hibiscus, the Japanese maples, and the dwarf lemon tree that grew among her flowers.

I stirred sugar into my tea. "Does your husband know that Andrea's claims are true?"

Tina looked into her iced tea and shook her head. "No."

"She was crushed, you know. You could have saved her a night of anguish."

Tina lifted her forget-me-not eyes, and I nearly gasped. The probability of blue-eyed Scott fathering Andrea with her black eyes was extremely unlikely, if I remembered my Biology 101 correctly. Not one bit of relief settled in my heart as I had anticipated. Andrea was still my daughter, and I was her she-bear, claws at the ready, willing to bite if necessary.

Tina said, "When you called just now, I expected her to be with you. I was going to apologize."

"She won't come here again unless I'm sure she will be welcomed." That came out more adversarial than I'd planned. *Lord, help me to do and say what's best for Andrea.* "Tina, I want to assure you that you have nothing to worry about in regard to Andrea. She's very grounded, yet optimistic in her expectations. I'd hate to see that change about her. She's rebuilt her life since her grandmother, your mother, died."

Tina looked beyond me to her house, twisting a diamond ring on her pinkie.

"Andrea's a gifted cellist," I said, hoping to awaken Tina's maternal instincts. "Her dream is to play professionally, and she has the talent to do it. For now, she's teaching music in the city for the public schools.

Her students love her." *Couldn't you?* "She's taught me so much. She's so wise. And although the piercings are a definite distraction, she's gorgeous. Tina, she has questions she hopes you can answer. That's all."

"How old are you?" she asked.

"Forty."

"So you were nothing but a girl when Scott married you. He was such a softy. He brought home countless dogs and cats—and me—until our landlord found out. Perhaps you are here to have *your* questions answered."

Yes! No! "I'm only here to ask you, one mother to another, to see Andrea just once, so she can satisfy her curiosity about you."

"Do you see much of Andrea in me?"

The blond hair? In the short time I'd known Andrea, she'd colored her dark hair with all-over red stripes and later with purple strands around her face. She had a sense of adventure where her hair was concerned. *So yes, that could be Tina.* The blue eyes? *No.* Her birdlike build? *Definitely.* The graceful line of Tina's collarbone, as delicate as a china cup? *Oh yes.* But Tina's lips swelled as if stung by a bee. *Collagen injections?* The self-protective fortress that surrounded Tina? *Never.*

"A little," I said, feeling stingy, but then I added, "Your builds are very similar, but Andrea's eyes and hair are almost black."

Tina's face flushed with a memory. Was she thinking of Andrea's real father? "I've lightened my hair for years," she said, lowering her eyes and tucking a strand of hair behind her ear. "How about Scott? Does Andrea resemble Scott?"

"Mostly in character. There was a time I doubted Scott was Andrea's father."

Tina's eyes shot up.

"But knowing or not knowing his role in her birth wouldn't change anything now. Andrea is a part of my family."

"You must think I'm terrible to go all of these years without looking for my own daughter."

Actually, I'd assumed Tina had called every relative looking for her mother and Andrea, and when she didn't find them among her family, I imagined her driving from one end of California to the other, looking for a place her mother would feel comfortable raising a child, a place where people were content to keep their secrets. "Few of us are the mothers we dreamed of being," I said. "Certainly not me."

Tina played with the hem of a place mat. "I wasn't well."

"And now?"

"George takes very good care of me."

"Will you see Andrea?" I asked.

Tina chewed on her lip before answering. "Tell her I'll contact her when George goes on a trip. He's going to Singapore in a few weeks. His absence will make meeting much easier for us. She lives in the city, doesn't she? I know a quiet place to have lunch."

Andrea needed more than a quiet place to have lunch. My chair screeched across the slate when I stood. I doubted I could remain in Tina's company much longer and not lose my cool. "I have to go. Thank you for the tea."

"Can you stay a moment longer? It will be so much easier to face Andrea if . . . Has she had a good life? My mother could be very rigid."

I remained standing. The sooner I left, the better. "Andrea adored her grandmother. She only talks in the best of terms about Victoria."

"And you? How are you doing with Scott gone?"

"It was terribly difficult at first. But I'm remarried now. My son—"

"*Scott's* son?"

"Yes."

"He got the son he wanted, did he?" Tina finally smiled. "Does your son play ball?"

"Yes. He's very good."

"Of course he would be. That's wonderful. I'm sure Scott was very proud of him. Do you have a picture?"

I sat back down and opened my wallet to Ky's school picture. Tina swallowed hard. "My goodness, there's a strong resemblance to his father." She closed the wallet and pushed it back across the table.

Scott loved this woman? She never tried to find Andrea. She considered a quiet lunch in the city a grand gesture. Still, she was my sister in grief for Scott. For a long moment, I squinted against the glare of the morning sun, reminding myself of my mission.

"I was terrible to Andrea when she first came looking for Scott," I said. "I wouldn't believe her about being Scott's daughter. In fact, I slapped her hard across the face when she told me who she was. I hated the idea that Scott had hidden her—and you—from me. At first because I was jealous, and then because knowing about his life before me shattered his image. I feared I had never known him. Andrea was nothing but an interloper until I got to know her. Then my anger turned on Scott for abandoning her."

Tina's eyes shot up to meet mine. "I was angry at Scott, too, for expecting so much of me. I wasn't the woman he wanted or needed. But those feelings have faded over time." She glanced around the patio. "I have so much to be thankful for." She leaned forward. "Tell me, did Scott suffer?"

"When he died? No. He died instantly. At least that's what the police told me. He rode his bike to work every day. He took chances sometimes. It wouldn't surprise me to learn that he'd darted in front of the truck, believing he could beat it across the intersection. I haven't read the accident report. I'm happier believing the sun blinded the truck driver. That's a pretty silly distinction, but it helps."

"And your new husband?"

"I'm very blessed."

"George is my third husband. There were no more children." As the day brightened, Tina's eyes took on the color of the sky on the horizon. "That was best for all concerned. I spend my time doing volunteer work at the local hospital. Nothing consequential. I deliver flowers and push a magazine cart around to the patients. Sometimes I travel with George, although I prefer the solitude of the house while he's gone. Does that make me terrible?"

Careful. "No . . . solitude can be nice."

"Before you go, let me write a note to Andrea and give her my cell phone number." She stood. "I'll be right back."

When she disappeared into the house, I walked the steps to the top terrace of her garden to take a closer look at the roses. The sun warmed my legs and awoke the sting of the duck's bite. I needed distraction.

Several of my favorite hybrid tea roses grew in Tina's garden, plus a few I didn't know—a speckled pink, a tricolored rose with lemony center petals that shifted to creamy white and red, plus a mauve rose with papery petals that reminded me of an antique dress. I turned over a yellow-spotted leaf to find velvety orange spots. The diagnosis was rust, a plant disease seldom seen in drier Colorado. Finding the disease on Tina's rose eased my plant envy just a bit. I cleared the liquidambar leaves that had collected around the base of the rose. Good air circulation would lessen the likelihood of another infestation. I added *neglectful gardener* to my list of disappointments in Tina.

"Hello? I've finished!" called Tina from the patio, waving an envelope.

I joined her. "Can you tell me the name of the tricolored rose on the top terrace?"

"I wouldn't have the slightest idea. The garden was installed by the previous owner. Maybe the gardener would know. I could ask him."

"Tell your gardener to keep the bases of the roses free of debris to prevent fungal diseases."

She stared at me as if I'd spoken a foreign language.

"Never mind," I said. "I'm sure he takes good care of your roses."

She extended her hand. "Have a good life."

"Have fun getting to know Andrea." But I doubted she would.

~~~

To me, the name *Mother* came with a long list of expectations. She was the one who cheered the loudest for your successes and brightened at your every homecoming. When classmates laughed at your Native American weaving project, only your mother could bury your pain under a plate of chocolate chip cookies and a glass of milk. A bad case of strep throat turned her into your fairy godmother. *Do you want round or straight noodles in your chicken soup? How about some tapioca pudding? Would grape juice be less irritating to your throat?*

Andrea read the note from Tina, then turned to me. "Have you read this? It has all the passion of a collection notice."

"We talked about this, Andrea. Tina is your mother, but being a mother doesn't make her motherly. You'll have to create a relationship that works for both of you, if that's what you decide."

Margot looked up from her book. "Sounds like good advice, sis."

Andrea tore up the note and threw the pieces into the air. "Want some tea?" She didn't wait for a reply. She filled the teapot with water and slammed it onto a burner. The gas flame came on with a *whump!*

Margot excused herself. "I need some fresh air." She grabbed a sweater and left. Nothing terrified Margot more than a good show of emotion.

Andrea stood cross-armed looking out the window to the street. "She wants to wait three weeks? And she's hiding me from her husband? Hello? This is the twenty-first century. We don't ostracize bad girls anymore. They get book deals." Andrea's chin touched her chest. Soon her shoulders bobbed. In a voice pinched with pain, she said, "I'm all alone."

∽

I woke up from my nap to Margot waving my cell phone in my face. "Larry wants to talk to you." Since the bathroom was the only private place in Andrea's studio apartment, I found a spot on the curb outside, under a colorless sky, barely noticeable between two parked cars. "I've invited Andrea to come home with me."

"You have?"

"She wants to see Ky and Louise, and she needs some time to think about what to do next."

"Did she quit her job?"

"Nothing like that. I went to see Tina this morning." I told Larry about our visit. "Andrea's crushed. She needs time with people who love her."

Larry allowed a beat of silence to pass before he spoke. "It's getting kind of crowded around here."

"We have the guest room."

"*And* the basement."

"We can't put her in an unfinished basement."

"Ky and I have been working on it."

The owner of one of the cars returned and started the engine. I stood to walk toward the rec center. "Really?"

"We're painting the walls today."

"What color?"

"Ky wants to surprise you."

Uh oh. "Are you okay? You sound . . . Are you and Ky getting along?"

"We're getting along fine."

I turned to walk back toward Andrea's apartment. "You don't sound fine."

"I miss you, Mib. You've been gone longer than you planned. And now you're bringing another complication into our lives. We never seem to get a break."

"Life *is* complicated, Larry." Try finding a private place to talk in San Francisco.

"You have to admit, things are a little crazy around here. We never get to be together—"

"Are you blaming *me* for that?"

"You didn't have to go to California or invite Andrea."

"Your mother doesn't have to be at the house every night, either, and you could look for a job with more reasonable hours. Maybe if you stayed up past eight, or better yet, stayed in bed until six, we'd have plenty of time together."

The phone went very quiet.

"You're right. We should talk about this when I get home," I said.

Silence.

"I'll get home faster. We won't take 50 again. I'll call when we get to Salt Lake to let you know when we'll be home. Okay?"

"I better get going if we're going to finish painting today."

"I'll be home after midnight on Wednesday."

"Wake me up."

*The most amazing stand of bamboo I
have ever seen grows inside the San Francisco
airport. Tall. Green. Straight. Every shoot a
limbo pole in the making.*

Margot stopped short of the security line at the San Francisco International Airport, a cathedral of sea-glass green and stainless steel. Above us, a flotilla of glass hulls sailed overhead in a wavy sea of trusses and beams held up by soaring pillars.

"Don't you want to get in line?" I asked.

"Not yet." Margot fidgeted with the hem of her blouse, a decidedly non-Margot type of blouse Andrea had convinced her to buy. Chiffon and satin with a lacy camisole underneath, with low-cut jeans and boots.

"You look amazing," I said. I wore a shapeless black tank top and drawstring pants—an outfit borrowed from Andrea. My overalls still hung drying in her shower. I knew how Quasimodo felt in the presence of his beloved Esmeralda. Frumpy.

"I shouldn't have spent the money."

This from a woman who wore designer sweats?

"There's a guy in the Cinnabon line checking you over," I told her.

She looked. "The pimply kid with the knit cap? Gross."

"No, the guy reading the newspaper. Look now."

"I'm not looking."

"He's not even pretending to read his newspaper anymore."

She looked, just like I knew she would. "Men reading tabloids with two-headed aliens on the cover don't excite me," she said, but she granted me a small smile.

"I'm sorry you don't have time to drive back to Colorado with us," I said. "The best hamburgers in the world are made in Green River, Utah."

"You can't entice me with hamburgers when I know you want to leave me stranded in some netherworld convenience store again. No, thank you."

I hate good-byes. Thank goodness the Transportation Safety Administration had made lingering good-byes passé. How many times can you say, *It was wonderful having you. You'll call when you get home, won't you?* Margot never called, no matter how many times I asked, and sadly, our good-byes were always awkward.

"I better get going," I said. "The parking lot charges by the nanosecond."

Margot stood on her tiptoes to scan the snaking line of travelers waiting to go through security. "The line's not moving very fast. Can you stay a little longer?" She offered the question like a naughty child offering her hand, expecting it to be slapped. "If you want to go, go. I won't stop you."

"I can stay as long as you like."

Margot turned her back to the security line. "I haven't exactly been open with you." She looked to the ceiling and sighed. "I haven't had a job in six months, and it doesn't look like I'm going to have another one anytime soon."

"Did you—"

Margot put her finger to my lips. "Don't talk. Just listen. Telling you is hard enough without having to play twenty questions." She sighed. "Orange Coast Health Group acquired the hospital on January first. I was assured to my face that my position was secure. 'You're our kind of administrator,' they said. 'You're one of the reasons Santa Monica Hospital was such an appealing acquisition for us.' Within twenty-four hours, I was cleaning out my desk."

"Why didn't you tell me?"

"I assumed something would come up. But it seems I didn't sow enough goodwill when I had the chance. I thought running a top-notch health facility was enough."

"What will you do?"

"I don't know, and it scares me to death."

I wrapped my arms around her, and she clenched me right back. "Don't worry about tomorrow," I said. "Tomorrow has enough worries of its own."

"That's the stupidest thing I've ever heard," she whispered in my ear.

"You won't think so when God answers the prayer I'm going to pray for you." I paused to give Margot a chance to push away, but she didn't. She settled her head onto my shoulder, so I prayed, "Father in heaven, here's your dear Margot. She needs to know she's not alone in this world, that you're more powerful than her deepest fears. Provide what she needs, Lord."

"I think people are starting to stare."

"All they see are two sisters loving each other the best they can and having a hard time saying good-bye. I'm going to finish my prayer now."

She nodded and her wet cheek touched mine.

"She's walked alone too long. Forgive me for withholding my support from her. Make me a better sister. Pour out your blessing on her, especially a bushel and a peck of love."

"Don't forget about a job."

"Father, guide Margot to a job where she will fulfill her life's purpose—a really great job where the people will care about her."

"Maybe you should pray for Mother, too."

"Good Father, watch over our mother, as lost as any lamb, and bring her home safe and sound. Anything else?"

"I have to sell my house."

"You do?"

"I've drained my savings account paying the mortgage."

"And Lord, provide a buyer for Margot's house."

"Does it matter that I don't believe in God?"

With a faith I didn't know I possessed, I said, "That's about to change." We stood with our foreheads touching, promising to call more often and to think of ways to draw Mother into our circle.

Margot whispered, "I love you," and joined the line of passengers filing through security.

I sat in the rental car for a long time thinking about what had transpired between Margot and me. After a visit with my sister, I usually inventoried my body and soul for wounds. Besides the duck bite on my shin, I felt fresh and clean, like a bed sheet billowing like a sail on the clothesline, warmed by the sun and threaded with the scents of the garden.

More than anything, I wished I could call my grandmother to tell her about Margot and me. I remembered the early mornings at my grandmother's house when I was a child, how the fog had quieted and softened the morning. The diffused light wasn't quite strong enough to release the color of the curtains or my bedspread. Dampness seeped through the blankets to my skin. My nose was cold to my touch.

While Margot slept beside me, I counted to ten, sometimes twenty, and pushed the blankets back to step lightly out of the room. I sat with my back to the wall heater, waiting for the heat to sharpen to pinpricks on my back. When I couldn't stand the heat one more moment, I sprinted to the bedroom. The heat kept its hand on my back as I dressed.

Sometimes I crawled back into bed to listen to my grandmother pray by her bed on the other side of the wall. She said Margot's and my names with great urgency as she asked God to woo us, cleanse us, to walk with us, and to cover us with His everlasting arms. Grandma had God awfully busy hounding Margot and me into heaven. I worried He wouldn't have time for anyone else. I was one of God's answers to Grandma's prayers. And I believed I'd seen the fingerprints of God on Margot's heart a moment ago in the San Francisco International Airport.

It was just a matter of time. But Grandma had died years ago without seeing Margot's heart soften toward the Father.

I wondered how she would have prayed for Ky.

Holy Jesus! Hear my prayer! Convict Ky of his sin before the night is here! Draw him back with cords of loving-kindness, Lord, and rescue him from the kingdom of darkness! Usher him this day into the kingdom of the Son you love! Do it now, Lord! Don't tarry! Unleash the hounds of heaven! In Jesus' name, amen and amen.

SEPT
15

The Autumn Joy sedum lives! The stubble the sparrows left is now a compact bouquet of fleshy leaves. Beautiful! Cover the poor thing next spring, for heaven's sake!

Sonny climbed the ladder to the rooftop of Margaret and Walter's house. "Don't forget to rinse the pads off real good," yelled Walter, sounding like a drill sergeant.

Sonny yelled back at him, "Did you remember to turn the water off?"

Walter's expression soured even more. "The doggoned water's been off for an hour," he said, although Sonny couldn't hear him. No matter. Sonny had turned his attention to removing the evaporative cooler's panels—the first step to winterizing the unit.

Margaret touched Walter's shoulder. "Why don't you go into the house, dear, and have a piece of that apple pie I baked?"

Walter watched Sonny working on the roof and huffed. "Make sure he unplugs the reservoir. I don't want no corrosion problems come next spring."

She reassured him that Sonny would follow his instructions. "I promise to let you climb up there after he leaves to check his work," she whispered and kissed his cheek. Walter seemed appeased. He climbed the stairs to the kitchen door.

"And make sure he puts the dad-blasted ladder back where he found it."

When the screen door slammed behind Walter, I turned back to the Don Juan roses that grew on Margaret's fence between the lawn and the sidewalk. The heap of red blossoms and burgundy leaves reassured me that wounds healed. I snipped a dead twig here and there and deadheaded spent clusters of blossoms. Gentle fall temperatures had encouraged the line of roses to push more blossoms. The replacement Don Juan I'd planted two years earlier nearly swelled to match the original roses.

Margaret followed me as I worked. "Sonny's been over here every Friday afternoon to help Walter around the house whether he wants the help or not. The minute he opens his eyes every Friday morning, Walter starts mumbling about Sonny's visit. I moved my baking day to Thursdays to have something to sweeten his attitude. Sometimes it works and sometimes it don't. But Sonny keeps coming. Who knew having an attentive son would be so much trouble?"

I zipped up my sweatshirt. "I wouldn't know."

"You haven't said a thing about Ky since you got back from California."

"He's as happy as a bug in a black basement."

"Now you're talking riddles."

"Larry and Ky finished his basement bedroom while I was gone. Larry asked him what color he wanted the room painted, and Ky chose black. He loves it."

"But you don't? That's no matter. You can paint the room any color you want when he goes off to college. I made Sonny's room into my sewing room—painted it the pinkest pink they carried at the paint store."

"The color isn't the problem. The basement gives Ky more freedom of movement and less accountability. I'm not sure he's ready for that much responsibility."

"Surrender—so easy to say, so difficult to do." She sighed. "Can you join us for a piece of pie?"

As much as I wanted to talk with Margaret about how a mother surrendered a sixteen-year-old son, a full day of clients lay before me and Ky needed picking up at school by three. I stomped down the contents of my pruning bucket and sheathed my pruners. "I wish I had time."

"Then let me send some home for your dessert tonight."

Blink lifted his head.

"Thanks for offering, but it's Andrea's last night with us. Louise is testing one more recipe on us. I sincerely hope she doesn't bring another Susan Paris creation."

"I'll wager Louise makes the Aloha Peaches and Cream dessert I wrangled out of Julie Coleman. The late peaches are heavenly this year." Margaret hugged me. "I hope you're going to rest over the weekend. You look tired, my dear."

"I'll be canning tomatoes with Connie tomorrow. The heirloom tomato is loaded." The thought of twelve hours of peeling tomatoes in a steamy kitchen nearly leveled me. "Come on, Blink."

He rolled onto his back to expose his belly to the warming day, his way of telling me he had other plans.

"Blink, come on."

He stretched and pawed the air before rolling onto his side. I stooped to scratch behind his ear. He leaned into the scratch. "We'll stop on the way to the Webleys' to get some coconut balls," I whispered into his ear. Blink heaved himself to his feet and trotted to the Daisy Mobile, where he danced his happy-dog jig, waiting for me to open the door.

In the Webleys' garden, after a long season of watchfulness, the black-eyed Susans had finally faded. By the time I finished deadheading the plants, I held a fistful of stems resembling chocolate drumsticks. Instead of dropping the stems into the pruning bucket, I laid them on the seat of the Daisy Mobile to include in a fall arrangement. On my hands and knees, I pulled at the runaway catmint I'd battled all summer.

"Will you ever forgive me for planting that catmint?" It was Elizabeth.

I tried to hide my surprise. "I owe you a debt of gratitude. I almost planted the monster in my rock garden."

"I know you're surprised to see me here, so you might as well say so."

I stood to brush the soil off my pants. "Well . . . yes . . . I am surprised to see you."

"Don't get your hopes up. I'm just visiting. I brought some lunch out for Gordon."

I was smiling. I could feel it.

"I'm telling you that I put arsenic in the chicken salad, so now you're an accomplice." She unsheathed her pruners. "Before I short-sheet his bed, let me help you with the hyssop and miniature roses."

"How's your daughter doing?" I asked.

"She's started her sophomore year, and she thinks she's in love. I'm calling my travel agent today to book a flight to Florida to talk some sense into her."

From our weekly visits, I'd learned Elizabeth's bravado outpaced her execution. "No you won't."

"No, I don't suppose I will."

We worked side-by-side in silence until Elizabeth removed her jacket. "I've promised myself to plant tulips this fall," she said. "I want something new and outrageous. Any recommendations?"

"For *this* garden?"

"Yes," she said, bending to rip a fistful of catmint out of the ground.

"You can't beat a black-and-white tulip bed for drama."

Elizabeth stopped working to look around her garden. "Oh yes, around the gazebo, don't you think? Early or late bloomers?"

"My choices would be Queen of Night and Maureen, both late bloomers."

"And deep red geraniums in pots on the steps." Elizabeth smiled and nodded.

I sheathed my pruners and removed my gloves.

"Let me see your hands," Elizabeth demanded. She held my hands, palms up, in hers. All of my cuticles bled. White blisters under callouses, some broken and bleeding, covered the pads of my palms and fingers. "What have you been doing," she asked, "plowing the north forty behind a mule?"

"Nothing so noble. Just catching up with my clients from my time in California." I blew on my palms to soothe their sting. "I've never been fussy about my nails or hands, but I've never spent fifty hours a week weeding and pruning and spraying and fertilizing and—"

"Stop! You need to do yourself and everyone around you a favor—go back to designing gardens. You're brilliant at it."

"Even if I can't make enough money?"

"Capitalism. If you let it, it will suck the life right out of you," Elizabeth said, sitting back on her heels. "I'm going to give you the advice I wish someone had given Gordon and me: if you can't make enough money to support the way you live, maybe you need to change the way you live." She turned to look at her house. "It's a pretty house, but it isn't worth as much as Gordon and I paid for it—and I'm not talking about dollars and cents."

⁓

I picked up Ky after school every day for one reason and one reason only—he was all mine for eight minutes, ten if the stoplight at Ninth Street turned red. I was determined to weasel my way into his day and life, even if it meant interrogating him about his school day, hour by hour. At first, he responded as I'd expected, with much gesticulating and grunting. I broke him down with sheer perseverance.

"How about third hour?" I asked.

"I turned in my essay on *Moby Dick*."

"I heard the printer running at about one-thirty this morning. You should give yourself more time for your writing projects."

"Writing the essay wasn't the problem. I totally got the whole man-is-his-own-worst-enemy thing. The problem was finding the scene between Ahab and Starbuck where the whale oil is leaking out of the barrels to cite. Next time, I'm choosing a much shorter book, and if I come across something interesting, I'm going to smack a Post-it note over the quote."

I wanted to stop the truck and cover his face with kisses. What he'd so casually spoken in a few sentences revealed amazing growth as a learner and a person. A tough assignment had been completed on time. He'd selected and developed a theme from a laborious tome pregnant with meaning. Plus, he'd exercised the patience to find the most convincing quote to support his thesis *and* sifted important lessons from the experience. I expected an announcement from the Nobel Prize Committee any day.

"You'll know next time," I said.

"For sure."

"How about fourth hour?"

By the time I parked the Daisy Mobile in the garage, I'd heard how heat affects aluminum, that Ky's first ceramic project had broken in the kiln, and that his U.S. Government teacher droned on for half of the class on the importance of students using their time wisely.

"And calculus?"

"A piece of cake," he said, yawning. "And I got most of my homework done in class."

"Before we go inside, I want to talk to you about something."

"What?" he asked as if cowering from a trap.

"How's your grief group going?"

" 'Kay."

"Do you have any questions for me or anything you want to talk about?"

"Nope," he said, pushing the Daisy Mobile door open.

If I'd known conversing with a teen would be like racing a starving man to the refrigerator, I would've worked on my sprinting skills. "You have been going, haven't you?" I asked, winded before we passed through the garden gate.

"Yeah. I have a friend who's in the group."

"Anyone I know?"

"Just my chem lab partner."

"So if Mrs. Silver needs you to melt aluminum cans, you and your lab partner can help her out."

Ky rolled his eyes, took the porch steps—all five of them—in one stride, and disappeared into the house.

"I'll see you in a couple hours!" I yelled after him.

Connie came to the door. "What time should we expect you for dinner?"

"Good question." I had two more clients in town and a business on Main Street. The Main Street account was a matter of watering indoor plants and dusting a fake ficus. "Two hours tops."

"Perfect! Don't worry about a thing. Larry will be home in time to help with dinner. Andrea's farewell dinner will be lovely."

I emptied the Daisy Mobile of bulging yard bags to make room for what I'd collect at my next client's. I wrapped my palms with strips of duct tape to hold my failing bandages in place. I'd just climbed into the driver's seat when I heard Louise's yodel.

"Yoohoo, Mibby? Did I hear you drive up? Yoohoo!" She stepped into the garage. "Don't gawk," she said. "I'm a woman in distress."

The only makeup on her face was a smudge of mascara under each eye and a remnant of raspberry lipstick. Her chef's hat had flattened her hair against her head. Louise being in public without makeup ranked with Lee surrendering to Grant at Appomattox, a great humiliation precipitated by great torment. Who knew how long Louise had weighed the cost-to-benefit ratio in her kitchen. Nevertheless, I looked at my watch before sliding out of the truck.

"Hey, sugar, you know I wouldn't bother you if I wasn't absolutely desperate."

"What's up?"

"I called to give my regrets to Andrea. I won't be able to attend her going-away dinner like I'd hoped."

The only other time I'd known Louise to miss a party was during her chemotherapy regimen—and then there was the grand opening of the new Safeway. "Tell me."

"It would be easier to show you."

Louise stopped abruptly inside her kitchen door. My mouth gaped open. A medley of mixing bowls smeared with sauces filled the countertops. Pans stacked within pans covered every burner of the stove. Heaped in the sink were roasting pans with greasy drippings and measuring cups and spoons. Canisters of sugar and flour and bottles of spices covered the kitchen table. Stained recipes hung from each cabinet door.

"What happened?" I asked.

"My committee mutinied, said they were tired of being in the kitchen all the time. Susan Paris, of all people, came to the front door with a tray of gritty fudge and delivered the proclamation. Bless her little heart, she has no business walking through a kitchen, much less thinking she has anything to contribute to a cookbook."

"Louise," I said as a warning.

"Don't worry your pretty li'l head. I don't have time for revenge. The deadline is rushing at me like a mad bull. I have two weeks to finish testing the recipes and to type them into the computer." She looked around the kitchen, her shoulders sagging with the weight of her task "Do y'all think I heard God wrong?"

"I think you'll feel better once we get the kitchen cleaned."

A faint light glimmered in Louise's eyes. "You're a good friend. I'll name my next three children after you."

~~~

Andrea had booked herself on the last flight out of Orchard City at 11:35 P.M.—way past my usual bedtime. We drove through the motel district toward the airport.

"What's with you and Larry?" Andrea asked.

"What do you mean?"

"You've been, like, married for less than six months and you barely talk to each other."

She was right. Larry and I lived in parallel universes, and in his universe, my voice droned out of his hearing range, completely indistinguishable from the ambient noise of, say, a wrestling match or a flyby of the Blue Angels. *Ho-hum.* No matter how many times I asked him if everything was all right between us, he said, "Sure," and flipped the channels between *SportsCenter* and yet another sad performance by the Rockies. Larry was snoring loudly by the time I crawled into bed each night, and I never heard him get out of bed in the morning. On the weekends, there was grocery shopping to do, the garden to maintain, and a huge pile of laundry, not to mention bills to pay, vehicles to wash, and church and Sunday school to attend. "We're both working hard; Ky's been a grade-A brat since we got married. Second-time marriage is just different, Andrea. It's functional and companionable."

"That sucks." We drove under the I–70 viaduct. "Connie says Larry wants to have kids. Maybe that would help."

I blinked rapidly and feigned interest in traffic in the rearview mirror. Doing so helped me hold my composure for about thirty seconds. That's how long it took for the anger to roil in my gut—first at Larry for changing his mind about having kids and telling his mother, then at Connie for blabbing the news to my daughter, of all people.

"Connie told you that?" I asked.

"Is this news to you?"

"Larry assured me before we married . . ." *What were his exact words?*

"He told you Ky would satisfy his need to be a father, didn't he?"

I nodded, which seemed less hazardous than actually speaking. Andrea caught on pretty fast.

"And because of your work schedules and Ky and Connie, you guys aren't hardly ever—?"

"Exactly."

She touched my shoulder with the gentleness of a prayer. "You have to talk to him tonight. Don't put it off."

"He's already in bed."

"Wake him up."

I changed lanes to turn toward the airport parking area.

"Don't you dare park the truck," Andrea said. "You're not putting off talking to Larry because of me. Drop me at the curb."

"No way. I want to see you off."

"We can instant message tomorrow night. You should have lots of news by then."

"Then tell me about Tina. You haven't said what you've decided to do about her."

The Daisy Mobile rumbled to a stop in the loading zone. Andrea put her hand over the keys to let me know she meant business about me going directly home. A van swerved to the curb in front of us. Men in suits, carrying briefcases, hopped out of the van and entered the terminal.

"I've prayed and prayed about Tina," she said. "God's being awfully quiet, so I'm taking His silence as a message to wait. If Tina calls, she calls. I can't make her love me."

"You made me love you," I said, barely able to hide my emotion.

"You're different." She slid across the seat to embrace me. "You have a heart that lives to love."

I tightened my hold of her. "When will we see you again? Christmas?"

"I'll book my flight the moment I get home." We clung to each other for a long moment. Finally she pulled up on the door handle.

"Wait a minute. Let me pray for you."

She nodded and held my hands. "Lord, give Andrea a safe and pleasant trip home. Bring her back soon. And bless her new school year . . . a lot. Amen."

On the curb, she stood on tiptoe to speak over the passenger window. "It wouldn't hurt to think about a baby. Maybe you've been reading too many child development books and not letting God show you how big He is."

On the drive home from the airport, I did as Andrea had suggested. I thought about having a baby. At first, the thought of a new life fluttering within me took my breath away. Then my synapses started firing questions: *Are you prepared to face the added risks to your health and the health of your baby? You're not a spring chicken anymore. What will you do if Larry prefers his own flesh and blood to Ky? How will Ky feel about you starting another family? Even more alienated? There's always Down's syndrome to consider. You've miscarried before.*

But there was one question that chilled my blood: what business did Larry have talking to his mother instead of me about wanting a child of his own?

In the dark kitchen, I followed the sound of Blink's tail thumping on the floor. His wet nose touched my knee. "Hey there, ol' friend. Is everyone in bed?" I flipped on the kitchen light and checked for signs of life in the basement. Not one glimmer of light shone, but I wasn't surprised. Ky had complained about his tough cross-country training that day.

I knocked softly on Ky's door. He didn't answer. I pushed the door open and stood over his bed nearly busting for joy over the miracle of his life. "You're enough for me," I whispered and kissed his sticky forehead. *Eewww.* I made a mental note to buy him some astringent and cotton balls. And then to convince him to use them.

Upstairs, I lifted the covers and slid into bed, moving carefully to avoid waking Larry, more out of avoidance than any concern for his need for uninterrupted rest.

"Did you get Andrea off okay?" he asked in a voice untouched by sleep.

I stiffened. "Uh-huh."

He clicked on the bedside lamp.

"Larry, turn off the light and go to sleep. This is the worst possible time for me to talk about anything. I'm tired. My hands hurt. Andrea just left. But mostly, I just don't know what to say."

"Let me see your hands first."

He unwrapped the bandage on my right hand. "You're working too hard." He kissed the only place on my hand without blisters or cracks or callouses—the tip of my pinkie—and rewrapped the bandage. He snapped off the light and lay down. I lay straight as a lodgepole. If my anger sprouted and bloomed in the leadenness of the night, it was only because Larry had watered it.

With a sigh, he heaved himself out of bed. "I'm going to watch television for a while."

Fine.

I added watching *SportsCenter* for the umpteenth time to my list of grievances. Although not one measure of the familiar theme song sounded from the family room, I pictured Larry slouched in a chair, pouting over our missed weekend getaway, my extended stay in California, my trouble-prone son, the ghosts of my first husband, and work schedules that allowed us no time together. Panic squeezed my chest when I realized his list was probably longer than mine when I added up all of the trouble loving me had brought to his life. Was he sitting in the dark, thinking he'd married the wrong woman? I threw back the covers and headed downstairs.

He sat in the glow of the muted television picture with his long legs stretched before him. I stepped over one leg to sit on the coffee table facing him. Even with the house closed tight against the fall chill, the clank of steel from the train yard reached us.

Start with the obvious. "It's late," I said. Larry didn't have one thing to say about the hour. "You were right. We should talk." His eyes focused on the wall behind me. "Larry?"

"I don't know what to say, either, Mib, except the usual. What have I done now?"

Finally, a question I could answer. "You've been talking to your mother about wanting a baby. I'm the one you should be talking to."

"And when would I do that?"

"Availability isn't the issue here. You assured me before we married that loving me and seeing Ky raised into manhood would be enough for you. A baby would only complicate our lives. You know that. And then talking to your mother . . ." I threw up my hands. "Do you know how that makes me feel?"

He thrummed the arms of the chair with his fingers. The clock chimed the half hour. A quick succession of scenes from the TV flashed off the walls. A silence as menacing as death settled over the room until Larry finally spoke. "I was wrong to talk to my mom."

"Have you really changed your mind? Do you want a baby? I don't know, Larry. What will Ky think?"

"What will Ky think? That's the whole problem here. We're operating a household based on what Ky wants. You feel displaced by me talking to my mother. You should try being displaced by a kid who considers himself the king of the universe. It isn't right—not for him or you or me. It's time we reevaluated our priorities. You can't play the role of God in your son's life—"

"I'm doing no such thing."

He drew up his legs and leaned forward. "Hear me out, Mib. When you work to shelter Ky from the hurt and disappointment he's due, you're stepping into God's sandals. If we believe God is all He says He is, He's big enough to shape Ky's life with the good *and* the bad that comes his way."

"And what are we doing during all of this—sitting on a beach somewhere sipping fruity drinks with straws and umbrellas?"

"Not at all. I'll be your husband and Ky's father. You'll be my wife and his mother. But our marriage comes first. Our marriage should be a source of strength for Ky, and that can only happen if we're acting like we're husband and wife."

Finally, the real issue. "So what we're really talking about is sex?"

"That's part of it," he said, his voice pressed with emotion. His face twisted in pain before he covered his face with his hands and shook his head. He stayed that way, breathing deeply, expelling long breaths. "I . . . I'm embarrassed . . . but it kills me, Mib, that you don't find me—" he expelled the last word with a sob—"desirable."

Seeing him doubled over in pain as surely as if I had thrust him with a spear stripped me of my anger. I fell to my knees to cradle him as he cried. What could be said of a woman who had been so consumed by her needs that she'd neglected the needs of her husband? Nothing good.

I couldn't claim ignorance. I'd been here before. There had been a similar time in my marriage to Scott. A new baby. Constant fatigue. Scott's demanding career. Church commitments and overcommitments. Ky's ear infections and food allergies. Tons of dirty diapers. And a house to take care of. Sex just plumb fell off our marital map. And it seemed as though Scott waited until my physical and emotional reserves had completely evaporated before he reached out to me. More often than not, I put him off, justifying myself with the usual litany: He pays more attention to his car than to me. When was the last time he asked me how my day was? I'm exhausted. The baby never sleeps. Scott never helps with the laundry. I haven't shaved my legs in weeks.

Newly married with a beautiful infant son, I'd never been more lonely. But the phrase "Do not deprive each other" from a devotional I'd read for busy moms dogged me. I resisted taking the initiative for quite a while, which only underscored my selfishness. I wanted Scott to make *me* feel beautiful and desirable and smart before I surrendered to his desire. It was out of desperation, really, that I gave myself to him. To create a bower for our love, I learned to nap when Ky napped and let the dishes sit in the sink. I exchanged baby-sitting with my friends from church so Scott and I could stay home and eat dinner alone. It was as if our lovemaking reconnected the scattered tethers of our relationship. At first, I felt guilty. I was giving myself only to get what I needed, but when I saw how contented Scott became, I considered our love dance a gift to him. So did he. Within months, our marriage had been transformed.

Shame on me for withholding the gift from Larry. I pried his hands from his face. "Nothing could be farther from the truth. I can't stop thinking of you all day long. When I hear your car in the driveway, my knees go weak. I long for the feel of you, the touch of you, the taste of you."

Larry's face still registered caution and doubt, so I quoted the Bible verse I'd memorized for our honeymoon but never had the chance to recite. "Awake, north wind, and come, south wind! Blow on my garden, that its fragrance may spread abroad. Let my lover come into his garden and taste its choice fruits." Definitely *not* an Awana verse but evocative just the same.

His face softened. We kissed. We entwined. We sighed.

"Larry, I'm so sorry—"

"Shh, I am, too."

SEPT
22

Rain, rain, and more rain! Woohoo!
Over an inch fell in the afternoon—a record!
Thanks, Father!

Larry lifted the edge of the living room curtain to look outside. "Mib, have you seen this carload of guys out front? A kid's sitting on the hood using a cell phone. Where's Ky?"

I joined Larry at the window. Sure enough, Jeremy's car idled at the curb with the radio blaring. The phone rang. Larry and I locked glances.

"I'll get it!" Ky called from the basement.

"I don't like this," I said.

Larry turned for the front door.

"Wait! Shouldn't we give him a chance to do the right thing?"

"And if he doesn't?"

"How much duct tape do we have?"

A door slammed in the basement and Ky's footfalls pounded on the stairs.

"The back door," I said, running to intercept Ky. Larry followed. Ky had his hand on the doorknob when we rounded the corner into the kitchen. "Ky! Hey, what's up?" I said, hoping to sound matter-of-fact. "Are you headed out?"

Connie looked up from the recipes she was proofreading for Louise at the kitchen table, red pen poised over the stack of papers.

Ky raked his fingers through his hair and looked up but not at us. "Yeah. The guys called. What's the problem? I have my license and I'm not grounded anymore."

"Remember what the judge—" I started but turned to Larry as we'd agreed I should when Ky required reining in.

Ky spoke first. "You don't have to worry. I'm going as their designated driver."

"That's the stupidest idea I've ever heard," Larry said.

Lord, give Larry discernment. . . .

Ky threw up his hands. "What? I'm just supposed to let my friends go out and get killed?"

. . . and give Ky an obedient heart.

"Driving a carload of drunken kids around isn't what you think. You're not going," Larry countered.

"But I *told* them I would!"

"You can tell them to call a cab." Larry took out his wallet and handed Ky several bills. "My treat."

He ignored the money. "What's the big deal? I thought you'd be proud of me for being so responsible."

"Your intentions are good," I said.

"Just not very smart," added Larry.

Quit with the insults already.

Ky took a step toward Larry. "Where do you get off telling me what to do anyway? You're not my dad!"

"You're right. I'm not your father, but I'm an adult and you're a kid." Larry's voice was a gravel road. "If you step through that door, your car will be gone within the hour, and it won't be coming back. What's more, if you go out with these guys you call friends, don't come back, Ky. You've made your choice."

What?!

Ky looked from Larry to me. "Okay."

"Wait a minute—" I yelled after Ky, but the door had already slammed behind him. When I tried to follow him, Larry grabbed me around the waist.

"Let go of me!" I yelled, struggling against his grasp. "Let go!"

"Shh, shh." He wrapped his arms around me and spoke softly into my ear. "He has to make this choice sooner or later. It might as well be sooner."

"You had no right to make an ultimatum like that." I broke from his embrace to move toward the front door.

He grabbed my arm. I tried to pull free.

"He needed a brick wall, Mib. One of us—"

"One of us, what? One of us needed to keep their cool? Use their head? Speak reason? I couldn't agree with you more."

"Don't say anything you're sure to regret, Mib."

"You've said plenty to regret already."

"I regret nothing."

My words burned my throat. "I'm asking you to please take your hands off of me."

Connie's eyes widened. She covered her gaping mouth with her hand. Larry released me. I backed away. When he saw how angry I was, he reached for me again.

"Don't touch me! We agreed you were to rein him in, not throw him out!" I ran for the front door and the porch. I looked up and down the street. Jeremy's car was nowhere in sight.

"Come back inside, Mib," Larry pleaded.

"I'm going after him." I pushed past Larry into the house. "I'm pretty sure I know where they go."

"All I'm asking is for you to take the time to think about what you're doing. You need to calm down."

"Calm down? You just told my son to leave and not come back, and I'm supposed to take that calmly? I trusted you. I stood back. And this is what I can expect from you? Bullying? Maybe you're the one who should leave."

He deflated before my eyes.

"Listen, Larry, I—"

His hand went up to stop me. "Come on, Ma, I'll drive you home."

Connie hesitated, looked to me, and watched Larry walk out the door. When she followed him, a suffocating silence settled on the house. I stood in the middle of the living room, shaking, running options over in my head. It all boiled down to protecting Ky from danger. I grabbed my purse. The party spot was in the desert near the airport. That narrowed the search area down to twenty or so square miles. The enormity of the task stopped me cold in the middle of the poop deck. Lit only from the kitchen window, the garden reflected my life, overgrown and out of control. The garden desperately needed pruning. Did my family need pruning, too?

Surrender Ky to me.

I fumbled in my purse to find the key to the Daisy Mobile. "I can't leave Ky out in the desert. Who knows what could happen."

Surrender him.

I stopped, hung my head. "I can't. You ask too much. Ask me anything else but this. Not my son."

The ram in the thicket.

I fell to my knees and onto my face. I didn't smell anything Blink had left behind, so I lay there, thinking I could resist the image of the lamb in the thicket, my Savior who bore my sins, and yes, Ky's sins, too. "Could I meet you halfway?" I prayed. I sensed no objection, so I continued. "I'm sorry, but I'm not willing to put Ky on the altar quite yet. You know me—I'm not too trusting that way. But there are a few things, little things, that I'm willing to surrender for myself, like the prestige I've enjoyed from having a kid too good to be true. Maybe Ky senses my disappointment. How awful for him, so I surrender my right to always be proud of what he does, and I ask you to heal him of any wounds my attitude has inflicted on him. And when other moms tell me about their kids' mission trips, I surrender my need to make excuses for Ky not attending youth group. You are the author and perfecter of his faith. I trust you to write his story. That's two things I've surrendered, Lord. I'm going into the desert to look for Ky now. Will you help me find him?"

I distrusted the testimonies of people who prayed only to be covered by a velvety blanket of peace—a little too mystical for my tastes. I liked rock-solid results. In this case, Ky arriving home in a fiery chariot would have sufficed. But not only did a velvety blanket of peace fall on me, but I was swaddled like a baby. No matter how hard I pressed against its softness with arguments and what-ifs, the peace held me motionless until I surrendered to its embrace. I didn't understand what had happened, was completely astounded by the power of its hold, but I liked it more than Strawberry Cream Balls. I savored the peace for several moments before I trotted off toward the garage to start my search-and-rescue operation.

I turned the doorknob to enter the garage and nearly planted my face in the door. It was locked. I never locked the door. Before I found the key on the ring, the lock clicked and the door opened. Ky, red-eyed and shame-faced, stood before me.

"What are you doing in the garage?"

"I don't blame you for being angry," he said. "It's just that I heard you and Larry arguing, and I . . . I've never heard you yell like that."

"I thought you went to the desert with your friends. I was coming to look for you." *Doesn't that explain my hysteria?*

"I'm so sorry. I didn't mean to cause problems for you and Larry."

My heart thumped at the sound of Larry's name, and I remembered the hurt on Connie's face. "We'll work it out. That's not your problem." I wrapped my arms around Ky, my head to his chest, and hugged him hard. "I'm glad you didn't go with your friends."

After a moment of hugging, Ky twisted gently out of my embrace. "Larry was right. It was stupid. I would have ended up in D.Y.S. for sure."

His reference to the Department of Youth Services made me shiver. Barbed wire. Cinder block sleeping cubicles. No doors. Jail for young people. "I'm proud of you. You made the right decision."

"You should thank Larry. I didn't wanna go with those guys. I just didn't want them bugging me 24/7. They never would've let me live it down. But when I told them what Larry had said, I got all kinds of sympathy for having a wicked stepfather."

"We'll both thank him when he gets back from taking Connie home."

~~⌒

With every minute Larry stayed at Connie's house, my regret over what I'd said to him deepened. I sat in Scott's chair with an afghan over my lap, waiting. The crickets' song slowed as the night cooled and draped the house with a disquieting emptiness, even though Ky's music throbbed in the basement and Blink snored at my feet. My body warmed the leather to release the reassuring scent of Scott. I whispered into the darkness, "I miss you so much—so very, very much."

During the barrenness of many Januarys I'd sat in this very chair for hours, thumbing through seed catalogs. Despite my experience and pragmatic thinking, the glossy pages of the catalog beguiled me with impossibly red astilbe, multicolored bouquets of painted daisies, and a cobalt-blue hydrangea, a thousand hues exaggerated from fact. Not one munching caterpillar disfigured a leaf. Not one wanton pigweed interrupted the suspension of disbelief. Pink Canterbury bells. August Moon hosta. A raucous tangle of daylilies, all in simultaneous bloom. Disneyland for gardeners. My reason tiptoed out for a cappuccino while I reconfigured the garden, too enraptured by the enhanced photos to exercise temperance in my selections. One time I ordered the Black Magic elephant ears and a spotted toad lily—an avant-garde yet striking flower—although both plants were doomed to failure in the western Colorado heat.

Sitting by a crackling fire in January, I didn't think about shoveling and heaving and bending and sore hands. In my imaginary garden, the sun warmed my back. A trellis rose from the woodpile at my bidding. Weeds hid in fear. Aphids sought safer respites. Gardening was easy. It wasn't until my shovel had barely nicked the hard-packed earth in spring that I awoke from my seed catalog dreams.

I believed a similar dementia had erased the toil of reconfiguring my life to be Scott's wife. Just as deceptive as the seed catalog illustrations, a parade of pictures enhanced by the passing of time played in my head. Scott sending flowers for no reason at all. Scott drawing me a bubble bath and preparing dinner after I had a difficult day with Ky. Scott presenting me with a black pearl necklace for our tenth anniversary. All but forgotten was the ironing board he'd brought home for our first anniversary, or that he'd planned a camping trip with his buddies on my thirtieth birthday. Marriage was hard work, only made more difficult by an enshrined ghost from a marriage past. Larry was as doomed as the toad lilies.

Not if I can help it.

I dropped a dusty box of photographs in front of Scott's chair and breathed in deeply to still my shaking before spilling the box's contents across the floor. On my knees, I pushed images of my life aside, looking for the one photograph that caught the strength of Scott's influence on Ky and me. When I found it, I propped it in Scott's chair. In the photograph, Scott knelt in the grass beside a gap-toothed Ky in his first baseball uniform—the Cougars. Scott looked straight into the camera, chest out, smiling proudly.

Tears welled and spilled down my cheeks. I blew my nose and hugged a box of tissues to my chest. "You were such a good husband and a wonderful father," I said to Scott in the photograph. "I can't tell you how hard it's been without you. Ky's changed. He's growing up, really pressing the boundaries. I thought I'd lost him tonight. But he's smarter than I gave him credit for. He's like you that way. So smart but so reckless. When he sweats, he even smells like you. That's weird, isn't it?

"Well, I figure you know that I got married a few months back. You know him. Larry from church—the big guy with the beard and hair. You went to a men's conference with him in Estes Park. He cleaned up real, real nice. If you were here, you'd be friends, I'm sure of it. He's honest and hard-working, a real tradesman. He replaced the water heater. And he remodeled the basement just like you wanted to. He's trying real hard to be a good husband and father. He loves Ky. But you know me. I'm so selfish—maybe even worse since you . . . left. I'm not proud of that.

"Anyway, I'm here to tell you that I will always love you, Scott, and that I forgive you for leaving me. But I have to move on. I hope heaven is even better than you'd hoped. Good-bye, my beloved."

I cried my way through the box of tissues and fell asleep curled in Scott's chair.

SEPT

23

Thinking about ripping every plant and blade of grass out of the backyard to make room for dahlias.

The delivery drivers from the Salvation Army hefted Scott's chair into the back of the truck and closed the doors. The man with his life story tattooed up and down his arms ripped open the last package of Sweet Suzy Strawberry Cream Balls before he climbed into the truck's cab. I called, "Thanks for coming so early!" When the truck pulled away from the curb, I felt weightless, like the first time you wear shorts in the spring and a breeze tickles the hair on your legs—a new-yet-old sensation. But the feeling passed quickly.

I leaned against a porch column and prayed, "O Jesus, please, please, please save my marriage."

I'd woken up in the chair only an hour earlier and ran upstairs looking for Larry. The quilt lay undisturbed across the bed, so I rushed to the bathroom. His towel was dry, the sink clean of toothpaste. I sat on the tub, afraid to breathe, knowing that the future of my marriage lay in what happened next. Questions and their elusive answers immobilized me. *Should I go to him? What if he isn't at Connie's? Does he want me to find him? Should I wait for him here or would that seem like I've given*

up on our marriage? Maybe he's on his way home now. If I left, we would
miss each other.

"Enough of that." I splashed cold water on my face and checked my
teeth for remnants of dinner. It had taken some pleading for the Salvation Army guys to pick up the chair on a Saturday morning. The
dispatcher had finally said, "Listen, lady, this better be some kind of
special chair. My boys will be there in ten minutes."

Gravel crunched under the wheels of the Daisy Mobile when I
pulled into Connie's driveway. I parked under a cottonwood tree and
put my head on the steering wheel to pray. "O Jesus, I should be too
ashamed to come to you, but I'm desperate. I've hurt Larry terribly. Like
the Good Shepherd you are, bind his wounds. And please give me
another chance to love him. I'm willing to forget every dream I've ever
dreamed; I'm willing to live in pain; I'm willing to be a beggar in this
world."

Are you willing to live in a trailer?

"A trailer?" I pictured myself eating alone at the kitchen table in my
showroom-floor kitchen. "A trailer would be fine, Lord. I just don't
want to live without Larry. I'm going into the house now to ask him to
forgive me. Please soften his heart toward me. Don't let my selfishness
and disrespect and . . ."

Fear?

"Yes, fear. I won't let any of that come between me and Larry again.
In Jesus' name, amen."

Connie and I stood on either side of the screen door of her porch.
Saturday morning traffic on Peach Orchard Road sped by behind me.
Connie wrung her hands. "Is the boy okay? Did Ky get home?"

"Oh yes. I'm sorry, Connie. I should have called."

"I could have called, too. It was a long night for all of us."

"Is Larry here?"

"Yes, out back with his dahlias." Connie tightened the sash of her
robe. "Before you talk to him, I think you should hear what I have to
say." She pushed the door open. I followed her to the kitchen. "I made
some coffee," she said.

My stomach was a giant ball of rubber bands. "I don't think I could drink anything. Not until I see Larry."

She stilled her trembling lips with her fingertips. "You're not here to . . . Are you? I'm the one to blame." Her shoulders heaved and her tears flowed freely.

I wrapped my arms around her and rubbed her back. "Oh, Connie, I'm so sorry I made you feel that way."

"I never meant to become a pest—"

"You *didn't*."

Connie stepped back to meet my gaze. With her eyebrows raised, she said, "How can that be? I annoyed myself."

"Well . . . maybe you were just a little annoying."

"You're a sweet girl and a terrible liar." She motioned for me to sit down when all I wanted to do was run to find Larry. But Connie had been a friend too long to leave the strings of our relationship untied, so I sat at the kitchen table and she joined me. Still, my legs bounced under the table. A chickadee sounded the nine o'clock hour on the birdcall clock above the table. Connie fingered her wedding band as she talked. "While you two were dating, I felt Larry drifting away from me. Now, don't get me wrong, I was happy for the two of you, but nothing could have prepared me for the panic I felt over being alone in this house." Her eyes glistened with tears. "I wanted to be the kind of mother-in-law who was a good friend. I wanted to help you wherever I could, share what I knew. But the truth of it was, I didn't want to be in this house by myself."

I reached across the table to touch her hand. "Connie, you—"

"Don't you dare give me an easy way out. I put you both in a terrible place. Larry trying to be loyal, you working so hard to be patient." She sighed. "I am sorry." She tilted her head as if to catch a sound. She hurried to the kitchen window. "You better get out there," she said. "I hear Larry's car idling."

I joined her at the window. Exhaust billowed out of the Datsun, but Larry wasn't in the car. The door to the dahlia shed stood open. I looked to Connie. "Pray," I said and ran toward the shed, stopping only to turn off the car and pocket the keys. The shed was empty. I looked for him among the dahlias and between the rows of sweet corn and inside the tool shed. When I turned to leave, Goliath jumped from the rafters, landed at my feet, and bolted outside. Surprise made my heart pound.

Love the cat?

Okay, okay, I love the cat. There was only one more place to look—the hybrid garden on the very edge of the property.

The dahlias were at their peak in September. Pom-poms of color, large and small, rose six feet in height. Pinks. Yellows. Burgundies. Blends of candy-store colors and startling whites tipped with red. I found Larry among his hybrid dahlias, his "surprises," as he called them, created by a chance meeting of pollen carried by bumblebees from one dahlia to another. He sat leaning against a shade-house post. His head was bent, but from the roll of his shoulders, I knew he wasn't praying. My heart sagged. He held a bouquet of dahlias the color of the predawn sky—the very dahlias he'd named in my honor: Mibby's Light.

It was as if a garden gate stood between us and my harsh words from the night before had locked it closed. It was Larry who had to open the gate. I prayed he would. "Larry?"

He looked up and seemed to grimace, but I saw it was really a smile, one that expected another round of pummeling. "I was cutting these for you," he said.

"They're awfully pretty."

He rubbed his eyes with the heels of his hands. "I've been out here most of the night. The sunrise was amazing."

I looked toward the east, more to ease the tension than because of any hope of seeing a remnant of the sunrise. Not one cloud hovered in the sky to hold my attention. "Can we talk?"

He unlocked the gate for me with a nod, so I sat across from him on the tilled earth. I sifted a handful of soil through my fingers as I searched back through the months of our marriage as you would trace a length of knotted yarn to find the free end, hoping there was a beginning to our troubles, a place where we looped over ourselves and the knotting began. Larry spoke before I found the end of my string.

"Did Ky get home okay last night?"

"He never left. I found him in the garage." I told Larry how Ky had appreciated using him as a scapegoat with his friends.

"Glad to be useful." He sighed—out of relief, I thought. "I'm sorry I didn't come home. I was angry, hurt . . . stupid."

"I don't think you're stupid, not one bit. I'm here to apologize to you, but I'm having a hard time knowing where to start."

"Mib—"

"Let me tell you what I did last night." I told Larry about saying good-bye to Scott. "He was a good husband for me while he was alive. I needed someone who had walked the trail ahead of me. His experience gave me all kinds of confidence. But I've changed. I'm not a scaredy-cat anymore. I need a husband who's strong and expects me to be strong, too—in all sorts of ways—as a mother, a wife, a friend, a woman of God. You're that man, Larry. You're perfect for me. I don't want or need anyone else."

He closed his eyes.

"Can you forgive me?" I asked.

He lifted the bouquet from his lap and turned the dahlias in the brightening morning. "Do you remember the day I showed you the dahlia garden and we talked about a name for this flower?"

August. Hot. Larry, sweet and flattering. Me, condescending and dismissive. Definitely *not* my proudest day, so of course, I remembered everything in stunning detail. "Yes."

"You made it pretty clear you weren't interested in me. I knew that very day I would never stop loving you, but unless I wanted to go crazy, I would have to give up the hope of ever being loved by you. So I renamed these flowers Surrender. Every leaf that unfurled, every bud that set, and every bloom that opened reminded me that you weren't mine to have. And then the killing frost came early. When I dug up the tubers and rubbed the soil from their roots, my heart nearly broke at the thought of the long winter ahead. That's when I came to see you."

"You helped me clean out Scott's closet."

"I remember," he said, handing me the flowers. "Maybe I rushed things a little. Maybe life would have been easier on Ky if I'd waited out the winter or if I hadn't gone to you at all."

"Don't say that. You had to come. I *wanted* you to come."

He took my hand and raised it to his lips. *Forgiven.*

I crawled to sit by him and lean against his shoulder. "I called the Salvation Army to come and pick up Scott's chair."

"You did? I *like* that chair."

"We can get another one."

Larry pulled me closer. "Maybe one of those big chairs we can sit in together."

"A cuddle chair? I'd like that."

My stomach softened and warmed. We sat clinging to each another for a long time, my head against his broad chest, listening to his heartbeat. The sun warmed the earth to release its sweet perfume. I rubbed the spoonlike petals of Surrender between my fingers. Such a soft and reassuring color reflected the nature of God's grace to anyone willing to trust Him. *Even me?* "Do you have a flower in this year's hybrids I could name Surrendering Ky—something that changes color according to the light and smells like a locker room?"

Larry laughed and kissed the top of my head. "When I surrendered you, I didn't lash you to an altar. I opened my hands. If you had needed me for anything, I would have been there in a heartbeat. The hard part would have been leaving you again."

"Don't ever do that. Don't ever leave me."

"You mean like storming out of the house and staying away all night?" He stood and pulled me into his arms. "I acted like a spoiled child last night," he said, his warm breath tickling my ear. "I promise that no matter how hard you insist that I go away, I won't. I'll stay until the foundations of the world crumble under my feet."

I already knew that about Larry, but his saying so was the greatest gift he had ever given me.

We prayed together then, surrendering Ky into God's hands, offering ourselves to parent him with the same patience with which the Father parented us. After the amen, he asked me, "You realize, don't you, that even with the perfect parenting of the Father, we act like jerks?"

I was more familiar with the concept than I wanted to admit.

NOV

4

We dug up the dahlia tubers today, later than ever. One more year of good performance by Surrender and she's going to the county fair. Come on, girl, you can do it!

Susan Paris pushed through the crowd of people toward me. "Where's Louise?" she called. "People are filling their plates with seconds. She needs to do her spiel before people start leaving."

After a quick check of the kitchen and the ladies' room, I pulled my sweater around me and stepped out into the startling cold. Louise stood with arms outstretched and her face turned up to the night sky.

"Louise, what are you doing out here? It's freezing."

"Drying my underarms. The cold feels heavenly." She kissed my cheek. "I can't experience an emotion without stoking the flame of a hot flash. I ignited over a grape juice commercial the other day. Tonight, seeing all those sweet survivors and remembering the ones who are walking with Jesus . . . Oh my, I nearly melted into a puddle."

Louise had invited half of Orchard City to the launch party for her cookbook. Many more than that had shown up. She gave the credit to the good Lord and the far-reaching effects of cancer on our community, and she was correct. But there was more to the story. There was Louise, beginning to end. People knew they would feel loved if they came to her party. Everyone needed a dose of Louise now and then.

"Susan wants to get things started," I told her.

"That girl makes the hare look slow." Louise locked her arm in mine. "It nearly killed me to meet the deadline, and sugar, you know I couldn't have done it without your help. I'll never forgive myself for not taking typing in high school. I didn't want to ruin my nails. What a silly whip of a girl I was."

A breeze rattled the few remaining leaves on the cottonwood trees, and I huddled closer to Louise.

"Do you want to know the parson's truth? I'm out here to lower my core temperature so I can fill my plate with Marilyn Mellecker's green chilies and pork. That dish lights a fire in me." Louise helped me into my sweater and buttoned it up to my neck as if I were three years old. "I like Larry's goatee. I do declare my finger would disappear up to the knuckle in one of his dimples."

A warmth spread across my chest as I pictured his broad smile and the deep hollows of his dimples. I'd left him inside Grange Hall with Ky. Both of them would have preferred to be home watching CU detassel the Cornhuskers.

"Have you tried one of Susan's Oatmeal Date Nut Cookies? They really are good. The dear had her mother send the recipe directly to me so she wouldn't mess it up."

"I'm not very hungry."

Louise raised her eyebrows. "*You* not interested in cookies?"

"Oatmeal Date Nut Cookies sound a little too healthy to me."

"You're not warming something in *your* li'l ol' oven, are you?"

Over a month earlier, Louise had baked a batch of lemon scones just for us. Under the influence of all that butter and cream, I'd admitted to her that Larry and I were considering the very remote possibility of adding to our family. Since then, Louise had studied me for "signs" as earnestly as a hunter stalked its prey.

"It's nothing like that. I helped Larry dig up his dahlia tubers today. We ordered a pizza with everything. I've been burping Italian sausage all afternoon."

"I see. Oh, looky there. We have a butterscotch moon on the rise."

The top of the moon's round face rose above the Grand Mesa. From inside, conversations hummed into the night air. The string quartet drew out a chord at the end of "Hark the Herald Angels Sing" and began the soothing strains of "Away in a Manger." I rested my head on Louise's shoulder. My muscles softened as the lullaby coaxed me toward a dream of my bed and downy comforter.

Louise startled me out of the dream. "You have to promise me, baby girl, that if I ever take on a project like this again, you'll get my daddy's bird gun out of the hall closet and shoot me dead."

"Okay."

"Just be sure I'm not having a hot flash. I don't want to die with sweat rings under my arms." We laughed and tightened our embrace. "I love you, sweet pea."

"I love you, too."

Inside the hall, a buffet table laden with entries from the *In the Pink* cookbook reached from one wall to another. Contributors, all wearing pink, scurried between the kitchen and the table, refilling platters and coffee carafes. Each table wore a shawl of pink over a white tablecloth, a bouquet of pink roses with tapers to match, and shades of pink jelly-beans in silver bowls.

Larry took my hand when I returned to our table. "You're cold," he said. He pulled my chair to him and wrapped his arms around me.

Ky leaned toward us. His plate held the remnants of corn chips and salsa. "Are we leaving pretty soon?"

"As soon as Louise speaks."

Louise tapped on the microphone. "Testin', testin', y'all." Shrill feed-back filled the room. "Goodness, I hope that wasn't a critic sounding off." The audience laughed while a technician made adjustments to the sound board.

"I just want to thank y'all for coming out on such a cold night to help us launch the *In the Pink* cookbook. Just in case a few of you wandered in off the street, let me tell you why all of the ladies wearing pink in this room are so happy you joined us this evening. Cancer is a life-changing event. All of the ladies in pink and I agree that kindnesses extended to us during our treatments were magnified in their blessing to us. A visit, a bouquet, a meal, and companionship through the long hours of being hooked up to an IV—all of these things say that cancer sufferers are still a part of the living world and that we matter. We would like to thank you from the bottom of our hearts."

All of the women in pink stopped what they were doing to applaud their support teams in the audience. How like Louise to turn the attention she deserved back to others.

"Good friends and dear families, the proceeds from this cookbook will go to the From Ashes to Beauty Foundation. If you're thinkin' you need another cookbook like you need another hole in the head, remember this is the only cookbook guaranteed to make your husband dance like Fred Astaire. So break out your beaded chiffon evening gowns, ladies, and buy a cookbook for everyone on your Christmas list! Thank you."

Ky asked, "Who's Fred Astaire?"

~~~

At home, Larry pulled off his tie, laid it on the kitchen counter, and started down the hall toward the stairs. He stopped. "Aren't you coming?"

"I want to see if Andrea has any news about her audition."

"I'll meet you upstairs."

SIT DOWN!! Drum roll!! Sound of trumpets!!! Ta-dah!!!! i got a callback from the symphony!!! yes!!!! Ok . . . so it's the san jose symphony, NOT the sf symphony, but it's a symphony! Pray I don't shake like this when I go back . . . must practice . . . callbacks are weds . . . have to get a sub . . . Darlia says to close my eyes & play for Jesus . . . how perfect is that? how was louise's party? i hated to miss it . . . tell her to send me a case of cookbooks to sell . . . are her lemon scones in there? if so send 2 cases . . . ha!

I flipped through my signed copy of *In the Pink,* looking for Louise's lemon scone recipe. Not in the index. I checked the table of contents under Breakfasts, Breads, and Desserts. No lemon scones.

"That Louise," I said to no one, a little miffed at the exclusion. But really, I'm not sure I would want to eat a lemon scone baked by anyone but Louise.

I wrote back to Andrea:

I'm so proud of you! Your Orchard City prayer team will be on our knees all day Wednesday. Call the minute you know something, ANYTHING!

The party was beautiful—lots of good food and company. Louise was the belle of the ball. Ky's favorites were the appetizers, especially the Grand Mesa Nachos. Picture a mountain of tortilla chips, salsa, and cheese. Larry kept asking where the meat and potatoes were stashed. Typical! I slipped a handful of oatmeal cookies into my pocket for lunch tomorrow. You would have loved the music—a string quartet playing Christmas carols. Louise didn't include her lemon scones in the cookbook. I'll talk her into baking a batch for Christmas morning. I'm soooo glad you're coming. Only 45 more days. Yeah! It's late. Talk to you soon, Miss Amazing Cellist!

Love, Mom

JAN
12

High of 54°! How can this be? It's too early to be worrying about fruit trees! Could we have some normalcy, please?

Ky sat cross-legged on the lawn of the high school beside a golden-haired girl, head to head, knees touching. The girl studied an oversized paper while Ky talked. He pushed his hair off his forehead. *Book a haircut today.* Leaves crunched under the Daisy Mobile's tires, and he held up a finger to buy himself another moment with the girl. The girl looked up, smiled, and turned her attention back to Ky. She wore a white blouse and black pants with a necktie draped over her shoulder. Ky slid the paper into a manila envelope and stood. He offered the girl a hand, which she accepted. She walked away from us down the sidewalk, looking over her shoulder once to smile at Ky.

"See you on Monday," he said, turning toward the Daisy Mobile.

I asked Ky, trying not to sound too curious, "Who's that?"

"A girl I know."

Expecting him to elaborate was futile. "Does she need a ride somewhere?"

"She takes the bus to work."

"I'm in no hurry."

He shrugged. "I dunno."

Sweeten the deal. "I'll let you drive."

He unfastened his seatbelt and pulled up on the door handle. "I'll ask her."

"Great," I said with no one to hear me. I slid into the passenger seat and pushed Ky's book bag onto the floor along with the manila envelope. Before I could peek inside, he opened the driver's door for the girl to sit between us. For the next ten minutes he fished the middle seatbelt from between the seat cushions. All the while the girl, Annie, and I chatted. By the time her seatbelt clicked closed, I knew she was Ky's chemistry lab partner, she attended the Presbyterian church, and she had invited Ky to the grief group—all good stuff to know.

"My sister was killed when a drunk driver ran a red light," she said in a practiced voice. "It's almost been a year."

"I'm so sorry," I said.

"Yeah, thanks. I'm real sorry about your husband, too."

Ky flipped the turn signal, looked over his shoulder, and gunned the accelerator. The Daisy Mobile lurched and died. His face tinted pink. "It's been a while since I've driven Mom's truck. The clutch is a little tricky." The engine roared back to life and Ky made a U-turn to head south. It was good to see him keep his cool under stress.

"Where do you work?" I asked Annie.

Ky shot me a glance that meant, *Don't ask so many questions.* I didn't have to. The girl with cappuccino freckles and eyes like a quiet sea considered conversation a pleasantry—nothing torturous or inherently sinister about it.

"I bus tables at La Fontenella. It's my aunt and uncle's restaurant. He's from Italy. They met in college. Aunt Sherry studied in Florence for a semester. You should try the restaurant sometime. The food is great. We've just started catering, too. If you ever have a big crowd to feed, we make it easy."

We neared an intersection where a cluster of cars had stopped for the red light. Ky maintained pressure on the accelerator way past my comfort zone. I tightened my grip on the door handle and pushed hard against the floorboard with my right foot. Ky finally braked. We stopped within an inch of an idling Volkswagen van. A tattered bumper sticker encouraged readers to visualize whirled peas. My voice was breathy when I asked Annie if her aunt and uncle served tiramisu at the restaurant.

"Uncle Paolo makes *the* best tiramisu in the world."

Ky jumped the curb with the back tire when he turned right onto Main Street. "I think the steering needs adjusting."

"I'll check into it."

In three city blocks I learned that Annie's birthday was three days after Ky's; her parents volunteered with Benevolent Friends, a support group for grieving parents; she was a junior like Ky; and since her sister's death, she'd decided to become a bereavement counselor to work with grieving teens and younger children. She had a cat named Ricky. I liked her.

"The group at school has meant so much to me," she said, working the knot of her necktie without a mirror. "They say misery loves company, but it really helps to know that other people understand what you're going through." She snugged the knot under her collar.

"I enjoyed your company," I said.

"Thanks," she said to me, and to Ky, "See ya." She disappeared into the restaurant. Ky watched her leave with a yearning that squeezed my heart.

"We should get going," I said. "This is a loading zone."

"Do you want to drive home? I saw you pressing the floorboard back there."

"You're doing a great job. I'm happy to let you do the driving."

He lurched the Daisy Mobile into traffic.

"She's a nice girl."

"Yeah."

We drove in silence down Main Street. A block from our house, he said, "I have something to show you when we get home. And don't worry. It's nothing bad."

We sat on his bed in his black bedroom—Larry had dubbed it the Bat Cave. Ky played with the clasp of the manila envelope on his lap.

"We finished an art project in grief group today. Mrs. Silver wants us to share the sketch with someone close. I'm warning you: my art sucks. Anyway, we were supposed to pick colors for the emotions we feel." Ky placed a drawing on my lap. "I used warm colors for emotions that make me uncomfortable and cool colors for things I feel good about.

"The circle represents my life. I drew it with a thin orange-red line because life feels fragile and that scares me and sometimes makes me angry. I don't get that, but Mrs. Silver says someday I will. Anyway, I made the house mostly orange because I'm confused a lot, but the blue windows are the times when stuff's okay. This is school. It's red and blue—blue because I like my classes and most of my teachers, red because so much of what goes on there is stupid."

"Like?"

"Kids think it really matters what you wear and who you sit with at lunch and where the next party's gonna be. There's so much more to life than high school. They just don't get it."

"You had to learn that lesson from a harsh teacher."

"Yeah, I guess so."

"Why did you draw a fence with a gate around the church?"

"I want to decide which church I go to."

"You don't like our church?"

"No, it's cool. At first I wanted to fence church off from my life completely. You know, quit going. The more I thought about it, what I really wanted was to go to a church where I wasn't poor little Ky whose dad had died."

"Like the Presbyterian church?"

"Good people go there."

"I'm glad you found a place." I looked back to the drawing. "So did you add the gate later?"

"Another reason I drew the fence was to shut God out of my life. I was pretty pissed at Him, and sometimes I still am. He could have done a million things to keep Dad from riding into that intersection, but He chose not to. I mean, God sees everything, and yet He didn't rescue Dad. Why not? And then I think, hey, everybody dies. We're finite, so maybe it's no big deal for Dad to die. If we believe in heaven, it shouldn't matter, right? God is definitely orange."

I'd thought of Ky's brain as a storm with swirling winds and occasional lightning strikes but no rain. I had no idea our journeys had been so similar.

"One time at youth group," he said, tapping the picture, "a girl stood up to say how wonderful God was because He found her lost dog. I nearly screamed, 'I lost my dad!' But I knew if I did, the room would get real quiet, and like, every eye would be on me. No thanks. I left instead."

"God is confusing, but the gate is still open?"

"I still want God in my life, but our relationship will never be the same as it was when I was a kid. Annie read the different accounts of the crucifixion in the Gospels. The stories showed her that Jesus understands the loneliness of being separated from His Father, even though He was going to see Him real soon. I've read the crucifixion stories in Matthew and Mark so far."

I had no idea. *Thank you, Father.*

A knock on the doorjamb startled both of us. "Oh golly, I'm sorry I scared you," Connie said. "I heard you talking down here, so I brought you some of my Best-Ever Oatmeal Cookies."

Connie turned to set the tray on Ky's dresser, but the impossibility of finding a clear place flummoxed her. I took the tray from her. "Thanks for the cookies, Connie. These are my favorites."

She looked to Ky and back to me. "Save room for shepherd's pie. We'll be eating in an hour or so." She left.

Ky grabbed a handful of cookies and called after her, "Thanks, Connie."

"You're welcome."

I returned to the picture. "There's a lot of orange here," I said.

"Yeah, well, life's been weird lately. Mrs. Silver says that's normal for grieving people, but even more so for teens. The biggest surprise for me was that I'm still grieving at all. Like, shouldn't I be done with this by now? I mean, in my head, when I think about how Dad died and that he's not coming back, it all makes sense. And then nothing makes sense. At least I don't think I'm going crazy anymore." He took the drawing from me and returned it to the envelope. "Mrs. Silver says most of my confusion will clear up in time, but the loss of Dad has marked me permanently. Eventually, I'll adjust."

"Ky, I appreciate your telling me all of this. You've given me a wonderful gift."

"Mrs. Silver said we had to."

"Yeah, well, thanks anyway." I brushed cookie crumbs onto the floor, where they'd never be seen again. I hesitated outside his door and turned back. Honesty deserved honesty. "Just so you know, the way I think about God and death have changed, too. You're right. We all get to die, but if death is just the threshold of heaven, then what are we afraid of?"

"Exactly. That's faith."

"Yep, that's faith."

MARCH

5

I have over 500 trees and 750 shrubs and thousands of bedding plants to take care of. I don't have time to write in a gardening journal!

Larry held up a key. "Do you want to open the door?"

"No. You do it."

He slid the key into the lock. "It won't turn."

"Press against the door as you turn the key."

"Nope."

"Jiggle it."

He stepped away from the door, hands up in surrender. "You try."

I put my shoulder to the door as Judith had taught me and turned the key with a jiggle, and the door opened. Larry and I stood at the threshold—not moving, barely breathing. "I can't believe we're doing this," I said.

He took my hand and we stepped into the sales area of the Walled Garden. Larry said, "I haven't been this excited or scared since I was fifteen and I got on the wrong ski lift at Telluride. There I was at the top of The Plunge. I stood there for an hour gathering my courage to point my skis downhill. What a ride."

With the grand reopening only two weeks away, we didn't have an hour to spare. Blink trotted past us to make himself at home sniffing among the aisles of pottery and seeds and gardening tools. My mind kicked into overdrive. "We should move the chemicals to the back of the store and flank the entry with seasonal displays, don't you think? I wonder if we can order summer bulbs this late."

"All I know is that a delivery from Wooters Seed will be here tomorrow. Then there's Hanson Pottery on Wednesday, and truckloads of plant materials start arriving on Friday. We need to get the shade houses covered. I'm thinking we better hire a guy—or two."

"Kathleen starts tomorrow. She'll walk me through the ordering process and help me reconnect with some of the old suppliers." I swiped a finger along a shelf of fall bulbs to collect a gray mat of dust. "We can toss these bulbs, and the shelves need a good dusting."

Larry sniffed. "What's that smell?"

"Probably the break room. Maybe the septic system."

He groaned.

I moved toward the checkout counter. "We should start a list."

He caught me by the hand. "Come here," he said and pulled me into his arms.

"Your heart is pounding," I said.

"It's all a little overwhelming."

"Are you sorry we bought the place?"

"No, not at all. I was ready to leave Sweet Suzy. Are you? You're the one who gave up your house."

When we'd closed on the Crawford Street house, I'd filled my pocket with tissues, expecting the flood of emotions to catch up to me when I signed over the deed of trust. The new owners sat across the glossy table, each holding a child—an infant and a red-headed girl who leaned into her father and watched us with cautious eyes. When she sneezed, I handed over my pocketful of tissue and the father held the wad over her nose and said, "Blow."

"It was *our* house," I said, "and we should have sold it sooner."

"Ky seems happy."

"Of course, he's five miles closer to Annie."

We held each other until the pounding of our hearts slowed.

"Hallelujah!" called Louise. "This is the day which the Lord hath made; we will rejoice and be glad in it."

A basket hung over her arm as she walked around the store, looking down the aisles and running her fingers along shelves. She held up a dusty finger. "This place is pure potential. A fresh coat of paint. A new counter for the checkout area—Mexican tile, I think, to complement the ambiance."

Larry's hand tightened over mine. "With the opening only a couple weeks away," he said, his voice pinched, "we have to put all of our energy into stocking merchandise. Cosmetic improvements will have to wait for our slow months. A positive cash flow would be nice, too."

Louise spoke with faith and confidence. "The Lord owns the cattle on a thousand hills. Tile won't be a problem for Him." She set the basket on the counter and my stomach gurgled. "And don't you worry about the grand reopening. My girls in pink will provide all the goodies. Y'all don't mind if we take a teensy weensy corner to sell our cookbook, do you?"

"What's in the basket, Louise?" I asked.

She pulled the napkin off with a flourish. "Lemon scones, anyone?"

Ky walked in holding Annie's hand. "Hey, Mom, Larry, did this place come with the front loader?"

"*And* a dump truck," Larry said.

"Cool, where are the keys?"

Annie spoke to Ky. "Chill. Give your parents a chance to breathe."

I really like this girl. "Shouldn't you be in school?"

"Pep rally. Last hour. Optional. No way. Hey, what about the golf cart Judith let me drive? Is that still around?"

I looked to Larry. He shrugged. "I don't remember seeing a golf cart listed on the inventory, but that doesn't mean it isn't here—somewhere."

"Shouldn't Mom be here by now?" I asked. "Maybe you should call her."

Ky reached for a lemon scone. Louise slapped his hand. "The party starts when Connie gets here, not a second sooner."

"Ky and I could go get her," Annie offered.

"Let's give her a minute," I said.

While we waited for Connie, we hunted down the source of the odor—a bottle of lime sulfur that had broken open in the storeroom. I blotted what I could with a paper towel. Larry mopped the rest with hot, soapy water. He kissed me when we sniffed the air and our eyes no longer watered. "What was that for?" I asked.

"We just completed the very first job of owning Walled Garden Nursery."

"That's a tradition I think we should keep."

And to seal our agreement, he dipped me and kissed me again. I preferred my new business partner. No tail. No muddy paws. No dog breath. *Sorry, Blink.*

"Oh man, does this place have a cold shower?" Ky asked. "Try to pull yourselves together. Connie's here."

We gathered near the pottery and held hands in a circle—Larry, Ky, Annie, Louise, Connie, and me. "I'll start," Larry said, and he prayed, "You are our Father, Savior, and Strength. We dedicate our service to you in this place. May we always honor you."

"Lord, this is just the sweetest thing you've done for my dear friends. I pray you would send them too many customers and bless their socks clear off."

"Dear Jesus," started Annie, "I know how hard it is to run a family-owned business, so I pray that you will bless the McManus family with wisdom and perseverance and love."

I caught Annie's eye across the circle and mouthed, *Thank you.*

Connie prayed, "Heavenly Father, thank you for my family and the love we share. Let this be a place where we reflect your love to the people who shop here."

"God, uh, Jesus, bless my parents and help us find the golf cart."

I wanted everything, the bigger the better, that my good Father had to give. Strength, courage, faith, wisdom—I wanted it all. "I need you. *We* need you. In Jesus' name, amen."

ACKNOWLEDGMENTS

The knowledge and experience of these generous people deepened the content of *In Every Flower*: Cheryl Ooley, Karen Jensen, Catharine Mudd, Hanneke Nelson, Leslie Holzschuh, and Susan Capps. Thank you, ladies.

Always and forever, I'm grateful for my friendship with Charlene Patterson, my editor at Bethany House.

For wise counsel and heartfelt cheerleading, my agent, Janet Kobobel Grant, is the best.

For six years of patient and very thorough critiquing of my manuscripts, I owe much more than a debt of gratitude. I love you Darlia, Muriel, and Sharon.

Paul Sparks walked me through his dahlia garden—*again*—on a beautiful October afternoon. His beauties towered above me and inspired me greatly.

Sara Oakley nearly convinced me to join her painting class. An amazing teacher, she made me believe a paint brush belonged in my hand, at least for the time I spent observing her class. Maybe . . .

Leslie Arroyo walked me through the juvenile justice system and seeded my imagination with new ideas. (A special thanks to my sons, Geoff and Matt, for *not* walking me through the juvenile justice system. I love you guys.)

To my readers, thank you for all of the enthusiastic e-mails. Your words of encouragement always arrive at just the right moment. I'm very grateful. Keep writing!

Be *the* first *to know*

Want to be the first to know
what's new from
your favorite authors?

Want to know all about
exciting new writers?

Sign up for BethanyHouse newsletters at
www.bethanynewsletters.com
and you'll get regular updates via e-mail.
You can sign up for as many authors or
categories as you want so you get only
the information you really want.

Sign up today